STEVE JACOBS was born in Port Elizabeth, South Africa, in 1955. He studied Law at the University of Cape Town, and after a year spent working on a kibbutz in Israel he worked as an Advocate in Johannesburg. He left the legal profession to concentrate on his writing. A collection of his short stories, *Light in a Stark Age*, was published in 1984 (Ravan Press). This was followed by two novellas, published as *Diary of an Exile* (Ad. Donker, 1986).

He has had a number of jobs since leaving the legal profession, including being a freelance reporter and a property administrator. He is currently Sub-Editor of *The Argus*, a Cape Town daily newspaper.

He is an active campaigner for human and animal rights, and has been a Trustee of Beauty without Cruelty, worked with squatters at the Crossroads township, and been a member of Koeburg Alert, an organisation opposing a nuclear power station.

UNDER THE LION

STEVE JACOBS

UNDER THE LION

HEINEMANN

Heinemann International Literature and Textbooks
A division of Heinemann Educational Books Ltd
Halley Court, Jordan Hill, Oxford OX2 8EJ

Heinemann: A Division of Reed Publishing (USA) Inc
361 Hanover Street, Portsmouth, New Hampshire, 03801-3912, USA

Heinemann Educational Books (Nigeria) Ltd
PMB 5205, Ibadan
Heinemann Educational Boleswa
PO Box 10103, Village Post Office, Gaborone, Botswana

LONDON EDINBURGH PARIS MADRID
ATHENS BOLOGNA MELBOURNE SYDNEY
AUCKLAND SINGAPORE TOKYO

First published by Ad. Donker, a subsidiary of Donker Holdings (PTY) Ltd in 1988

First published by Heinemann International Literature
and Textbooks in 1993

Series Editor: Adewale Maja-Pearce

British Library Cataloguing in Publication Data
A catalogue record for this book is available from the British Library.

ISBN 0435 90588 0

Phototypeset by M. M. Fourie, Johannesburg
Printed and bound in Great Britain by
Cox & Wyman Ltd, Reading, Berkshire

93 94 95 96 10 9 8 7 6 5 4 3 2 1

To the memory of
my mother

I

A bell tolled. A man wearing a heavy grey overcoat picked his way between the colossal pillars of sound it constructed on the pavement, his face set stern. Only a flicker of his eyes betrayed the impact of each beat. 'Dolente, dolente,' the chimes mourned. It was a grey day. Drops of rain left dark patches on his shoulders and ruffled his hair like the loving fingers of a mother or a wife. He walked, erect as a lawyer, through the streets of Eisstad, through the bell's steady clangour, through the swish-swish-swishing of logs being slid over ice, and the padding of lions. I have walked here, he thought. I have walked here almost every day of my adult life and some part of me has become identified with these concrete blocks. An essence of me, Josef S, lives on even when I have passed; the negative image of a man may be seen on moonlit nights, walking, walking, walking. Or does a person leave no imprint of his passage through this place?

He glanced up, over the city, into the mist, but the mountain refused to come out of hiding. He thought of the lions, but they had gone, irretrievably, irrevocably. All that remained of those frail beasts was this mountain that bore their name. Did they prowl, ghostly at night, on the slopes, contemplating a revolution against the humans who had eradicated them, shot by shot over the years, until the last battered, toothless one died alone in the bushes? Did the rains disturb their footprints, long moulded into dusty paths? Did each fresh storm stir new longings to get up, lashing old muscles to new efforts? Josef S imagined tawny shapes come down from the mountain, haunting the streets, peering around the corners of buildings, slinking catlike after those people who were careless enough to walk through town at dusk.

Thud, thud, thud. The noise intruded into Josef's daydream. It drummed out the lions, erased the columns of the bell, released the vision of a huge articulated truck, white and red like a wound. Thud, thud. Hard dark missiles were being propelled from the doorway of a shop, across the pavement, a rapid-fire of fish frozen solid as blue metal, leaving a trail of wetness and scales. The lawyer put a hand to his eyes as if blindness threatened; he seemed, momentarily, to stumble. When he took away his fingers, a workman materialised, in overalls, gloved against the cold, hurling the fish into the truck's dark hold. Inside, two fellows collected the bouncing, thudding projectiles and stacked them, as efficiently as armourers: Josef could not see their faces. In the window of the fish-shop, the catch of the day stood up, splayed on its gills, naked except for a garland of leaves that it wore around its neck. An old bent woman with a shopping basket welded into the crook of her arm prodded its mottled surface irreverently with her eyes. It stared back glassily. The thick lips clenched on an apple.

A newspaper vendor, a small boy, saw Josef approach and let loose a bloodchilling yell of advertisement, not readily identifiable with the product he was peddling. His newspapers served as both merchandise and work-table; they were covered in black plastic to keep out the rain. As if he recognised the lawyer, he skipped out of the shelter of his doorway, grinning his old man's grin, extending the newspaper like a hand in greeting. Josef gave him a few cents too much. The grin grew wider and the boy returned to his shadow. In his short pants and barefoot, he was apparently impervious to the cold wind that blew in from the sea. A jingling of money, a happy sound, contradicted his appearance of poverty. Josef stuffed the newspaper under his arm and ran the remaining two blocks to the bus-stop, suddenly afraid as a child in the face of the encroaching night, afraid that he would miss his bus, afraid that the darkness would slide from the child's doorway and wrap around him before he could escape. The boy would not give in to that kind of fear. He was a child of the streets; he had been exposed to everything. He would survive.

Josef chose a seat towards the back of the bus. The passengers were mainly commuters returning home. A young woman, a secretary or shop assistant, in the seat across the aisle, was reading a paperback novel. Perhaps she aspired to the fiendish ambition of the heroine of the title, who had risen from the poorest of beginnings to become the mistress of a dynasty. The girl was utterly absorbed in this fictional climb to power; a necklace with a teardrop ornament hung over the pages like a divining pendulum. The bus smelled of vinegar.

Josef unfolded his newspaper as the bus jerked alive. But he did not read; he did not even look at the headlines. Instead, he stared out of the window at the passing city: it seemed dirty and trapped. The mountain could not escape either. Veils of rain covered its face like folds of lace. The newspaper vendor was in another world now, somehow happy with his tip, whereas Josef, secure in his world, was

8

disturbed. As they progressed, stop after stop, the bus filled with grey refugees from the rain, who eventually displaced the bus's sour smell with a musty one of their own. They lurched and swayed with the vehicle's motion.

For a moment, Josef thought he saw Robert's face on the cloud. The boy's sensitive eyes were glazed by the mist, were looking at sights that such soft eyes should have been spared. A beret fitted militarily on his head. Josef turned quickly away. An elderly couple sat in front of him, unspeaking. They did not need to talk; they were safe with each other, an institution, a bastion against the world. They had withstood this life together, had weathered its storms, and nothing could frighten them now. They would die within days, or weeks of each other, so interlocked that living apart would have been impossible, like tearing the heart out of that old lion and expecting it to survive.

CARS STONED IN VALHALLA, Josef read, and immediately turned the page. Did he only buy the newspaper to please the boy from the shadows? But the economic news was no less disturbing: business confidence in the Republic was fading as the country slid towards civil war.

A boy stood next to him: he wore short pants and sandals and a short-sleeved shirt. He looked up shyly at the lawyer, trying to catch his eye, and a smile touched Josef's mouth, slight as the dab of a make-up brush. Encouraged, the child brought out a toy: a blue plastic model of a comic-book super-hero, and, aware of the adult watching, twisted the movable parts into various battle-positions. Robert's fair hair fell over his face as he laughed, as he lifted his toy pistol and aimed it at his brother. 'Pow,' he said. Josef fell on the grass, holding his head, pretending that the shot had hit him. Robert danced around his brother, waving the gun and chanting childish war cries. The newspaper seller sneered at toys; life was full of real struggles, he had no need for vicarious turmoil. Or, fascinated, he watched the moving limbs of the blue warrior as the child on the bus, godlike, manipulated them, fired the little man's laser gun at the storm. The bus lurched and a woman took her son away. Josef curled his fingers in a wave: the boy hid his face in his mother's skirt and made super-hero noises: 'Pow. Boom. Pow,' as he followed her down onto the pavement, into the deluge.

The rain formed drops on the window, the drops rolled into one another, gathered force, picked up stragglers, and were plucked off by the wind. For a moment, Josef saw his reflection in the bus window: a long pale face with shadows where the eyes should have been. Was this how the world saw him, a gloomy haunted figure? Or could a smile alter the effect completely? Perhaps when the rain lifted. Each window had its rolling raindrops that cut the bus off from the tree-lined streets with their comfortable houses, motor cars in good condition, recent models: the war had not yet reached the suburbs. The rain tumbled from the sky as if it would wash away these houses and cars. The boy in the doorway, the hundreds of vagrant boys around the city, merged with the rain as if they belonged to it, splashed in it with their hard bare feet which felt no cold, as the freezing drops streaked down their wrinkled aged faces.

The elderly couple got off at the next stop, supporting each other. They opened an umbrella, and, like one large animal, lumbered off into the storm, without haste or the fuss that many of the younger passengers showed, exaggerated gestures of needing to be protected from the rain.

Josef folded his newspaper and stood up. He stumbled to the front of the bus as if he were walking uphill. Someone else took his seat. It was a relief to be on the wet pavement, to have left the mustiness and the fictional intrigues, the short, cosseted, introspective ride. As suddenly as the cloudburst had begun, so the heavens healed. Josef was not released into darkness as he had feared, but into a fresh post-storm corridor of trees and grassy footpaths. Walking to and from bus-stops was his principal exercise. For the first time, the tensions of the day began to drain away. Lions did not leap into his imagination, litigation and contracts belonged to another world, and the security of his house beckoned.

Dorothy appeared from the kitchen when she heard his key in the lock.

'How was your day?' she asked as usual, and, without waiting for an answer, approached him with an assurance that was not derived from her position as wife of a prominent lawyer of Eisstad. She was a tall handsome woman with reddish-brown hair. She was wearing corduroy slacks with a camel mohair jersey. Her voice was rich as red wine: it was one of the qualities that had attracted him to her in the beginning. Sometimes he could not imagine what she found attractive about him, a haunted and overworked man, who, often, could hardly spare time in the evenings even to talk to her. He put down his briefcase and took her in his arms. Their lips touched. For a moment, he wanted to hang onto her, like a child to its mother, and have her absorb some of the residual tension, but she pulled away from him and returned to the kitchen. Something was simmering there, something with a rich fragrance which only she could create, which he knew he had no ability to conjure. So are dependencies manufactured.

'Fine,' he said at last, too late, as Dorothy disappeared. He opened a door and his wife's dog, a pure white bull terrier, ran at him, full of joy and strong as an ox, its enormous chest heaving with pleasure.

Josef pushed away the animal with an irritable: 'Get down Lex.' They had bought it because Dorothy was lonely during the day when her husband was at work and she was at home, writing. He thought of it as her dog even though he had named it whimsically after his profession. The dog represented something different to each of them: to her it was a stubborn, faithful companion; to him, a watchdog for his wife, a guardian, defender of the law. And the dog? It was splendidly unaware of Josef's symbolism. It would follow him round a room with the eyes of a naughty child, needing only the smallest encouragement to come barrelling after him with an over-abundance of goodwill. Dorothy kept the dog locked up. She feared that it would run into the road and be killed or that, in its exuberance, it would bite someone and they would be ordered to put it down. So Lex remained a prisoner of Dorothy's good offices. She smothered it with kindness, fed it with the best cuts and would stroke it endlessly while she read, its huge head resting heavily on her knees. Of course the dog was filled with energy because it did not have enough exercise, but the husband did not interfere: it was not his business, he decided.

Josef changed into casual clothes and took his evening's work from his briefcase: the usual batch of contracts or pleadings or opinions. He often brought work home from the office; it was something to do and it was money, and Dorothy did not complain. He went into the dining-room, put his files and his dictaphone on the table, and unfolded the newspaper. But before he had begun to read, Dorothy was there, leaning against the door frame, a dishcloth hanging from her fingers as if she were about to disown it.

'Do you want to go out tonight?' she asked.

'I've got to prepare for tomorrow,' Josef hedged. 'You should have asked me earlier.'

'I'm feeling cooped up,' she said. 'The rain.'

'I'm sorry. Not tonight.' He turned a page, unread. 'You go if you want.'

She retreated, and her silence hinted at the gulf that had opened between them. Josef had the sensation of being in water, of water covering his face up to the level of his eyes and ears, so that his senses were distorted. He could not cope with her upsets. At the end of the day, he did not have the emotional armoury to deal with domestic trauma. He wanted to come home to peace after the battlefield of his work; he needed to regain his strength on the home front, pour medicines on the psychic wounds so that he could re-enter the battle on the next day, more or less healed, more or less prepared for the continuing struggle. At nights, often, he was haggard from the strain of a hectic office; his face was sallow and lined. He wanted his wife to be serene, to assist him to prepare the balms. He could not withstand further onslaughts from the quarter which was intended to provide salvation.

'What's wrong?' he asked reluctantly. She stood with her back to him in the doorway and he saw that she was crying. The dog whimpered, and nuzzled her legs. Josef approached her, without touching her.

'Tell me,' he said, looking at her back, at her neck as her hair fell aside to expose its pale curve. Why could he offer her so little at the end of the day?

'Something . . . happened today,' she stammered, as if she had borne this thing alone only until he came home so that she could unburden it on him, but found him wanting.

'What? Are you hurt?' Still, he could not touch her.

'No, I'm all right . . .' She hesitated.

'Well, what?' he asked impatiently.

'There was a knock at the door, and I went to answer it . . .'

For some reason, although he knew that he was not guilty of anything, Josef S suddenly pictured policemen in his house, confronting his wife, demanding to know things about him. 'Who was it?' he asked, his voice harsh.

'A woman,' she said.

He stepped back in relief, even though his wife was still distressed. Immediately, he saw the selfishness of his reaction and regretted it, hoping that Dorothy had not seen; but she was too absorbed in her story.

'It was a woman,' she repeated, 'begging.'

'You should have given her something,' he said. 'Food, old clothes . . . Eisstad is full of beggars; there's one on every street corner . . .'

'She wanted work and I was too scared to let her in and Lex was barking and she looked so sad.' He put his arm round her shoulders then, but when he looked at his hand, it was not his, but his father's. He was his father, comforting his wife. Slowly, so as not to alert Dorothy to his vision, he moved away, and she continued as if she had not noticed. 'The woman told me she'd come in from the country with three children. I couldn't understand her properly: it seemed as if she'd left them in a toilet in the township. She was frightened of the police and of the comrades in Valhalla. I gave her some money and food and sent her back into the rain. I should have asked her in, but Lex was barking his head off and I couldn't think clearly. What could I do? I felt so helpless.'

'I'm sure you did as much as you could,' her husband said, trying to reassure. His hand was normal again; he stared at the veins and hairs that could have been his father's. In the distance, he thought he could hear the echo of the bell.

She shook her head and spoke very softly. 'I'm sorry. I didn't want to trouble you. It's just that I felt so guilty. If our positions had been reversed, would she have treated me any better?' The dog whined and she patted it abstractedly. 'She was grateful for my kindness, but when she saw that I was prepared to give, she kept asking for more. I sent her away. I closed the door in her face.'

He had a glimpse of her deep green eyes, as inscrutable to him then as the forests on the northern border where Robert was. Did he see sadness, a need to be held as he, earlier, had a craving to be held by her? Or perhaps hers was a defiant look, telling him that she could have done no more for the woman at the door, justifying her actions, based on fear, that ran counter to her principles. Josef sat down, feeling defeated. He could not speak.

'I have everything I need and she has nothing. If I was alone and scared in Valhalla, wouldn't she have taken me in?' Dorothy hesitated in the doorway, perhaps waiting for him to give her guidance, a word of comfort, but he had given too many words of comfort at work; he had none left for his wife. When she saw that he was not going to answer, she walked away, back into the kitchen. The rich smell now vaguely nauseated him.

Josef S took up the newspaper, avoiding the political and economic columns, and turned to the metropolitan section, paging without thinking, using his father's hands, mentally searching for his wife in a forest of cooking smells and sounds. The rain had started again, and its pattering on the window-pane slotted into the gaps

13

left by the kitchen noises.

PUTTING THE LEEU BACK INTO LEEUKOP caught his attention and he stopped.

'A local zoologist plans to reintroduce lions to the Leeukop,' he read with increasing interest, 'although he expects an uphill battle against the authorities.

'Dr Duncan Foster has applied to the Executive Committee of the City Council for exemption from the provisions of Municipal Regulation 4(b) of Proclamation 96 of 19— which prohibits the introduction of wild animals into a municipal area.

'Dr Foster, who last year resigned from his post as professor in the Department of Zoology at the University of Eisstad for "personal reasons", is currently involved in raising lion cubs on his farm outside Eisstad. He told the *Evening Times* that it is his "mission to put the lions back where they belong."

'He said: "Lions lived and bred and hunted on the mountain undisturbed until the Settlers came. They shot every last mother and cub they could find. Now, the humans have taken over the mountain and they pretend nostalgia for the 'wild old days' when life was somehow purer and more exciting. They've used the lions' name for the mountain and the Tourist Board entices visitors to Eisstad with a story that a last lion remains."

'Dr Foster believes that the lions have been glorified in their absence, and compares their extinction to that of indigenous tribes who suffer at the hands of colonists. He intends the release of the lions to be a symbol of the struggle of the people to be free.

' "No one wants to allow the lions to return to their original home," he said. "I intend to change that. I will fight City Hall all the way to the top."

'Dr Foster did not specify what he meant by "the top", but it is understood that he will take the matter to court if the council turns him down.'

Josef realised that he was stroking the dog, rubbing his fingers in the short hair behind its ears. Lex had a vacant expression, probably of bliss, in his brown eyes.

'Supper's ready,' Dorothy called. Dog and man went obediently.

Shrieking alerted him. But when he looked for the source he could see nothing. He stood in a vast dust-bowl that went on for ever in all directions around him. Bones of animals which had died and rotted away in the desert lay half-submerged in the sand: rows of

14

spines, barrels of ribs, empty-eyed skulls which warned of what might happen if he slipped, if he did not rise in time, if the sand was allowed to enter and eat from the inside. The wind raised small swirling devils on the plain; they spun soundlessly. From such a storm, a human figure emerged. It stood with its back to Josef and he knew that he should make contact; it possessed answers to some of his questions. But at the same time, he feared this manifestation so greatly that he had to escape from it. Small shapes, no bigger than dots, moved on the dusty plain, in the distance, too far away to make sense. Josef stared, trying to understand, but the shrieking distracted him. The dreaded figure turned around and Josef could not look at its face.

Fire flickered through the closed shutters and he heard the popping of burning wood. Josef sat up in bed. Dorothy slept beside him, breathing regularly; she had not wakened him. He had woken at the jerk of his foot; he had been falling. And now, there was fire outside his window, and voices. He stood, and, naked but still warm from bed, walked carefully through the darkness to the window. The curtains were partially drawn and the window was open behind the shutters. With the back of his hand, Josef moved the heavy white material aside and peered through the slats. Across the road was an open area of tarmac, forecourt to a group of parking garages. Recently, a nightwatchman had come to live in one of these to oversee a construction site in the street. Josef heard a clap of hands and a cough, then a brief burst of laughter like a spurt of gunfire. Self-consciously, he hid behind the curtain, although it was unlikely that anyone could see him. Two men sat before a black drum in the middle of the parking lot. Two women walked about, talking animatedly. The drum, which had holes punched in it, was filled with burning logs, and the men, wrapped in greatcoats, were trying to keep warm on a winter's night. They alternately held their hands out to the fire and stuffed them in the pockets of their coats. Josef began to feel the cold and he shivered. As he returned to bed, he looked at his watch; it was 3.30. A low mumble of talking rocked him to sleep.

In the morning, as he was dressing for work, Josef asked his wife: 'Did you hear them last night? The people across the road. Or was I dreaming?'

'I heard nothing,' she replied. She lay in bed and watched him dress. Usually she was up before him; today she was quiet. The dog was lying on the bed, something Josef would not allow while he slept. Her fingers stroked the broad head mechanically, almost listlessly, while Lex grunted and nipped at a spot inside his hind leg.

'It was rather absurd,' Josef said. 'In the middle of the suburbs, in the very heart of urban civilisation, where light and heat are flicked on by a switch . . . is it not absurd that people are keeping warm in front of fires in drums?'

He felt her eyes examining him, as if she were wondering where this sudden insight came from. She did not say: 'I'm the bleeding-heart liberal. Remember? You're the tough corporate lawyer. I explore the nature of our society; you exploit its conflicts by knowing the rules.'

He wrapped his tie about his neck. 'I felt that I was looking at something very primitive last night,' he went on despite her inspection. 'At our core of light there is a primitive darkness which threatens to eat our civilisation, bit by bit, until we are as dark . . .'

'I don't believe you thought all that last night,' she said eventually, and turned her face to her pillow. 'You've never cared about anyone except yourself. You're just talking for the sake of it, Josef,' she said, and got up. The dog stirred, then lay back luxuriously in the bed clothes, its tongue lolling out of its mouth, frustrated in its attempt to lick the woman once more. 'Breakfast will be ready in good time. The wife is still in harness, you'll be pleased to hear. Don't talk, it's not necessary.'

He wondered, as she put on her dressing gown, what he had done to upset her this badly. Apart from his observation about the night-watchman, he had behaved no differently from normal, from all the other mornings of marriage. He realised that he was not particularly interested in the answer. Nevertheless, he did not speak at breakfast and he did not tell her his dream about the figure on the plain.

The watchman sat bolt upright on a straightbacked chair, shaving with a basin and mirror as if he were camping, applying the utmost concentration to his task. He wore a vest and blue trousers. A black pot rested on the burning logs of the fire-drum before him; steam rose from it into the cold morning air. The woman had on a pink nightgown; she was taking care of whatever domestic duties could occupy her in a parking lot. Neither of them took any notice of Josef as he dallied on his verandah, caught between a curiosity to observe and a reluctance to pry. They had slept in the garage, the swing door of which was half open, revealing an unmade bed. Around them, workmen were beginning to set the day's building in

16

motion. Nondescript men in blue or green overalls piled bricks into wheelbarrows. Slow feet trudged in the direction of the construction, a lifetime of labourers, as anonymous as ants, men who left the proof of their activity all over the country and then disappeared as mysteriously as they had arrived.

On his way to work, Josef thought about the newspaper seller and the couple who lived in the garage: they seemed to belong to a special breed of human beings, toughened in a way that urban man found difficult to comprehend.

The morning newspaper bore the headline, VIOLENCE IN TOWNSHIPS: 7 DIE. The story reflected a world that had nothing in common with the lawyer's: a world of teargas, bullets, armoured police vehicles called Leeus, a world of terror that existed only in the pages of his newpapers.

The press had been reporting on this turbulence for months: sometimes it seemed to get better, sometimes it got worse. Names of people appeared, and then were no longer mentioned. Perhaps their owners had been arrested, or murdered, or had left the country. Sometimes the same name was prominent for a longer time, sometimes the activists demanded that someone be freed, sometimes the Government clamped down on its enemies. Josef S followed the general pattern of the thing. On any given day, he might have been able to chronicle the events of the previous week, but after months, the newsprint blurred into general headings: PETROL BOMB ATTACK, MINISTER SPEAKS, TEARGAS USED ON CAMPUS, MINISTER'S SPEECH REJECTED, LANDMINES DETONATED ON NORTHERN-BORDER FARMS, CONSUMER BOYCOTT CALLED TO PROTEST DETENTIONS, POLICE BREAK UP MARCH ON PARLIAMENT, ACTIVIST MURDERED . . . The accumulation ultimately numbed the reader who was not involved. It would have been different if he had experienced these events personally. Perhaps a specific incident would have stood out in his mind, a confrontation, something as real as the face of the boy on the street who sold him his newspaper. But the State kept the two worlds apart; the townships could have been on another continent.

Josef smiled at his receptionist. Surrounded by clients and ringing telephones, she had time only to nod back. The waiting room was already filling. Clerks and secretaries and messengers emerged from doorways, preoccupied, and vanished as quickly, creating a tapestry of movement that indicated a normal morning's business. A touch of nausea suddenly gripped Josef; he shut his eyes for a moment as the whirling office dance threatened to tilt him off-balance.

'Good morning, Mr S,' said a timid voice beside him. 'Are you all right?'

'Yes, thank you Ben.' The boy was on his way to the photostat room carrying a folder. I have created an industry, Josef thought, and it rolls on, with a momentum of its own, even if I'm not here. What would Dorothy say about this new insight? Perhaps that I am only now seeing the obvious, things that she has known for years? 'Have you contacted the witnesses in the Forsyth case yet, Ben?' he asked.

'Yes, Mr S,' the young man said, and for the second time that morning, Josef felt that he was under scrutiny. This time from Ben. Which was difficult to believe. Ben was a timid soul. He had a soft face and twitching eyes. Josef had never thought he would be a lawyer, but, to give an impression of liberalism, as a token, the firm had decided to hire him. 'They're coming in this afternoon,' Ben continued, and Josef realised that he must have been the same age as Robert.

'Good,' said Josef, and walked away quickly, aware that Ben was staring at his back as if certain things that should have been discussed had been left unsaid. He accepted a pile of messages from his secretary and pushed open the door of his office. The familiar smell struck him, the smell of his leather-bound books, of dust and sunshine. His office caught the sunlight at midday and the sun seemed to remain embedded in the furniture. This office was his more than anything else in the world. Here he did not have to pretend, did not have to accommodate any desires contrary to his own. Here he held court, and his subjects bowed to his superior knowledge. With a feeling of coming home, a feeling akin to love, Josef S closed the door and sat down in his chair. He put his briefcase on his desk and closed his eyes. At once, the buzzer of the intercom disturbed him.

'Please, Linda, hold calls,' he said sharply.

On the far wall, a shaft of sunlight rested like a spotlight. Dust motes floated on the beam. Josef S closed his eyes again, and breathed deeply. Immediately, an image of Dorothy came into his mind, the picture of a woman lying on a bed with a white dog across her legs. Her fingers played on the animal's flank and the dog was looking at her with the complete trust only animals and babies have. How long was it since he, Josef, had looked at his wife with that sort of expression? Had he ever done so? Had there been time?

With a quick burst of panic, he realised that he could not remember their courtship. Had they walked together on the Leeukop picking flowers and holding hands as lovers were supposed to? Had they sat on beaches at sunset sipping wine from crystal glasses, watching the small waves lapping on the sand as gently as cats' tongues? Had they taken day-trips into the country and lain together in vineyards or pine-forests, wrapped around by a stillness that bound them more closely than words?

He rubbed his eyes, but he could not link these romantic images to anything he had ever done, as much as he now wanted to. What, then, could he salvage from the past? Her voice, rooted deeply in those days, saying: 'I don't want children, do you?' And his answer: 'Not at all.' And her response: 'Books will be my children.'

Had she been attracted to his ambition, or to his iciness? Or simply to his desire not to have children? Did ten years of marriage rest on such a negative foundation? Had the domestic routine so ground down their union that all pretense at civility had gone and only bitterness was left?

He remembered another comment of hers: 'My parents want me to get married and have a family, but my career is too important.' Perhaps the answer lay in this, perhaps she had married him so that she could be supported while she wrote. And now that her name was established, she was anticipating the time when she would no longer need him.

Only the physical boundaries of his office were safe: as soon as he closed his eyes, that other world, inside, burst into life and demanded attention, wanted explanations from him that he could not give. Ben had recognised his weakness, timid Ben. But Ben could not help him. No one could; the rot was too deep. His clients waited outside but the lawyer could not see them yet. He turned the pages of his newspaper, avoiding the zoologist's latest plans for releasing lions on the mountain.

FOREIGN MP'S SEE PARADOXES IN REPUBLIC appeared on the editorial page. Josef read, disinterestedly. His reading was a nervous tic, a fidget, a device to keep the outside world at bay for a few more minutes. He learned that a group of foreign politicians had been visiting Valhalla and had given a news conference at the Eisstad Airport the previous day, before their departure for their respective home countries. Mr Gustav Brown, Chairman of the International Humanitarian Society, had said that his group had been struck by certain paradoxes in the country. Wearily, Josef found out

19

what they were. 'The Republic claims to be a democracy,' Brown had told the press, 'yet opponents of the Government disappear. President Buth points to an independent judiciary and an apparently free press, yet Raymond Mkhize of the Flatlands Democratic Front was detained last week and no one knows where he's being held. On the one hand, you are allowed to express your disapproval, on the other, opposition is suppressed. We have spent many comfortable days in Eisstad in a luxury hotel being served by waiters who go home to the ghetto of Valhalla. Most of the guests at our hotel, in fact most of the citizens of Eisstad, have never been to the townships. The Government refuses to talk to the leaders of the opposition . . .'

The lawyer sighed. He stood up and his gaze passed over his framed diplomas hanging on the wall like war-medals on a veteran's chest. In the corner was an ancient typewriter that had been his father's. Its primitive structure was an anachronism in the modern office; it was tough and uncomplicated. That was why he kept the machine: it gave him the feeling that he was in touch with a simpler world, had only to reach out his hand and beat a message for a different age. Typewriter, grey overcoat and memories: these things were a father's legacy to his elder son. Today, that son was reluctant to see clients, to allow strangers into his sanctuary. He walked to the window and looked down at the pigeons resting wherever they could find an outcrop of concrete. Eventually, he called to his secretary.

'Linda, you'd better let them in.' Within moments there was a knock at his door, and, fixing a professional smile on his face, Josef went to answer it.

The sun was shining although a cold wind blew. It was a weak sun, watery as the eyes of an old man. Josef walked slowly in the park, toying with the sandwiches that Dorothy had packed for him. Was it wise to begin a new venture in the present troubled circumstances? His last client before lunch had not been concerned with political vagaries; he wanted to float a company. Josef restricted his advice to legal technicalities, had not discussed his doubts with the man who wore an ostentatious gold ring on his finger, an open-necked shirt, checked sports jacket, but no tie, as if he were not bound by the same constraints as his lawyer. To Josef S, he seemed to operate on the edge of social conscience. He would not read articles on Valhalla in the *Daily News* but would turn straight to the share prices, paying no more attention to the arrest of the Secretary of the FDF than Josef would pay to the gossip columns.

Secretaries and clerks sat on the park benches, holding hands and library books; everything was normal in the city of Eisstad. Wherever trees did not block the view, Josef could see the mountain that rose above the city. His own house nestled in its foothills. He imagined Dorothy, alone, with only Lex and her books for company. She would have closed the door behind the char, who only worked in the mornings, and sat down to lunch: a salad and freshly-baked bread set out like a work of art on the white kitchen table. She would be thanking her muse for the morning's labour of love. Josef pictured the creature as a cross between a falcon and an angel, sitting on her shoulder, claws dug in, whispering into her ear, nuzzling her neck, stroking her to produce fictions. But lately a look of dissatisfaction had crept into her eyes, and she had taken to staring into the room, distantly, as if she were trying to foresee her own future in the same way that she plotted the destinies of her characters. Sometimes he watched her, surreptitiously, as she bent over her work, and he marvelled at her ability to extract stories from the air, while her red hair fell over her face. She had a faraway expression when she wrote, and sometimes her feet twitched like those of a dreaming animal. He wondered at her talent to invent new worlds, or interpret old ones, but at heart he was glad he did not have her need to create: the tension was often unbearable, especially when she was not producing well. It was an isolated life for Dorothy, at home with her pens and paper and typewriter, her only interactions being with the dog and the char. Josef had never understood her solitary lifestyle, had always felt it to be incomplete. Yet when she was writing, he had seen, she was so absorbed that the outside world did not exist for her. He dared not intrude: when she was interrupted, the ferocity in her eyes could be frightening. Once he had asked her about the fantasy world she brought to life, enquiring if there were characters in her imagination that she did not allow to see the light, and whether this was tantamount to abortion. She had smiled without answering and he had not asked again.

Two lovers leaned against a railing, arms interlocked, admiring a bed of roses. A municipal cleaner rested on his outstretched brush. A squirrel pursued peanuts thrown by a group of school-children while a pigeon pecked at a dirty corner the cleaner had overlooked. Its companions stood on the head of an early statesman immortalised in stone, who had advanced the interests of civilisation by going to

21

war with the indigenous tribes and bringing the survivors the benefits of Western rule and religion. Josef smiled. Had humans perched on the great man's shoulders, shitting down his coat, they would have encountered the anger of the authorities. Pigeons were exempt from Governmental and municipal decree.

In one corner of the park, two women stood silently, facing the Houses of Parliament, wearing overcoats against the chill and braving the law. About a hundred people, a lunchtime crowd, milled around keeping a respectful, or frightened, distance from these protesters. Both had placards on their backs. CHILDREN ARE BEING MURDERED BY THE POLICE, read one. WE ARE HORRIFIED AT THE DEATHS, said its companion. As the lawyer edged closer, he saw that the women had chained themselves to the fence that separated the park from Parliament.

'Go home and look after your own children,' taunted a woman in the crowd.

'The police are upholding law and order!' a man shouted.

But the women did not respond, and after a while the crowd was affected by their silence and itself grew still. A few onlookers joined what had now become a vigil. Others left. Josef stood by, watching and waiting, aware that these women expressed the current of township feeling. It was the first time he had seen it demonstrated publicly: the law prohibited political gatherings even if only two people were involved. Josef looked for faces he knew in the crowd — many of his colleagues walked in the park at lunchtime — but he recognised no one. With a sudden surge of bitterness, which was new and surprising to him, he reflected that the commercial lawyers of Eisstad were too conservative to associate themselves with such an exhibition.

'Why don't they talk?' someone asked.

'They are standing in silence to commemorate the dead,' a voice answered. Josef turned. The tall young man was casually dressed in a white shirt and blue denim trousers. He had short hair and a slight shadow on his chin, as if he had neglected to shave. As soon as he had spoken, he seemed to shrink into himself. There could be no doubting the intensity of his feeling: his words had a harsh ring to them. But he seemed to regret them immediately and eased himself from the crowd with the comments of some of its members following after him like arrows. He did not defend himself, but walked briskly away, gangly and awkward.

The crowd had found its voice again and turned its venom back to the protesters. 'Subversives,' an elderly woman spat, jabbing her umbrella towards the sky. 'They want to give it all away, everything we have. They should be ashamed of themselves.'

'Traitors,' someone else agreed, but no one moved any closer. The women's passivity held the crowd at bay as effectively as if a wall separated them, an invisible barrier that no one dared to breach except for journalists who are trained not to respect boundaries. When the press arrived, the crowd parted and allowed them to approach the women without hindrance. Note pads and cameras gave the journalists a mysterious authority; their presence indicated that something important was happening, an event that would be recorded in the late edition of the *Evening Times*.

One of the reporters saw Josef and smiled at him. 'Good afternoon, Mr S.'

'Good afternoon,' Josef replied, recognising the man from court. 'How's the Esselmann case going?'

'Postponed . . .' He hesitated. 'But I'm not covering it any more.'

Josef feigned interest. 'Oh, why?' he asked. He remembered that the man's name was Wilson.

'I've been transferred to the townships. It gets dangerous and the news editor only wants senior reporters to go in.'

'And what's it like today?' Josef asked politely, feeling the inadequacy of the question, as if he were enquiring after someone's health, and aware that, not having been to the townships himself, he would not be able to relate to the answer.

'The police sealed off all roads to Valhalla, Sonnestraal and Vrede this morning,' Wilson said. 'The children have been boycotting classes and stoning cars.'

'Why is it always the children?' Josef asked. I have no children, he thought. I don't know how children reason. What prompts children to violence?

'Because they're the ones who are going to inherit the system. They see how their parents have failed. They have the energy, and nothing to lose.' Wilson rubbed the side of his face (he had bad skin), adjusted his spectacles, and indicated the messages on the women's backs. 'So of course they are the first to be shot in police actions. Some people can't live with that knowledge,' he said, looking round at the faces in the crowd, 'and some are so self-absorbed that they refuse to understand the grievances of others. That's the pity of it.'

'These women are going to be arrested,' said Josef suddenly, and as if in immediate confirmation of his analysis, a siren sounded near-by. A murmur of expectancy rose in the crowd. One or two people moved away, as if fearing to be involved in a confrontation.

'Oh yes,' said Wilson, 'that's part of their statement.'

'How do you know?'

'They spoke to me earlier; they wanted us to cover their protest.' Wilson met the eye of one of his colleagues who was gesturing to him. 'Please excuse me,' he said, and began to move away.

'Before you go,' Josef asked, catching hold of the journalist's arm, 'please tell me. Do the women have children?'

'Yes. They're protesting as "mothers".'

'I see,' said the lawyer as Wilson walked up to the demonstrators, and without talking to them, stood and waited for the police to come.

When he had entered the field of law as a student at the University of Eisstad, Josef had not thought very much about 'justice'. Law was to be a job, a way to succeed where his father had failed. Being a good lawyer meant learning the rules, not questioning their morality. Knowledge of the law was a powerful tool to make money, not a key to understanding the inequalities of a society. Those who cherished justice, like Wilson, were not necessarily those who had learned the law.

Three policemen, dressed in blue, seeming inevitably to be larger than they actually were, looking solid as the Leeukop, walked up the avenue. The crowd melted as they advanced. The men approached confidently, accustomed to a clear access. They were relaxed, this was an easy amusing duty, this was far removed from petrol bombs in the townships. They are so young, Josef thought, and they have the authority to make decisions of life and death; they are the custodians of law and justice. The most senior of the three, wearing a sergeant's stripes, straightened his cap, and addressed the silent women.

'Ladies,' he said, 'you must unchain yourselves and leave here.' The woman with the umbrella was nodding vehemently. 'You are constituting an illegal gathering in terms of Section 48(1) of the Public Safeties Act.'

But the protesters did not move and it was Wilson who answered. 'These women have instructed me to tell you that they are involved in a silent protest, and will not speak to you,' he said. 'They have thrown away the keys of the padlock, so they cannot free themselves.' He gave the impression of someone relishing his role. 'That, gentlemen,' he said smugly, 'is your job.'

The policemen withdrew and conferred; joking had given way to an ominous seriousness. Then one of them, a constable, strode away. He was gone for about five minutes while the crowd grew, even though it was almost two o'clock and the end of lunch-hour. People were muttering, though not loudly enough for their comments to be heard: this was live entertainment, the pictures from their television sets projected in the flesh during a dull working day. The constable returned, carrying a hacksaw, and while the lunchtime crowd reluctantly diminished, drifting slowly away, eking out the last morsel of the drama, the man laboured to cut the women loose. He worked as if they were not present, since they had absented themselves from the proceedings. But his task was awkward, because the women were standing close up against the fence. The most obvious place to work on the chains was inside the grounds of Parliament, but there were spikes on top of the fence and none of the men seemed prepared to risk injury in scaling it. The constable's frustration was evident, causing some titters from the onlookers, while the photographers were making merry of his growing discomfort. After a while he called to his companions. He had succeeded, somehow, in slipping the women's hands free. Still they said nothing. If they had been hurt they did not show it. A patter of wry clapping indicated that the crowd was no longer awed; they had seen that policemen were fallible. As the silent women were led away, the sergeant, belatedly, took the posters from their backs.

'It's war!' bellowed a tramp who had surfaced with a drunken grin on his rubbery face. The crowd was a buffer between him and the policemen who might otherwise have locked him up for his impertinence. Josef gave him what remained of Dorothy's sandwiches and walked thoughtfully back to his office. The tramp's words: 'Bless you Master', rang in his ears like mockery.

That night, the *Evening Times* carried a picture of Gille Sutton and Sally Patterson, clearly showing the slogans on their backs. The events in the park had become the city's news. Was the newspaper-seller aware he was helping to disseminate the information as he dashed between motor-cars, collecting coins and counting change in the moments before the traffic lights turned green? Josef S again tipped the boy, who grinned broadly and performed a little dance of joy, as though welcoming his patron to some new religion. But this notion was absurd and Josef hurried on his way.

25

While he waited at the bus-stop, he read the story of what he had seen: WOMEN ARRESTED AFTER CHAINED PROTEST. The article gave the full text of the women's statement to the press before their demonstration: 'We are mothers. Our children are privileged and protected, while in the townships children are being murdered by those who are supposed to uphold law and order. We cannot live with this knowledge. Their deaths appal us.' The women had been charged in terms of the Public Safeties Act, Section 48(1), which prohibited 'illegal gatherings', and they had been released on bail. They were to app'ear in court at a later date.

A curious snippet appeared in the Features Section. An astrologer from a country town had predicted the sudden death of a prominent figure and forecast that the death would create turmoil on a national scale. The astrologer was not named.

Josef felt a wave of heat pass through his body.

As he opened the front gate of his house, workmen passed, running to catch the buses back to the townships, calling throaty farewells to one another. He shivered as clouds extinguished the weak evening light. Across the road, the garage door was up and Josef could make out paint tins, a cupboard, chairs and a bed. The watchman was carrying an armful of wood towards the black drum; he met Josef's gaze and the lawyer turned sharply up his stairs. There was neither animosity nor pleading in the look, but Josef fled as if the man were about to ask something of him: a meal, money, the use of the bathroom. The woman was nowhere to be seen.

Dorothy greeted her husband cheerfully, kissing him on the lips. 'It went very well today,' she said, her voice husky.

'I'm glad.'

'The threads came together. I think my unconscious must have been working on the problem. Perhaps that's why I've been so moody.'

Nobody could have been more different from the woman he had left in the morning. Josef hugged her and she smiled a dazzling smile; her green eyes were moist. She had a cigarette in her fingers which she held away so that she would not burn him. For a moment, he felt a stirring of the old desire for her.

'I'm sorry,' she said. 'I'm sorry if I made things uncomfortable, but you know it has nothing to do with you. It's just these tangles in my mind when I'm trying to put my stories together.' She was so talkative that she seemed drunk, but it was an intoxication born of

26

writing, not alcohol. She was as excited as a child, and he wished he could share her excitement; she had obviously been waiting for him to come home so that she could tell him about her day. But he felt flat and listless. He could have told her about the women he had seen arrested, but her need to talk was greater. Her encounter with the beggar had been forgotten; excitement had defeated depression. 'It happens like this,' she had once told him. 'The depression and the elation come in waves, one following the other, as regularly as day follows night.' Now she said: 'I have cooked. I hope you're hungry.'

He nodded, although he did not have much appetite. 'Let me put my things down,' he said, 'then we can eat.'

In their bedroom, while Lex watched him curiously, Josef wearily took off his jacket. It seemed to him as though he had always carried that weariness around, but that he had only become aware of it today, and that the cumulative effect of the years of warding it off had finally worn him down. He sat on the bed and could not find the power to rise. Lying back, he thought how foolish he must appear, and wondered why it had to be so, why he had to be strong and whether his wife cared anyway.

'Josef,' Dorothy called, 'are you ready for supper?'

He could not answer. He lay on his back and looked at the patterns on the ceiling. She called again. There were squares on the ceiling; he tried to make some sort of sense of their arrangement. If there was a meaning, it eluded him.

The shivering lasted for a week. Dorothy had helped him to bed, supper and stories forgotten, and he slept and cried and sweated and dreamed. Dorothy moved into the spare room while Josef grappled with his illness. Sometimes he woke at night as wet as if he had been out in the rain, and as cold. His sheets were clinging beasts that would allow him no peace.

The fat men were seated at a round table. They were bankers, they told him, and insurance salesmen. One was a lawyer. 'I too am a lawyer,' Josef S began to say, but he was silenced by a gesture from one of the men, possibly the leader of the group, who put his forefinger to his lips, and Josef closed his.

'Lunch will soon be served,' said the man, 'and we have important business to discuss before the waiters disturb us with the clatter of their dishes. You may sit on that chair, in that corner, if you wish, but please do not say anything.' His voice had the texture of honey, oozing from his mouth in a smooth, thick flow of sweetly spoken words.

Josef, as chastened as if he were a schoolboy, sat where he was told. He folded his hands in his lap and let his head droop onto his chest. He stared as his shoes, at the knots in the laces. The businessmen were conversing in what seemed to be a foreign language. Dimly, he heard their mutterings. Snatches of phrases, segments of dialogue, words here and there penetrated his thoughts, which seemed to be concerned with knots. Most of it he could not understand, until he heard the one who was a lawyer say: 'I must tell you, I could hardly believe it, but he was smiling when they burned him; he seemed to be relieved to accept the punishment for his guilt.'

'What guilt?' asked a banker through clouds of cigar smoke.

'The guilt of being an informer of course,' answered the lawyer, 'a traitor to his own people.'

'He was supporting the greater good,' interjected the banker. 'He had no right to smile. He should have objected most strongly.'

'What "greater good"?' Josef S burst out, unable to keep his new opinions to himself.

'Shush,' warned the leader. 'Haven't I asked you to be quiet? Speak only when you are addressed, or we will have to send you to bed.

'The good of the State,' explained the banker. 'The State demands blind obedience, does it not gentlemen?'

'Hear, hear!' the others chimed. 'Blind! Blind! Blind!'

The chanting swelled, battering against Josef's eardrums. The fat men were carried away by the passion of their conviction. 'Blind! Blind! Blind!' Through his muffling hands it began to sound like 'Dine! Dine! Dine!' The men were banging their thick tumblers on the table in time to their words. Josef wanted to leave. But he did not want them to know that they had driven him away. He cowered ever lower in his corner, while the words beat him like the blows of a hammer. He saw the men stand, in unison, and raise their tumblers to their lips. They disappeared into the mist of cigar smoke and then suddenly reappeared, stretching out their heavy glasses until they touched in a toast. Like balloons, their stomachs almost met across the table. Josef uncovered his ears.

'To law!' shouted the lawyer.

'To order!' shouted the banker.

'To the State!' they declared together.

'Now let us eat,' said the leader. Everyone sat down. 'Come,' the leader beckoned to Josef. 'Come and join us. Be one with us. You have strayed, certainly, from our fold. Your stomach is half the size of ours. But we will accept you with all the love we can command. And that is substantial. We are the receptacles of love and joy. Dig into our beneficence and you will find a mine of love. Go over to the other side and there is only hatred. We have the power and the wealth to dispense love.'

'Waiter!' a voice yelled. 'Bring us food!' A waiter appeared, and another, followed by a third. Each man carried a tray, laden with steaming plates; a procession of penguins, dressed in black and white.

'Fish!' they fluted and squawked. 'Fish for lunch, gentlemen,' and they began handing out the plates to the diners.

'Fish gives you brains,' said the lawyer, picking the pale corpse from his plate. He squeezed it against his lips, so that the grease ran down the corners of his mouth. Soon his fingers were soaked with fat, his thumbnails shone. He sucked loudly on the soft meat and the sound was echoed by the other mouths.

'Come, Josef,' coaxed the leader. 'Come and join us. Look! They've brought you a plate.'

The others had forgotten that Josef S was there at all; they had buried their heads in their meals and were eating with assorted crunchings and slurpings.

'I'm sorry,' said Josef. 'I must go.'

But the leader had turned to his own meal with such ferocity, such fixed attention, that he too appeared to have forgotten the slim, quiet man in the corner.

'Meat next! The lamb!' someone shouted. 'Waiter! Where are they? Food! Food!'

The cry was taken up by the others, who began to beat their knives and forks on the table in a terrible rhythm. Grease-stained mouths opened to roar: 'The lamb, the lamb! Waiter, the lamb! Bring the lamb!' The knives were poised like fangs, the forks were claws. The lawyer was salivating: foam collected round his lips and spilled onto his jacket. The jacket had been a neat pin-striped lawyer's jacket. Now it was soiled with food and spittle.

The swing door to the kitchen opened. In the doorway stood one of the penguins, looking apologetic. His drooping eyes and sad mouth suggested that he was about to burst into tears.

'I'm sorry,' he said, 'but we have no more lamb.'

'What?' cried a man whom Josef knew to be a sheep farmer. 'No lamb? How can you tell us you have no lamb?'

At that, the fat men jumped up from the table with surprising alacrity. Tripping over the chairs, bumping into one another and brandishing their knives and forks, they charged at the waiter. 'Carve him up!' yelled the lawyer. 'Tear strips from him!'

The waiter fled with the mob at his heels. They struggled to fit through the doorway: they squeezed and trampled one another, and moans and farts escaped their bloated bodies. The waiter's fearful yells could be heard in the distance. There was a crashing of plates and a clatter of pots inside the kitchen, and then the last of the fat men had passed through the swing-door. Josef S was left alone, amid the chaos of their meal.

He had not known that he had so much sweat in him. At nights he woke sodden, the hair on his body sticking to him like the coat of an animal caught in the rain. Beneath the dark hair, his white skin was stretched tautly over his bones. He hated to look at himself as he stood, cornered by his delirium, driven by his illness from the treacherous security of his bed. Not wanting to wake Dorothy, he would remake the bed, swallow pills to numb the growing pain in his throat and crawl back, dreading the onset of the dreams.

The pain in his throat developed on the fourth day of illness. He said to Dorothy: 'Swallowing is like scraping a knife-blade over a raw wound. Perhaps this is my punishment for being able to eat while others are starving.'

She smiled and put her hand to his forehead to feel how hot he was. The pills were not much protection against the pain, and at nights, sometimes, he would wake suddenly and sit up with the certainty that he was a fish which had just been hooked in the mouth, and the hook was the seat of a pain that was unparalleled in his experience of pain. He would reach for his pills and his water and try to anaesthetise himself. On one occasion when he switched on his bedside light, his outstretched arm emitted steam, and he recalled a time when as a child he had been present at an early milking on a farm: the cows had risen at the prompting of the herders and the mud where they had lain had steamed in the chill air.

Josef became angry and frustrated at the restraints to his freedom of movement, and he wished to be well again. What anger and frustration do the people from the townships experience, he wondered. The laughing policemen, the silent women, the bitter young man and the jabbing umbrella haunted his waking state as the fat men tormented his dreams.

The builders seemed to pass to and fro outside his window banging a drum. Josef noticed this at various levels of consciousness for four days. Dorothy came and went, in command, bringing medicines and food. The spectral family he had acquired in the park paraded around the room, re-enacting the arrest, and his sense of injustice increased.

It was night: the builders had gone and Dorothy was asleep. He lay and stared at the cover of an unopened law report. Even though the fires in his body had cooled he could not concentrate on reading. The night was completely still. He closed his eyes, and saw a comforting vision of a lady convalescing on a terraced lawn, sipping tea, while a benign sun shone warmly and a bird chirped in a tree nearby. White garden furniture stood emptily on the green terrace. A peacock strutted across the lawn, its tail fanned magnificently, staring blindly at the lady with its manifold eyes.

Josef thought, as he lay in the darkness, that if he told Dorothy his dreams, she could write about them. Perhaps she could use them as images in her stories. But he had never told her his dreams. He drifted into sleep and slept his first full night in a week.

He woke weak and listless. Dorothy told him that his partner and senior clerks were sharing his work between them as well as they could in his absence. He remembered that he had been given this information before, but during his illness he had not known what to do with it. Now he felt relieved but redundant. How easy it is to be replaced by others! And of what value is your own work, indeed your life, when others can step in and take over as if you had never existed? The whole week had vanished and what had been gained? It must simply be written off, Josef S thought, a bad debt. He began to cough and to sweat again, but not badly, and he knew that soon he would have to stand and face the world again.

'A man is sitting outside in a white car with an official number plate,' Dorothy told him. 'He's pretending to read a newspaper.'

With a touch of sarcasm, Josef asked: 'Do you think we're being watched?'

'Of course not,' she replied sharply.

'Your writer's imagination is playing up again,' he chided her. 'You may not like the police, but that in itself is not a crime.'

'Not yet,' she said, and the words chilled him. In Valhalla they shot children. Why not add a lawyer and a writer to their hit list? Did there have to be a reason? Perhaps something she had written . . .

'I'm quite certain that the man in the white car isn't spying on us,' he said in his most convincing lawyer's manner. (He still remembered, he still had the skill. It was like riding a bicycle; you did not forget.)

Dorothy left the room, and he hoped that he had not hurt her. When she was vulnerable, he could hurt her in so many unwitting ways. In time, she would retaliate. 'I looked after you when you were ill,' he imagined her saying. 'You were as weak as a baby, and I nursed you. I mothered you. Without me, you would have starved. And as soon as you recovered, you relapsed into your old cruel ways. I am sorry.'

But when she returned, she simply said: 'You were right. The man has gone.'

Lex rested his head on the bed for Josef to pat.

Later Dorothy drove Josef up to the mountain, to the end of the road which petered out in a car park. He was too weak to leave the car. He sat and looked out over Eisstad and the sea. The rain had fallen steadily while he was sick, and now a rainbow was out. It spanned a full, brilliant arc, one foot in a suburban garden, the other in the purple sea beside a black rock, over which white spray was foaming. What a riot of colour! After the sameness of his room, day after day, disturbed only by his dreams and the labourers, the external stimulation was deeply satisfying.

With the thirst of a dehydrated man, he drank in the scenery. The sea was flat, at sullen peace with the shore. And Eisstad gleamed as if it had been freshly polished: the white houses nestling in the foothills of the mountain, the office blocks in the city centre, and the old City Hall in the square. In its day it had been the outstanding building, now it was dwarfed by the monstrous slabs around it, its clock tower chiming for a past age. Josef S identified his office and the Court, and the vicinity of his house below.

Behind the car, the mass of the Leeukop rose, awe-inspiring, its head lost in the clouds. From the car park, a path led up the face of the mountain, and Josef S imagined lions stalking down to the houses. But when there had been lions, there had been no houses, only a trading post fenced off from the threat of the interior. He could see the area beside the harbour, known as Waterfront, where the old fish factory stood, and he resolved to walk through it when he had fully recovered; perhaps an exposure to history would help him to understand the present.

32

He strained to see the townships, Valhalla, Sonnestraal and Vrede, but they were lost in the depths of the interior hidden by cloud. Is it not strange, he thought, that they are shooting children there, that flames and anarchy are the governors of those places, while twenty minutes away, by car, the suburbs are peaceful and the inhabitants virtually unaware of their neighbours' predicament? Which is worse, he wondered, being confronted by violence as a fact of life, or having to endure the nightmare of imagining it, waiting for it to come closer, waiting for the day when the anger would spill into the suburbs of Eisstad and destroy its icy tranquility for ever?

Dorothy was quiet. Their breathing was the only communication between them. Old antagonists, yet familiar ones. He took her hand and held it and she did not resist. Something approximating a feeling of peace descended, as though the mountain had laid a massive hand in blessing on them, soothing away their small worries with its timeless grandeur. Like two warriors who have declared a truce, they sat staring at the city and the sea.

A little way below the car park, a path led to a cannon which pointed to the harbour. The Department of Parks and Forests had cleaned up the old weapon, repaired the holes in the long barrel, painted it silver and put a chain around it. A neat silver pile of recently cast cannon balls formed a pyramid, a memorial to the wars of former ages. The path had a gentle incline, down which week-end hikers and hordes of children on school outings trooped to inspect the weapon that had once protected the fledgling community against attacks from the sea. Josef found it hard to believe that its range was capable of reaching the sea. Surely every firing would have caused the risk of sending the balls (were they silver in those days too?) crashing into the gardens, or roofs, of the burghers of Eisstad. Now the weapon sat, gleaming, proud, useless, a spent force watching over violence of a different nature with its black blind eye; violence that came from the land, violence with its roots as far back into history as the cannon itself. Whatever death or discomfort the cannon had caused was long forgotten. The weapon had outlived such memories; it was simply a handsome plaything for the children, a place to eat your sandwiches before you began the ascent of the Leeukop. Someone had scrawled the initials M.S. onto its surface, and on a nearby stone someone had painted in red: JEROME LOVES CINDI.

'Let's go,' Dorothy said. 'I must feed Lex.'

They drove past a small white building near to the car park. The early lion hunters had used it as a base for their expeditions on the mountain; recently it too had been renovated for the tourists.

A flood of tiredness poured over the invalid and the rain returned, covering the city in a mask of water.

The sole was lightly fried; Dorothy had made it as he liked. He squeezed lemon juice on the meat and pared a piece from the bone. He was chewing slowly (it seemed the first thing he had eaten in a week) when Dorothy spoke. She had not touched her food, but had been fidgeting with her napkin.

'Josef . . .' she began.

He looked up and saw that her eyes were misty.

'What is it?'

'I've been thinking . . .'

'Tell me,' he said gently.

She took a deep breath. 'Josef, I want to have a child.'

The lawyer sat back, put his fork down and said calmly: 'You didn't used to.'

'I'm changing, Josef. My writing isn't fulfilling me as it once did.' He said nothing and she went on, not looking at him, staring at her hands. 'Josef. Do you understand? If I don't have children soon, it'll be too late.'

'There's still time,' he said reluctantly.

'No, Josef. It sounds paradoxical, but despite my age, I still feel that a part of me is a teenager. And I imagine that people are looking at me and saying: "That's Dorothy Knox the author. She has no real children, only books."'

'Of course they're not saying that,' was all he could muster.

'Josef, I'm beginning to feel biologically useless.'

'But Dorothy, we agreed in the beginning . . .'

The expression on her face changed. As if a new person had suddenly entered her body, the sadness disappeared and she smiled, an icy, glazed smile. 'It's all right, Josef. I know what we agreed. I'm sorry I mentioned it.' She cut a piece of fish and put it in her mouth.

Dressed in his father's overcoat, Josef S walked. Clouds packed the sky, but they seemed to be high up and, although they turned the day grey, it would not rain. Probably he should not be exposing himself to the cold so soon after his illness, but he had promised himself this excursion. Behind him, the Leeukop dominated the city, almost black, its head lost in cloud.

Josef walked with his hands stuck in his pockets and his face obscured by a scarf. He had not yet gone back to work, and he felt like a schoolboy playing truant.

The streets were empty. Had the city been evacuated without his knowledge? Had the war in the townships torn through these streets too, and whipped away the people with the force of a hurricane? As if to negate so preposterous an idea, a young boy dashed out of a building, followed by a dog. They disappeared into a sidestreet. It was a glimpse of normality, succeeded again by silence, as if Josef were walking through a dream. Sometimes scenes from his delirium returned to him, and he imagined that, behind these walls, fantastic banquets were taking place, and he had only to step into any of these buildings to find a group of fat men stuffing fish into their mouths.

The sea air was brisk and smelled of fish. He thought of the frozen blocks he had seen scudding across the pavement. As the Republic's harbour city, Eisstad was of course a fish city. It had been built on the bones of fish dredged from the sea, tons and tons of them over the years; it was surprising that anything was still left.

As a child, when his mother was still alive, Josef S had gone fishing with his father. On Sundays, they had walked out on the pier, where the other anglers stood already connected by fine lines to the sea. He remembered sparkling, endless waters, gently swelling, so that the pier felt like a tilting boat; and sometimes angry breakers heavy with sharks. His father would bait his hook for him and throw the line out. Then there'd be the thrill of small mouths pulling on the lure, the knowledge that you had made contact with something alive in that great depth, something invisible but drawn to you by a secret signal.

The boy had never wanted actually to snare these teasing mysterious presences, and was always relieved when, as usual, he brought his hook up, stripped bare, catching nothing. He enjoyed being with his father, doing 'grown up' things, and experienced a secret shame at his compassion, which he kept well hidden.

Once, to his father's delight, he hooked and landed a kob as long as his arm. He brought to the surface a creature which had previously known only the soft folds of water smoothing past its sensuous body, and watched it die on the hard unyielding concrete. He did not want to touch the corpse, although all round him on the pier anglers were sticking their fingers into the bony mouths of their catches, caressing the pink flesh as though it belonged to infants. The boy cried for the death he had caused, but allowed no one to

35

see the tears. After a while, he stopped going to the pier with his father, and was obliged to invent excuses, as his motive would not have been understood. Where had the compassion come from? He had certainly not acquired it from his father. His mother had never taken sides on such issues; he did not know what she had felt. Was it a trait inherited from earlier generations — something stored in his genes for use at an appropriate moment?

He had not been to Waterfront for years. He was interested, but not surprised, to see how the political grafitti that was a mark of the times had taken hold here — a small overflowing of anger from the townships: THIS IS CIVIL WAR, RELEASE MKHIZE, PLEASE BUTH, GET THE POLICE OUT OF OUR TOWNSHIPS, BOYCOTT. The latter had been spraypainted in huge white letters on a concrete warehouse wall. There was no indication of what its author wanted to boycott; perhaps, Josef reflected wryly, everything.

A man in a black overcoat and checked cap made his unsteady way down the street, carrying a brown paper packet that betrayed the shape of a bottle. He lurched across the road towards Josef S, and the lawyer's pulse quickened. He was still too weak to run away if he had to: even from a drunk. The man managed to position himself in front of Josef, blocking his way. He had red eyes, thick lips, irregular teeth and a scar on his forehead. Words tumbled from his mouth, unjoined, to create a pattern of unhappiness in the air between them: 'Hungry . . . no job . . . can't think when I'm hungry . . .' The lawyer thought of retorting: 'Can't think when you're drunk, either.' But instead he put his hand to his pocket, aware that the red eyes were following the movement in an unfocussed way, and retrieved a few coins. 'Here,' he said, not even checking their value.

The man accepted them and stepped aside, allowing Josef to pass, as if he were the gate-keeper to a forbidden city. Even though the drunk had not been threatening, Josef felt relief, as if he had escaped from danger, if only temporarily. However much one gives, he thought, there are always going to be more beggars. Behind him, he heard: 'Thank you, sir . . . God bless you . . . God be with you . . .' Josef turned. The man had his hand to his cap: he lowered it to cross himself clumsily, and bowed. Then he shuffled away. Beggars and tramps seemed to have a direct line to the Almighty.

The buildings were drab: some were obviously houses, others showed nondescript facades and could have been offices or factories. In the grey light of the middle afternoon, few buildings stood out. There was a uniformity of style as though the builders had been forced to contend with adverse economic conditions, or as if the appearance of the buildings had not been considered important. Waterfront was an oppressive place; all the life seemed to have been squeezed out of it. Once people had thronged the streets, once a community had lived here. But the people had been cast out, sent to the townships, and their homes had been converted to warehouses. The place seemed to have a surly will of its own. As Josef walked, the buildings glowered at him and he hurried to be away from the deadness.

The Waterfront absorbed Josef S as it had always absorbed the lost. Had he really expected to learn something here about the troubles in the country? Perhaps he could decipher the activities of the past inhabitants: workers tramping from the docks, shouldering duffle bags; sailors released onto land in search of earthly delights denied them at sea; children playing games in the streets; women hanging washing from the upper windows, so that the bleak walls of the buildings would be gaily decorated; public airings of private disputes, with passers-by taking sides, one group supporting the husband, the other the wife.

Events like these had happened here. Perhaps the knowledge was embedded in the stones, causing these images to flow into his mind. Eisstad's Waterfront should have been a lively place, but the cold sea air flowing between the gaps in the buildings carried a sense of desolation. Where once the smell had heralded the appearance of fish-sellers, marketing their merchandise from barrows, now their cries were absent and only his footsteps rang on the cobbles of the streets. Perhaps it is Friday, Josef S thought, and everyone has gone home.

Where were the workers? Even though the city had expelled some of its citizens, it still had to have workers: flower and fruit sellers, men on construction sites, stevedores, employees of the railways. Admittedly they no longer lived in the city, but they still worked in it. Where were they? They could not have vanished as if they had been sent to the moon. But the streets of Waterfront were empty: the further Josef went, the worse it became.

A poster on a wall presented the sole spot of colour in the grey sameness. Its edges were torn; obviously someone had attempted, unsuccessfully, to remove it. The message, however, was intact and provided the reason for the desolation: SUPPORT THE BOYCOTT, in large black letters on a red background depicting an armoured police vehicle and a group of children running. Smaller letters along the bottom of the poster declaimed: POLICE OUT OF THE TOWN-SHIPS. FREE DETAINEES. The date given was, Josef saw, that day's. He realised that there had been no deliverymen in the streets of the suburbs, nor had the builders hammered outside his window.

When he had left his house in the afternoon, the watchman had been sitting on a yellow chair. They had nodded at each other and a touch of a smile had played at the corners of the man's mouth. He was pulling on a pipe; the woman, bent double, was washing clothes in a plastic tub. Did he know about the boycott? Did sitting on a yellow chair in the middle of the afternoon constitute a boycott of his own? If he was dismissed as a result of his action, would he be sent back to Valhalla? Did he agree with the boycott, or was he forced to participate by what the Government called 'radical agita-tors'?

In the middle of the Republic's intense political activity, he, Josef S, was a shadow, who passed over the earth leaving no mark of his passage. A spell of faintness made him pause for a moment; he had walked too far for a convalescent. He leaned against a wall. The roar of the sea sounded in his ears, and the shouts of the ghosts of former inhabitants filled the space of the street, echoing from wall to wall: they were shouting about fish, freshly caught, and newspapers and fruit. He heard shrieking but could not locate its source.

A cold wind was whirling papers in the gutter. Josef sat for a while, dizzy and unwilling to stand until his strength returned. Imagine if any of my colleagues were to see me now, he thought, sitting in a gutter in Waterfront. What would they think of me? What would Dorothy think? But he knew it did not really matter. Order and sys-tems were being turned on their heads in the Republic. Josef knew that he was being swept along on the tide of change.

A pamphlet among the papers in the street caught his eye. SUP-PORT THE BOYCOTT the red letters proclaimed, echoing the tat-tered poster on the wall. 'We must show our anger at the system that has thrown us out of our homes and given us an unequal education . . .' Josef crumpled the paper and stood, propping him-self against the wall. The smell of fish was stronger and he knew he was close to the water. He walked without stumbling, his strength returning, through the corridor of buildings until suddenly he was at the edge of the sea.

On his right lay the harbour with its flotillas of tugs and yachts and oil tankers, sleek as swords, in the slate-grey water. Cranes, metal birds, dipped their noses towards the water in search of cargo while predatory seagulls circled overhead, squawking from their red maws, diving when their sharp eyes located something edible.

To his left a row of houses, run-down and empty, overlooked the water. Their front walls were numbered: 30, 28, 26, 24; then a vacant lot with grass growing waist-high and wild, in tufts, like hair on a partially bald head; then 20, and so on. Faded notices decorated some of the walls. On one sign was written: STICK NO BILLS. On another: TO LET.

The fish factory stood tall and gaunt, its red bricks pocked and pitted by the assault of the sea air. A grand wooden door was set back from the street, reached by a flight of stairs; it had huge brass knobs, green and tarnished. An opaque glass pane positioned high up must have allowed a modicum of light to enter the building. Josef remembered the previous door, thick rusty steel that had clanged shut as solidly as the door of a cell or a bank vault. When he was a child, the city's treasures were processed behind these red walls.

'How long has this building been here, Dad?' the boy asked.

'About a hundred years,' replied the big man beside him.

'Fish for a hundred years!' exclaimed Josef. 'So many fish!'

The man laughed, a lion's roar: 'This factory is the second . . . It's built on the site of an even older factory which was made out of stone.'

'Who built the first one?' the boy asked.

'The original settlers. They built it as a store to supply passing ships with fruit and vegetables.'

Josef had reached the topmost step. As he stood there, he almost stretched out his hand to the tall man in the grey overcoat.

'An inventor called Gomez tried to freeze vegetables and fruit but he couldn't stop the ice from melting. He knew that freezing would keep food fresh, but people laughed at poor Gomez because he couldn't get his theory to work. He was too advanced for his time.' The voice from the past began to dim.

'What happened to Gomez? Tell me what happened to him!' the boy insisted.

'No one knows. He disappeared. People think he was driven away by the mockery of the burghers, and that he went to hide on the Leeukop and was eaten by lions. There were still lions on the mountain in those days. But his body was never found, nor his bones. Maybe the burghers were afraid to go and look. They turned the

39

building into a factory for fish and no one tried to freeze food any more. Not for hundreds of years.'

'But people didn't forget him, did they Dad?' The boy demanded that his father bestow immortality: the story, often repeated, gained the quality of myth, and the reassurances were always there.

'Oh no, Josef, of course not. He gave the city its name: Eisstad, the City of Ice. It was a joke at first, I suppose, but it stuck. Before Gomez, the city had no name. In fact it was not even meant to be — originally it was just going to be a place for ships to stop on their long voyages round the coast . . .'

No one knew what Gomez looked like. There were no pictures: he had simply been an obscure settler whom no one would have remembered at all if he had not wanted to keep vegetables on ice. A statue to the man, dressed in the clothes of the time, but featureless, stood overlooking the town square. What sort of heritage is this, Josef would wonder, when the most important man in our history has no face?

Every day had been a holocaust at the fish factory: the clatter of machinery, the winches, the flowing silver bodies, rivers of death to be gutted and packaged, or smashed and ground into meal. Now the factory had become a shell with the atmosphere that old prisons or old concentration camps wear, places where immense suffering has occurred, places that exist in the hearts of cities, where people know and condone.

'What about the people who lived here already?' the boy asked. 'What happened to them? Didn't they have a name for the place? Aren't there statues for them?'

'Their descendants live here in Waterfront, Josef,' the voice replied faintly. And were moved out to ghettos with euphemistic names on the Flatlands by Buth's Government, reflected the lawyer, where they cannot taint us with their presence. They went, leaving ghosts behind, leaving empty buildings and streets populated by a few tramps and beggars. And the ghettos breed youngsters who know how to throw stones better than to write their own names, and Peace and Sunshine are littered with the bodies of children, killed to preserve a cold and callous system.

Suddenly Josef saw that the fish factory was the centre of Eisstad: the cold heart of the city. Perhaps that was why he had been drawn back to it now, in this time of upheaval. No clatter of machinery greeted him as he stood on the threshold of this dark place. The red brick, though it might have been intended to make the place cheerful, was ominous and stark, no improvement on the stone. The heart of Eisstad, begun with hope and enthusiasm, had become a death factory, was itself dead. And the decay had spread through the city, and through the Republic. As a body dies in stages, so the Republic was thrashing and kicking in its death throes. What would take its place? Would this building have any part in the future? 'Will it, Dad?' Josef urged. 'Tell me, what will happen?' But only the wind spoke, flicking the tips of the waves to white froth.

Josef S pushed on the door, not expecting anything to happen. He was surprised when it moved effortlessly on its hinges. There was a scurrying inside, the noise of small animals. The interior was lit by a few candles which flickered as he entered with the wind; voices whispered. The huge dark hall, its smooth floors once covered in scales and blood and crates, and shouting men with hoses, was now silent as a museum with the pitter-patter of rats' feet, scavengers in the darkness.

Intellect told him to get out: he was still at the door, he could still escape. But curiosity kept him inside to face any danger. The light outside was too weak to penetrate the few windows; perhaps most of them had been painted over to exclude light. As his eyes grew accustomed to the darkness, Josef walked in further, and came into the light of the candles. His footsteps made little sound on the stone floor; he held his breath.

Suddenly, a group of seven or eight boys surrounded him, chattering like squirrels, none of them taller than his chest. Feeling like a large animal surrounded by small predators, Josef lifted his hands to show that he carried no weapons. The leader (he was the biggest, a fat boy) stood right up against Josef's chest; he smelled, a smell of the streets. Josef saw something in the boy's hand gleam in the candlelight, but strangely he had no fear. Instead, exhilaration overwhelmed him and he grew light-headed with joy.

'Do you live here?' he asked, and the shapes rustled around him, ghosts returned to life, menacing. Josef began to laugh recklessly, abandoning himself to whatever fate lay in store. The rustling receded uncertainly. He heard someone say: 'This one is mad,' and he saw no reason to refute the allegation.

'Who are you?' the leader asked.

'A friend,' said Josef S. 'I mean you no harm.'

'What do you want?'

I want to find something to believe in. I want this heart of ice to beat with blood again, but not with the blood of death. I want life

41

to return to the veins of Waterfront, and lions to roam on the slopes of the Leeukop, and the statue of Gomez to grow features overnight, sculptured by the spirits of Eisstad. I want the Government to stop murdering children in Valhalla; I want them to release Raymond Mkhize of the FDF. I want my brother to return unharmed from killing; I want to love my wife, and be able to put up with the dog . . . Is that enough?

'Nothing,' said Josef S. 'I want nothing. I heard a noise and came to investigate. That's all. I mean you no harm.'

At this, the leader put away his knife. As if it were a signal, the circle dispersed; the boys seemed to forget that Josef was there. They howled and bullied each other and plunged into physical games, sometimes illuminated by candlelight, sometimes in darkness. The menace was gone. Is it so easy, Josef asked himself, to win them over? These are the children for whom the women chained themselves in protest: perhaps their friends have died, but they are still children. What stupidities lead to the deaths of children?

'Where are your parents?' Josef asked.

'We can't stay with our parents,' the fat boy said. He stood back, inspecting his captive by the meagre light.

'Do you come from Valhalla?'

'Valhalla, Vrede, Son. Him!' the boy pointed into the darkness. 'He ran away because his father gets drunk and hits him.' He indicated himself. 'Me, my parents are dead and I've got to look after all of them.'

The candles flickered, the children shrieked and jumped about; they formed circles and danced, leaping onto one another's shoulders.

'Give us some money' the fat boy demanded. 'We're hungry. We want to buy bread.'

Josef S searched through his pockets, found a note and gave it to the boy, who scrutinised it closely and then let out a yell of delight, and dived into the pack of his mates, flourishing the windfall. While the children scrummaged furiously, squealing and flailing their arms, Josef let himself out of the building, escaping from the oppressive darkness into the cold streets of Eisstad.

A light rain had begun to fall and Josef hunched into his coat, walking quickly to be away from this dreary place. A man on crutches hobbled past. One of his legs had been amputated at the knee. He wore a white cap, a nondescript navy coat and brown trousers with one leg pinned above the stump. He was making slow progress towards the harbour, holding a brown case in the hand that straddled one of the crutches like a guitarist's hand resting on his instrument. As he passed an advertisement saying: WE BUILD YOUR FUTURE — BANKEIS, the wind meddled with his coat and his trouser leg, but he seemed inured to cold. He was one of the unheralded pillars of Eisstad. Once, Josef S would not have noticed this man. Now the lawyer stopped to watch, wondering where the cripple found the will, day after day, to struggle to work and home again, so determined that he was even prepared to defy the boycott.

A boy scuttled out from a doorway behind the low wall of a verandah. He thrust a roll of peppermints at Josef S. 'Want one?' he grinned.

Taken aback, the lawyer shook his head; the urchin pulled a sweet from the roll and stuffed it into his mouth, which seemed to contain its fair share of mints already.

'Maybe *he* wants one,' Josef said, gesturing after the cripple, who was almost out of sight down the road. The boy, barefoot and snot-nosed, leaped after the man. Waterfront was still capable of surprising: in the nooks and crannies of apparent emptiness, behind the shuttered windows and barricaded doorways, people lived and moved like the small ecosystems one finds in the corners of a garden, perhaps under a discarded mat where multitudes of small creatures have chosen to build a temporary life, under persistent threat of eviction stubbornly clinging to their territories.

A car was approaching. It caught up with the man in the overcoat and drew alongside him as he walked, a yellow police van with its blue insignias and wire-mesh over the windows, protection against the stones in the townships. The driver, leaning out of his window, gave the bedraggled figure a hard look. Josef S returned the stare.

'You all right, sir?' the policeman asked.

'Yes, thank you, I'm fine.'

'Well be careful. You know they're causing trouble today. You don't want them to stone you.'

'No, I'm sure I'll be fine. There's been no trouble.'

'Do you want a lift, sir?' the policeman insisted. 'We can put you in the back.' He laughed.

'Yes, I know. Thank you, I'll walk.'

'Good afternoon, sir.' The policeman accelerated at breakneck speed up the empty street, as if to show how little he minded having his offer spurned, his professional advice ignored. In the wake of his departure, silence washed back. Both the boy and the cripple,

Josef noticed, had vanished, as mice do when a cat appears.

As if he were returning from work, Josef S bought his evening newspaper and, as usual, caught a bus. He sat reading about a man, a Doctor Albert Poynter, who was fasting in the Hunting Lodge on the mountain behind the car park, fasting for peace. Dr Poynter ran a clinic in Valhalla. He had treated the teargas victims and the bullet wounds, and he was using his fast to draw attention to the conditions in the townships. There was a picture of the man in front of a huge candle which had been lit at the launch of his fast. The caption announced that he was going to fast for three weeks.

The idea of Home tugged at Josef with a promise of sanctuary after his discoveries in Waterfront. He walked briskly from the bus-stop, pausing to nod at the woman who lived next door; she smiled back from behind her window boxes. He did not know her name and he doubted whether she knew his, although Dorothy might have spoken to her; she had never mentioned it. The woman was a survivor from a different time, an older time when children were sacred and did not swarm in the shell of an abandoned fish factory; a time when children had been cared for, not shot in the streets, when no one had to fast for peace because peace already existed. Or was such a time simply an illusion which this woman with her white hair and lopsided grin had created? Did she have children of her own, grown up and gone away? Perhaps she would have liked to look after the lost boys the city bred, caring for them as lovingly as she watered her plants. Or perhaps she was mad, and chattered to her reflection in the mirror, only emerging in her lucid periods, incapable of looking after anyone. Certainly she had no idea of the violence being perpetrated no more than half an hour away from her.

The light was brilliant. Rain poured down from a purple sky, as if to purify the blighted earth. The leaves of the fig and orange trees were bright green, lit by the dying sun. The orange tree was in flower, but the rain had quenched the smell that had recently invaded the kitchen. Josef stood before the open window and looked out at the golden wall at the end of the garden.

'God, but it's been raining,' Dorothy said, and when he did not answer, continued: 'Did you have a good walk? You were gone for longer than I thought you'd be. I began to worry.'

'I was trying to rediscover my childhood — I don't know how well I succeeded. Perhaps I simply got caught in the rain.'

'You should be careful. You've been sick. Where were you walking?'

Josef began to tell her that he had fainted down in Waterfront. Then he realised that she would merely worry, and that no purpose would be gained by her knowing. Silence breeds misunderstanding; suddenly you are talking past each other, if indeed you are talking at all.

'Downtown,' he answered non-committally.

'Come and eat,' she said.

'Yes,' he responded. A double line of ants on the kitchen ceiling moved simultaneously in opposite directions. He watched their organised disorder. Everyone is looking for food, he thought. Yet my wife wants to feed me and I don't wish to eat. He went reluctantly.

'Someone is fasting for peace,' he told Dorothy. 'I read about him in the newspaper.'

'I hope he finds peace,' she answered, deliberately misunderstanding him.

'Yes, I hope so,' Josef said, and a feeling of terrible sadness came over him. He wanted to tell Dorothy of the women who had chained themselves to the fence of Parliament, but he could not. 'What is our neighbour's name?' he asked eventually.

'The old woman? That's Iris Milner.'

'Do you see her at all? Socially, I mean.'

'Sometimes we have tea together,' Dorothy said, 'but not often. I haven't been over for a few weeks.'

'Does she ever come here?' he asked, startled by the notion that this woman, who was a stranger, had been into his house.

'Occasionally. Why?' Dorothy asked sharply. 'Would you rather she didn't?'

'No, no.' he said hurriedly. If she came more often, he thought, perhaps she would bring her aura of peace to stay. Perhaps peace would slip off her, like an old skin, and find a new home here.

'I thought it might be a good thing if she spent time with us,' he said. 'She probably gets lonely . . . all day alone with her plants . . .'

Dorothy failed to answer, implying that the conversation had become absurd and could be taken no further. The dog thrust his jaw into his master's lap, looking up with adoring eyes. Josef patted the ugly head absent-mindedly, Lex stuck out his tongue and Josef pushed the dog away with the back of his hand, trying to concentrate on his food. He had no appetite for supper: sole again, this time grilled and covered in butter sauce. He forced the white meat into his mouth. In the dream, their mouths had been running with grease, their fingers had glistened. Their sucking noises had echoed through into his waking.

If Dorothy noticed his abstraction, she did not comment. She ate, then stood and went to the kitchen to fetch the dessert. Josef fed his fish to the dog. By the time his wife returned, the crocodile jaws had snapped shut and Lex was happily licking his lips. Josef felt a twinge of guilt at wasting a good supper; he thought of the children in the factory and wondered what they would eat that night. Dessert was fruit salad and ice-cream.

He thrust himself home against her, forcing himself to climax by imagining that he was hurting her, that his passion would cause her to haemorrhage, that she would climax again and again until she could not breathe and died beneath him. They were two opposing armies, sweating, trapped in battle against each other. He lay on top of her, and she accepted that his need had ended; she waited for him, stroking his hair as if she cared. He smelled her on his fingers: an old battlefield, another battle. He looked painfully into her eyes and saw a mysterious wanting, although she said nothing. She asked for nothing, and he had nothing to give. For a moment, again, his hand was his father's, down to the shape of the wrinkles around the knuckles, and the fingernails. It seemed obscene that this hand should have been sexually involved with his wife. Later he saw that there was blood on his fingers — she had not told him that she was bleeding — and on the sheets. He caressed her mechanically and she responded, and gooseflesh rose on his arms. He got up and washed, then returned to sleep.

The shrieking that woke him was the telephone ringing. Josef S rose cold and confused. Dorothy moaned and reached out for him. In the darkness he stumbled against a chair: the thick white curtains cut off any light from the street. If the curtains were drawn, no noise could intrude from across the road, the man who slept in the garage could not keep them awake with his midnight stampings, and the flickering from his fire-drum could not enter the room. Josef lifted the receiver. Lex howled at the disturbance.

'Josef!' The voice was abrasive, young.

'Robert?' Josef asked, hazily. 'Robert, is that you?'

'Yes, Josef, hello.' He offered no apology for calling in the middle of the night.

'Where are you? Is anything wrong?'

'I'm in Eisstad.' The voice slurred, as if its owner had been drinking. 'Can I come and stay?'

'Of course you can. Do you want me to fetch you?'

'No. I can find my way to your house. I'll see you now.' The phone went dead. As if the receiver were a dangerous object, Josef S put it down carefully, and went back to Dorothy. He stroked the soft hair on her neck for comfort as if the storm was gathering and he was powerless to withstand it.

'Robert is coming to stay,' he said. 'He was drunk.'

'He's welcome,' she answered. 'We haven't heard from him for so long . . .' She stopped. She might have said: 'I thought he was dead.'

2

The young man, hardly older than a boy, sipped the hot drink that Dorothy had prepared. He reclined in a lounge chair — he was so drunk that he could not sit up — and rested the coffee on his chest, folding his hands around the cup as though every bit of warmth was welcome. He wore a thick blue fisherman's jersey, faded blue denims, and army boots; his fair hair was tousled as though he had not washed or brushed it for days, his bloodshot eyes tried to focus on the cup, but closed intermittently. He had brought no bag, had simply arrived, rough and bleary, at the door, half an hour after the phone call. He must have walked; no sign of possible transport was in the street when Josef looked. The night was cold and peaceful, the stars glittered icily in the black sky, and the boy had leaned against the doorpost, his head too heavy to be supported on his frail shoulders. One of my wishes has been granted, Josef thought, but is he indeed unharmed?

The Leeukop brooded over Eisstad. Josef had almost expected to see bright lights, lions' eyes, gliding through the bushes, old dusty forms come to life in the midnight, preparing to prowl through the peaceful streets. Would Mrs Milner be strong, or silent, or insensitive enough to avoid the attention of these roving beasts, as their talons raked through the darkness, as their bodies, propelled by ropy muscles tight as springs, launched into the air? Would the night-watchman, sleeping peacefully in his garage across the road, wake to see a snarling golden red-bespattered presence sent in by the night?

Dorothy stood above the young man while Josef sat and watched, wanting to know his brother's story, but reluctant to intrude before it was time. Dorothy wore a white dressing gown. Her red hair fell like fire on her shoulders and her green eyes burned. Her voice was husky with sleep, and Josef reflected what a mystery she was to him. She had taken Robert under her wing with the protectiveness of a fiery bird; suddenly the mystery of his wife sparked his interest, and he wanted to stand up and put his hands on her hips, and run his fingers through that flaming hair until they caught fire. He wanted to cup his hands on her breasts beneath the gown and force her onto the couch.

'We've made a bed for you in the spare room,' Dorothy said. 'You

48

can bath if you like.'

Robert sat silently, staring at his cup. Lex lay in a corner of the lounge, strangely subdued, bewildered by this midnight disturbance. Then the young man began to laugh, just a quiet chuckling, as if some absurdity was too great to be left unacknowledged.

'Thank you,' he mumbled, and the brashness was gone. 'Yes, I'll bath. I haven't bathed for quite some time. It will be good to bath,' he said, repeating the word like a charm. He got up, unsteadily, unwinding like a roll of string until he stood taller than the others, head still bowed. Josef was struck by how young he looked, and how old; a tired spirit inhabited the boy's body. A chill passed through the lawyer: what were they doing to the youth of the country when even a bath had become an exotic concept?

'Come on then.' Dorothy took his hand and led him to the bathroom. 'I've got a towel for you.' He went, accepting her authority as if she were his mother.

'I'll see you in the morning,' Josef heard himself say. 'Dorothy will take care of you.'

Was he abrogating his responsibility? But the woman had it all under control, the woman knew what to do, the woman had the ability to tread the delicate paths surely and with steady steps. Where he would have been awkward, she was gentle; where he would have been clumsy, she was firm. If Dorothy had not been there, how would he have dealt with this raw boy, stripped naked by the army? She will care for you like a mother, he wanted to say. She will wash you with her gentle fire, and you will be cleansed. It may take days or weeks, my brother, but Dorothy will undo what they have done to you. She will dig out the ignorant weed they have implanted, and with her gentleness, she will cultivate a new seed.

'Goodnight, Joe,' the boy slurred, and, turning to the dog: 'Goodnight, Rex.' The bull terrier's ears pricked up and then relaxed, and he whined. Did he sense the presence of lions in the house? Almost boastfully, Robert added: 'I'm really drunk, aren't I?' As though drunkenness were the gate to normal life.

'You seem to be,' Josef said. 'Don't fall asleep in the bath.'

Again Robert laughed; the sound got caught in his throat like a cough. 'What a way to end it,' he said. 'After everything, to drown in my brother's bath. Don't worry, Josef, I've survived worse . . .'

He seemed on the point of telling a story, but then thought better of it, or perhaps tiredness got the upper hand, and he went down the passage. Soon, there was a sound of running water.

Josef returned to bed. After a while, Dorothy climbed in beside him.

'Did he talk to you?' Josef asked. 'You handled him well.'

'He didn't say very much,' she answered. 'I showed him to the spare room.'

'I wonder how long he's going to stay. He's changed.'

'Of course he's changed. He's been in the army for two years.'

'They've made him unrecognisable. Who is he now?'

She snuggled up to him. 'He's drunk, Josef. In the morning, he'll be your brother again.'

'But did I even know him before he went in?' Josef mused. He stroked her arm, but the desire he had experienced earlier was gone and he could not coax it back by the effort of his will. He tried to recall the thoughts which had so attracted him to her, but they refused to reveal themselves; they lay as dormant as the erection he had lost. So easily, he could have touched her as he had wanted to earlier, and she would have responded to his need (as always), but now that she was close enough, he could not. Did she sense the conflict in him? If she did, she hid the knowledge behind her mysterious facade. Perhaps it found expression in her writings, perhaps he was the villain in her stories, or the puzzled anti-hero. How did she see him? She never said, just as he did not tell her of his thoughts. They kept their secrets from each other.

'I'm going to work,' he said. 'I feel better.'

She lay in the darkness, her face in the pillow. She may have been thinking that he was leaving her to look after his brother, that he had chosen to return to work because his brother would be home, and he did not want to face him all day long, that he was shirking his responsibilities. She may have been angry that she would have a distraction at home which would interfere with her work. He had no idea what she was thinking. She moved her head to breathe, and said: 'Yes, I think you're better. You must sleep if you're going to work.'

'Yes,' he said, 'I must sleep,' although there was not much sleep left in the night, and if he had peered through the curtains, he would have seen the new morning infuse the sky with blood, which had already begun to settle on the land and to drain into the sea.

Ben stood at his desk. 'I'm glad to see you back, Mr S,' he said.

'Thank you, Ben,' replied Josef. 'How have you been?'

'Fine,' the clerk said hesitantly, shuffling his feet into the carpet, and staring at his shoes.

'Is anything wrong?'

'No, not really, sir.' But he remained where he was.

Usually, Josef S did not have tolerance for this kind of hesitation, especially in the middle of a working day, when eliciting statements from hesitant people was part of his job. Perhaps his sickness had left him weaker and feebler, and more open to listening to the complaints of his clerk. Before, he might have snapped, been abrupt, and the boy would have crawled away, tail between his legs, but today, on the day of his return, he listened. And Ben seemed to feel free to approach, as if his employer possessed a new softness.

'Is someone bothering you at work, Ben?' Josef asked, prodding at the boy's nervousness.

'I want to take a day off next week, Mr S.'

'Have you asked Mr Parry?'

'He won't let me go.'

'Why?'

'Mr Parry was angry with me because I stayed away yesterday. Because of the boycott. I couldn't come to work . . . it was dangerous. They were stoning the cars leaving Valhalla and checking people on the buses. Mr Parry phoned me and told me to come in, but I told him it was too dangerous. He didn't believe me, Mr S. He doesn't know what it's like in the townships.'

Ben's words were part of a different fabric; they expressed a reality that was as alien to Josef S as if it were taking place on the moon. He read of these things in the newspapers, but he could not put pictures to the words. It was a shock to realise that timid Ben lived out Josef's nightmares; daily, Ben had to endure war at home while his employers returned to their safe streets.

'Perhaps Mr Parry does not understand,' Josef offered.

'Mr Parry does not want to understand,' Ben said, and suddenly Josef saw bitterness and anger in the young man's eyes. He had never seen bitterness in Ben's eyes before, he had never thought of him as a political animal. The order was changing, the ice was melting as a hot wind blew in from the ghettos.

'The comrades were going from house to house in the townships yesterday, Mr S,' Ben said, 'checking to see if the men were at home. They were asking the women where their husbands were, and if the men were at work, they threatened to burn down the houses. Mr Parry does not want to understand these things because they interfere with his idea of what the law should be. The only law in the

51

townships these days is the law of the gun and the law of fire.' Ben was no longer looking at his shoes; he was staring into his employer's eyes with the anger of fires. The burning townships were reflected in his eyes. 'Gangs went through the factories in Waterfront yesterday, warning the workers to go home or they would burn down the factories. And Mr Parry phoned me to come to work.' A sound like a grunt forced itself from Ben's throat. 'In the next block, a man I know was shot by the police. That's why I want a day off. His funeral is next week.'

'Why did they shoot him, Ben?'

'He was standing outside talking to some people and they drove past and saw him, and they chased him into his house.' Ben put a hand to his eyes and was silent for a moment; then he recovered. 'They kicked down his door and followed him into his house and shot him in the back in his kitchen. His wife was hiding under the table with the baby, but they didn't see her. They just wanted blood, so they shot him. Next week is his funeral. Our whole suburb is going, everyone who knew him: we have a very close community, Mr S. Everyone is mourning him.'

'Has his wife laid a complaint?' Josef asked.

'What good will that do?' Ben replied. 'Does a lion investigate the harm done by its claws?'

Curious, thought Josef S, that Ben should use the analogy of the lion. 'I'm sorry, Ben,' he said, and his words sounded hollow, devoid of meaning, the stuff of cheap greeting cards showing pictures of wheatfields blowing in the wind. 'I'll talk to Mr Parry. As far as I'm concerned, you can have the day off.' He closed his eyes as a moment of weakness passed over him, as the hot wind from the townships flushed through him. 'I'm sorry, Ben,' he repeated. 'I'm sorry that your friend died and that I can do nothing to help. I'll talk to Mr Parry.'

'Thank you,' Ben said quietly, and turned to leave. He stopped at the door and spoke, but did not look back. 'One day, maybe, you can do something. You are not helpless. You can choose.'

The sunlight seeped, like the beginnings of a tide, into the room: spring was on its way with the hint (or threat) of new structures. He thought of Dorothy at home with Robert, and tried to imagine them together. Would they talk easily? Would the soldier and the liberal writer find common ground? Would she tell him about her writing and hear of his adventures on the northern border? Would they establish an intimacy that he, Josef, had lost with her? Would Robert unburden himself in a way he could not with his brother?

The phone jangled him back into reality.

If Josef S had been questioned about it in the witness box, he would not have been able to answer how or where he first heard: whether it was a report on the radio, or the screaming headlines of the newspapers, or the babble of the office staff. Everyone knew at the same time, all the mouths of Eisstad were saying simultaneoulsy: 'Someone tried to assassinate the President!'

The story was not clear: had the President died, who was responsible, had the killer been caught? Excitement, the fear of an economic crash, fantasies of a true democracy at last: these were some of the first reactions. The radio played sombre music during the day as it became apparent that the President had been stabbed in the chest and was fighting for his life in an unnamed private hospital in Eisstad, and that a bishop had been brought in to pray for his recovery. As softly as falling rain, news trickled out: a suspect had been arrested by the security police and was in custody; his name was being withheld. The scene of the crime was the President's favourite restaurant where he had been dining with the First Lady. A knife had been found.

And finally, the whole story was revealed: in a relaxed moment, those entrusted with the care of the most important man in the Republic had let down their guard, and a waiter, bending over Buth while serving him, had plunged a sharp knife into his chest. The police were investigating whether the suspect had acted alone or was part of a conspiracy. In a fit of zeal, the restaurateur had been arrested as well, and charged with complicity to murder, or, alternatively, with negligence. Meanwhile, to the accompaniment of the darkest, most funereal of melodies, the President fought for his life somewhere in Eisstad, while the people of the suburbs prayed for him to live and the people of the townships prayed for him to die.

Josef S felt an overwhelming indifference to the saga. It did not matter to him whether President Buth recovered or not, whether the waiter was employed by foreign powers or revolutionary groups within the Republic, nor what the police were doing to him now that they had him in their charge. ('In their care' was a phrase the press liked to use.)

'I feel sorry for him,' Robert said in a voice that did not contain any sorrow.

'For Buth?' asked Dorothy. 'Who could feel sorrow for that old

53

tyrant? He's got what he deserved. I'm not sorry at all.'

'No,' said Robert, 'for the guy who did it.'

'Why?'

'They'll beat the shit out of him,' Robert said matter-of-factly.

'How do you know?'

'They always do.'

No one asked him if he had acquired personal experience in these matters. No one said anything about the army, and he had not volunteered any information, as yet.

The meal continued in silence except for the sombre music. Suddenly a bleep interrupted the programme and a woman's voice announced: 'President Buth's condition is critical but unchanged.' Josef leaned over and switched off the radio.

Robert's attention appeared to be totally on the food: he seemed fascinated by food. Dorothy was intent on serving him. And Josef sat back and watched as if he were unwilling or unable to be involved, as if the effort of participating had become far too strenuous. The others ignored, or pretended to ignore, his withdrawal. And so the evening passed.

A terrible shrieking aroused Josef S. He looked for the noise: it floated in the air, it was renewed stridently at regular intervals as its maker drew breath.

Josef stood on a hillock and below him were smaller hillocks which appeared to be bowing down to him. Another noise, a chanting, tore itself from the all-pervasive shrieking and ultimately gained dominance; it rose up to him. Dots turned into men; they walked in a long column, a dark winding river. In the heat, the dust, kicked up by tramping feet, rose until it reached knee height: the men were floating on a carpet of dust. Those leading the procession carried six long black boxes on their shoulders. The boxes rested on the tide of men as if they were being swept along on a fast-flowing river. He wanted to go down to join this waterway of men, to throw himself into their ranks and disappear. Someone raised a banner, another a flag, and Josef took his first step to join them.

One of the hillocks became a human figure and Josef, wrapping his grey coat around his shoulders, felt a chill in the heat of the day.

The statue of Gomez dominated the square. It stood on a pedestal of huge stone blocks, its sightless face yearning for the sea. Beneath the widebrimmed hat and the flowing, curling hair, the blank stone presented its mysterious surface to thousands of tourists annually. Gomez was adorned in a long robe with wide sleeves. One leg strode forward, a telescope rested in the crook of an arm. A plaque on the pedestal announced: ARTUR GOMEZ INVENTOR FOUNDER OF EISSTAD. What would Gomez have thought of this description, the lawyer wondered. Gomez had invented nothing (at least nothing that history had recorded) and his only contribution to the 'founding' of the city was the mocking reference (by his contemporaries) to his attempts. Perhaps the unhappy man might have gained a wry satisfaction from the fact that he was remembered and revered, while those compatriots, righteous doubters, were as forgotten as the dust.

A further irony was that this innocent was identified in the popular mind with the worst of the imperialists. In the event of a revolution, Artur Gomez would, together with Buth and his Cabinet, be the target for the popular rage. Driven mad by the laughter of his fellows, seeking some kind of refuge on the dark bulk of the Leeukop, Gomez had fallen to wild forces, a victim of the dark land to which he had tried to bring light. Would he be safe from the lions this time? Or was Gomez destined to sink into oblivion at last, as mobs, their muscles tight from swinging picks into the earth, smashed his statue into dust?

A group of schoolchildren walked down past the old City Hall, singing. People looked at them curiously; their angelic presence was infused with menace. They passed Gomez's statue without glancing at it; it was as much a part of the landscape as the trees. Like a small army they marched towards the bus terminus, in their ragged uniforms, arms swinging, their song floating across the empty space of the square. They could have been singing a dirge for the death of their friends; they could have been tramping over the cobbles with hatred in their hearts for the citizens of Eisstad who sent their police force into Valhalla to kill children. Their gentle melodies revealed their true feelings no more clearly than Gomez's blank face could expose his.

Josef S, unable to concentrate on his work, had asked his secretary to cancel his appointments, and had found himself walking through town. He had become a walker, he needed to see things with new eyes, to re-examine his city and his past.

'Robert has come back, Dad,' he said, 'and I don't know him. He's a stranger. I wish you were here to take care of him' The grey wind whipped some newspaper across the cobbles, and the mournful cries of the flower-sellers mingled with the shrieks of the seagulls. The children were gone, swallowed up by buses bound for the townships.

'He was a child when they took him, Dad; he was a sensitive boy. I couldn't be a father to him; I was too young, too involved in my career. And Dorothy wasn't interested then. He needed a stable family framework so that he could cope with the army. But we couldn't give it to him. He was soft when he left but they coarsened him; he was malleable, and they created stone from the material they took from us. We should have resisted them, Dad, because they used him up and spat him out, old and hard and angry, and we have to live with the thing that they have created.'

The wind threatened rain; a few drops spattered against Josef's face warning him to return to his office before the storm burst. But later, he was drawn back to the square as though he had not seen enough, as though the cobbles, laid in an earlier time, still breathed an air of the past. In the fading evening light, he stood before the City Hall which was separated from the square by a row of palm trees. It was a three storey sandstone building with a central clock tower, adorned with pillars and arches, and topped by a dome, rising like an assertion of the age which built it. Steps led to a pillared entrance, but municipal bureaucrats no longer ascended them on their way to the offices behind the rows of arched windows. The City Council had moved to one of the new monoliths, leaving the old building to fulfil more cultural functions.

The Leeukop squatted behind, brooding in cloud, as if waiting for the signal to rise and lumber off further into the Continent, to find respite from the affairs of men. Seagulls drifted down, their chests polished white like enamel, and picked in the cracks of the cobbles with their merciless beaks. One stared at Josef with a small blue eye, its webbed feet splayed wide over the pointed top of a bollard, perhaps assessing its chances of obtaining food from the man: even the birds had become beggars in Eisstad.

A group of tramps made a noisy effort of bedding down in the doorway of a shop adjoining the square. They prepared their cardboard and plastic as naturally as Dorothy made the bed at home. The seagulls did not bother to seek out food from that quarter: they knew not a scrap was spared. And so another aspect of Eisstad, this understanding between tramps and seagulls, had revealed itself to him, another small current in the secret flow of the city. The tramps ignored him, and no one else was about, except for the birds, which were also losing interest.

56

Josef started to dream as he stood in the middle of the city square, in the middle of the darkness gathering round him like the folds of a curtain, watching the apparent peace, with only the scraping of the beaks on stone, the occasional caw of bird or swearword of tramp to disturb the tranquility of the approaching night. He dreamed that the square would be filled with lions come down from the mountain. And the lions would sit down before the statue of Gomez the dreamer, and the seagulls would pick at the cobbles unmolested; there would be no tramps, but any humans in the square would not be disturbed, and the lions would lick their massive paws and watch over the city for the night and return to the mountain in the morning, harming no one on their soft padding way. Then, at last, there would be peace in the Republic.

As he stood there, a small panel van drove up and parked in the street next to the square. A group of young people tumbled out, and, with a few curt instructions, a woman dressed in an anorak and jeans, her hair tied back in a pony tail, organised them into a working party. Josef watched with growing interest as those in the back of the van began passing what looked like human bodies to those standing on the pavement. The bodies were dressed in trousers and shirts, yet appeared to have neither feet nor hands. Nor were they particularly heavy because their bearers took them easily, one under each arm, and carried them to the centre of the square, sitting them up against the pedestal of Gomez's statue so that they resembled the drunk tramps nodding off in their doorway. When the party had finished its work, Gomez was surrounded by ten limp figures whose heads rested on their chests as if they were asleep or dead. Josef approached these 'corpses', tingling with excitement, not knowing if he risked harm from those who had placed them there. He was hardly surprised to find that, like Gomez, they had no faces. The faceless shall share the night, Josef S thought.

'This is an "art reaction" to the killings in Valhalla yesterday,' the young woman who had given the orders said defiantly, as though she needed to explain her actions to someone whom she perceived to belong to the establishment.

How pretty she is, Josef thought, like a little bird, fierce with energy and conviction. 'I'm relieved,' he said.

She scrutinised him suspiciously. 'Why?'

'When you arrived, I thought you must be one of those death squads the papers talk about,' he said, 'and these were your latest victims.' He smiled. 'It's comforting to know that someone is still exercising restraint . . .'

'You're making fun of us!' she interrupted. 'If . . . if it wasn't for peaceful protest like this, the whole situation would sink into chaos. We're committed to non-violence.' How could someone who had delivered such barking orders have such a soft speaking voice? Her stutter intrigued him.

'That makes me feel a lot easier,' he joked. 'I'm pleased that public order hasn't yet disintegrated completely.'

'The police killed ten people yesterday,' she retorted. 'In the townships, public order *has* disintegrated. We *have* to make the public aware.'

'We?' Josef inquired.

'SFJ, Students for Justice; have you heard of us? We're affiliated to the FDF.'

'Of course,' said the lawyer, although he had not.

'Come on,' a voice shouted from the van. 'Let's get out of here already.'

The young woman walked away quickly. 'Goodbye,' Josef said after her, but she did not answer. The engine of the van was running and the driver revved impatiently. Did these 'art guerillas' expect to be arrested for putting dummies in the square? The woman's dark eyes had flashed in anger, yet they retained a vulnerability, as if her emotion could turn equally to fury or to tears. Would she be able to control the lions if they were allowed to prowl in the streets of Eisstad?

A tramp, disturbed by the noise, sat up in his plastic bag, next to one of the palm trees where the flower sellers had left their boxes and tins for the night. As the van disappeared, the tramp rearranged his bedding and lay down again. The clear plastic was like the body-bags one saw in war films. If the man died during the night, they could remove him with the minimum amount of fuss, all wrapped up, neatly packaged for disposal.

Robert sat in a chair staring into space. 'How was your day?' Josef asked.

'Fine,' the young man answered non-committally. He did not lift his eyes to acknowledge the entrance of his brother.

'Are you happy here?' Josef asked. 'Is there anything you need?'

'I'm fine,' Robert repeated, and then, abstractedly, almost as an afterthought, said, 'Thanks.'

'Do you want to talk about anything?'

58

'No, nothing, I'm fine. Please don't worry about me. I'm all right.'

'Good,' said Josef, sitting down with his newspaper. He tried to concentrate on the litany of stonings and arson, on the report of Buth's attempted assassination, but his attention returned to his brother, pale and sober, staring at the wall as if he would light it up with the images he had in his mind. How long was he going to sit like this? 'Good,' Josef repeated, vainly trying to stoke some conversation out of the ashes of silence. There was a brief flicker in Robert's eyes, as if he had seen the lions move in for the attack, but then his eyes went lifeless again. Josef read: PRESIDENT'S CONDITION UNCHANGED.

Abruptly, Robert stood up. 'Goodnight,' he said. 'I'm going to bed.'

'Goodnight,' Josef answered reluctantly. He did not want his brother to leave, especially as he seemed to have driven the boy away by his presence. How did a parent deal with a reticent child? How could Dorothy even contemplate having children? The door of the bathroom shut softly.

Had Robert been sullen before he went into the army? But the lawyer could not remember: he had been working too hard then to pay much attention to the shadow who had occupied the spare room in his house. 'What must I do with him, Dad?' Josef asked. 'How would you have handled him? Would you have even noticed that he was unhappy? You left me with the problem when I could hardly cope with my own life.' But as his thoughts became increasingly bitter, he turned back to the newspaper.

'They've released the restaurant owner,' he told Dorothy, who had come in and was stacking plates in the sideboard. 'But they're still looking for a conspiracy. They're even trying to find an astrologer who predicted that Buth would be murdered ... Do you know how many children Buth has?'

'I have no idea,' she said rather shortly, as if she resented him breaking into her thoughts.

'So much that one doesn't know,' he mused. 'So much to know, so much to learn, and so much time and effort to get answers. And while you're unravelling one mystery, the others slip away like clouds on the mountain.'

'What do you want to know?' she asked.

'How many grieving children the President has, and what Gomez looked like, and ...'

'Gomez?' she asked, perplexed, as if she had heard the name, but could not recall in what connection.

'The "Founder of Eisstad",' he said. 'Artur Gomez.'

'Oh,' she said, '*that* Gomez . . .'

'And if there are lions left on the mountain. And what my father used to think about after my mother died. And what's wrong with my brother.'

She sat down on the chair where Robert had sat, and looked closely at him. He felt his heart skip at the beauty of her green eyes. Her gown had opened, hinting at the shape of her breasts. He had an overwhelming desire to touch her, as he had had the night that Robert arrived, and the desire was so strong that he closed his eyes. He could not touch her only when he desired her, and then be cold to her afterwards when his lust was spent.

'What's wrong?' she asked, taking his hand in hers.

'I'm tired,' he said. 'I'm tired to death.' He felt two tears roll down his face, as hot as lava, and he wiped them away with his free hand, wishing that she had not seen.

'It's the aftermath of your illness,' she said, but he knew that she was only partly correct.

Lex waddled in, licking his lips, looking coyly at the husband and wife with his small eyes, seeming to intimate that he was pleased to have been fed but that a little more would go down as well. At the click of Dorothy's fingers, he came to her and stood under her hand, getting the affection that might have been directed towards Josef, had he allowed it.

'I'm sorry,' he said. 'I'm sorry I'm behaving like this. I'm under a lot of strain.'

'Do you want to tell me?'

He shook his head. Did she think that he had another woman? 'I can't. It's a general feeling, it's in the air. Nothing I can label.'

'And you want to know what's wrong with Robert!' she said accusingly.

Two silent brothers, trapped in their own minds, sitting on sofas and staring into space . . . Father, what sort of offspring have you allowed into this world?

'Robert is fine,' Dorothy said.

'Does he talk to you? Does he tell you about himself? You're with him during the day. What do you talk about?'

'Sometimes he tells me some small incident from his army days, nothing much. Day to day things, like some of the people he knew. Apart from that, he reads or listens to music or spends time with

Lex. I write and make lunch. It's usually at lunch that he tells me his stories. I don't pry. He washes up, he offers, and I think he's pleased to have something to do. He doesn't seem to be unhappy. He's actually very kind to me. He takes an interest in what I'm doing.'

'But he can't just sit around all day long.'

'You did when you were recovering from your illness.'

'He's not ill.'

'Isn't he? I believe that in a way he *is* sick, and he's come here to convalesce.'

'But you said he's not unhappy.'

'Don't cross-examine me,' she snapped. 'We're not in court. I said he *seems* to be happy: he hides his feelings. Just as you do. Lex comforts him.' Was there a flicker of uncertainty in her eyes?

'Does he really hate me? I wish he'd talk to me.'

'He'll talk when he's ready. I wish you'd talk to me.'

How could he tell her that he no longer loved her, that sometimes he felt waves of the old passion for her, but that love had slipped off like a dressing gown that no longer fitted? And what was this 'love' that he no longer felt? How could one quantify it? Were there degrees of it that one felt more or less of as the years passed? Or was it an absolute, either existing or not? Could one say: 'I no longer love the person I loved yesterday?' He was still discovering what this absence of love entailed; whether it meant that he had to seek love elsewhere, whether he could remain with her, whether he should tell her and how to do so. She might even know already, by virtue of his attitude, his silences.

'I can't,' he said. 'I'm sorry. I know it's hard for you.'

She shrugged and he could see that she was about to leave. He felt the despair of separation then, as if he would never again be able to rely even on the habit that had kept them together. For a moment, he wanted to get up and follow her, to put his hands on her shoulders and turn her to face him, to bury his head in her breasts and beg forgiveness, to let the tears roll unashamedly down his face and down her body, to take her to bed and recreate the enthusiasm of their first months together. But his impulse to start from the chair after her was nullified by his inability to act. He continued to sit, holding his newspaper, and as she walked out of the door, he was overwhelmed by loss.

Josef woke with a start and sat bolt upright, as if he had been looking into the face of disaster and had managed to escape just in time. He was surprised to find himself in bed, next to his wife; she was watching him. The curtains were partly drawn and the cold light eased in through the shutters.

'You were moaning in your sleep.'

'I was dreaming,' he said. 'About dust.'

'Come here.' And she wiped his face with a corner of the sheet. 'Your eyes are watering. You're crying.'

'Yes,' he said. 'That's all I remember . . . Dust.'

'Tears and dust,' she declared. 'Apocalyptic dreams.'

'I suppose we're living in apocalyptic times,' he said quietly.

'Robert must be up by now.' She slid out of bed. 'I'd better get breakfast ready.'

'It must be difficult to wake up in a room when you're used to a tent.' His tone became angry when he recognised her concern for his brother. Outside he heard the noises of the builders, the usual thudding as the nightwatchman chopped wood, preparing his own breakfast fire: the world was returning from darkness.

'Don't be hard on him,' Dorothy admonished, and for a moment Josef thought she meant the man outside. 'He had no choice. They would have sent him to prison if he hadn't served. You know that.'

'Yes, of course,' he said. 'It's simply that they have turned him into something alien, and I sometimes feel that we may have a spy in the house. One of *them*.'

'We seem to take turns to be frightened,' she smiled. 'Don't we? He's just confused. He needs love and understanding to help him adapt to the normal world. He is a gentle man. There's nothing sinister about him. Believe me, I would have sensed it if there was. My writer's antennae are highly developed . . .' She seldom discussed her writing these days. But now, it was as if a bond between them had been severed, and she could be freer without fear of hurt.

'It's difficult for me,' he said. 'I was almost a father to him in the last years, and now we can't even talk. He's become like a tortoise. I know he's soft inside, but he's surrounded himself with hardness. God knows what they've done to him.'

'But you're not his father. You're not responsible for him like a father, only like a brother. Wait for him to come out of his shell. He will when he's ready.'

'Perhaps I expected too much from him,' Josef mused. 'Perhaps I wanted him to drive himself as I drive myself. I don't know.'

There was little conversation at breakfast. Coffee, butter, salt, were passed in silence. It was a relief to be out of the house. Josef nodded to the nightwatchman in his yellow chair, shaving, and the man returned the greeting with a flick of the razor. Josef decided to walk into town rather than take a bus: the soft sunlight of early morning made the prospect pleasant. Besides, he was early, and he would be able to go past the square.

People were standing around Gomez, gazing at the dummies. A ripple of laughter threaded continuously through the watchers, taken up by one lot after the other.

'Buth's family,' a man in overalls was repeating to anyone who would listen. 'All dummies.'

Josef S could find little humour in the sight or the comments. He thought about those killed by the police, and the purpose of this demonstration, about Ben's friend shot in his kitchen while his wife watched, about the faceless victims represented by these limp creatures. The girl from the night before was in the crowd, nervous as a sparrow. Their eyes met, but she did not acknowledge him. Perhaps she was playing spy games; perhaps she suspected the sombre man of being a security policeman. Nevertheless she did not leave. She stayed and mingled with the people, perhaps listening to the comments, remaining inconspicuous, until she had made her way to Josef's side. In keeping with the game (he was convinced that she must have recognised him), he said nothing, but pretended to ignore her. Yet he was very conscious of her presence. She came closer to him, and then said quietly: 'They're coming. Just . . . just take it easy.'

Josef looked round cautiously. A yellow police car was parked at either end of the square. Four policemen were walking towards its centre. The crowd began to diminish and the laughter with it. People melted into the entrances of the shops bordering the square. Josef felt the impulse to run, but reminded himself that he had no reason to flee. Besides, he was curious. He wanted to ask the girl if her confidence meant that she trusted him, but when he looked for her, she had disappeared, and he could not locate her in the thinning crowd.

'*Here* are Gomez's children,' someone said as the policemen closed in upon them. For a moment, Josef imagined that they would rush up swinging their batons wildly, or firing their police revolvers, or whatever they did when they felt threatened, but nothing of the sort occurred. They stalked in, economically as cats, anonymous behind dark glasses, hands seeming to brush their holsters. The policemen in court, those men who announced the arrival of the judge and ordered everyone to stand, were tame creatures compared with their colleagues of the streets.

'Hey,' one of the policemen said to the man in overalls who had put on a cheerful expression. 'Who put these . . .' he pointed to the dummies, '. . . these dolls here? Did you see who did it?' His colleagues were going through what was left of the crowd, asking similar questions.

'No,' the man said jauntily, taunting him. 'I saw nothing.'

The policeman glared at him in disbelief and turned to Josef as if he would be a more reliable witness. 'Did you see who put those dolls there, sir?'

'I've just arrived,' replied the lawyer, avoiding the lie.

'Are you sure, sir?'

'Are you suggesting that I'm a liar?' Josef exclaimed. 'My name is Josef S and I'm a lawyer, an officer of the court. I won't be interrogated as if I were a criminal.'

The policeman stepped back in self-defence. 'I'm sorry, sir. I'm only doing my duty,' he said. His eyes were black mirrors; they reflected Josef's face briefly in the early light before he turned to rejoin his companions.

The workman slapped Josef on the shoulder. 'Well done, mister, you put that bastard in his place.' But Josef was not happy with his victory; in his burst of anger, he had divulged his name. Besides, he did not like to make a spectacle of himself. But something deep within him, a sense of outrage that he hardly knew he possessed, had provoked this reaction at the policeman's arrogance.

'Thank you,' he said. 'Somebody has to, I suppose.'

'Did you read what de Wet wrote in the paper?' the man asked.

Josef shrugged; he did not want a long discussion with anyone.

But the man persisted, insensitive to Josef's reticence. 'He said that his policemen can see who is a criminal just by looking at his face.'

'That's convenient,' the lawyer conceded.

'No wonder they act like animals,' the workman said. 'They think they're God.'

The crowd was swelling again, as curious passers-by paused to see what was happening. Laughter rose and jokes were cracked. Josef stayed on, even though he was once more late for work. The four policemen had retreated to one of their cars and the sergeant was speaking into his police radio. Josef had no illusions about the effect of his outburst: these men probably did believe that they could identify a criminal by looking at him. Had they seen guilt in his face?

'Who do you think's behind it?' asked a man who stood nearby.

'I've just arrived,' Josef repeated. 'They were already sitting there.'

'It's the agitators,' the man said. 'They're stirring things up. It's not safe to go home anymore, you get rocks through your windows, and it's all because of them.' He jabbed a finger at the dummies, as if those inanimate forms were to blame for the political instability. 'This country is going up in flames, and it's all because of the agitators.'

'I see,' said Josef, not bothering to argue. Politely, he inquired: 'Where do you live?'

'Valhalla,' the man said heatedly. 'The buses weren't running this morning because of the rioting and I had to walk for miles. Most of the windows are broken anyway. And you know who throws the stones?' He grew increasingly excited with the telling. 'It's the children. That's why the police shoot them. The other day they threw a stone into the bus and it hit a woman on her head. She had blood and glass in her hair, and they had to take her to hospital.' He straightened his tie angrily. 'And when you can get a bus, the wind blows right through and it's bloody cold this time of year.'

Josef could have asked him many things. Why are the children rebelling? Can you stir up emotions where there is no grievance? Where did your family come from? Waterfront? If they were still allowed to live there, surely you could have walked to work like I did, without needing a bus. What kind of a man are you who turns his back on his own people? And what sort of man am I that I can condemn your attitude and feel more for the plight of your people than you can? Why does my anger rise at your conviction? Is it not ironic that we stand at opposite poles, each supporting the views of the other's group?

But the lawyer did not ask these questions, because there was no point. In the safety of his house, his wife waited, looking after his brother; this man ran the gauntlet of the newspaper stories, day after day.

The man now said: 'I have a child in high school, but they've closed the schools. They aren't learning, so what will happen to him? I want him to have a better life than me, but how can he if he has no education? He says he's fighting for his rights . . .' the man spat, '. . . but what's he going to do with his rights if he knows nothing except how to throw stones? Even the smallest ones know how to throw stones. When you walk in the street you see them pretending to throw. One of the boys they shot, they said he had rocks in his pockets . . .' Obviously he thought that the lawyer was listening sympathetically, and he prodded him with a sharp forefinger. Josef did not want to talk to this man. What if he was from the Security Branch, planted in the square as a trap? Had he not witnessed Josef's confrontation with the policeman? Wasn't he protesting too much? Josef might have answered: how can your son have a better life than you when he cannot leave Valhalla? But he said nothing.

'These people who cause this violence are filth,' raved the man. 'Filth!'

'I'm sure you're right,' the lawyer said, excusing himself; he had had enough. But as he turned to leave the square, a patrol van drew up, and he hesitated. Two policemen got out, and, together with the four who had summoned them, walked towards the statue; good humouredly, the crowd let them through. One of the newcomers carried a camera. While his companions watched, he positioned himself carefully to take pictures of the dummies where they sat.

'Smile!' someone shouted. 'Say cheese for the uncle!' The crowd howled.

Unsmiling, the policemen bent to pick up the lifeless forms, like farmers harvesting a crop. They ignored the raucous comments of the onlookers as they carried the offenders to the patrol van and slung them in the back.

'They're arresting them!' spluttered a woman with a peal of laughter.

'Under the Public Safeties Act!'

'They're a threat to the peace!'

'An illegal gathering of dummies!'

'Lucky they're not alive or they would have shot them.'

'Political dummies!'

The man who had spoken to Josef was walking away, a slight figure in a smart suit. He disappeared into one of the streets bordering the square. Josef watched him go, but the man made no contact with the policemen standing next to the patrol van. 'I'm becoming suspicious of nothing,' the lawyer thought. 'That's what this system is doing to us; it makes us fear even our own thoughts. One cannot live with fear. One cannot become crippled. I must be able to reach out.' He walked off briskly to his office; his shoes rang on the cobbles.

Getting agreements of lease stamped was Ben's job, but all at once it became important for Josef to handle this matter himself. He wanted to walk again, to be on the streets with people in the sunshine. The Department of Inland Revenue was a squat, ugly building, contrasting bleakly with the baroque elegance of the old City Hall. Something about the way it sat reminded Josef of the man in overalls he had spoken to earlier in the square: both were part of this place, inextricably, indivisibly; both had a claim on the land. The lawyer wondered if he also belonged, or if he was an aberration, a misfit, like the protesting women whose action had resulted in an arrest that was more sacrificial then effective: a few columns in the newspaper, a picture, hardship. The State remained intransigent.

Did the grieving parents of the murdered children take any comfort from the women's stand? When the tide rose out of Valhalla, would these good women not be swept along with it, as might Josef S and his family? Perhaps a refugee from the north would recognise Robert and point to him in positive identification. It was that man! He killed my brother! It would not be enough to say, I am sorry! I am sorry for you, that you have suffered, and for Robert, my brother. He did not know what he was doing. He was a child when they took him and used him. He did not pull the trigger: they did. He was only part of the gun.

That tide, when it washed out of the townships and swept away buildings like the Department of Inland Revenue, and the fish factory, and the City Hall, might find that Josef S and his wife and his brother were carried along above it, light as leaves on the swollen currents, floating above the graves of President Buth and General de Wet.

Now, in the late afternoon, the Revenue Building was virtually empty. Its grey tiled floors, black doors and mustard coloured walls were an odd combination of oppression and light. In the entrance hall stood a heavy black iron statue of a pot-bellied man and his dog. For the first time (and he had been to the building often enough), Josef stopped at the statue. Had anyone besides its creator ever examined the ugly thing before him? He wondered if the eyes of clerks were fixed on him, watching his scrutiny with a scrutiny of their own, looking for signs of criticism, of sedition.

The man represented in the statue could have been an executioner, a warrior, or a feudal lord. He wore a helmet, which fitted against his face like a mask, and a suit of armour. He had one hand on his hip; the other held a staff which was planted firmly into the metal earth. The dog had an armour-plated back and cloven hooves. It was fiercely muzzled. Man and dog stood beside an apparatus that could have been a plough or an instrument of torture, with its sinister range of wheels, ratchets, gears and blades. And yet Josef had never noticed it before. Was the fat, protected man a blatant symbol of the ruling class, the dog a naked manifestation of the State's power, the machinery a reminder of the mechanism of torture and confinement? Was everyone so blinded that they did not recognise this joke on them? There was no caption to the statue, but Josef could supply one: POWER TO THE RULERS, TO THE DESCENDANTS OF GOMEZ, TO THE COLLECTORS OF TAX, TO THE PROPONENTS OF FORCED REMOVAL, TO THE CHILD MURDERERS, TO THE ARRESTORS OF DUMMIES, TO THE ICE MEN.

Perhaps, Josef S thought, he should bring Robert to see this statue, force him to look at it, stand beside him and say: 'Is this what you were risking your life for?' Perhaps he should bring Dorothy, and beg her to write stories about power and its excesses, to employ her talent in this direction. But you could not tell a creative writer what to write; Dorothy had made that quite clear to him. The statue would continue to gloat until the enraged mobs, having finished with the hapless Gomez in the square, hopefully turned their anger on this, the true focus of their fury: the dark face of the Ice Men.

Josef handed the lease to a sallow-faced clerk, nattily dressed in a green suit and wearing a small moustache, who slouched behind the counter labelled 'Revenue Stamps'. As the young man calculated the amount of stamps needed, his pencil broke.

'That's Government pencils for you,' Josef said drily.

'Yes, but I've got lots more,' the clerk laughed, and passed the lease back to the lawyer with a sum of money pencilled in the top right-hand corner. Josef tried to pay him, but the clerk refused to accept the notes. 'You must buy the stamps from the cashiers,' he said. 'They're only here in the mornings until one o'clock.'

Josef began to protest, but what was the point? This man, backed by the forces represented in the statue, did not have stamps. Only the cashiers, who, for some bureaucratically imponderable reason stopped work at one, could take money. And so the business had to remain unresolved. Ben would have known that. Josef would have to send him in the morning.

After work, the lawyer decided to walk home since the weather was mild. The clouds had receded for the afternoon and the late sun bathed the Leeukop in a mysterious orange light that turned its grey-green surface black. The mountain was as inscrutable when fully illuminated as when packed with cloud. Who in the city could even imagine what life forms crawled or strutted in those shadows?

Josef bought a newspaper and stopped at the entrance to a park. A blue ball came bouncing down the street and he stepped aside to avoid it; he could not see where it had come from. He watched the ball disappear, then he went into the park and sat down on one of the benches. He felt buffetted by the events in his private life; in the political life of the Republic, he was like a branch in the wind. The bench was reassuringly solid beneath him.

He was alone in the park. A swing, a jungle gym and seesaw were like lonely children waiting for playmates: lifeless metallic frames, longing to be touched. The grass was well-kept, the park was neat: the Department of Parks and Forests still operated normally even in times of political upheaval.

Josef flicked through his newspaper, scanning the headlines, dipping into the stories. The front page announced that the condition of President Buth had improved considerably and that he had been taken out of intensive care. But unrest was sweeping the Republic. Arson and stone-throwing had occurred at various places, apparently sparked off by the attempt on Buth's life and in sympathy with his alleged attacker. The facts and figures were presented starkly; read together, the statistics of those wounded, killed or arrested meant nothing, even when the names were given. They did not take on life, flesh did not crawl onto the bones of those scant words, faces did not materialise onto the letters of the names. And so, when a child died, or a father, when a breadwinner was arrested, leaving the family destitute, when a stone-thrower was shot and taken to hospital under police guard, the reader could not feel the individual pain. The eye skimmed over the facts, irritably perhaps, because there was no story, and one was left with frustration at missing the human drama and having to make do with the skeleton.

Duncan Foster was in the news as well. It appeared that the Executive Committee of the City Council had decided to turn down his scheme for reintroducing lions onto the Leeukop. According to the article, accompanied by a photograph of the zoologist in a pen with lion cubs on his farm outside Eisstad, the City Council had given no reasons for its decision, but had simply 'noted' Dr Foster's application. The caption below the photograph declared that these cubs would have been the first lions released. 'I want to give them their freedom,' the zoologist was quoted as saying. 'I want to return these wonderful animals to their natural home.' Asked what the lions would eat if released, Dr Foster had said it was his intention also to populate the mountain with small indigenous antelope. He dismissed any danger to humans from the lions, saying that if necessary he would erect a fence around the base of the mountain at his own cost. Perhaps Foster was a latter-day Gomez, another dreamer. Clearly, thought Josef, his idea was too dangerous and impractical to be allowed. He wondered at the newspaper even publishing the story.

The end of the article referred the reader to the letters page where two letters put the case of the 'Lion Man': one for him, one against. The issue was being taken up by the citizens of Eisstad, and their views were as might have been expected: the objecting citizen discussed the danger of having lions prowling the mountain and refused to acknowledge the symbolic aspect; while the proponent expressed no fear although he lived directly below the mountain in Leeuwenvoet, Josef S's suburb. He might even have been a neighbour; Josef could not tell from the bare 'I.M.' with which he signed the letter. To I.M., the freedom of the lions was a symbol of the freedom of the workers, those who had been oppressed and banished to the townships. He applauded the Doctor's initiative in the struggle for freedom and referred to the statements of Foster which Josef had read previously in the press. I.M. had lived in the wilds; to him, the lion threat was totally exaggerated.

Finally, Josef turned to the article on the dummies in the square. A police spokesman was reported as saying that the police had found ten dummies in Artur Gomez Square and had taken them to the Eisstad Police Station where the rightful owner could claim them. Eyewitnesses stated that the 'dummies had been arrested'. The article further noted that 'about 500 people' had watched the police action 'with amusement'.

In the park, a gum tree bled; its red sap had clotted on the trunk below the wound. A squirrel leaped, chattering, up the tree, in that state of madness peculiar to squirrels. Josef S got up slowly and walked the rest of the way home. A neighbour's child was talking to the man on the yellow chair; they were so absorbed in their conversation that the nightwatchman did not greet the lawyer. A feeling of dread came over Josef. In his house, the lights blazed through the shutters. All at once he did not want to go in.

Dorothy appeared as he opened the front door, her face slightly flushed. She smiled at him. Why don't we fight anymore? he thought. At least when we were fighting, there was some life to this charade. Now there is nothing but a dead pretence. He smiled back at her and put the newspaper and his briefcase on the table.

'How was your day?' he asked Robert, not expecting any more of an answer than usual. Lex lay at his brother's feet.

'Relaxing,' Robert volunteered. 'I'm starting to see more clearly now.' But the answer sounded as if it were tailored to please; it did not ring true. He nudged the dog with his toe and stared up at the ceiling, avoiding contact with Josef's eyes. The dog lifted its head, regally, at the touch, and licked its lips, a picture of domestic happiness. At least someone in the household was completely comfortable.

'I'm pleased,' said Josef. I wish I could see more clearly, he thought.

When they had eaten, Josef washed the dishes. This was their arrangement. Dorothy cooked because she was at home and because cooking gave her pleasure and gave him none; he was content to clean up afterwards. They did not even discuss their respective roles in the kitchen; they knew them too well to need to talk. Robert had not offered to wash the supper dishes since his arrival. Perhaps he helped Dorothy to cook; there was no way in the present state of non-communication that Josef was likely to find out. Whatever happened while he was at work had come to be their secret and he was not a party to it. A touch of the childish fear of exclusion came over him, but the feeling passed as he wiped the plates. What did it matter if his wife and his brother found comfort in each other, as long as this comfort made life easier for both of them?

He entered her, blindly in the mole darkness, going into an infinity of tunnels, going in for ever. How alone each one was, how isolated from each other. Only their sweat and flesh joined; their thoughts and experiences of this intimacy were as separate as if each partner was in a different country.

Josef S was no longer intimidated by Ed Parry's size, by his intense brown eyes, by his alien baldness. Parry's big blunt hands stroked his naked head as he listened to Josef's plea on behalf of Ben.

'We can't give in,' Parry said. 'If they see us giving in, they'll move in for the kill.'

71

'It's not a defeat, Ed, and they're not animals.'

'They behave like animals, Josef.' Parry stood up and began to pace about the room. His clothes did not fit well; he seemed too big for them. 'They stoned Gareth's car on the airport road yesterday. The brick hit his bonnet. An inch or two further back . . . He would have been dead, Josef. For what? Because some hooligans took it into their heads to have fun on the freeway.' He stared at his partner with eyes that had melted witnesses and turned judges' stomachs, unpredictable eyes; as though he could persuade by the force of his will alone. 'Have you gone soft, Josef? What happened to that hard-arsed fighter?' He slapped his partner's shoulder.

Josef shook his head, and rested it in his hands. One had to fight against the weariness, against the confusion: one had to find the correct answers to the accusations. For every debate, there were answers and counters: it was a game, and if you knew more than your opponent, you might succeed this time.

'Edward,' he said, 'you're not giving in by letting Ben go off for a day to attend the funeral. I can tell you this: by refusing to allow him to go, you'll create a resentment out of all proportion to your refusal. People are angry, Ed. That stone had generations of hatred propelling it, and if you persist in believing that it was mere hooliganism, you're deluding yourself. Call me soft, whatever you wish, but I'm telling you that there's a terrible sickness in this country, where children are murdered by police and mothers are arrested for showing their concern at the killings.'

Parry turned like a cannon aiming to fire, but when he saw Josef's bowed head, when he discovered that the enemy he was looking for had adopted an unaggressive posture, perhaps even a submissive one, and he had no one at whom to direct the power of his eyes, he appeared to lose ground. 'I'm concerned too, Josef,' Parry said, 'but what must I do? I've worked hard, I've built up whatever I have by the sweat of my labour. And now I see it in jeopardy.'

He guffawed; it was a gruff attempt to cover up his admission of fear. The idea of Edward Parry being scared was ludicrous, and yet fear was the force behind so much of the righteous indignation in Eisstad. The people who had been exiled to the Flatlands, to their dismal townships, were stoning their way back. And the fear of their return was bringing out the less charitable side of men like Ed Parry.

He relaxed his big round shoulders when he saw that there was to be no battle and went to sit in his chair, opposite Josef. Another battlefield, Josef thought, another person close to me who has become an adversary. Why was it that those you cared for most became your enemies? The tramps, the meths-drinkers of Eisstad, those wretched unloved mockeries of people, fought with one another over trivia. He had seen it happen, time and time again, a group screaming obscenities across the city's polite streets, while the cultured citizens looked away discreetly, pretending they hadn't heard, distancing themselves physically and emotionally from the drunken battle in their midst. And as those withered people with faces like lettuces hustled one another, the world paid no attention until someone called the police who bundled them off for disturbing the peace. And, in a more subtle way, Josef was doing the same.

'That's why,' Edward Parry broke into his thoughts, 'that's why I'm against those hooligans.'

'Ed. We've known each other for how long?' Josef asked. He did not wait for an answer. 'I'm appealing to you as a friend. Let Ben go to the funeral. For my sake.'

Parry rubbed his head again. It was a tic; he did it in court when he was thinking. You could tell when you had Ed Parry in a spot because he would start to caress his baldness, as if in search of comfort. But then he spread his arms magnanimously: 'All right, Josef,' he said, 'for you. Ben can go and mourn and come back a stone-thrower.'

'Thank you, Ed,' said Josef and stood to go out.

As though he had suffered a defeat and had only just realised it, Parry threw a passing shot but not with his eyes; Josef was avoiding eye-contact. 'If a brick hits my car, I'll thank you, Josef,' he said quietly.

Somewhere in the city, a siren went on, a desolate noise. No one switched it off. It blared endlessly, as a bell might have tolled, to warn the people of Eisstad and the Republic that uncontrollable forces were at work, that they should look over their shoulders, sniff into the wind, be of swift foot, like antelope as the lion approaches through the yellow grass of the Leeukop, as he pads softly past the silver cannon and the love graffiti painted on the stones around it, and stares out over the suburbs, while a wisp of smoke rises from somewhere in Valhalla. No one is going to put out the fires.

Josef told his secretary to find Ben and send him in. While he waited, he tried to apply his mind to the documents piled on his desk. The paper was growing as if it had a will of its own: leases, opinions to draft, preparations for trial, heads of argument, advices

73

on evidence, new law reports, all lying before him, the baleful re-
minders of his responsibilities. He took a folder from the top of the
pile and was about to open it when Ben knocked.

'I've spoken to Mr Parry,' Josef told him. Ben shuffled on the
carpet. His anger was no longer evident; he had become, again, the
boy that Josef thought he knew. 'He's agreed to let you go to the
funeral.' Ben smiled soberly. 'But he's not happy. He believes that
you are going to become a stone-thrower. Maybe I shouldn't be telling you this, Ben, but I warn you to tread lightly around Mr Parry.
He's feeling threatened.'

The young man looked incredulously at Josef, as if it were incon-
ceivable that he could pose a threat to anyone. But he did not say
anything: the smile was the thank you, and there was a hint of the
other thing, the barrier that he had erected, the point to which he
would allow himself to be pushed, and no further. It was a new
thing; Josef was beginning to recognise it in the people he encountered in the street, a defiance that had been epitomised by the
attack on Buth.

'Will many people go, Ben?' Josef asked. 'After all, it is on a week-
day.'

'There will be thousands, Mr S. People are prepared to lose their
jobs to go. It will be another stayaway.'

'Would you have left this job if Mr Parry refused to give you the
day off?'

'Yes,' said Ben without hesitation.

'Well, I'm glad I persuaded him then,' said Josef, and Ben smiled
again in gratitude.

'Here.' Ben took a thin, folded newspaper from his inside pocket
and put it on Josef's desk. 'You must read this. You can keep it.'

'Thank you, Ben,' said the lawyer, looking despairingly at the
waiting files begging to be read. He picked up the gift, if it was indeed a gift and not a warning, and began to page through it. When
he looked up, Ben had gone, as if he had never been there. Josef
glanced at his father's typewriter, wishing it could provide him with
a touchstone, going back many years as it did, to a reality that would
make sense to him. The skeletal machine stared back blandly, chal-
lenging him to try and tap the answers out for himself on its ancient
keyboard.

The newspaper was called *The Voice*; Josef had never heard of it.
The Voice was only eight pages long, and he suspected that its size
was limited by a shortage of funds rather than an absence of voci-

74

ferousness. It was illustrated throughout with photographs of the 'Protests'. A policeman stood with a shotgun before a burning truck, a sea of hands was raised in defiance at a student meeting, a gutted building provided a background to two boys holding a banner on which was painted: UNITE! But the article which he found most poignant was entitled: FIRST-AID HINTS. According to the author, people injured during the protests were often arrested when they went to hospital for treatment. The purpose of the piece, prepared under the guidance of a group of sympathetic doctors, including Dr Albert Poynter of the Valhalla Clinic, was to instruct people in the affected communities in the home treatment of minor injuries suffered during police action. Separate sections were devoted to injuries caused by whips, birdshot and buckshot, teargas, rubber and real bullets. Advice was given on the administration of antiseptics and dressings. Josef read: 'These serious injuries MUST go straight to hospital: Head injury, if unconscious or drowsy or having fits, loss of vision (blurring or double vision), paralysis, vomiting. Chest injury, if difficulty in breathing or short of breath, coughing blood, pain inside chest. Abdomen/Back if . . .'

Josef stood and took the newspaper with him. And Edward Parry was worried about a brick on his bonnet! He dropped *The Voice* on Parry's desk (the man was not in his office) and walked out. He doubted whether his partner would even look at it.

Outside, the Leeukop presided over everything, forever. It did not matter who was in power, it did not matter what went on in the affairs of men. The mountain was constant; it did not change. That keel-shaped silhouette would dominate the skyline in a thousand years' time. Houses might encroach up its foothills, or be demolished; lions might be reintroduced, or the last lion might spring from a rock and find its mate in the tawny grass, and repopulate the mountain. But the mountain would remain in control. Pink clouds floated past, as if the mountain were a black keel cutting through a pink sea.

The cartoonist from the *Evening Times* had caricatured the arrest of the dummies. In a courtroom, he had a policeman telling a dubious magistrate: 'I arrested the accused for forming an illegal gathering in Artur Gomez Square last week.' The 'accused' were the dummies, slovenly as drunkards, propped up in the dock, their eyes expressing their amazement at the absurdity of this situation.

Buth's condition was unchanged and there was no news of his assailant; nothing to bear out or disprove Robert's gloomy forecast.

The man had disappeared into the depths of their security system as surely as a stone into a well. The reporter's inquiries had been met with a curt 'No comment'.

Josef walked past an antique shop. Two big, floppy dummies of the kind used in the demonstration sat on a bench outside. They gazed at the passers-by with an indifference born of despair through their bland button eyes. The lawyer felt a thrill of identification at these mute participants in a revolution. They fitted strangely well into a background that included old teapots, irons, jugs and platters. But the pleasant, country atmosphere created by the shop was rudely broken by a woman collapsed against a wall further along the street. She was as limp, as expressionless, as the dummies. A meths-drinker, she was out cold on the pavement. She wore running shoes, a white scarf on her head, a filthy bandage on her hand; her blue trousers were wet. Pedestrians stepped over her as if she were not there. Josef stopped (she breathed shallowly; she was alive) and folded a coin into her fingers so that it was invisible from other, thieving eyes. He could do no more. At least, when she woke, she would have the wherewithal to proceed to the next stage. For her that might be shelter, food, more drink: that was her business. Eisstad was a city of beggars and tramps: they were as permanent as the mountain.

He boarded his bus, and was transported through the clinically ordered streets of the suburbs to his home.

It occurred to him gradually that something was different. He looked around, listened, as if he had become one of those antelope and the lion was stalking him through the streets of Leeuwenvoet. Then he knew; the nightwatchman was not there. The yellow chair was gone; the woman with her domestic manner in the parking lot; the piles of sand. The renovations were done and the man had been taken away together with his cooking drum and his bed and his hat and white bag, shipped out like the people of Waterfront, perhaps to face the turbulent townships. The small reprieve from the turmoil was over, unless the builders were going to use him to guard another site. A small sadness touched the lawyer when he thought that he would never again see this man whom he now regarded as his neighbour, who had even gained the trust and friendship of the children of the suburb. The garage door was open, and inside was empty.

A wind was coming up, and as its first gusts caught at his legs, Josef S hurried inside.

He woke: the wind was rushing round his house, the roof creaked and the windows rattled. There were lulls while the wind gathered in the distance, like a locomotive building up steam before hurtling down a track. Then the storm was upon him with a massive concussion, and, as suddenly, abated in time for the next gust.

'Josef,' Dorothy said. 'Josef, what's happening?'

The wind is unsettling, it disturbs one's equilibrium, it makes one nervous, insecure, he might have said. Instead he pretended not to hear her. He pretended to be asleep. What's happening, he might have echoed, to us, to the country, to people we care for? Don't ask me, he would have said. I don't know the answers.

The wind was making the day unpleasant and unmanageable: pedestrians were being blown all over the streets like litter; shop fronts cracked and glass exploded onto the pavements; branches were torn off trees, sometimes onto cars parked or passing below.

If you stood in the parking area on the Leeukop and looked out to sea, you would have seen the wind stripping back white layers of water like a cook peeling onions, and the sun shining through the spray made rainbows for the moment it took the water to settle. The gusts built up and then subsided; shipping was disrupted, flights delayed. It was described as the worst wind-storm in ten years by those who claimed to remember the last one.

'It's a sign of the times,' said Ed Parry.

'God blowing the winds of change?' Josef asked sardonically.

Parry answered seriously: 'Perhaps. You never know. Just because you don't believe . . .'

'You don't either, Ed. Have you begun to?'

'I think I should. Do you know that on the airport road the police are guarding the bridges? Because of the stone-throwers. It's a sobering thought. It's never been this bad, Josef. We've had riots before, but this . . . I dreamed last night that I was swimming in a sea, and that all the people in the water with me were floundering. Suddenly I had got through the waves, and I was wading up onto an island. We'd all been heading for this island. I don't know if anyone else made it.'

'Was I there, Ed? Did I make it?'

'I don't remember seeing you, Josef,' Parry said.

'Perhaps I was already there,' Josef laughed. 'And I was waiting for you.'

Parry did not answer: he simply looked pensive. 'When's this funeral?' he asked.

'Tomorrow,' said Josef. He did not add that he was going to be there. He had told no one.

The idea of going had crept up on him stealthily through the long grass and had caught up with him at night when he slept. He was hardly aware of it himself. It revealed itself as he spoke, popped its wild head out of the underbrush of his thoughts and faced him in all its intensity. He knew then that he had to go, that it was his duty as a concerned citizen of Eisstad to show his sympathy with the mourners.

'I read that newspaper,' said Parry. 'I presume you left it for me.'

'Yes, I found it humbling.'

'But what's the alternative, Josef? Do you have an alternative?'

'I'm a lawyer, Ed. Not a politician. No, I don't know the answer, but an answer must be found . . .'

'You see, Josef, one mustn't be naive about this. Of course people are getting hurt. Children *are* being shot. We all know that's happening. But look who's in charge of maintaining order. I mean, Josef, you or I wouldn't do it. You have to attract a certain type of person to do the dirty work, and that's what you get.'

'Are you comfortable with that, Ed?'

'I'm more comfortable with it than with bricks on my bonnet,' Parry growled.

'What sort of solution is that?'

'I don't know, Josef. I don't know. But something must be done.'

'Whatever's being done is all wrong,' said Josef. 'Whenever they overreact and shoot someone, they make matters worse.'

The big man glowered. The wind howled outside, and beat on the sides of the building. 'These children are not innocent as everyone tries to pretend: they're quite responsible for what they're doing.'

The faces of the boys in the fish factory came to Josef, those hard brutal old faces, shared by the newspaper vendors and the beggars: the street people, uprooted by the Government's removal policy, exiled to the Flatlands and ultimately returning to drift on the streets of Eisstad.

'Do you think so, Ed?' Josef rubbed his eyes.

'Parents have no control, Josef,' Parry said. 'They've abrogated their responsibilities to the hooligans they've raised.'

The lawyers were circling each other in the passage like dogs. Josef managed to escape into his office.

The pile of work on his desk was rising out of control and he could not deal with it. He tried to attend to the urgent matters, to apply his mind to those documents which had to be filed within certain time-limits. But he felt that events were slipping by him faster than he could hold on: like a man falling over a cliff and clutching at bushes that came away in his hands. His partner had not said anything, but surely Josef's neglect was obvious. Clients must have been complaining, soon the pile of briefs would even out and then, perhaps, diminish. To survive as a lawyer you had to inspire confidence, you had to churn out the work. If you got old and weary and could no longer produce, you were sent to slaughter like a milk cow whose daily outpouring was worth less than the cost of its feed. Josef was spending too much time thinking about what was now being called: 'The Situation'. The work on his desk seemed irrelevant compared to The Situation.

He walked out into the streets again and bought a newspaper. A tall beggar smiled at him. Josef smiled back. Encouraged, the man slouched over towards him, and a stink of wine made Josef step back. The man had so few teeth that when he spoke, spittle sprayed all over the lawyer. 'I need two bob,' he said. 'I have to get to the station.' All at once, Josef felt a camaraderie with this derelict who had nothing, not even the guile to tell a decent lie. They stood in a doorway while the wind tried to tear the newspaper from Josef's grasp, and whip away the words between the man and the child-man. 'I won't buy drink,' the tramp said, but Josef did not care what he did with the money. He dug into his pocket (he seemed to have been doing so much of this recently: a small redistribution of wealth) and gave. 'Bless you,' the beggar mumbled.

'Will you?' Josef asked tiredly.

'I will pray for you,' the man said emphatically, and Josef did not bother to wipe the spit from his face. We are in this together, he thought, your spit and my spit, we must share because we only have each other. As if this derelict could stop the slide, as if he were not just another bush clutched despairingly on the way down.

'What will you pray for?' Josef asked.

'I know what to pray for,' the tramp said, and put his arm around Josef's shoulders in a bear hug. Josef did not object: he allowed the child-man to fill him with primitive energies. Perhaps the beggar was diseased: certainly Ed Parry would have feared for his partner's competence as a lawyer if he had seen this interaction. But Josef needed whatever it was that this man was able to give him.

'Pray well, my friend,' he said, and the two went their separate

79

ways into the wind.

Only on the bus, battered and missing windows, did Josef unfold the newspaper. Cold fingers iced his back: small bumps lifted on his skin. LAWYER MURDERED shrieked the headline. He looked around at the other passengers; they were sunk into themselves like dummies, shrunken against the wind that raged so viciously through the open windows that he could only read the front page. The newspaper was uncontrollable: it was possessed by its own life, it wanted to tear itself from his hands and fly like an eagle around the bus, alerting all these dummy people to the fact that a lawyer had been murdered.

She was based in Valhalla, Josef read. He had not known her but the name was familiar: a Mrs Idini. A group of men had waited for her in a white car outside her house in Valhalla when she returned from work. As she was walking up her driveway, in full view of the neighbours and her children, the men, wearing balaclavas, strode up to her and shot her at point-blank range in the head. Then they fled, leaving her in a pool of blood.

Mrs Idini had been a well-known civil rights activist on the Flatlands and had defended a number of political prisoners during her career. It was learned by the newspaper that she had, on that day, accepted the legal defence of the man who had stabbed Buth. Shocked witnesses spoke of her 'contribution to justice' and the irony that she should have been murdered because of her work in attempting to secure a peaceful society. In an editorial comment, the newspaper deplored her death, and the existence of what it termed a 'right-wing death squad' operating against opponents of the Government. Such a development would only polarise attitudes, the editor warned, and appealed for calm on all sides. The comment concluded: 'We trust that the police will act with all haste in apprehending the killers so as to scotch rumours that the authorities know more about the murder than they care to admit.'

A separate article chronicled the usual daily mayhem emanating from the Flatlands and from various townships attached to rural communities. General de Wet attributed this violence to the work of 'hooligans and thugs', and appealed to all 'law-abiding citizens' not to become involved, but to continue with their 'peaceful pursuits' while the police worked at 'normalising the situation'.

A few passengers sat on the floor of the bus to get out of the wind. An old woman shivered into her scarf. 'Normality' would be long in coming, the lawyer thought.

For one horrific moment, Josef imagined that Robert, his silent brother, had been one of the killers. The young man was sitting in the lounge in his usual position with the dog's head cradled in his lap. Who knew what he did during the day? Josef was too tired even to try to start a conversation, and was surprised when Robert spoke, in reply to his nod.

'Dad wasn't a very good father, was he?' Robert said.

The question was as startling for its suddenness as for its content. Josef sat down in the armchair across from the settee which Robert occupied and put his briefcase and newspaper on the floor. He bit back the sarcastic rejoinders which immediately demanded to be expressed, and tried to answer as sympathetically as possible.

'Why do you say that, Robert?' he asked.

'Well, he never spent much time with us after Mom died. He just got drunk and left us to ourselves, didn't he? I know you did your best, but you aren't my father. You couldn't take his place.'

'He was broken by Mom's death,' said Josef, 'I suppose he never really recovered from that.'

'I used to think about him a lot when I was in the army; I still do. I see him as a small grey man sitting over that old-fashioned typewriter you have in your office, with a bottle of wine on the floor next to him. When I try to twist him into other positions, he won't go. I try to turn his arms away from the typewriter. Sometimes I try to stretch his legs and make him walk down a street. But he won't go.'

'He was a very obstinate man,' Josef chuckled.

'Once I was in a hole, and they were shooting at us, and I was really scared, and I called to him to come and help me, but he wouldn't come.' Robert looked shy as he added: 'Then I called you, and you came, and I felt better.' He looked intently at the dog which stared back, love in its small brown eyes.

'Who was shooting at you?'

'The enemy,' Robert answered shortly. His eyes were fixed, unseeing, on Lex, as if he had removed himself from the conversation, as if his brother had intruded too far into a private world where he did not belong.

'Which enemy?' Josef persisted. 'Who were you fighting against?'

'Oh, it's the war on the border. Don't you know?' said Robert vaguely.

'On the border,' Josef repeated. 'Tell me.'

'It's nothing to worry about.' Robert brightened. 'There's enough of us up there. You're safe, Josef. You and Dorothy. They can't get through. We're better trained and armed than them. You mustn't worry,' he said, with a mixture of pride at having been a participant and reluctance to reveal too much.

'Well, I'm pleased that I answered your call,' said Josef. 'Was I much help? I couldn't imagine myself in battle.' The joke fell flat. Robert did not smile.

'I said I felt better.' The shutters came down then. He had spoken, he had revealed something, and now he was back behind his screen of silence.

'Where were you today?' Josef asked carefully.

'Here,' said Robert reluctantly, as if he had volunteered all the information he needed to for that session. 'All day. Why?'

'No reason,' Josef lied. 'I just wonder if you get bored, sitting here day after day.'

Robert's raucous laughter brought Dorothy into the room. She put her head in at the door. From her glassy expression, Josef could tell that she had been deeply involved in her writing.

'Bored!' Robert sneered. 'I've got enough movies in my head never to be bored again, ever. I just run them over and over, you see.'

'Oh hello Josef,' said Dorothy. 'I'm sorry, but I got carried away with my work. I haven't made supper. I didn't realise it was so late.' She put her hand to her mouth apologetically, as if she expected to be chastened, like a child. She had on a sandy-coloured tracksuit; her husband noticed that she was not wearing her wedding-ring.

'It doesn't matter,' he said. 'I'm not hungry anyway.'

'I've been on a creative streak; it's difficult to stop.'

'Then go on.' He regretted her interruption; he had broken through Robert's defences and had elicited this sharp reaction. He wanted to press the advantage before his brother withdrew again. He almost waved her away, but stopped himself. 'I'll talk to Robert,' he said as gently as he could. 'You write.' And she went. 'Tell me some of the movies,' Josef coaxed. The young man blinked as he vacillated between reticence and disclosure.

'They make you aggressive,' Robert said. 'They make you hate. I suppose it's the only way. Otherwise you wouldn't be able to kill . . . There was a boy called Fowler. They picked on him because he was weak, he never said much. They called him "Chicken", making fun of his name. He used to go red and you knew they were getting to him. The Corporal used to make us hate him . . . He would say: "Chicken's mug isn't clean, so you must all run around the camp as punishment." So we all hated Chicken, even though he was just an ordinary guy. They did it on purpose, to teach us how to hate. So every time we got punished because of Chicken we used to take it out on him, you know, make him slip in the shower, cut him up a bit, make him go red and then some of the guys used to crow at him like cocks.'

Robert looked down at his long fingers, perhaps in shame at the recollection that he had been part of this bullying mob, perhaps because he thought that his story sounded ludicrous in the luxury of a suburban home in Eisstad. Certainly, Josef could not detect much shame: his brother appeared to be completely emotionless, almost as if this story was being told by someone alien to the situation described.

'They used to put their faces right up next to his and crow and he just went red and said nothing at all. But you could see he was upset. It made him go a bit funny,' said Robert. He rubbed the dog's spine harder than before and Lex jerked his head excitedly, biting the air. Robert stilled the dog with the pressure of his big hand.

'There was a curfew,' he continued, 'six till six. The people from the villages weren't allowed to be out during that time. If anyone broke the curfew, they'd be shot. They knew that. Anyway, one night, Fowler went out at about four, I thought he was just going for a piss, but he didn't come back until seven, and he didn't answer when I asked him where he'd been, and some of the guys, the ones who used to tease him, crowed because it was dawn. Fowler just got into bed and pretended to be asleep although he wasn't sleeping. At breakfast we heard that Chicken had shot an old man during curfew. When we asked him why he had done it, he said that he had never shot anyone before and he wanted to see what it was like. So he went to find someone to shoot. This old man was walking around his hut . . . That's one of the movies, Josef.'

'I see.'

'Do you want to hear another movie?'

'Yes, if you want to tell me.'

'We were in the bush, on a patrol. I was walking next to a guy, his name was Carl, and there was a shot from a tree, and he fell down. They'd shot his head off. When we'd all got off the ground and the tree had been shot to pieces — I mean,' Robert's words came out more quickly, 'that tree had as little left of it as the bloke who'd been sitting in it — when we took Carl back to the helicopter, it was horrible because his face had gone . . . the guy in the tree had shot

Carl's face off.' The young man laughed as the adrenalin pumped through him again, for a moment. 'And I just kept on thinking that it could have been me. You know, if he'd shot just a little to the side, he would have shot *my* face off and then I wouldn't be here, Josef. They would have knocked on your door one day,' (Josef thought about the white car parked outside) 'and told you that I'd been killed in action, defending our country, and that you should be proud of me because I'd helped make the Republic a safer place for everyone. Just like they told Carl's parents, I suppose. And then they'd have buried me without a face, and you and Dorothy would have come and they'd have blown a bugle . . . Why was it Carl, Josef? Why was it Carl and not me?' Then, for the first time since he had arrived, Robert showed emotion; he put his face in his hands and shook his head from side to side. After a while, he looked up; his eyes were red although he had cried silently. 'Why will I live to be old when Carl's life ended there? I don't understand these things, Josef.'

'I don't know either, Robert,' his brother said, and thought: how can a twenty year old understand death when he has not even begun to grapple with life? How can he know that Carl's death had no more meaning than Gomez's: both rendered faceless in pursuit of a dead ideal?

'I should go back, Josef,' Robert said, 'and take my chances.' He smiled briefly. 'It's more exciting than Eisstad.'

Josef's eyes narrowed. 'When we didn't hear from you, we thought . . . we thought something might have happened. We didn't know.'

'I'm not much of a letter writer,' Robert smiled, 'and I didn't think you'd be interested in the army stories. Usually we just sat round and waited. Sometimes we had contacts . . .' His voice trailed off.

'Of course we're interested,' Josef began, but Robert was speaking again.

'Sometimes we came upon bones of animals, skulls and ribs and bits of skin still sticking on, like clothes, as though the animals hadn't completely undressed, that's what it looked like.' He mumbled his words, apparently embarrassed at the metaphor, as though he were not sufficiently out of the army's clutches to be easy in a civilian milieu. 'And you thought about death, and how those bones could be you. Underneath your uniform and the rifle and the bullets, you are just bones . . . Do you know what I mean?'

Josef nodded.

'There were some crazy guys up there: this boy I know, called Jack, he was mad. His company was attacking a village because terrorists were hiding out there. The village was in a valley, and a machine gun was set up on the hill. As Jack's mates marched down the valley and the people ran up into the hills, they were mown down. Jack walked through streams of blood, he told me afterwards. He said he felt like a viking. All round him, people were crying and bleeding and dying, and Jack said, for the first time in his life, he felt really good. He was dealing with people in a totally new way.'

Robert spoke with such conviction that Josef wondered whether he was talking about himself. Was he 'Jack'? But Josef did not want to question his brother, did not want to determine his 'guilt' in this war game. Robert had admitted to shooting in self-defence, not to murder, and Josef did not want to know: it was difficult enough for the young man to adapt to 'normal' life without having to suffer the accusations of his brother.

'. . . Jack came back with a box of ears. He made a necklace from them,' Robert said without looking up to see his brother's reaction. 'He strung them together and used to wear them even in camp. He didn't talk much to anyone. Only sometimes to me. He was discharged a few months before me and we heard that he had got a job at a hospital in a small town as an orderly so that he could get drugs.

'We have to do it, Josef,' Robert continued. 'If we don't, they'll destroy this country. They'll destroy Eisstad. All the madness up there is for a purpose.'

Despite himself, despite his resolve not to be critical, Josef exclaimed bitterly: 'Is it? Do you uphold civilisation by slaughter?'

'I did it for you and Dorothy,' said Robert, his face white as if he had been slapped.

'Of course,' Josef responded immediately. 'I'm sorry.' He stood up and walked absent-mindedly about the room, stopping at the bookcase, and then before the ornament-cupboard with its fine figures of ladies carrying umbrellas, and boys riding bicycles: remnants of another era when such trivia must have been important. He had a sudden violent urge to sweep his hand through the lot and bring it crashing down in a pile of shattered glass, to mirror, externally, the chaos in his own home, as some way of restoring the balance. But he did not do so. Instead, he resumed his wandering, while Robert sat quietly, stroking the dog, appearing to have regained his composure.

Josef stopped before a picture of a faded man with a pointed beard who had his arm around the shoulders of a pretty woman in a white gown. They stood there, stiffly, posing for their wedding photograph with whatever hopes they had for their future locked behind those silent features. How could they have suspected then that the future would not bring the happiness that they anticipated, that perhaps they craved? Or did they not even think in terms of happiness? The woman had died when Robert was a baby, crossing the street, and the man had withdrawn into a loneliness from which he refused to be enticed. He had identified the body of his pretty bride and he carried the shock of that night on his face for the rest of his life: Josef remembered him looking startled when disturbed at his typewriter, as startled as a rabbit, always startled and withdrawn. Or drunk. What could have been so absorbing in a clerk's work that he should bring it home night after night, and, wrapped in his grey overcoat, devote himself to it rather then to his children? Josef did not know. The two ghosts haunted his wall.

'I'm going to bed now,' said Robert with the air of one who has finally sung for his supper, one who has now, at last, earned the right to be left alone.

'Goodnight,' Josef replied. 'I'm glad we've spoken.'

Robert did not acknowledge this remark. With Lex at his heel (he seemed to have commandeered the dog), he went into his room and closed the door.

'I am no longer going to eat meat or fish,' Josef S told his wife that night. 'I find the idea of putting flesh into my mouth repugnant.'

Her ring was back on her finger: a broad gold band. He wondered why she had removed it earlier: perhaps to put cream on her hands, or to bath. Perhaps she had taken to removing her ring when she wrote as a way to emphasise her identity as Dorothy Knox, the author. He did not ask. Her hands were strong. He could not bear to imagine them caressing another man.

3

The familiar shrieking once more warned him. But he could not escape, no matter how much dread he felt. No matter that his nemesis stood at the lip of the Abyss, looking down as the procession emerged.

The priest raised a short spear and pointed it in the direction of the marchers. The dust bowl was the surface of the moon; the fine dust filtered into eyes and noses, and people covered their faces with scarves as they tramped. Their feet raised the powdery matter to head height until they were invisible and only a white haze lay over the plain. The priest, spearpoint of the anger, disappeared into the dust-cloud together with the placards: IN LOVING MEMORY OF OUR DEAREST BELOVED . . . MURDERED IN THE CAUSE OF PEACE . . . REMEMBERED BY HIS FAMILY . . . REST IN PEACE . . .

They were bathing in dust, covering their bodies with it, throwing it into the air in handfuls so that it hid them, rubbing it into their skins as if it were water. He took a step towards them and they waved him closer with their wild hands that appeared from inside the dust like swans' heads from ponds of water. He heard laughter from inside the dust cloud and he did not know if they were laughing at him. At least the laughter displaced the shrieking.

Valhalla was dusty: as in the dreams. A dirty wind blew sand into the mouth and eyes and under the flaps of clothes. It was not sand from construction sites — there was no construction — but from untarred streets and pavements. The houses were not individual, as in Eisstad, but were clones, extending, it seemed, for miles in every direction, drab boxes that must kill the spirit. And yet, paradoxically, there was more feeling, more spirit, in those bare streets than in their counterparts in the shadow of the Leeukop. People seemed to live more in the streets than in their houses: children, more often barefoot than not, played or ran, or waited on street corners, watching as he drove past. He expected rocks to thud against his windscreen, to form spiders' patterns in front of his eyes. He was a foreign organism travelling through the veins of a body, waiting for rejection. But it did not come. The eyes were sometimes suspicious, sometimes excited (he drove slowly enough to see their eyes), but no one lifted a finger against him. Housewives, usually wearing aprons, and scarves on their heads, stood at front gates, shouting to one another across the narrow streets, communicating in a way that was not done in Eisstad where the houses were bigger, where people had telephones, where entertaining was conducted inside. How strange that the very conditions that should dampen the human spirit seemed to bring out the magic of a community, whereas opulence so often caused sterility.

This was Valhalla: principal supplier of Eisstad's workforce, people forced by law to live here. It was criss-crossed by roads rutted from bad drainage, a bleak urban desert from which there was no escape. In the distance, if he turned his head, Josef S could see the Leeukop, in outline, ghostly as a dream, presiding over the people who created these laws, hardly even a part of the world of the people of Valhalla. Except that the dispossessed wanted to return. Not all of them. Only, as Buth's propaganda machine would call them, the 'radicals', the stone-throwers so feared by Edward Parry, the children murdered by the police. Josef drove with the guidance of a map of the township on the seat beside him.

The address of the deceased, where the funeral procession would begin, was in the newspapers; he had not had to ask Ben. Nobody knew he was there. Dorothy thought he had taken his car to perform an inspection in a case on which he was working. He had called his office with a similar excuse.

The roads were not even named, but had numbers: VA57, VA5, and so on, in no obvious numerical sequence. They were intersected by grandly misnamed 'avenues'. The dead man had lived at the intersection of 12th Avenue and VA27. Ben probably lived close by. As he drove, Josef tried to picture the events that had led up to the killing: people massed in the streets, the stayaway causing a Sunday atmosphere; workers debating whether they would be paid or fired from their jobs; children boycotting the schools, running from group to group passing on messages: a bush telegraph. 'They're coming, they're coming this way, no that, up 25, down 26. Stones ready, Comrades'. The warriors remain while the others flee into their houses and barricade the doors. And the Armoured Personnel Carriers, the Leeus, used by the riot police, trundle down the streets, yellow and blue, their squat ugly shapes pitted with the holes of previous stonings, vehicles developed for use in the bush country up north, to patrol the borders, now redeployed in the Flatlands where roads have replaced the bush and the enemy has become the people.

All of this Josef S pieced together from what he read, day after day in the newspapers, the words supported by photographs, and now the photographs substituted by the reality of the places where the pictures had been taken. With the mountain a hope in the background, and the citizens of Eisstad unaware of this reality, the Government's plan was blindingly simple: remove the people from areas like Waterfront and relocate them in the sprawling ghettos on the Flatlands where they can be sealed off, so that the Leeus do not have to disturb the peaceful suburbs.

And then the stones begin to beat on the armoured sides: lion against lion, and the response is immediate. Cannisters of teargas are fired, and birdshot, and rubber bullets, and into the resulting war-haze policemen like troops descend to take their revenge for the assault on law and order. Ben is there perhaps, not the nervous clerk, but an angry young man wearing a red scarf, his books put aside for the lure of rocks, his law for the attack on law, waving his fists and singing freedom songs, and then running as the shots pepper the backs of his Comrades. Or perhaps Ben is hiding in his mother's house while the chaos explodes, wondering if he will ever become a lawyer or if the opportunity has been snatched from him as surely as life from the body of his neighbour whom the police have chosen to be the victim, for whatever reason.

Freddy Pietersen, 26, is a rugby player, married, one child. Perhaps the police have taken a dislike to an article of clothing he wears, a headband, a colour: who can say? He makes a final dash into his house, no ball in his hand, hurtling for a goal line that will not save him. Behind, the opposition, disregarding the rules completely, breaks down the door and bursts into the kitchen: a rifle is raised, or a shotgun (the newspapers did not say), and the bullet destroys all dreams, all hopes, everything, ends the game, leaving only the wife's tears, the community's anger and the funeral.

By the time that Josef drove into VA25, he had no need for his map. The people were coming. They were coming like a huge snake, winding through the narrow roads, twisting round the houses, the tail hidden from the head.

Josef parked his car and got out to join the procession. An excitement which he had never felt before leaped into him like a drug: the newspapers could not convey the energy that this mass of people generated. What relation could the words 'There were an estimated twenty thousand people at the funeral' bear to the scene that was unfolding before him now? The coffin was carried on a bier at the front of the procession: a long black box draped with the flag of the FDF. It was held up by arms interlinked in a complex pattern, a wonderful sculpture carved out of the living flesh of a hundred hands all crowding to touch the wood, all seeking to be part of the grief. The mourners chanted and punched the air with clenched fists: 'Power to the People!'

Josef had to turn away: the spectacle was too enormous to comprehend all at once. A plastic bag caught by the wind high up hung in the air as motionless as if it had been painted there. In a yard without a shred of anything green, a yard made entirely out of dust, children were throwing a ball to one another. A woman with a headful of yellow curlers sat on a verandah watching the entertainment. A boy on crutches with both legs in plaster was moving awkwardly but quickly to join the crowd. Josef wondered if he would see Ben, but there was very little chance of that. The procession swelled as it moved down the road picking up people, perhaps not a snake but a flood of water being fed by incoming tributaries until it began to mount the dusty pavements.

A man with a megaphone, and wearing a yellow FDF T-shirt, tried to maintain order. 'Keep behind the front row, Comrades,' he urged. 'Please keep off the pavements. Join at the back.' People were too excited to obey. Ululations took flight like shrieking gulls from the gut of the crowd.

Josef S waded into the river and was swept along in its heady current. He was next to a man who wore a red scarf and a woman in a white blouse and black skirt. The dust rose up to the knees and when Josef looked down, he could not see his feet. He had the impression of floating on this river together with a mass of human flotsam, and he found himself chanting with the crowd: 'Power to the People, Power to the People, Power, Power!' The mourners accepted him as naturally as if he were one of their own. Even if they knew that he came from the Ice City, nobody cared. He was accepted: one drop in a massive swelling flood, all identity given up in a common pursuit that was larger than any individual: a huge affirmation of faith in the human spirit.

An army helicopter was circling overhead, throbbing the air with its rhythmic palpitations, low enough to offend, to extort the raising of angry fists from some of the marchers. 'They agreed to keep away,' said the man with the red scarf. 'They agreed to keep their Leeus in their cages today so we can bury our dead in peace. But still they want to show us who's boss.' He shook his fist at the mechanical insect above. After a while, it flew away in the direction of the mountain. The chanting continued.

A mangy horse trudged by in a side street, blinkered, dragging a vegetable barrow with what seemed to be the last of its strength, as encased in dust as the silent driver who whipped the animal from time to time with the reins. The heat rose from the ground with a force that made breathing difficult; there were no trees to shield the marchers. Did trees refuse to grow here or had nobody bothered to plant any? Winter appeared to have deserted Valhalla. Josef could imagine what the wet winter did to these streets: one either lived in a dust bowl or in a swamp. Yet the people smiled at one another over their front gates and absorbed him into their throng, and did not lynch him. He realised now that he had taken his life into his hands by coming here, he had had no idea what he would find: and yet, despite the things which had been done to these people in his name, they accepted him.

The sports stadium was suddenly there in the middle of the narrow streets. It was called Valhalla Park, the name adorning the single grandstand, a large concrete structure which gaped like a mouth in mid-bite towards Eisstad. A wall surrounded the ground. The procession entered the stadium through one of the traffic gates. Cars had been parked across the access roads to the stadium and marshalls, wearing yellow armbands, buttons, and FDF T-shirts, diverted traffic. The T-shirts proclaimed: FDF LIVES! Nor could anyone deny that the FDF controlled Valhalla that day. Even babies were decked out in FDF paraphernalia: the children were being prepared for the struggle against Buth's Government.

'Please get off the pavements and the walls,' the man with the megaphone appealed. He wore an FDF sticker upside down on his shirt. 'Please join the march from the back.' He was running backwards and forwards in a state of great excitement. 'Please, people, enter the stadium in an orderly fashion.'

Banners, proud as sails in a stiff breeze, unequivocally declared the political direction of the marchers: DEATH TO THE ILLEGITIMATE GOVERNMENT. POLICE OUT. BUTH: THE BLOOD IS ON YOUR HANDS. One of the banners showed a stylised fist holding a stylised gun, and affirmed: FREEDOM IS IN YOUR HANDS. Freedom, Josef S wondered, can it be sustained if it is purchased by violence?

The river was flowing firmly into the stadium. Even if Josef had

had a change of heart and wanted to turn back, the current would not have permitted him to go. If the police had arrived then, there would have been pandemonium: people would have been crushed to death against the stadium walls. The heat pressed its red palms down onto the heads of the marchers: Josef was sweating as badly as when he had been ill; his clothes were as sodden as his bedding. And then he was thrust into the stadium.

The coffin rested on its bier on one of the goal lines. A row of men, the orators or members of the family, sat solemnly on stiff chairs in the in-goal area. Between coffin and men was a microphone on a stand, lethal as a spear. The mourners sat cross-legged facing the coffin in semi-circular rows that fanned out on the playing field. Josef chose to stand, leaning against the concrete wall of the stadium opposite the speakers. A child played in the dust in front of him and drew white marks on her face with a piece of soft white stone, as if putting on war-paint. She appeared to be perfectly happy.

Four or five camera crews from local and foreign television stations recorded the events. The men looked like war correspondents: they had a world-weary air about them, occasioned not so much by the heat as by the cynicism of reporting on sufferings and injustices day after day, year after year, all around the world. Some of these pressmen had stickers on their clothes or their equipment: FDF UNITES on a camera-bag or DON'T MOURN, MOBILISE worn as an armband, perhaps more as a passport through the townships than from any deep-seated conviction at the cause advertised. Others wore fatigues and boots as if they saw themselves as soldiers. Their job was to publicise the conflict to the world, they had no commitment to any particular situation: these soldiers were mercenaries. Josef pictured one of these men, tired and burned out, sitting in an office in one of the world's capitals, in ten years' time, sending out the next generation of prematurely old men on a further round of disaster reporting. One of them might write a book about his experiences and become comfortable and famous; another might end up defeated in a bar somewhere, finally overcome by the horror he had witnessed during the course of his career. Josef recognised the same weariness in his brother. But Robert was young enough to adjust, to grow normal again; these men had progressed so far that they could not turn back.

While the helicopter pulsed above the stadium, the orators condemned the presence of the police in the townships. To Josef S, these speakers were indistinguishable from one another. He had not heard of any of them: religious and political leaders, family of the deceased. Their words seemed to flow into a stream that mingled with the heat and filled the spaces between the mourners. Speaker after speaker stood and denounced the system which legalised removals, which forced people to live apart, which had caused Freddy Pietersen to be shot in his own home. Ben must have been present, but where? Was he sitting in front with his arm raised in anger every time a speaker made a pertinent point? Did his eyes glow in that same strange way that Josef had seen in his office? Who was this boy, called Ben, who was such a different person from the timid clerk in an icy world?

'They won't stop us with Leeus!' the microphone spat. 'We are flesh and blood and bones, and we can be destroyed physically, but they won't destroy our spirit. A thousand, ten thousand, fifty thousand of them can come into Valhalla, but they will not crush us. We must be united in the struggle! If you sit on the fence, you will get hurt; you must be involved.'

The orator, dressed neatly in a dark suit, seemed to materialise from the haze, from the background of the other speakers, and stand there, clearly outlined in the sunlight, and Josef S was forced to listen. The man was short and slim, but he bludgeoned the crowd with his voice. He was aggressive and unsubtle, and the mourners drank in his words with the thirst of people stranded in a desert. The words chipped away through the heat and the dust. Sweat lined Josef's face and he had to sweep it out of his eyes.

Echoing the words on one of the banners, the speaker cried: 'Buth! The blood of the children is on your hands!' and he waved his finger. 'Buth! I want you to know that the people have long memories, and that when the people rule, you will be tried for your crimes before a court of the people. I want you and your generals to know these things, Buth. Let your spies, who are among us today,' the mourners cheered and waved their fists, shouting: 'Power! Power!', 'take this message back to their masters.'

The mourners erupted into applause. Josef S could hardly absorb the enormous presence that filled the stadium, the fact that all these people, thousands of them, were opposed to Buth's Government, and that the people of Eisstad, on the whole, had no idea of this popular resistance. No doubt journalists from the local newspapers were present, but their reports and photographs could not convey the atmosphere of a funeral of this magnitude, could not, on paper, suggest the electricity created by this speaker. Only television could transmit the urgency into the homes of Eisstad, but ETV refused to show footage of the troubles on the Flatlands. An exasperated columnist in the *Evening Times* had recently compared ETV's news broadcasts to the snippets of information printed on the inside of bubblegum wrappers. He believed that the official mouthpiece of the State was creating a dangerous illusion of security. Now, for the first time, Josef understood the nature of the complaint. What he was seeing was beyond anything he had been prepared for, either by the bland non-reporting of ETV, or the daily lists of horrors printed by Eisstad's two independent newspapers.

'I call on you, Comrades, to stand up against the system. So many of our brothers have been detained and shot. We can't stop now. They can ring our streets with steel, they can kick in our doors, they can shoot us in our kitchens but they will never crush us. We have waited for three hundred years to gain political rights in the country of our birth, and we are on the brink, Comrades, on the very brink of success.'

He sat down, to thunderous applause and shouts of 'Power!'. The world's television cameras panned the mourners, the raised fists, the FDF T-shirts. Only the Republic's viewers would be deprived of this energy and anger. Of course, the orator's conclusion was debatable: how close the people were to success. But the audience believed him, passionately.

'Thank you, Reverend Lode,' said a priest who was acting as the Master of Ceremonies. 'You have given us all hope and inspiration today, a sad day, a day on which we are to bury our brother, Freddy Pietersen. We should not despair however, Comrades. We should take courage from the sacrifice of our brother and move on to fight this unjust regime.'

'Power! Power! Power!' chanted the rows of mourners and Josef S was tempted to join in the chanting, but was it not inappropriate to embrace a cause to which he had so recently been exposed, a cause the pursuit of which would have enabled people like Edward Parry to label him a traitor? Was this really his cause? Could he chant slogans which were part of a movement which threatened his own security and privilege, and those of his family? Again, his eye rested on the shimmering ghost of the Leeukop; it dominated everything, even in its ephemeral form. He imagined shimmering lions lying on its surface.

'Brothers and sisters,' said the Master of Ceremonies. 'We will proceed to the cemetery. Please leave the stadium in an orderly fashion. We will walk in rows of six. Please keep to your row and do not walk on the pavements. We must present a united front.'

'Power! Power! Power!' was the echo. It thudded against the grandstand in waves; it rose like a series of machine-gun bursts through those seated. Again, the helicopter appeared, and flew monotonously, a prehistoric impulse masquerading in a modern skin. The sky had become white hot. The machine clung tenuously to its place in the heat, spinning around, feigning importance, but Josef knew that the only matters of import were on the ground: the groundswell of movement from the dispossessed who were marching their way out of the townships to reclaim what they believed to be theirs.

Perhaps it was the heat and the sweat running into his eyes; perhaps it was the vision of his brother shooting bullets into flesh; perhaps it was the thought of the blade cutting into Buth's chest as he bent to eat; or the man who had stuck that blade, bent now under the ministrations of his interrogators. Perhaps it was simply the fact of seeing and experiencing these people, united in a common cause. Josef cried. He did not sob, but tears came to his eyes and welled up there. He had to press his fingers into the corners of his eyes to expel the water, and he smelled salt. He wiped his face with his handkerchief hoping no one would notice the tears, yet knowing that no one would care. He felt that his pale face was red from the heat and the crying and his embarrassment. He walked through the exit with the first of the crowd and stood against the wall of a house watching the people emerging. They came and came and kept on coming, their shoes tramping the ground, crunching the gravel like an army going to war. They were dressed in the yellow, red and green of the FDF or in white because their intention was not to mourn but to rejoice in this reason for their unification.

A group had hitched a ride on a horse-drawn cart as the procession, with Josef S now in it, filled the road, stopping traffic, banners and flags waving. A poster of Mkhize had been raised, with the words FREE MKHIZE printed over a photograph of his face. The journalists were filming the march from any observation point they could find; one man with long yellow hair and baggy clothes had climbed onto a bus shelter and was training his camera on the river flowing below him. By nightfall, these events would be relayed to every part of the world except the part in which they had occurred.

The procession took ten or fifteen minutes to pass any point, the stark black coffin luring all those people to follow; the twined hands held the bier towards the sun. Josef's clothes were wet, his skin felt as if it were caked in salt. His arms were bruised from the buffeting of the crowd. He had long since taken off his jacket and wore it slung over his shoulder, his tie stuffed into a pocket. His shoes were white from dust. The dust had even stained his dark trousers up to the knees: from afar, from a dream, you might have gained the impression that the crowd was levitating, rising above tedious reality. The people climbed into the sky before Josef's eyes, gravity lost its control of them. They floated with their coffin towards the sun, and the lion-skinned priest jabbed his short spear, piercing the flank of the dust that rose with them. Not even the helicopter would stop that procession which would walk right through the metal as if it did not exist, driving a wedge through reality.

The entrance of the cemetery was not wide enough to accomodate the march as it was constituted and the tenuous order that the marshalls had established broke up. Those mourners who elected not to go in dammed up the streets; others, impatient to be part of the proceedings, jumped over the cemetery wall or sat on it.

The cemetery was an unkempt jumble of graves. The place had an air of neglect as if the community could not afford its upkeep, or had lost interest: headstones were unpolished; jam-jars which might once have contained flowers lay dirty and empty, now litter rather than adornment; clumps of yellow grass sprouted randomly from the dust; one grave was surrounded by a green picket fence and the grass grew wildly within that private garden to which no one could have had access for years.

The priest who had been Master of Ceremonies at the stadium took control of the microphone. 'Please get off the walls,' he directed, and one or two of those perched like cats obeyed. 'The walls will collapse and people will get hurt. Please come into the cemetery. There is still room.'

But anyone wanting to see into the grave pit had to find a vantage point. The graveside was tightly ringed by priests, family and journalists; it was impossible for anyone else to get close. Two television crews had clambered with their equipment onto the roof of the small stone chapel beside which Freddy Pietersen was to be buried, and a few enterprising mourners lay sprawled like leopards along the branches of three bare trees. Greenery appeared to be forbidden in the wasteland of Valhalla.

'Let the family approach the grave,' pleaded the priest, but it was a forlorn request.

Josef sat on a gravestone. He was very weary: the heat, the emotion, the walk, had drained away his energy. Behind him, a group of men was hoisting a banner as laboriously as if it were a tent, using guy ropes to keep the wooden struts upright. The message was intended for the cameras: FREDDY PIETERSEN. YOU DIED FOR US ALL.

The priest was chanting monotonously into his microphone. Josef's concentration wandered with the ululation. He thought of dust, rising from the waving yellow grass as feet stamped on it; he thought of men dressed in lion-skins brandishing shields, warding off militaristic evils with the most primitive methods, and then of the Leeus, rumbling down the township roads, and the helicopters above.

The journalists on the ground were struggling to take photographs: too many people blocked the way. The tall cameraman whom Josef had seen on top of the bus shelter was in the thick of the crowd. He was the epitome of Josef's image of a war correspondent: long hair framing a rugged face, camouflage trousers tucked into army boots, an FDF sticker on his camera-bag. His camera was raised at arm's length above his head, aimed blindly in the direction of the grave, stealing shots over the heads of the mourners. It was indecent: these predators would even follow the coffin into the pit to photograph the mourners, a 'corpse-eye view', so to speak. Yet they were tolerated, because their pictures were destined for international consumption.

The bier, a bed frame with long legs, was taken away, hand over hand, and disappeared somewhere. Josef S did not see the coffin lowered into the pit because of the crush at the graveside. He saw a ladder and heard men digging Valhalla sand into the hole. Sand thumped onto the box, and, at the same time, bunches of flowers were passed overhead towards the grave. Even the journalists helped in this chore and for a moment, the war correspondent, his camera slung around his neck, held a bunch of roses in his hand.

Josef S closed his eyes and cupped his hands before his face. Was it not strange that he could hear no signs of grief from those at the graveside? The funeral was a circus, a political rally, a mass gathering in a country where most other gatherings were illegal. A member of the dead man's family thanked the mourners for supporting them in their time of loss, and then it was all over. Two men approached Josef and shook his hand. From their nodding and the look in their eyes, he understood they were expressing appreciation that he had made the effort to be with them.

'I wish to thank all religious denominations for coming,' announced the priest, 'and please, people, stick together. We will march down 16th Avenue. Walk on the left side of the road and don't disperse into side roads.'

Josef walked back next to the procession, at a slightly faster pace: he wanted to go home. Suddenly a group of men and boys broke away from the march and, adjusting their scarves so as to disguise their faces, swooped to pick up rocks from the dusty pavement. Their movements had the natural grace of sportsmen, bending on the run to pick up a ball from the turf. For a moment, Josef feared that they were coming for him, that they knew he was from the city of the hated oppressors, that the speeches during the course of the day had stoked the fires to uncontrollable heights, and that he was about to become the target of their anger. But they ran past him and disappeared down a side road where the object of their attention was hidden.

Josef S walked soberly to his car. The sun was beginning to go down; he had been in Valhalla all day, one of the most exhilarating days of his life. He was exhausted but strangely fulfilled. As he drove out of the township past the Valhalla Police Station, Leeus in army colours were entering; he noticed troops garrisoned in the grounds. The funeral had been peaceful; he could not have imagined it any other way. Why the troops? It was only when he was on the freeway heading back for Eisstad that he realised the significance of what he had seen: there had been *soldiers* in the township. Up until then, there had only been police.

He bought a newspaper from a small boy who, apparently unperturbed by the events in the country, was blowing tunelessly on a mouth organ and jiggling his bag of change to keep up some kind of beat. Or perhaps the boy was acutely in tune with the discordant nature of the Republic. He gave Josef a conspiratorial smile as though they were party to a secret which the lawyer still had to learn. Not long ago, Josef S would not have noticed the boy from whom he bought his newspaper: a newspaper seller would have been part of the scenery, of no more importance than an automatic vending machine. Now they were exchanging knowing looks, contemplating together the upheavals that were shaking the Republic.

Did this child have parents? Were they drunkards, or dead? Did the father fall into such violent rages that it was safer for the boy to leave home? Did he sleep in doorways? Or was he part of the gang that lived in the fish factory? Or did he sell himself to Eisstad's lonely at night? As Josef drove away, the thin sound of the mouth organ followed him, as ephemeral as the wind.

In the beginning, Dorothy had not wanted children; her writing was too demanding, too urgent, left too little time. Once, despite her precautions, she thought she was pregnant. Her husband had feared for that imagined foetus floating like a blind fish inside her. He feared for the spark, which, if allowed to mature, would have to endure the burden of life. What right did a man and woman have, he wondered, to bring into the world a package of nerve ends that would have to suffer pain? How could anyone take on such a responsibility? To his parents, childbirth was a natural extension of marriage, an animal function. And the result? The dark and brooding Josef S and his brother, the viking, wading in rivers of blood. What a terrible force could be unleashed upon the world, shaped by pain! Had one seed, determined to survive against enormous odds, managed to circumvent the devices and traps that had been laid in its way; had it swum on a ridiculously hazardous journey, propelled by a biological necessity, counter to the desires of the man and his wife; had it succeeded in its mission, no less explosive (he thought) than a submarine threading its way through enemy waters to strike at the Capital? The announcement that it had not, after all, had left him euphoric with relief, a relief so great that he had not even considered that his wife might have felt differently.

Josef glanced at the headlines: TROOPS MOVE INTO TOWN-SHIPS. He parked in a quiet street and rested the *Evening Times* against the steering wheel. Squirrels frolicked in the trees overhead and pigeons flopped heavily to pick up scraps from the tarmac. He read that, as a result of the worsening unrest situation, troops were now being stationed in the townships to assist the riot police. General de Wet denied that this was an act of civil war. Asked to comment, he stated that the troops were simply there to maintain 'law and order', to be a back-up force to the police who were being confronted by too many incidents to be truly effective.

An ambulance sped past. Josef was less than surprised to see the wire meshing attached to its windscreen. The situation had deteriorated to the extent that even ambulances were under threat. And yet, he had been perfectly safe. The magnitude of his experince in Valhalla was breaking over him like waves over a breakwater, and he needed to be alone somewhere to think things out, to gain a perspective on the events of the day before he went home to explain himself to Dorothy. He dropped the newspaper on the seat beside him and drove to his office.

Josef S put his father's typewriter on his desk and sat down. He stared at the bars and the keys and the spaces, trying to retrieve some measure of order from the spare black frame. He tried to visualise his father's fingers tapping out numerical messages night after night, with the lovely face of his wife hovering at his shoulder, driving him to communicate just as Dorothy's muse forced her to invent her fictions or the Reverend Lode's anger compelled him to spit out his frustration into a stadium full of chanting people. Ought these communications to be evaluated according to social relevance? Did a private sorrow have any less importance then a public one? The ancient machine could give no answers. It simply existed, and the viewer put his or her interpretation onto it, in accordance with his or her perspective at the time.

Perhaps, once, Josef S had seen the typewriter as a symbol of a failed human being and father, its spareness indicative of the barren personality that worked it; perhaps now he saw it as an example of the determination of a man who had stubbornly held his grief at bay. 'So far and no further,' the old man might have said to the emotion that was crippling him. And he had communicated his sorrow by numbers for the rest of his life. Again, the question returned: was the old man's grief, relayed in this way, any less relevant to the human condition than the Reverend Lode's impassioned speeches? Or Josef's growing anguish at the pain of the Republic? How could he communicate his pain as these others had? Perhaps this was the solution: that he needed to convert his private grief into public action.

Feeling at last as if crucial pieces of a puzzle were falling into place, the lawyer left his office and drove home. It was already dark.

'Where have you been?' Dorothy demanded. 'My God, we've been so worried. I called your office and they didn't know . . . they said you hadn't come back yet from wherever you were . . . What a mess you're in!'

'The inspection took longer than I thought,' Josef said softly. His eyes were closing; it was a burden to fight that exquisite feeling of release. He was drifting, drifting with thousands of people, swallowed up into their massed ranks, like driftwood taken up in the sea and swept along by the currents with no control over its destination. He was not an individual, but part of a great movement.

'My publishers accepted my book, Josef,' Dorothy said. 'They loved it.' Her voice was husky with pride, and relief that her husband was home. She stood before him with an air of childlike joy at her achievement and waited, even now, for his approval.

'That's wonderful,' he answered from inside the waves. He smiled, trying to find joy for his wife amid the confusion. 'I'm very happy for you,' he said.

She came to him and embraced him, and he buried his head in her flaming hair. As he did so, he was aware that Robert had entered the room and was staring at them; it was something he sensed rather than observed.

'Aren't you happy for Dorothy?' Josef asked the presence, as a way of revealing that he knew they were being watched, and of sharing the responsibility of Dorothy's happiness.

'Who are you talking to?' she asked.

'Robert,' he said.

'Robert's gone out,' she said. 'He's not here.'

Josef felt a sudden coldness in his neck. He looked at the door, where he had felt Robert to be, but no one was there.

'I'm sorry,' he said. 'I must have been imagining. It's been a long day.'

'He's taken Lex for a walk.'

Josef changed the subject. 'We'll go out to eat tomorrow, to celebrate,' he offered. 'I would take you tonight, but I really am too tired.' Through her hair, the world seemed to be on fire.

Later, when he lay in bed, he wondered if the events of the day had made him invent ghosts or whether someone had indeed been spying on him. It was also curious that Dorothy had not questioned him more closely on where he had been: perhaps her excitement overshadowed suspicion.

'*Stories of Exile* by Dorothy Knox,' his wife said beside him. She wriggled in satisfaction and her body rubbed against his. But he had no desire for her. He tensed when she touched his arm. 'As a lawyer you receive recognition every time a client walks in the door and says "Please take my case", and if you win you feel even better. But I work alone for years on a book, and I never know if I'm on the right track. When my publishers see it and like it, all the pain of creating becomes worthwhile. All those years have not been wasted . . .'

'I know,' he said in the darkness. He remembered a time when he had been able to identify completely with her joys and sorrows as if they were his own, when he had looked into her green eyes and his heart had melted, when he had run his fingers through her hair and experienced a thrill of wonder that another person could inspire him so much.

'There's another aspect too,' she murmured. 'If I could help to create awareness through my books, I would feel that I was contributing to the struggle in a small way. It's all I can do. I'm not an up-front person.' She kissed the side of his face and he did not possess the callousness to push her away. In her time of acceptance, how could he reject her? The thought of Robert watching their intimacy was a seed which had taken hold for no good reason: he tried to uproot it, but he felt it was there to stay.

At breakfast, Josef said: 'There are troops in the townships. The border has moved south to the Flatlands.' This observation was directed at Robert, who began to butter his toast too intently, avoiding the bait that was floating in his direction. 'What do you think of that?' Josef asked pointedly at last.

'I'm not in the army any more,' Robert said. 'I've done my service.'

'But you'll be called up for camps,' Josef pressed. 'Will you go?'

'Why not?' Robert fended reluctantly, spreading fig jam on top of the butter.

'Because you'll be fighting against your own people, fellow citizens,' said Josef, and to him the comment was so self-evident that it was almost unnecessary. But the effect on Robert was revelatory. He slammed the knife down.

'Savages!' he snorted. 'Do you know what they do to each other?' The calm he had maintained for so much of his stay dropped away like a cloth from a statue that had been unveiled. His eyes were hard and staring, looking into scenes that Josef did not wish to imagine. The picture of his brother, automatic rifle held in the crook of his arm, striding through valleys awash with blood, an image culled from a genre of substandard war films, flickered through the lawyer's mind. 'Do you know?'

Josef shook his head, taken aback by the venom, even though he realised that he should have expected it; he had prodded and jabbed until it had been released.

'I've seen what they do to each other. I don't sit at home and make up liberal theories. I've seen with my own eyes. They're savages and we have to save them from themselves. The troops have gone in to keep order, to keep the peaceful ones from being hurt.'

His face was dark with anger. 'I'd be proud to protect "my people" if you want to call them that, from the revolutionaries.'

'So is it all the work of a few revolutionaries?' Josef S asked. 'All the disturbance?'

'Of course,' glowered Robert.

'Is that what they told you?'

'I've seen what they do to each other,' his brother repeated.

'Not in the townships, surely,' Josef tested. 'Remember the troops have only just gone into the townships. Or did you go in too?'

'No, I wasn't there,' Robert answered, but the words slunk out of his mouth like beaten dogs.

Dorothy came in then with plates of eggs for the brothers. Her face glowed with contentment, as if she had learned that she was pregnant, and her husband suddenly saw how she would look when she grew old: a kindly old face, crinkled with the creases of concentration that it took to create new worlds. Did she still want children, or was the acceptance of her book fulfilment enough? But Josef knew that, in time, the discontent would return, as it always had.

'Coffee, gentlemen?' she asked, ignoring the tension that charged the space between her husband and his brother. Perhaps in her euphoria she did not notice, or perhaps she intended to deflate their anger.

'Please,' said Josef, but Robert shook his head. The interruption was sufficient to allow him to regain his composure, to raise the veil again. As if he had not been stirred at all, he returned to his breakfast, while Josef forced himself to attend to his. Robert's eyes were focussed on his plate, refusing to meet his brother's. Dorothy brought coffee for Josef and herself. She was smiling into the distance.

Winter was relaxing its grip on Eisstad and Josef came upon sudden explosions of colour in suburban gardens. He bought a newspaper from a vendor and flipped through it on his way to work.

THIRTY THOUSAND PEOPLE AT FUNERAL declared the headline, followed by a bland account of the events Josef had witnessed in Valhalla the previous day. A second story, titled TROOPS SURROUND VALHALLA, revealed that the Reverend Mr Lode had been detained after the funeral. A Leeu had stopped outside his house, and the Reverend had been bundled into the back. Eyewitnesses claimed that he was bleeding from a cut on the head, but a police spokesman denied this. A photograph on page five showed three armed guards leaning against the outer gate of the hospital in which Buth was recuperating. The men were in plain clothes, and carried submachine guns. They were laughing, sharing a joke. Two of them appeared to be in their late twenties, one a boy barely older than Robert. Josef wondered if they had been involved with the group which had murdered the lawyer, Mrs Idini. It was reported elsewhere that restrictions had been placed on her funeral: no political speeches were to be made, only members of her family were allowed to address the gathering, and the procession was to be escorted by the police. A spokesman for the FDF condemned these curbs as 'an attempt by a desperate Government to halt the people's movement towards freedom.'

Josef folded the newspaper roughly and lengthened his stride. He walked quickly without looking at the bright blossoms of spring which were inappropriately cheerful.

'Thank you, Mr S,' Ben said. 'I was prepared to give up my job to go to the funeral.' Surely this boy, standing on the carpet before Josef like a pupil in a headmaster's office, could not have been one of the youths chanting 'Power!' and waving fists? But then might the headmaster himself not have been one of the mourners in the hot, dusty procession?

Josef said: 'I read about it in the newspaper.'

The young man's eyes, which could look innocent, even angelic, if they were raised as now, in amusement, shone. Angels, thought Josef S, leading the Revolution. 'The newspaper said thirty thousand people, Mr S,' Ben said, and added wistfully, 'I wish you'd been there. So you could have seen what's going on.'

Josef pointed to the folders on his desk. 'That's what's going on, Ben.' How long ago had all this begun? It seemed as though years had passed since he had encountered the women in the park, protesting at murders he had only vaguely been aware of. 'Do you know how far behind I am?'

If the question was a hint for Ben to go, he did not take it. His hands were folded in front of his body like those of a politician about to make a speech. Was this small, timid clerk going to be part of the power structure in the post-Revolutionary Republic? They would need every educated person they could lay their hands on, Josef thought.

'Do you know?' Ben began, but then altered his course. 'Yes, I suppose you do, if you've read the newspaper: the troops have entered Valhalla. They sealed it off last night. There was a ring of steel around Valhalla.' The angelic eyes twinkled. 'It's war, Mr S,' Ben said. 'They've declared war on us.' (Josef noticed that the clerk did not say: '*You've* declared war on us.') Then the young man echoed the Reverend Lode: 'You can't be uninvolved. You've got to take sides.'

'What are you telling me, Ben?' Pupil and teacher were swinging round each other like the opposing ends of some infernal machine. Ben did not answer his employer directly.

'The police barged into our houses. They sealed off streets and searched our houses, one by one. They ransacked cupboards: they even searched one woman's fridge. What did they expect to find in the fridge, Mr S? When the soldiers left, the little children ran out of the houses shaking their fists and shouting "Power!" '

'What were the police looking for, Ben?'

'There was a rumour that they were looking for guns. People were so scared, Mr S. They were burning pamphlets before the soldiers came. There were bonfires in the streets. It was very beautiful, especially in those parts where there is no electricity.' Ben was smiling, perhaps at the incongruity of coming to work in the calm centre of Eisstad when his home was on fire. 'It's an occupation force, Mr S. We are at war.'

'I saw that Lode was detained,' Josef was moved to put in.

'How do you know Lode?' Ben asked sharply.

'Just what I read in the newspapers.'

'Yes, Lode was taken, and many others.' He shrugged. 'It is the way now. There will be many detentions, many deaths, but that can't be helped. Many will fall in the struggle,' he said, repeating the Revolutionary jargon that Josef was hearing so often now. Then he added, nonchalantly, so casually that Josef was taken by surprise, 'Are you?'

'Am I what?' the lawyer asked, his eyes hooded.

'Are you prepared to enter the struggle?'

'It's not my struggle,' said Josef slowly. 'I'm one of the oppressors, one of the privileged minority. How can I enter your struggle?'

'It's a people's struggle,' Ben countered, 'a struggle for democracy. That makes it your struggle too. If you're not a democrat, why were you at the funeral? Are you a police spy?'

Josef sat back, stunned, as if he had been nailed to his chair. 'How on earth did you know I was there?' he managed to say.

'Our people keep a look out, Mr S,' said Ben, 'and because we know many things, we also know that you are not an informer. If you were, you would not have got out of Valhalla yesterday.'

The implications of this network of information (if indeed it existed, if Ben was telling the truth and not making up wild stories) were astonishing to Josef S. The thought that his life had depended on its reliability was terrifying. A picture of men running by, holding fist-sized rocks, while he stood immune in the middle, an island in a rapid, flashed into his mind. How naïve he had been! How absurd to consider that he could enter the political arena as a novice and make judgements. The people had only been peaceful because he presented no threat. 'What do you want me to do, Ben?' he asked now.

'I want you to defend William Ngo.'

'Who is William Ngo?' Young men, fleet as a river, swept up stones and flowed past him, a rock in their path, and slung their missiles with the force of floods on those impeding their course.

'He's the man accused of attempting to murder Buth.'

'Oh yes,' said Josef distractedly. 'Yes, I remember now.' He glanced at the typewriter for assistance. All he saw was a structure of metal and spaces, of positives and negatives: a machine with the capacity to spell out messages, but without an inherent message of its own. Like everything else, it was open to interpretation, an ambiguous oracle. He tried to conjure up his father's face from the keys, but, for the first time, no image came. Instead the face of Raymond Mkhize, secretary of the FDF, hovered over the machine. 'Why do you want me?' Josef asked. 'Why me?'

'Because no one else will take the case, Mr S. Everyone else is scared after Mrs Idini's death. Do you understand?'

'And you're asking me to appear in the centre of this political stage, a fair target for every right-wing madman?' Josef said. 'Why shouldn't I also be scared?'

'It was a hope, Mr S,' said Ben. 'William Ngo is not a member of the FDF. But we want him to have the best defence possible. We know that you will fight for his life. We don't want William Ngo to die in the struggle. After the Revolution, he will be a very important person in the New Republic.'

'What about the FDF's usual lawyers?' Josef persisted. 'I cannot believe that you have no one else.'

'Our usual lawyers are either in hiding or have been arrested, Mr S. Besides, those who live in the townships are much more vulnerable than you are. At least you're protected by your status.'

106

'I'm glad you think so,' Josef said wryly.

'And there's another thing, Mr S. William acted independently when he stabbed Buth. This was not an FDF initiative. We cannot be linked with him.'

'I'd have thought you'd want to take the credit.'

'On the contrary,' said Ben. 'If the Government could prove we were involved, they'd ban us immediately. It would be the excuse they've been looking for.'

'A non-violent stance,' Josef remarked sceptically, 'for a Revolutionary organisation. It doesn't follow.'

'We're a peaceful organisation, Mr S,' said Ben, smiling sweetly. 'The Government is responsible for the violence.'

'What would Ed Parry say?' Josef laughed raggedly. 'The firm of Parry and S at the forefront of the struggle . . .'

'The people are relying on you,' Ben said, as simply as a child.

'And what if I fail?'

'We are confident that you will do you best.'

'All right, Ben,' said Josef S. 'I'll take the case.' There was a stampede in his head as if all the stone-throwing youngsters in Valhalla had got in, leaping around with the force of lion-wildness. 'You'd better arrange an interview for me with Ngo. I presume he's in the Tower. Find out the date of trial, if there are any witnesses, people who can testify to his good character. Arrange the appointments — look in my diary.'

Ben was smiling broadly. 'Yes, Mr S.' The young man was now bolder than he had ever been; he might yet make a lawyer, Josef thought.

'By the way, Mr S, don't worry about your fee. We have plenty of money at our disposal.'

'Money was the last thing on my mind,' said Josef S.

Josef parked in the lot below the wall of the Leeukop. A path through the bushes led to the small white building inappropriately named the Hunting Lodge. Darkness was rushing down the mountain with wild bounds and leaps. Josef had no torch and he stumbled on loose stones. He held his hands out in front of him like a sleepwalker.

Throughout the day, his conversation with Ben had returned to him, had been taken out and examined from every angle. What sequence of events had he set in motion by agreeing to defend William Ngo? Could he have taken a different course? Was it still possible to turn back?

He had gone home on a bus blackened and pocked from petrol bombs and stones. Wire meshing protected the driver's window but most of the others were missing so that draughts swept through, leaving the occupants chilled; it was as well that winter was on its way out. A sprinkling of glass had been swept into one of the back corners, crunching underfoot as he walked to his seat. 'You can measure the course of a revolution by the state of the country's buses,' a wit sitting beside him had said.

He had taken the car keys from the basket next to the telephone. Neither Dorothy nor Robert was home, which was curious, but Josef had been relieved rather than concerned. On the spur of the moment, he had decided to visit the doctor who was fasting in the Hunting Lodge. He drove through the empty streets, half expecting to see Dorothy and Robert walking together. But by the time he reached the parking lot, he had forgotten them. He was excited at meeting someone else from Eisstad who was involved in the struggle, someone so much closer to it, someone at the heart of the matter.

He approached the door with trepidation. Was the man there? What would his reaction be to strangers? Would he be too weak to talk? The single window in the wall facing the path glowed and flickered with an orange light.

Albert Poynter sat, sunken into an enormous green armchair, presiding over the small room; the size of the chair made him look smaller than he was. His legs were covered by a blanket, giving the impression that he was ill, but he stood up when Josef entered and extended his hand in greeting. His eyes were almost lost in red puffy cheeks, the result of starvation. His hair was tousled, adding to the appearance of sickness. Josef recognised the man from photographs he had seen in the newspapers, many of which, together with articles detailing the progress of the fast, were pinned up on a notice board beside his chair. The draughts from the opened door disturbed the musty smell and set the candles flickering; light and shadows careered around the room, danced over Poynter's face, turned him upside down so that Josef almost lost his balance as he shook the bony hand.

'Hello,' the man said. 'I'm Albert.' He smiled widely but the light distorted his features; what might have been angelic in a consistent light became confused and shaded. 'Albert Poynter.'

'Josef S,' said the tall man in the grey overcoat.

'Sit down.' Poynter gestured to one of the chairs arranged round his armchair like courtiers round a throne. He returned to his own seat and tucked himself in underneath his blanket.

A quick glance about the room revealed that the Hunting Lodge possessed two windows (both closed), a wooden floor, a fireplace over which was a mantlepiece, a few candelabra which provided the only light and two wooden beams across the ceiling, possibly designed to give it a 'hunting' ambience. However, apart from a few photographs of men with guns, the room was free of trappings glorifying the hunt. Instead, FDF pamphlets, stickers and T-shirts were displayed on a small trestle table, and posters were fixed on the walls. Two people, a man and a woman, sat near the door, with their backs to Poynter, huddled in conversation.

The draughts had settled, and with them, the wild shadows. When Josef S leaned back, he felt his eyes closing from the room's stuffiness and the fatigue of the day and he had to force himself to stay awake. 'I read about you,' he said, explaining his presence. 'I admire your commitment. I wanted to meet you.'

'Thank you for coming,' said Poynter. 'I've had almost a thousand visitors since I've been here. People have been very kind.' Any inclination one might have had to think that the man was sick, because of his obvious weakness, he seemed to want to dispel. He spoke enthusiastically, brightly. 'Do you work in Eisstad?' he asked.

'Yes,' Josef S replied. 'I'm a lawyer.'

'I'm glad we're getting across to the professions as well. The FDF is often dismissed as a violent revolutionary organisation with no popular support. That's the picture Buth's Government wants to paint of us, because it makes it easier to clamp down. They're trying to ban us,' he smiled again, 'but we're very strong, and we're growing stronger all the time.'

'I know,' said Josef S. 'I was at the funeral yesterday.'

'Poor Freddy,' said Poynter. 'He brought his wife into the clinic a few weeks before I began my fast. She had an infection . . . Was it a good funeral?' His blue eyes twinkled mischievously at the sacrilegiousness of the question. 'I read that thirty thousand attended.'

'And then the army closed off Valhalla,' the lawyer added. But his words rang fraudulently in his ears; he had just come into the situation and was already sounding off like an expert.

'Yes, that is frightening, isn't it?' Where did this half-starved man find the strength to continue to promote the organisation he represented? Only total commitment to his cause could have given Poynter the will to go on. 'Do you know what that means?' he was saying and Josef shook his head. 'It means that if I'm called up – I'm still liable for army camps for another five years — they can post me to Valhalla and I may have to shoot the people I've been treating at my clinic.' The twinkle had gone from his eyes; they now burned into Josef's. 'We treat the bullet wounds because people can't go to the hospitals. Every day I see the consequences of police brutality. How can I put on a uniform and serve in the townships?'

'Why can't they go to hospital?' the lawyer asked; he had read an explanation, but now he had an opportunity to question an eyewitness.

'They're arrested,' Poynter said.

'Arrested?'

The doctor shifted in his seat and rearranged his blanket. The couple at the door continued their whispering. From time to time the candles sizzled and flared; the windows presented pictures of blackness. Josef felt that he was dreaming, catapulting through night in this little room.

'The police claim that anyone who is shot in the townships was involved in unrest,' Poynter said. 'Even if he was just an innocent caught in the cross-fire.' He gazed at the black square of a window on which the candle-light flamed. 'Anyone with a bullet wound is charged with public violence. The hospitals are forced to hand them over. That's why the wounded prefer to come to the clinic.'

Josef rubbed his eyes. 'Don't you have to hand them over too?'

Poynter smiled. 'We don't always do what we're supposed to.' He reached for his jug of water and a glass. 'My only sustenance,' he explained, laughing. 'I have water cocktails: tap water, and Perrier water, and somebody has even brought me water from the top of the mountain. If I mix them together, it makes the taste less boring.'

'Aren't you drinking anything else? Fruit juice?'

'Nothing but water,' Poynter grimaced. 'Yesterday, a woman asked me if I was going to fast until peace was secured.' His grin grew so broad that his eyes almost disappeared completely. 'I said I was making a point, not planning suicide.' He leaned back and spoke, but not to Josef. 'I've still got work to do at the clinic,' he said as though he were confiding in someone who was absent, or in himself. 'They've released me for three weeks, but they need me, especially now that the troops are in Valhalla. The violence is only going to increase.'

'Then you'll have failed,' Josef murmured. 'If you're fasting for peace.'

'No, not at all. On the contrary, I think we've been very successful. You see, this fast is a group effort of the FDF to focus attention on what's happening on the Flats. I'm only the front man in the campaign. We decided to hold a fast because virtually every other type of protest is banned.' He clenched the blanket so tightly that his knuckles turned white. 'We've got to look for new ways to protest all the time. The Government is forcing us to become very inventive.' He sighed and sat quietly for a moment.

'I hope I'm not tiring you,' Josef said, 'asking all these questions.'

Poynter looked at the lawyer then as if he had only just noticed him. 'I'm used to answering questions,' he said. 'That's what I'm here for: the FDF public relations department.' The smile returned (it was never far away), mischievously. 'I never know which of my visitors will take back interesting titbits to de Wet. Even you, Josef S, may have a tape recorder up your sleeve.' Josef shook his head involuntarily. 'It doesn't matter. Perhaps it will teach them something.' Poynter stared into the darkness. 'I doubt it though. If they haven't learned by now . . .'

'I'm surprised they haven't harassed you,' said Josef, reflecting on an image of a man in a white car, waiting and watching; for him that image was one of the symbols of the times.

'In the week before the fast, I laid low. Now that we've attracted a lot of media coverage, I think it'll be all right. They wouldn't dare arrest me now. Afterwards, perhaps . . . maybe they'll want their pound of flesh, maybe they won't bother. Who knows? In the first week of my fast, I didn't leave the Lodge at all, except when John there,' he pointed to the man in the corner, 'whisked me off to his house to shower. But now I go for regular walks outside. It's very beautiful here. I've picked a good place to come and starve myself.' He chuckled. 'And one of the blessings of this Hunting Lodge is that I don't have a telephone to tap.'

Suddenly Josef S wanted to ask Poynter if he had seen the last lion during his days on the mountain, or heard it roar at nights, roar in exultation at the forces that were on the move on the plain below. Instead he commented: 'I stay in Leeuwenvoet. If you want to bath or rest, you're welcome . . .'

'Thank you,' Poynter smiled again, 'but John's taking care of me while I fast. It's very kind of you.' He pulled the blanket closely round him. Josef saw that, despite his thick jersey, Poynter was shivering. 'It gets cold sometimes,' he explained.

'Do you have access to a doctor?' Josef asked, concerned. 'Without a telephone . . . if you become ill . . .'

'John's a doctor. He watches every move I make.' Poynter's face glowed impishly in the candle-light. 'In fact I've become his guinea-pig. He's doing research into "fasting medicine".' The shivering spell was over; Poynter clasped his bony fingers together near to his face as if he were praying. 'John says I've lost a bit of weight.' A dry laugh escaped from thin lips. 'But I can't get rid of this roll of fat round my waist . . . Maybe I should fast for another few weeks.' Josef did not answer; the room had assumed the intimacy of a chapel.

A noise outside snapped the tranquility. The lawyer started, not from guilt, for he was doing nothing wrong, but from a touch of fear of the wild forces which might have been prowling on the mountain at night. Poynter glanced absently at his watch, out of habit, or as if the time would reveal the identity of the visitors. 'It's stopped,' he said, almost apologetically. 'It's automatic and I'm not moving enough . . . But time isn't important.' he added when he saw that Josef was trying to read his own watch in the shifting light. 'I've still got a few days here.'

The woman who entered, setting the candles dancing madly again, wore a scarf and carried a shopping basket packed with groceries. She put the basket down and approached the fasting man like a shambling bear, her enormous backside wiggling with pleasure.

'Amy!' Poynter exclaimed, standing to embrace her. 'How are you?'

'You look wonderful,' she enthused, not bothering to report on the state of her own health. To Josef, they were two exiles from a war, meeting in a peaceful country to reminisce.

'I've been getting a lot of rest,' he said. 'Actually, I haven't. It's been very busy here. I've had so many visitors, and the press, and the doctors.' He nodded towards John, and announced to everyone in the room: 'John has been fasting with me for the past two days.'

Josef S observed the rakelike figure at the door with new appreciation. Here were people so committed to their cause that they were making bitter personal sacrifices while the rest of Eisstad wallowed in petty domestic squabbles and grubby affairs of the heart.

Amy chose a seat next to the lawyer. She smiled and introduced herself. Josef S shook her hand.

'Isn't he wonderful?' Amy asked, referring to Poynter as he were not present. 'He's so clear, his eyes and his speech. Can you believe that he's fasting?'

'It's difficult,' said Josef, embarrassed.

112

Now John and his companion came over and sat down too. Albert Poynter was the centre of the circle, the focus of attention: he was the event. Invariably, all the eyes fixed on him, even when he was silent. Without him, the group would have disintegrated into a collection of individuals.

The young woman's name was Margaret Spears. Josef recognised her: it was she who had helped to place the dummies in the square. For no clear reason (certainly she did not seem to remember him), Josef's heart thudded in greeting. He seemed to have been yearning for her unconsciously, and his desire was like a bomb, primed to explode when next he saw her. He feared that everyone in the room could hear the blood rushing to his head.

'I'm fasting today,' Amy was saying, 'and it's difficult enough just fasting for one day; I don't know how he does it.' But Josef's attention was on Margaret: on her brown eyes, which sparkled and flared as the candle-light caught them; and on her features, which were strong and finely fashioned. The sculptor who had carved Margaret's face should have applied himself to Gomez to create a perfectly featured founder of Eisstad.

When Margaret caught him looking at her, she smiled quickly and then turned away, as though a secret existed between the two of them. As she moved her head, her dark hair stroked the shoulders of her cotton dress. The soft white material suggested a vulnerability which was at odds with the determination in her face. Sometimes, the candle-light threw shadows over her eyes, highlighting a mystery created by her brooding, bruised expression.

Amy did not see that Josef was hardly listening to her. She was saying: 'You know, it's disgusting what those policemen do. They were in their Leeus yesterday, handing out forms to the children, and telling them to complete them.'

'What forms?' Josef S heard himself ask, though the hammering in his chest seemed to drown his words.

'Forms to fill in their names, and schools, and hobbies, and all that,' Amy protested. Her lower lip quivered. 'I told the children to tear them up.' The exasperation in her voice implied that she felt she was conducting a lone battle against the police for the minds of the children. 'Sometimes, you know, they stop and give the children marshmallows and sweets, and the children climb up onto their Leeus as if they're all one big happy family.'

Why had she chosen to tell him? Perhaps she saw in the solemn figure someone closer to the authorities, someone who needed to be taught the lessons that Valhalla could offer. 'One day, last week,' she said, 'some children took over a bus — well the driver actually offered it to them — and they parked it across the road as a road block. I had been driving behind it. The police came and attacked us all with rubber bullets and teargas. I had to jump out of the car because I was choking. The teargas made my head feel twice as thick and I ran towards a house. A rubber bullet broke the window as I got to the door. I knocked, but they wouldn't open up. But the people at the next house let me in and I fell on the floor. It took me half an hour to recover. For a few days afterwards, I was so depressed from the teargas that I could hardly work.'

'What work do you do?' Josef asked, reluctantly. He did not particularly want to hear Amy's story; he wanted to talk to Margaret.

'I teach nutrition to people who can't afford meat or fish. I teach them how to have a balanced diet and how to cook vegetables tastily. I'm just doing my job, Josef, and I must put up with this nonsense! Can you believe that a woman like me must run away from bullets?'

'I read about it, Amy,' said Poynter, 'in the *Evening Times*.' and Josef S was relieved of the responsibility of answering. He could not imagine Amy running, even with bullets flying past her head, and he could not think of a suitable response to her account.

'The *Times* is very good,' Amy said. 'They've been giving you full coverage, haven't they?'

'Did you read today?' Poynter asked. 'De Wet is slandering both this campaign and the FDF. He said that a fast for peace is subversive and calculated to make people violent.'

'They twist everything,' Margaret said, giving Josef S an excuse to look at her again.

'Well, we haven't too long to go now,' said Poynter. He turned to Josef. 'Are you coming to the Peace Rally?' When the lawyer shrugged in ignorance, Poynter explained: 'On the last night of the fast, we're having a mass meeting in the City Hall. We have permission from the Council. We'd wanted Mkhize and Lode to speak, but they've both been detained. We'll have to get someone else.'

'Who do you have in mind?'

'We're not sure yet.'

'Yes, of course I'll come,' said Josef. 'I've seen no publicity . . .'

'The press will carry the story, and posters are going up. We're expecting busloads to come in from the Flats.' Poynter grinned. 'It'll be fun.'

Again the door opened. This time a cold breeze entered with the visitors: a photographer (his camera hung around his neck), and a tall cleric, awkward as a grasshopper, wearing a grey suit and white collar, carrying a book under his arm. Poynter stood up again and shook their hands. 'Hello Mike, Douglas,' he said, motioning to the two remaining empty chairs. 'I'm getting so many visitors that the time is going very quickly.' The men sat down. For a while the gangly cleric stared at Poynter who beamed like a patriarch at his family, in all the excitement seeming to forget the cold. Then Douglas turned his attention to his book, his lips moving as he read; sometimes his voice came through in a whisper. 'How's the thesis going?' asked Poynter, addressing the bent head.

'No, I'm reading through it, Albert,' the awkward man answered, without looking up.

'How are things at home?' Poynter asked. 'Have they quietened down?'

'The people are very unhappy,' Douglas replied. 'I spoke to them yesterday. They organised a march to protest against rent increases but the police shot teargas at them. A baby girl, Nomsa Moloi, whom I christened a few months ago, she suffocated. Her parents want to have a funeral for her, but the police have imposed the usual restrictions. You know, Albert, there is no way to protest any more: any little gathering draws the police. I have prayed for guidance. I have prayed for the right words to use when I go back. What must I tell them? That they must love their enemy? That God will come down to help the humble? What am I supposed to tell my people to give them hope, and to lead them away from the violence that so many of them want to take up? They tell me that they must answer violence with violence. I have been reading the scriptures, Albert, looking for passages to guide me.'

'I'm sorry about the baby,' Poynter said. 'We're living in difficult times. We have to make sacrifices.'

Amy knelt before him and rested her hand on his shoulder. 'Bless you, Lord, for Albert's love,' she prayed, 'and for the community he's serving. Give him strength.' She stood and kissed his forehead.

'Amen,' the cleric responded. Poynter appeared to blush, but the flush of red in his face could have been a trick of the light.

Josef felt as if he were prying. Amy's gesture made him uncomfortable; it was too intimate. And, of course, Dorothy was waiting at home for him, wondering where he was. 'I must go,' he said, pushing his chair back.

'Thank you for coming, Josef,' said Albert. 'Please sign the visitors' book on your way out — it helps us assess the extent of our support in Eisstad — and I hope you'll come to the Peace Rally. And maybe some of these folk want a lift with you?' He looked around at the people sitting.

'Can you take me to the station?' Amy asked.

'I stay in the city,' Margaret added. 'Near the station.'

Josef S nodded, fearful of the circumstances that were pushing him and Margaret together. He stopped at the door to sign Poynter's book. He briefly considered writing a false name and address. But, he reflected, it was too late for that. He was already involved. As he wrote, he glanced back into the room. Douglas was reading again, his head swallowed in the pages of the thesis, desperately searching for guidance. Mike was taking a photograph of Albert sitting in his arm-chair; it was just as well he did not know that Josef S had agreed to defend William Ngo. The Revolution created instant heroes, and Josef preferred to stay in the background for as long as he could.

As Margaret opened the door, a pigeon flew in. It flapped blindly round the room, battering its noisy wings against the wall above Poynter's head. For a moment, no one moved. Then the bird beat its frantic way out. 'There you are,' said Albert, as though this was to be expected. 'A symbol of peace.' Josef pulled the door to and the orange room disappeared like a ship sinking into a black ocean.

Margaret had lit a candle. By its flicker they left the Hunting Lodge and made their way to the parking lot. The stars were icy. The black absence existing in a certain portion of the sky was the rock forming the head of the Lion.

Margaret's flat was simply yet tastefully decorated in blue and white. Josef made a quick tour of inspection, feeling more than faintly guilty when he looked into the bedroom and saw her bed. When last had he been into a strange woman's bedroom? It was a big bed, covered with a blue patchwork quilt. He longed to lie down on it, no matter what the consequences. It was foreign territory, as alien as the soil of the countries that Robert had trodden on; but where Robert had stepped with impunity, his older brother was only too careful not to put a foot wrong.

The lawyer sat on a white settee in the living room. He took off his overcoat, and for the first time in longer than he could remem-ber, felt at peace, blissfully at peace. He melted into the settee as though that was where he belonged, as though all along he had been

changing the subject; Josef allowed himself to be
ntent of the conversation was less important than
 down the road,' she continued. 'He's sixty-six and
dent man I've ever met. He walks to visit me, and
p with my friends drinking and talking politics. He
e sits in the corner, in that rocking chair, and
 said that if we get raided, he'll run like hell. He's
a foot in their jails, he said. I love him to bits . . .'
 any other family?' he asked when she stopped
w had to be maintained.
 if he had woken her and there was a trace of pain
 wiped it away with her hand. 'My mother's dead
ther, living abroad,' she said. 'He left rather than go
 wants me to join him, but I'm committed to being
 for change.'
ther too,' Josef reflected. 'Unlike yours, though,
 been through the army. He's told me some hair-
is hand shook a little as he lifted his cup, and tea
aucer. Finding the subject too distressing to pursue,
oes your father cope without his wife?'
ld you he's independent. My mother died five years
ontinued his interests. He reads a lot. He was a
 retired now.' She smiled. 'Maybe you could intro-
ur father. The two old gentlemen might walk to-
eachfront, look at the sea, and wonder where this
, and discuss the fact that they will not be a part of
d Josef S detect in her a longing for an old age in
e would be almost over? Or was that longing his?
ead,' he said flatly. 'After my mother died, he locked
 his work and his liquor for ten years. Robert and I

 why I told you,' he said. His hand was still trem-
ually talk about it.' He lapsed into silence and drank
 looked at him. He was aware of her scrutiny. The
and he could not think how to start it up again; he
e whether he wanted to.
t your brother,' she asked at last. She was fiddling
r finger; was she bored with him?
shook his head. 'Robert resents me. I don't know
thinks I was too hard on him, that I didn't give him

---

shamming, pretending that home was with his wife and her books,
whereas in reality it was here, in the living room of a woman he did
not even know, but who thrilled him in a way that Dorothy no
longer could.

'Would . . . would you like some tea?' she asked, slightly nervously
he thought, as if she suddenly realised that she had a strange man in
her flat. 'Or coffee?'

'Tea would be fine,' he said. 'Can I help you?'

'No,' she answered. 'Thank you.' She went into the kitchen and
he had a chance to survey the room. In a corner was an antique
chair made of a dark wood and partially covered with a reddish-
brown fabric. A porcelain cat stood haughtily on the mantelpiece
next to an empty cut-glass vase and a silver tray which leaned against
the wall. The bookcase contained titles Josef did not recognise, but
which had a political ring: *The Republic: The Lost Hundred Years*,
Military Adventurism: Protection of the National Interest, *Rural
Development*, and so on. Beside it was a corner of potted plants —
ferns and geraniums — which had a gentleness that offset the severity
of the books. On the bureau were writing paper, pens, and pictures
of cats. A guitar leaned against the wall. How carefully was Josef
treading? Or had he already slipped?

He stood up when she returned with the tea tray, formally, aware
that in her circle of acquaintances informality might well be the
standard of behaviour. He discovered that the act of receiving a cup
of tea from a strange woman held a curious fascination: whereas he
would unthinkingly accept meal after meal from Dorothy, and indeed expect to be served, one cup of tea from Margaret was a thrilling
event, bringing with it all sorts of possibilities. He knew Dorothy so
well that nothing she could do would surprise him. To him she was
a flat character in a novel; he always knew what she would do or
say next. But Margaret was unknown. He would observe the way
she held her cup, the way she sat, whether her body seemed to invite
or reject him, the way *she* observed *him*, the colour of her eyes, her
smell: animal things, a challenge; as a lion might stalk an antelope
on the mountain; as a fisherman might hang out the bait, so he felt
the thrill of the hunt. It was possible that she was enjoying a similar
chase.

'Sugar and milk?' she asked. Her hands were strong and capable,
like his wife's. He was attracted to women with strong hands.

'Milk, no sugar,' he said, reflecting that Dorothy would not have
had to ask. He sat back, holding the cup to his chest almost defens-

ively. He was suddenly at a loss for words. He wanted to say: 'I'm sorry, I don't know how to flirt. I've forgotten how to court a woman. I feel ashamed of myself being here when I have a wife at home and a brother for whom I should be setting an example. I am in love with you. As a lawyer, I am supposed to be always in control, and yet now my pulse hammers uncontrollably, my mouth is dry . . .' But he said nothing, and simply stared at her, overcome by the suddenness of his feelings, by the strange descent of this madness that left him weak.

'I admire Albert, don't you?' she asked, a line of conversation so simple, so obvious, that he was astonished at the range of possibilities it opened, and that he had been unable to conceive of it for himself. Perhaps she was more skilled at this game than he. Perhaps she was a better angler, perhaps (and this possibility was the most frightening of them all) she was not interested in him as he was in her. What grounds did he have for expecting her to be? She had smiled at him once or twice and accepted an offer of a lift home. She had approached him twice in Gomez Square, and had appeared to recognise him the second time: that was hardly a basis for anticipating love. A cat, tawny as a lion, sauntered into the room and jumped onto Josef's lap as if it belonged there.

'Albert is a couragous man,' Josef answered, and, referring to the cat, Margaret said at the same time: 'He likes you.' The two statements collided, and an embarrassed silence might have followed, except that the woman salvaged the situation. At that moment, such a rescue was completely beyond the lawyer. She laughed in a self-effacing way and reassured him: 'Walter's very independent,' she said. 'He's a fighter; he's wary of strangers.' Again, the dexterity of her response took him, leaden-mouthed, by surprise.

'My wife has a dog,' he said, clumsily, and knew, as the words tumbled out, that he should not have mentioned Dorothy.

'What kind?' she asked without batting an eyelid.

'A bull terrier,' he said. 'It's very ugly but my wife loves it.' Perhaps he needed to talk about Dorothy, to have Margaret accept the fact of her, to exorcise her image from his mind. The cat purred; he stroked it and it settled into his lap, languidly sticking out its pink tongue.

'I prefer cats,' she said. 'Since I spend so much time away from the flat, I must have an independent animal. Dogs need too much attention.'

Josef was moved to defend the species even though he felt little

allegiance to it. 'But dogs
Dorothy's dog loves lemon

'Lemons?'

He nodded. His courage
reasserting itself. 'If Lex se
top of the fridge, he'll sit a
down to him. He won't mo
he said: 'I saw you on the s

'Yes, I know,' she replied

'Is that why you attacked

She evaded the question
tered.

'I'm a lawyer; I rely on m

'You might be an informe

'So why do you speak so

'Because I don't believe t
to sneak around like a crim
more aware. I have to be op

'It seems so unfair, doesn
steadied as he spoke; he wa
and you speak out in the op

'Well, we have our backg
he was reminded of the in
spoken. 'Just as some of the
works out equal in the end. I

Strange, he thought, that
thy: 'up front'. 'I'm not an
that why he could not find h
only contribute to the strug
Had he been so fired by the st
as a partner someone who wou
Or was this merely an excuse,

'What exactly do you do
asking. Besides putting dumm

The corners of her mouth
work in an advice office, I m
Students for Justice, I liaise
get arrested for my work.' She
leave much time for Walter.'

'I wouldn't imagine so. I cert

'I named him after my fath

was deliberately
diverted. The c
its flow. 'He liv
the most indep
then has to put
doesn't mind.
watches. Once
not going to pu

'Do you hav
speaking. The f

She blinked
in her eyes. Sh
and I have a br
into the army.
here, to workin

'I have a b
Robert has ju
raising stories.'
spilled into the
he asked: 'How

'Very well. I
ago, and he's
teacher, but h
duce him to
gether on the
country is go
its progress.'
which her stru

'My father'
himself up wi
hardly saw hi

'I'm sorry.'

'I don't kn
bling. 'I don't
his tea while
flow had drie
was not very

'Tell me a
with a ring o

'Robert?'
why. Maybe

enough love. But in those days, things were tough. My father died leaving nothing. I had to support Robert at the same time that I was building up a practice . . . I didn't have enough time for him. I couldn't be his father.' The lawyer's eyes were like caged animals trying to escape. Margaret met his wild stare; her dark eyes soothed as if she had laid her fingers comfortingly on his head. 'My father was a clerk,' Josef said. 'He worked hard for someone else but he made no money. Whatever I have, I made for myself. I put myself through university while I was doing my articles; I went to night classes. When my father died, we looked after Robert, Dorothy and I. We don't deserve his resentment.'

'Perhaps he's not angry with you,' Margaret suggested. 'I've seen the trauma of adaptation before. At the Advice Office sometimes we see soldiers who've finished their service. They're often very confused. The army gives them a power which they could never have dreamed of, the power of life and death. When they're discharged, they have nothing. They're just boys, let loose onto the streets. It's a big adjustment. Probably his anger has nothing at all to do with you.'

'Why do they come to your office?'

'The ones we see are thinking of joining the FDF.'

'Robert wouldn't do that. He's still enchanted with the army. I think he found acceptance in the army; it was the first time in his life he felt wanted. He got very little love from anyone as a child. Although Dorothy is being very kind to him now. And I'm trying . . . But he does nothing at all, just sits at home and broods.'

'He'll sort it out in time,' Margaret reassured him. 'They do, one way or another. It's very unsettling going from all that regimentation to a completely non-structured life, from the importance of the uniform to no status at all. A few days ago, I saw an army Leeu drive past. There were about six young soldiers sitting up there, like royalty, waving at the people in the streets. How will they feel when they have to get off their high horses and come back to earth? That's what your brother is going through . . .'

'He said that they felt like vikings, wading in rivers of blood, when they walked through the villages of the people they had killed up there.' He glanced at his watch, and with a jolt realised that it was nearly ten o'clock. What would Dorothy be thinking? He could phone her, but he did not want to confront her over the phone, especially as he had resolved nothing with Margaret. He was hovering between excitement and extreme tiredness. He wanted to go home, and yet he could not tear himself away. The cat stretched its legs and the tiny crescents of claws extended just above his knee. Without touching him, the cat sheathed its claws, licked its shoulder and curled into a ball. Josef laid his hand on its back, acutely aware of how sensuous the stroking must appear to her. He felt a scab on the animal's rump. 'I fear that I'm boring you with my stories,' he said, and, although she was shaking her head, he asked her to tell him more about herself. His own background rang too sombrely in his ears and he did not want her pity.

'What about?' she asked.

He picked a topic at random. 'Your mother,' he suggested, forgetting that the woman was dead.

'My mother,' she said lightly, as if this were the beginning of a new game. 'Well, my mother used to think of herself as a patron of the arts. She surrounded herself with "interesting people", writers and artists. Sometimes things got pretty wild at home . . . the parties could go on all night. I suppose that I learned to be very adaptable. If I wasn't, I'd be in a corner blowing bubbles by now: my life requires a certain amount of flexibility . . .' She laughed, and her lips puckered in slight self-consciousness, and he felt himself melting inside. Every time she looked straight at him, every time she displayed emotion, the effect on him was devastating. 'Although, of course, it may not have been the environment; I probably picked up enough of my mother's genes to make me like her. I carry too much of my mother in me to worry about insecurity.

'And my father was so wonderful about it all. He would come into the drawing room and look around, and sometimes join in, sometimes go off to prepare his lessons. Nothing seemed to disturb him. He let her have her fun. He was the perfect balance for her . . .' Margaret frowned, then smiled as if at a private joke. 'But he couldn't balance her in the end. She fell out of a second floor window at a party — she was drunk — and broke her neck on the driveway. She'd had a good life: she always wanted to fly.'

'I'm sorry I brought up this subject,' Josef was saying, 'I didn't mean to make you sad . . .' Everything he touched turned to ashes.

'And now my father comes by and has a drink with us while we discuss the Revolution,' she continued, as if she had not heard him. He says the Revolution is being fueled by a certain semi-sweet white wine, and that if the Government finds out, they'll ban it.'

He had not made her sad. Like Albert Poynter, she persisted in her optimism, while he, the lawyer, the representative of stability, was sinking. He wanted to ask her if he was just unorthodox enough to appeal to someone who took a delight in the unusual. Perhaps he was hoping that, like her mother, she had an appreciation of artists. Why else did he offer: 'My wife is a writer'? Only because he believed that it would increase her interest in him, however vicariously. He could think of no other reason. Margaret raised her eyebrows dutifully, encouraging him to say: 'Dorothy would like to have come from an interesting background. She would like to tell stories of outrageous parties but her father is a lawyer and her mother a housewife, and to make up for the excitement she missed, she's created a fantasy life for herself.' Dorothy had done nothing to earn his bitterness, but it came flooding out, and he despised himself for it. 'My wife writes books. I read one or two when she began, but they didn't appeal to me, and rather than argue, I decided to leave her to it. Even though she's published, she still needs me to support her, which she hates. I don't mind supporting her: after all I pledged to do so. And it doesn't matter that I'm indifferent to her writing. Perhaps I've just lost interest . . . Look,' he tried to regain control of his speech before it unravelled completely, 'here I am telling you my most secret thoughts again.'

'What's your wife's name?'

'Dorothy Knox.'

'You're married to Dorothy Knox?'

Josef nodded.

Margaret clasped her hands together in front of her face. 'But Dorothy Knox is a wonderful writer!' she exclaimed. 'Do you really not like her books?'

The room began to turn upside down. He wondered if the cat would dig its claws into his leg, trying to hold on as gravity endeavoured to hurtle it down to the ceiling. He would come loose from his chair and together they would plummet into the abyss . . . '*The Raiders, Under the Castle*,' Margaret was saying. He had exposed his philistinism while appealing to the patron of the arts in her.

'Her new book has been accepted by her publishers,' he offered, '*Stories of Exile* . . .' But it was too late to redeem himself. Margaret's disappointment in him burned in his cheeks. His voice beat in the hollow of his skull, a drum roll on bone.

'I'd be proud of her if I were you.' Proud of her? Yes, he had once been. 'It's a pity that you've become so cut off from each other.' Was she taking Dorothy's side? Did she see him as a monster who had no tolerance for his wife's art?

'We don't talk about her writing,' he tried to explain. 'She's very sensitive to my criticism. I don't want to spark off an argument. So I leave her alone with her stories and she leaves me to my law. It's better that way.'

Did Margaret realise that she was rubbing a raw patch? Was the burning visible like clowns' spots on his cheeks? For, suddenly, she dropped the subject. 'Why don't you come and visit the Advice Office one day?' she said. 'I work in the afternoons after lectures. You may find it interesting.' Perhaps she was so preoccupied with her own concerns that she could not dwell on his problems. She put her head in her hands for a moment, and the action made her seem so vulnerable that he wanted to go over to her and cradle her. But if he tried to stand, surely he would fall: the room was still spinning. He wondered if his brother, the viking, would have rushed in where he feared to tread. She folded her arms across her breasts as if she were warding off the ghosts which came to her for advice after hours, after the office had closed, at home, when she had nothing more to give. But then she smiled and he had lost the opportunity if he had ever had it. He felt heavy and clumsy, somebody's husband in a strange woman's flat at an inappropriate hour.

'I would like to visit,' he said. 'Where is your office?'

'On the Waterfront,' she replied, and named the building. It was in the same street as the fish factory, overlooking the harbour, one of the seemingly deserted buildings in the warehouse district. 'The rental isn't too high,' she explained. 'We had to take a moral decision on whether to base ourselves in an area from which the people had been evicted. But, as we're helping, we decided in fact that it was a particularly suitable place to work.'

'I was there recently,' he said. 'I went to see the fish factory. I met some boys who live in the building. And some beggars.'

'The dispossessed.' She shuddered; perhaps the ghosts had grown more insistent.

'I'll visit you,' he promised.

They had come no closer to physical intimacy. Margaret had given no hint that she wanted to be closer to him. And he lacked the courage to make any advances. At least she seemed to have forgiven him for not appreciating his wife's work. Or perhaps it was not important to her.

'I had better go,' he said, prompting her to invite him to stay. But she did not. He tried to move the cat from his lap but it protested

124

loudly. It at least had adopted him, even if she had not. He would have to explain himself to Dorothy. How much would he have to say? That he had decided to defend William Ngo? That he had been to see Albert Poynter? That he had fallen in love with Margaret Spears?

She reached over and took the cat from his lap. 'Come on Walter,' she said. He smelled her perfume and felt her fingers brush against his legs. She clutched the cat to her breasts, and he breathed out, very slowly.

'Thank you for the lift,' she said, and he felt the emptiness of her rejection in his stomach. 'I've enjoyed talking to you.'

'And I to you,' he said, taking his leave formally and without touching her, even though he was burning to. 'Goodnight.'

As he left, he saw her smiling again, her thick dark hair framing her face and falling to her shoulders. The people involved in the struggle smile a lot, he thought, as if they have found a salvation which I am seeking but can never have.

The stairwell was narrow and dark: he stepped out into empty space. Limply as a puppet, hands dangling loose and trailing strings, he plummetted into the darkness, his great grey overcoat ballooning above his back as it filled with air, but unable to retard his fall.

4

'Where on earth have you been?' Dorothy demanded. 'What's going on?' As in the cartoons, she might have been waiting at the door with a rolling pin while he slunk in, the epitome of the dissolute husband. In fact she sat white-faced and tight-lipped on the settee. The dog waddled up to him, then stopped and sniffed, squinting suspiciously through its pink-rimmed eyes.

'I went to see Albert Poynter,' he said truculently, knowing that this information would be insufficient, making her drag the answers from him. Suddenly he remembered that he had promised to take her out to celebrate the acceptance of her book, but it was too late for that now: another entry in the catalogue of blanks that their marriage had become.

'Who's Albert Poynter?'

'The man fasting for peace. I've told you about him.'

'So late?'

'We were talking. There was a woman from Valhalla, a nutritionist. She was telling me some horror stories . . .'

'Well I've been hearing some horror stories, Josef.'

Did she know about Margaret? Had someone seen him entering or leaving her flat? Robert? Casually, he began to walk around the room, pretending to examine the photograph of his parents on the wall. 'What?' he challenged when she remained silent, perhaps disturbed by his movements. 'What horror stories?'

'The press have been phoning all night, Josef,' she said, as if that were enough. He was bewildered.

'The press? What do they want?' He turned suddenly on her, and saw a shadow in the kitchen. 'Robert, is that you?' The hackles rose on Lex's back and a high whine escaped from his mouth.

'Robert's gone out,' she said.

'Someone was in the kitchen,' he answered, 'unless I'm going mad.'

'How could anyone get in?' she asked. 'The back door's locked.'

Two sharp knocks rapped like gunshots from the kitchen. Josef strode across the living room: the kitchen was empty, but the back door was open. 'Dorothy,' he said softly, and his voice was shaking. She stood up, and walked stiffly to join him. The dog was moaning

126

like a person in pain.

'Oh my God,' Dorothy exclaimed, putting her hand on her husband's shoulder to steady herself. Lex ran, barking, to the open door, and made small leaps at the puppet-figure dangling over the threshold.

'And so it begins,' the lawyer said. Dorothy turned away. She was sobbing. 'I'm sorry,' Josef murmured. 'I'm sorry I called you. I'm sorry for everything.'

A black and white cat, a stray perhaps, fur unkempt, hung by a rope attached to the top of the door-frame; the noose around its neck. A nail, driven into the woodwork, held up the rope that had strangled it. A note, printed in a red wax crayon, saying YOU'RE NEXT, was tacked to its body.

'They've violated my house,' Josef whispered, but his words were lost in the angry noise that Lex was making. 'They've frightened my wife. What sort of people are they?' He stepped gingerly towards the grim messenger and nearly tripped over the dog.

'Go!' Josef yelled, but Lex was too excited for that. He was bouncing, stiff-legged, into the air, warning the carcase not to release its evil into the house. Kicking at the dog, Josef tried to prise the nail free with his fingers, but it was too deeply embedded. The cat's face was on a level with his: its small mouth was open, its tiny cone-teeth grinned, its bluish swollen tongue stuck out at him mockingly. 'Get away Lex! Dorothy!' But his wife stood, paralysed, watching her husband and the dead cat circling in a macabre dance. The cat knocked against Josef's chest; its rigid legs caught his overcoat, holding him with outstretched claws. He pushed the animal away but it swung back, determined to embrace him. Its marble eyes stared emptily, stiff in its head; he could not look. He lashed at the dog with his foot, but it came back as well, too determined and powerful to be brushed aside. 'Dorothy! A knife!'

She jerked into motion, stung by the harshness in his voice. She walked across the kitchen as if the floor were rolling on a heavy swell, and took a bread knife from the cutlery drawer. Keeping her eyes averted, she handed it to Josef: her face was colourless, her hair a wildfire on an ashen landscape.

Carefully, using his height to avoid contact with the stiff body, Josef sawed though the rope. He held the severed end at arm's length, a fisherman displaying his catch. The dog postured and snarled from deep inside its throat, baring its teeth. 'What do you do with a dead cat?' Josef asked, and when his wife did not reply, he ordered: 'Dorothy! Bring me a plastic bag.' She rummaged in a cupboard under the sink and produced a black plastic garbage bag. 'Please hold it open for me,' he said testily. 'I can't get it into the bag with one hand.' And then suddenly he began to laugh. In response, the dog howled. The cat jigged and twisted at the end of the rope as Josef's body shook, as if they had decided to continue their dance but at a faster tempo.

'What are you laughing at?' she snapped. 'Be quiet, Lex!'

Weak from laughing, his trembling hand manipulating the dancing cat, he answered: 'I'm very tired.'

'Here,' insisted the woman. Tears rolled down her white cheeks as she stood, a party to the undignified ritual, the garbage bag opened, her red hair tousled and childlike round her face. He dropped the corpse into the bag, and for a moment she held it, her arms bending at the full weight before he took it away from her. Still shaking, he knotted the edges together.

'It's the first time you've laughed in weeks,' she said.

'I'm going to dispose of the body,' was his only response as he hefted the dead weight. The dog followed him through the house into the street, its head as erect as a soldier's.

The parking lot where the nightwatchman used to sit was black and empty. It's a pity that you're no longer here to protect me, Josef S thought. I need some protection. Somewhere up on the Leeukop, a man was fasting for peace in the gathering darkness: a monastery of light keeping a dark age at bay. Lions prowled in the night, and the small building on the mountain was an outpost of hope in the wilderness.

Josef carried the bag at arm's length as though it might contaminate him. He dropped it in a municipal refuse bin at the end of the street while the dog, pleased at a job well done, smiled: the evil had been removed.

'Peace has been mutilated,' Josef told Mrs Milner through her dark closed shutters as he walked back up the street. 'Your illusions of peace can't keep out the violence. It's arrived in this street, and it's not going to end for a long time yet.' He closed his front door firmly behind him.

'Where's Robert?' he asked Dorothy. She stood in the kitchen with her arms folded, hugging the shivers that threatened to tear her chest open. 'You said he'd gone out. He never seems to be here when I'm here.' He did not add: Unless he's spying on me. 'Does he hate me?' He looked round the room in the silence that followed his question, and asked: 'Have you seen the pliers? I must get the nail out of the door-frame.'

'You're acting for that killer, aren't you?' she countered.

He looked at her closely, the search for the whereabouts of both brother and pliers forgotten. 'Which killer?'

'The one who stabbed Buth.'

'He isn't a killer,' Josef answered, puzzled.

'Yes he is,' she said. 'Didn't you hear? Buth died this afternoon.'

'Oh God.' He sat down. At the funeral, the Reverend Lode had warned that when the people ruled, Buth would be tried for his crimes. Well, the President had escaped such a trial. Now, if a divine justice existed, Buth was on his way to meet it, to explain why he had condoned, even authorised, events which had earned him the condemnation of an entire section of the community.

'No, I didn't hear,' Josef said. 'I had no idea.'

'Well he's dead. And you're acting for his killer.'

'How did you hear?' Even in his weariness, he knew he had not told her. Who had? How much did she know, if indeed there was anything to know? So much had been happening to Josef, it was almost impossible to separate what was public knowledge from what was not, what Dorothy should know from what was secret. And even why anything should be kept secret at all. Ben had known that Josef had been at the funeral. Dorothy knew he was acting for Ngo. 'How?' he repeated.

'The press have been calling, I told you. They want to ask you about Buth's death and that man you're defending. I told them you weren't in, but I didn't tell them that I didn't know where you were. I didn't tell them that I thought you were with another woman. I didn't tell them that you're a stranger to me now, and I don't know anything about you anymore.' She was holding herself more tightly than ever and her face was pinched and drawn: she looked old, older than anyone he knew, older, even, than his mother would have been now. 'I didn't want the press to know the intimate details of our lives. But if you don't come home, I don't know how I'll keep them out. They're like rats: they creep into the smallest holes if there's a story . . .'

He dropped his head into his hands; his fingers were cold as metal on his cheeks. The sawn off segment of rope hung over his head like a threat, or a curse. He could not answer her accusations. He was too tired, too drained: Ben, Poynter, Margaret, the cat hanging from the door-frame, and now this.

'They'll find out whatever they want to know, once they're interested in you. Why didn't you tell me that you were taking the case?' Her hands were on her hips now, driven there by anger. 'Why didn't you ask me if I minded having my home invaded, if I object to dead cats and reporters? Do you think I don't read the newspapers?' She was pacing the room with short quick steps. 'Do you think I don't know that woman lawyer was murdered? This doesn't only involve you, Josef. But if you want to be a hero, you might have to be one alone: I don't want to be caught in the cross-fire.' Her shoulders slumped. 'And I don't care if there is another woman: in fact I'd pity her. You're too selfish to love anyone.'

Josef found a pair of pliers in a drawer, and applied himself once more to the problem of pulling the nail out of the door-frame. Was it worthwhile even to answer her allegations? He did not know what the truth was, if there was a single truth. He was suddenly tempted to leave Dorothy in the house and drive back to Margaret. He would ask her to take him in . . . 'I suppose I should tell the police about the cat,' he said.

'They probably know all about it already,' she retorted, 'and more than they'll ever tell you.'

'New locks?' he asked, fending the accusations.

'They opened this lock. Why bother? They must have special keys.'

The nail came out; Josef swayed as triumphantly as a dentist with an extracted tooth. 'Tomorrow, I'll call in a carpenter to put bolts on all the doors.' He threw the nail and rope into the bin. 'If it's going to be a siege, then so be it.'

'You sound happy at the prospect.'

'Please let's go to bed,' he said. If he had expected her to object, refusing to touch a suspected adulterous husband who had not even bothered to defend himself, he was wrong. Wordlessly she led the way to the bedroom. She wore her white nightrobe, and although her body was outlined beneath it, he had no urge to touch her.

Did the shrieking come from the figure who stood before the Abyss, looking in? Josef thought he recognised its back: was this person in pain?

The men had clambered out of the Abyss. Like their ancestors, they wore full tribal regalia. They were burying their dead.

Josef stood and watched: it did not matter that these deaths had occurred; deaths are inevitable in conflict situations. But the men saw him, and they whispered among themselves like the whispering of the wind though the cracks in the rocks. They waved their skin shields as their ancestors must have when the settlers arrived. They wore skins of lions on their bodies, and necklaces of teeth, and bangles of claws about their wrists and ankles. They stamped their naked feet on the flat dry earth until the dust rose in white clouds like flour and obliterated the sun.

The shrieking stopped, and the figure turned towards him.

'You were moaning in your sleep,' Dorothy said, as though nothing had happened the night before.

'I was dreaming.' His voice was early-morning thick, and his heart was hammering in his chest. His hands were burning. It took him a good few minutes to recognise his infatuation. He lay there, knowing that he had no place in bed with his wife, but the changes were coming too quickly: he had to deal with them at his own pace. He was aware of Dorothy's green eyes boring into him, as if she were trying to pull out the truth with her eyes.

'What did you dream about?'

'The political situation,' he said unwillingly, dragging the words out like a prisoner lugging stones. Quickly, before she could speak, he asked: 'Where is Robert? Did he sleep out? I didn't hear him come in.' The burning of infatuation was so strong that he wrung his hands, and then swung himself out of bed.

'I don't keep track of Robert's movements,' Dorothy said, a little too sharply, and added: 'I wish you'd reconsider your decision about that case.'

'Will you phone the carpenters to put in bolts or must I?' was his answer.

She smiled sadly, shaking her head. 'I'm having no part of your game,' she said. 'You organise it if you want. Don't count on me for anything, Josef.'

Is this how love dies, he wondered, a slow strangulation? The noose tightening, bit by bit, day by day, while the two antagonists, battle-scarred, knowing where each other's weaknesses lie, prod the tender places, inflicting as much hurt as possible, creating as much hatred as the fragile relationship will bear before it implodes, and the adversaries fall, dragged down by their own hatred?

'If you see my brother, tell him that it's impolite to eavesdrop,' he said. It was a tentative, exploratory jab; he sensed that Robert was a tender subject.

131

'What do you mean?' He could almost see her lifting her shield to ward off the blow.

'The other night when we were talking about your new book, Robert was there listening, wasn't he?' Josef wrapped a towel round his waist. 'It's just something that's irked me . . .'

'Tell him yourself!' she snapped. Her hands, the hands that created stories, that had once made love to him, that had held him and stroked him when he was sick, were clenched into fists on the bedclothes. Strong hands, he saw again, absently, as she too might have been noticing things about him while their duel continued. Love and hate: so closely linked that it is possible to entertain both simultaneously. While he was hating her, he continued to notice aspects that he had once loved. And he was already mourning their absence from his life because they could not continue to be there.

'Maybe I will,' he said, his point made. The blow had got through: her reaction had betrayed her, the shield had not covered the soft place adequately. And she knew it, because she looked up defiantly, and said nothing. Was she still capable of surprising him? He did not think so. But his body burned for someone else. Wounded himself, he sought refuge in the bathroom.

BUTH DEAD and CITY LAWYER TO DEFEND NGO? were the headlines that greeted Josef when he ventured tiredly into town. Someone had leaked the news, one of Ben's comrades, he supposed, or perhaps someone from the security services who had infiltrated Ben's movement. There was an old photograph of Josef, thankfully almost unrecognisable, that someone had found in the newspaper archives. It had been taken when he was leaving Court years before. He could not even remember which case had drawn this attention then.

'Is Mr Parry in yet?' he asked the receptionist, and when she shook her head, he said: 'Please tell Ben to come and see me.'

She put her telephone down and winked at him. 'We're becoming famous,' she jibed. 'Everybody's talking. You're acting for Buth's killer.' She pointed to the newspaper, as if he did not know yet.

'I want you to take all my calls,' he said to her. 'If any journalists phone, tell them that I have no comment to make. Only put through callers who genuinely need to speak to me.'

For the first time, it seemed, he noticed her bulk as she sat behind the reception desk. After all these years, she had merged into the furniture, and become a voice at the end of a telephone, a plump hand to which he passed messages and from which he received them. But now, suddenly, she became a solid mass between him and all those who wanted things from him; a buffer between the privacy of his office and the hostile world beyond. He needed to elicit her sympathy, needed her on his side. He smiled at her, possibly the first time he had smiled at her with his eyes.

'Julia.' He leaned on the desk, on his balled fists, and looked at her. His intense, brown-eyed stare fixed her in her place so that not even a ringing telephone intruded. 'You're right. Everybody's talking. And they're going to be bothering me, and I want you to keep them out. Some of the calls might be abusive, but you mustn't take any of it personally. It's directed at me. Maybe it's not fair of me to inflict this on you, but somebody's got to act for William Ngo and I've decided to. If any of the calls are threatening, just put the phone down.'

'Yes, Mr S,' she said. There was no fear in her clear blue eyes. She was staunch, a rock, a woman who would take his interests to heart, who would protect him fiercely. 'Don't worry, keeping them out is my job.' She smiled back at him, all the mockery dropped: her iron-grey hair brushed straight back seemed to symbolise her strength. 'I must answer this call, excuse me.' He retreated, paced to the wall and back to her desk. 'Good morning, Parry & S,' she said and after a moment of listening: 'No, I'm sorry, he's not taking calls, but he's instructed me to say that he has no comment. Goodbye.' She flicked the appropriate switch.

'You're going to have to say that quite a few times in the next few days,' he warned her.

'Don't you worry,' she said sternly.

He smiled again at her, went into his office and closed the door. He did not open his briefcase: he unfolded the newspaper over his desk, put his head in his hands, and, thus propped up, surveyed the news. Buth's death, sudden as it was, was greeted with shock by conservative elements and with indifference (officially) by his opponents. A spokesman for the FDF said that it did not matter who was at the helm of the ship of state, since, unless the Republican Government was removed, the majority of the people would continue to suffer. It was of no concern to the FDF who replaced Buth; the Generals were in power in any case. They controlled the Republican Party.

General de Wet, the Republic's Commissioner of Police, responded that these allegations were nonsense, and that the FDF was using a tragic occasion to sow further mischief. President John Buth had been an honest upright man, a benefit to the Party and the Republic, and his death was a severe loss to the country.

The hospital where Buth had been treated issued a terse statement to the effect that his condition had been improving but had deteriorated rapidly due to complications and that he had died at midday.

The front page was dominated by a photograph of Buth, bold, powerful, arrogant, seated at his desk, his eyes smiling and defiant behind gold-rimmed spectacles. Behind him hung the flag of the Republic. Josef's photograph appeared on the bottom half of the page. The caption read: 'Josef S, the lawyer who is to defend William Ngo, accused of the President's murder.' In the accompanying article, it was mentioned that the previous lawyer who had undertaken to defend Ngo had been slain outside her home; also that Josef S had not been available for comment. Josef S, it was added, did not have a history of criminal or political work, and it was surprising that he had agreed to take the case.

Josef lifted the intercom and buzzed Julia's desk. 'How's it going out there?' Even though he should have expected the press reaction, it came as a shock. He had an impulse to withdraw from the case and from the public spotlight, to leave Dorothy and go and live somewhere peaceful with Margaret.

'You've had more calls,' Julia said. 'I'm taking messages. I'll send them through with Ben when he gets in.'

'Fine,' he answered. He checked in the telephone book and dialled a number. 'Mark,' he said. 'Josef S here. I need some bolts put onto my doors. Can you come after work today?'

'I'll say you do, Mr S.' The rough voice at the other end of the line cackled like a chicken's. 'How many doors?'

'Two,' said Josef S. 'Front and kitchen. Can we make it at five?'

'Sure, Mr S. And how is Mrs S?'

'Nervous,' said Josef. 'Five it is then,' and he put down the phone.

What do I do, Dad? he asked the typewriter. The silence of the machine was ominous.

The typewriter was solid and black, with the make inscribed in faded gold letters, so faded, it was almost illegible: only the end of the word '. . . wood' could be discerned. Today, it seemed more complex than ever before: the gears and ratchets and springs, the black keys surrounded by gold, the black paint peeling off the frame, parts he had no name for and which seemed to have been omitted from modern typewriters, or at least hidden, expressing a complexity his father had known, but which Josef could not decipher.

The airconditioning soughed gently, simulating the wind; he felt comfortable in its artificial embrace. Here, life was controlled, or at least controllable. Here, the elements did not intrude, but a perfectly comfortable environment was manufactured. Here, routine kept you in control, like an ox in harness, and you could not stray too far in metaphysical pursuits. Outside, it seemed to him, there was nothing to stop the mind from floating freely, and the thinking, when left uncontrolled, turned in on itself and devoured the thinker. Uncontrolled thinking was as dangerous as barbed wired ingested, twisting and slicing at your insides.

Sitting in his office, with the door closed, surveying the wall-high shelves of law books, with the Leeukop a hint through the blinds that half-obscured his window, he felt the tension drain away from him. Margaret, and William Ngo, and Dorothy, and the press and even Buth (when the newspaper was folded) disappeared. Secure in the knowledge that Julia was holding calls, he dozed. A flight of gulls screeched past his window, but the wildness outside did not bother him.

He woke; someone had knocked on the door. He had slept for an hour. He stood, combing his hair with his fingers. 'Who is it?' he asked.

'Ben.'

'Come in.'

Despite his apparent prominence in the FDF, the clerk was still in awe of his employers. 'You wanted to see me,' he said diffidently, as if he were assessing Josef's mood in order to know how forceful he should be. Perhaps he took courage from Josef's dishevelled appearance. Before the lawyer could answer, Ben placed a copy of *The Voice* on his desk. The community newspaper also carried a picture of Buth on its front, devoting the entire page to the coverage of his death under the title : WHAT NEXT?

'The editor of *The Voice* has been arrested,' Ben said. 'They didn't like his article.'

'How did the press learn that I'm acting for Ngo?' Josef S asked, feeling that he ought to be angry, but with a curious lack of interest as to the answer. He opened the blinds and the day entered his office.

'I don't know, Mr S. Phones are tapped. Maybe somebody from

the police tipped them off, just to put pressure on us. But they don't know for sure. Here.' He picked up *The Voice* from Josef's desk and sought out a passage as if he had memorised the whole thing. 'Here,' he pointed, but Josef did not look and Ben read to him: ' "It is rumoured that one of Eisstad's leading lawyers, Josef S, has accepted the brief to defend William Ngo, accused of the murder of President John Buth. Yesterday Mr S was not available for comment." You see? "Rumoured". The press couldn't confirm it: we don't have an informer, otherwise they'd have been certain . . .'

'Ben, Ben . . . Take a seat.' Ben slumped into one of the high-backed chairs that stood about awkwardly in the office. 'They know, Ben. And it doesn't really matter to me who told them. But from now on, if you want me to go ahead with the case, you're going to be very discreet. Watch what you say on the phone, don't give any secrets away to anyone, not even to your mother. People talk, and the information gets to the wrong ears. Now, what have you done?'

'I've arranged a consultation with William in the Tower for Monday at ten.'

'Good. Any witnesses? Character witnesses? Teachers who know him? Priests? Get onto it.'

'OK, Mr S. You might want to keep *The Voice*. It's for you.'

'Thank you, Ben. You know,' he mused, looking towards the old City Hall and Gomez Square, where the city's 'founder' stared out facelessly to sea, as if longing to return to the country from which he had come, 'I get the feeling that this place has no history. There is so much turmoil now, but sometimes no sense of belonging. I feel that I'm living on borrowed soil in borrowed time. That one day, I will have to give back whatever I own, and that, like Job, I will have to stand naked and wait for judgement.'

'That's not so, Mr S. You're participating in the struggle. You're helping to sow the seeds of our success and you will harvest the fruits.' The rhetoric was familiar by now, and Ben was beginning to warm to his topic. 'You won't be disinherited: you'll be honoured . . .'

But the lawyer interrupted. 'I won't live to taste those fruits, Ben. I foresee a long civil war, a bitter struggle that will produce many martyrs on both sides. The Republicans aren't going to lie on their backs and kick their feet in the air and give it all up, not a damn. I fear that the struggle will destroy the country; the Republic will bleed to death.'

'If you are to be judged, you will be judged favourably, Mr S,'

Ben persisted. 'We believe that the situation in our country will be normalised in time . . . Things won't deteriorate as you predict.'

'Christ, Ben, you can't even keep information to yourselves. But what the hell . . . Try not to leak too much to the press.'

'Yes sir.' The clerk stood to go.

Josef smiled wanly, as if he were peering through a thick mist. 'Thanks for the newspaper.'

'I'll try to keep you informed, sir,' Ben said, and let himself out.

The intercom buzzed. 'I've got a Dr Foster to see you, Mr S. He doesn't have an appointment, but he's insisting. He's not from the press . . . It's something about lions. Do you want to see him?'

'Yes Julia, send him in.'

As Josef waited for the client, he noticed *The Voice* lying like a flag advertising his 'conversion' and he swept it into a drawer. There was no need for anyone to know what he read. He rearranged the items on his desk — diary, stapler, letters — ordering these random objects with his long nervous fingers.

The squat man who came in wore baggy white trousers and a white shirt, buttoned only halfway up his chest, exposing a heavy gold medallion and chain. He had a square face, wiry grey hair thinning at the crown, thick sideburns and wide nostrils. Josef stood in greeting and extended his hand. The handshake was firm and dry, the hand as solid as its owner whom Josef motioned to sit.

What can I do for you, Dr Foster?' he asked.

'I want to sue the City Council.' Foster's voice boomed as if he were lecturing to students.

'And why do you want to do that?' Josef looked the man over carefully, his fingers drumming lightly on the table-top.

'I'm a zoologist,' Foster said. 'I want to introduce lions onto the Leeukop . . . legally if possible, with the Council's consent. But they've turned me down so far. I want to take them to court . . .'

'I've read your views, Dr Foster,' the lawyer said, 'and I sympathise with your motives: symbolically, releasing the lions would express solidarity with the people. But my advice to you is to forget it.'

Foster narrowed his eyes and put his hands behind his head: a challenge to attack him, unguarded. 'And why d'you say that? I read about you in this morning's newspaper. That's why I came to see you. You've taken that case when nobody else would. I thought you'd be the perfect person for me; a maverick like myself, a dreamer.' He brought his arms, heavy as hams, to rest on his stomach.

'You believe in justice even at personal risk.' He beat his chest with his flat hand. So do I! So why don't we campaign together?'

'I'm sorry, Dr Foster,' the lawyer said politely. 'I'm extremely reluctant to expose anyone to the danger of having lions prowling in the streets. And I suspect this will be the dominant view of the residents . . .'

'I have a copy of a letter that appeared in the newspaper, from a resident backing me!'

'I'm aware of the letter, but I think you'll find its supporters are in the minority: a radical fringe. My advice is to forget it. If you want to work for change, go and do something useful, something practical.' He lifted his eyebrows searching for an example. 'Go and help Albert Poynter. He's a doctor at the Valhalla Clinic. He needs all the help he can get. Go and work on an adult literacy programme; there are a hundred things you can do . . . This symbolism of yours is all very well as an idea, but it's practically useless if not dangerous.'

'I'm sorry you take that attitude, Mr S,' said Foster. Sulleness had fallen like a veil over his face; but it was transparent enough to reveal an underlying cunning. He was a cornered animal, planning its next move. 'Art is very seldom practical and my work is a form of art. I thought you would be only too willing to carry the struggle onto new fronts, right into the heart of Eisstad. I thought we could be allies. I was wrong, I see.' He put his stubby fingers to his face, hiding his expression.

'Right into my backyard, you mean!' Josef protested. 'I'm not here to be anyone's ally, nor do I care for your strange concept of art. I'm a lawyer, and my duty is to give the soundest possible advice. That's my job. That's what you're going to pay me for. I would be failing in my duty if I was to give the go-ahead to a hare-brained scheme that could, no, I'm sure *would*, land you on a murder charge as soon as one of your symbols ate somebody . . .'

But Foster did not seem to be listening. He had a faraway look in his eyes; in the sunlight they glinted yellowly: the colour of the long grass on the mountain in the dry summer. 'I've brought up those cubs,' he murmured. 'They are my children.'

'Do you understand me?' Josef asked.

'That's the trouble with most liberals,' Foster asserted as if he had forgotten his earlier observation about Josef's willingness to place himself at risk. 'They're all theory: not prepared to put their skins on the line.'

'I'll not expose myself or my family to senseless danger,' the lawyer retorted. Yet Dorothy considered it was dangerous to take Ngo's case. Where did one draw the line?

'I'm talking about showing the bourgeois suburbanites what danger's all about,' Foster thundered. 'What it's like for the people in the townships! How they have to live with Leeus on their doorsteps!'

'That's not what you've been saying all along, Dr Foster, is it? You've been talking about symbols. You've even offered to put up a fence, and to populate the mountain with indigenous antelope. You've never spoken about intentionally introducing a source of danger. That would be an aggravating factor . . .'

'I'm going,' said the zoologist, slamming his fist on the table, threatening the order that Josef had created. 'I've heard enough . . . I'll do what I have to do.'

'And what's that?'

'Don't you worry about it.' Foster pushed back his chair and stood heavily. He extended his hand, the model of courtesy even to an adversary. Josef S shook the hand. He felt a perverse affection for this man, this fanatic who wished to bring about his own brand of justice.

'If you foresee the possibility of the death of a person and you proceed recklessly with your course of action, and if such a death occurs, you are liable for murder. I want you to be quite clear about that before you do anything rash.'

'Thank you for your advice, Mr S,' Foster said. 'I'll pay your cashier on the way out.'

'We don't have a cashier. Pay the receptionist.' And then the big man was gone, walking very lightly, almost on the tips of the toes of his blue canvas shoes: he wore no leather, the lawyer noticed.

Josef took *The Voice* from the drawer and turned the pages restlessly. What would Foster do now? Josef had no doubt that he had advised the man correctly, and that he was right not to become involved in a mad exercise. Nevertheless, he was touched by a momentary misgiving, as if a blemish had appeared on his new armour of commitment: was he in fact not prepared to risk his life? Was the struggle simply a game for him, an escape from a marriage that was no longer working? Ironically, Dorothy came to his rescue: she would aver that he *was* prepared to undergo dangers, and in the process to endanger her as well.

The Voice declared: FDF REFUSES TO SEE LION-MAN A top representative of the FDF had turned down an application by Foster for a meeting. A spokesman for the organisation said simply that the two parties had nothing of common interest to discuss. This disclosure added even more poignancy to the epithet, maverick, that Foster had given himself. Josef S could only hope that all these rejections would not twist the man's mind completely.

On the leader page, *The Voice's* cartoonist had turned his talents to commenting on the life and death of President Buth. Under the caption SEVEN AGES OF A MAN appeared seven drawings: the artist's impression of the main stages of the ex-President's life. In the first, a baby with the seventy-year old President's face lay in a crib, howling. The second showed a boy, possessing the same face, playing inside a cow trough; a piece of straw protruding from his open mouth was a cruel reference to the President's provincial up-bringing. In the third, the young man with the now familiar face stood on a fruit-box delivering a speech; the words: WE WILL DIE TO UPHOLD OUR PRIVILEGE were prophetically attributed to him. The fourth depicted a middle-aged Buth entering a polling-booth, clutching a ballot-paper on which the X was marked against his name: no other names appeared on the paper. In the fifth cartoon, the elderly President held court from a royal box, waving a royal mace and wearing a crown and an ermine coat. The sixth picture portrayed the dead President lying in state in his coffin, some of those filing past him were crying, others smiled. The last frame was a scene in heaven, where the spirit of the dead man (still wearing the same face) was being tried by a court consisting of God the judge (drawn as an old man with a beard) winged angels as the jury and a late, leading member of the FDF as prosecutor. For those who did not know, the prosecutor wore a name-tag: GAVIN DAVIDS: DIED IN DETENTION. Buth, shackled in the dock, was being defended by the devil.

A longing for Margaret Spears interrupted Josef's reading. She came to him as an aura which penetrated his fingers and set them alight, which settled in his bones, causing them to ache as if with fever. She was a mysterious, beautiful witch who had cast a spell on him with her quick movements and burning eyes. Had he ever felt this way for Dorothy? He could not remember; he could not even remember their courtship although there must have been one. His love for Dorothy had died for no particular reason; why should a new love not die as well? 'No,' he said to the despair that tried to extinguish the fire in his hands, but it persisted, reminding Josef that he could not put faith in love, that he had never been able to.

Why should the next lover (Josef already thought of Margaret as the next) be any different? 'No,' Josef repeated above the rushing in his head. 'No.' He had to see her. Only by seeing her would he still his demons: desire and despair. He wanted to cradle her head in his hands, to ease away the pain he had glimpsed in her. Somehow by doing that, he would make his own pain more bearable.

'Has Mr Parry come in yet?' he asked Julia.

'Yes. He wants to see you. I said you're busy. Must I send him in?'

'Please.'

Better get it over with, Josef thought. But the strain was breaking through; presenting him with a vision of decay. He saw an old man sick in bed, plants turning brown and dying in the corners of the room, peeling wallpaper, the fly-stains on the walls giving the outward impression of an illness as severe as that from which the man was suffering. A yellow, spotted mirror revealed, partially, the face of a visitor, but there was no possibility of a clear identification. Who was the sick man? His father? Buth? The country? And was he the visitor? Perhaps the haunted brown eyes staring back from the cracked glass gave the game away. Or perhaps the visitor was Ed Parry, and the sick man was he, Josef S, old and lonely, wife gone, left to die alone by the friends he had alienated throughout his lifetime. Perhaps his wife and brother and partner would come by, once in a while, to gloat over his fall, to pretend concern, to water a sagging fern, to puff up his pillow, pat him on the head and then leave, satisfied that he was suffering for the hurt he had caused during his dealings with them. And he would stare at the floral design of the wallpaper, trying to make sense of it.

Parry opened the door, and Josef clamped his jaw tightly. He turned slowly from the window; he had been staring at the mountain without seeing it. He indicated one of his chairs and Parry sat, shoulders hunched tiredly.

'Hello Ed,' his partner began. 'I presume you read the paper.'

'You know,' said Parry very slowly, balancing his weight, as if he were scared that he would break the chair, or that he would fall and injure himself. He put his hands over his eyes and drew them down his face, caressing his cheeks with his palms. 'You know,' he repeated, 'when I started practicing, I used to do a lot of work for the FDF.' He peered at Josef from under his raised eyebrows, his head tilted down. 'I've never told you that . . . I wasn't hiding anything, I just didn't think you'd be interested . . . You've never been concerned with political work before. I appeared for them in their early

141

days, mainly in sedition and public violence trials. I was personally friendly with Gavin Davids who was then the leader of the FDF. I remember,' Parry rubbed his bald head, 'once we were driving up country together, I had to defend someone from the FDF, and Gavin told me that when the FDF got into power it would only be a matter of time before the radical wing deposed the moderates. He saw himself in a caretaker capacity. He warned me to leave the country while I was still young, to take my family and start again somewhere else.

'I didn't follow his advice and I'm still here.' Parry's eyes looked into a half-forgotten distance.

'They detained Gavin without charge, you know. And then they killed him: he was found hanging in a cell by his trousers. I only managed to represent him at the inquest. Death by suicide, the magistrate decided, no one was responsible, even though I got the security police to admit they'd beaten him on the night he died. He'd once told me that if he was detained, he'd never kill himself.

'I had a bit of publicity then — the press hysteria was nothing like it is now — and I received a couple of death threats, and thoroughly sick and tired of it all, I left that kind of work for commercial practice. I reckoned I was endangering myself and my family for no good cause. I wouldn't get any justice through the courts and if the other side overthrew the Republicans, well, I was in for it anyway. Now I believe that my first duty is to myself and my family. Don't be naïve, Josef. When they take over, they'll be no better than we are: mark my words, there'll be tanks in the streets, and a blood-letting such as you can hardly imagine. I believe the arsonists and stone-throwers must be stopped now. I admit, the police *do* sometimes over-react, but then they're under stress and you can't expect them to behave like gentlemen. There're always bound to be excesses . . .' Josef was staring at his father's typewriter, making it obvious that he had withdrawn from the conversation.

'Josef . . . Listen to me. The Ngo case is hopeless: the boy did it. He's going to swing, he probably wants to be a martyr. He knew what he was doing. Why expose yourself and the firm in this way? For nothing. For personal pride, to clear out your guilt. Whatever your reasons are, it's not worth it, Josef. I admire your courage but I insist that you think very seriously about what you're doing . . . for the firm and for yourself. Let me warn you: the lunatics on the right don't care who they hit. It may be you, or Ben, or Julia, or me; it may be a bomb in the building, and then you'll have that guilt on your shoulders as well.' Parry put his hands on his knees and stood up heavily. 'I'll leave you with those thoughts, Josef,' he said, and walked out without looking back.

Josef put on his jacket slowly as if he were moving in his sleep. For a moment he allowed his fingers to rest on the typewriter keys, then he left the office, glancing at the mountain, ancient watchdog of Eisstad, before he closed the door. As he passed Julia's desk, he nodded. 'I'm going out for a while,' he said, and she smiled sympathetically.

'Ah, Mr S!' a voice called in the street. 'I've been looking for you.'

'I have nothing to say,' the lawyer flashed back angrily.

'That's what your receptionist's been telling me all morning,' Wilson complained. 'But I'd like to ask you one or two questions if you don't mind.'

Josef S hurried on: he understood then why celebrities were known to assault journalists who pestered them. The man wore a tweed jacket even though the day was hot and the perspiration flowed freely down his face. His acne had not improved.

'What prompted you to take William Ngo's case?' Wilson asked, striding after the lawyer. 'Especially after Mrs Idini was murdered . . .'

'Listen Jonathan, why don't you play the story down for my sake? If you don't splash it all over your front pages, maybe I'll live longer. Have you ever thought of that?'

'But Mr S,' the man protested, 'mine is not the only newspaper. If we don't run the story, that won't stop the others from doing so. At least if you give me the correct version, we'll have that on record and we can refute any stories the others might come up with.'

'Why should the others come up with anything? It's "no comment" to all of you. Now please stop bothering me.'

Wilson accepted defeat. 'Good luck, Mr S,' he said, giving up the chase.

'Thank you.' Josef escaped. His jacket was weighted with stones, pulling his shoulders down. The sun laid a heavy hand on his unprotected head, forcing his eyes towards the pavement. It was some time before he noticed the posters advertising the meeting. Attached to lampposts, plastered to walls, they must have been put up overnight: PEACE RALLY in black on yellow backgrounds, CITY HALL. ALBERT POYNTER, FDF SPEAKERS. He imagined FDF workers, quiet as mice, observed only by tramps and seagulls, fingers tangled in quick knots and sticky from slapping glue, pressing into the shadows when a police van cruised by, scurrying to complete the job before the hand of authority scattered them.

Again, the Waterfront. Again the seemingly deserted buildings, behind whose blind eyes you suspected that multifaceted life went on, beyond the scrutiny of the law. The sea air was tart and a light rain began to fall. A minute ago the sun was in command, now the clouds had cemented the sky and the rain came down; it seemed to rain whenever Josef S went into Waterfront. Perhaps, he thought, the rain fell permanently on Waterfront, a celestial mark of mourning for the removals that had taken place there. Seagulls, fat from their pickings on the harbour, ruffled their wings and stalked across empty lots. A man in a blue tracksuit was returning from his daily battle with the sea, his fishing rod balanced as comfortably as a spear in his rough hand.

The rain was not heavy enough to make the lawyer uncomfortable, but he was relieved when he came to the building he was looking for. Thankfully, he skirted the dishevelled men who stood in the doorway, smiled at the shabbily-uniformed attendant in his information booth and told him where he was going.

'Seventh floor,' the man mumbled, making a note on a ruled page he kept on a clipboard, and Josef S stepped into a lift that smelled of stale sweat. He brushed his damp hair with his long fingers.

Her office was the antithesis of her home: it was furnished with the barest of essentials which seemed to have been scraped together from the cheapest sources without any homage to decor or taste, as if she, or her organisation, did not consider it necessary to waste money on things when so much was needed for the Cause. There was a green metal cabinet, the open doors of which revealed stationery and files, a desk cluttered with papers, a table with pamphlets, and three bare, unpolished chairs standing on a tiled floor. FDF posters regaled the walls, depicting Leeus in townships, lists of detained and dead, photographs of people who were possibly prominent members of the organisation. Margaret was not in, but a man sitting in one of the chairs appeared to be waiting for her return. He was staring stoically straight ahead at the spot where she would have been sitting. He wore a tired black suit, probably his best, and clasped his battered hat deferentially to his stomach. When Josef nodded to him, he nodded back, meeting the lawyer's eyes, unsmiling. With him was a boy in his early teens, wearing slacks and a tracksuit top. The boy (his son?) lacked the dignity of the older man; he had undisciplined eyes that searched the room for stimulation. What did he make of his father's stoicism? Would his youthful

144

energy be blunted during the course of a life of frustration until he too looked at the world with eyes that had no hope?

The lawyer picked up a pamphlet entitled: 'Know your Rights'. About 'Gatherings', he read: 'Outdoor gatherings of any number of people are prohibited under the Public Safeties Act. Therefore, during pamphleteering and signature collecting, there should be no communication between volunteers . . .' He skimmed through the sections detailing what information an arrested person had to furnish to the police, confiscation of property, right of access to lawyers, and so on, and stopped at the paragraph on 'Detention'. 'If, instead of being arrested and charged, you are *detained* under certain sections of the Public Safeties Act, you do not have the same rights of access to a lawyer and do not have to be brought to court within any particular period of time. These sections are primarily intended to enable the police to hold people for long priods of time for interrogation.' (And, as in the case of Gavin Davids, to remove them completely, Josef S reflected, despite Ed Parry's conception of the benevolence of the regime in comparison with the system the FDF would impose if they took power.) On the table was a copy of *The Voice*, and a pamphlet: 'Let us Pursue Justice'. Again, Josef read extracts: 'The Republican Government has attempted to smother legitimate protest as all those who oppose it have been subjected to varying degrees of harassment and intimidation. The FDF especially is under continual attack. Our meetings are banned, our leaders have been detained or murdered, our members are being threatened or arrested. By sending troops into the townships, the Government has declared war on its own people. We cannot allow ourselves to be bullied into silence by institutionalised brutality. Our townships are besieged, our schools invaded, our children killed. We have a duty to protest against these things . . .'

'The history of our times is written in newspaper reports and pamphlets.'

The familiar voice cut into his concentration. 'Hello, Josef S.' She wore a blue skirt and a white blouse. Her breasts, outlined by the material, were like small birds.

'Hello, Margaret Spears.' He felt light, released from stress, even though everything in this office reminded him of the repression in the land. Here he did not have to explain or defend his motives. Here he was accepted as one of those involved in the struggle. 'How are you today? Did you sleep well?'

145

'Perfectly,' she smiled. 'Thank you again for the lift home.' She turned to the man and the boy. 'George. I got through to the lawyers. Daniel has been arrested on a murder charge. We've got a meeting with the lawyer on Monday morning.' The man shook his head tiredly, an old boxer rocked by another blow from a system that has had him on the ropes since birth. 'He is no murderer,' he said. 'My son didn't kill anyone.' The boy seemed not to have heard or to have understood. He continued to look round the room at the posters, making his own sense out of this reality, perhaps already abandoning his brother, now lost to the struggle, cutting him off like dead wood so as not to impede his own entry into the fray. At best, Daniel would become a martyr; at worst, he would simply be forgotten, one of those nameless, numberless ones who, like insects, have sacrificed themselves for a perceived greater good for their kind, the aristocracy of absence. Or perhaps Josef S was ascribing too profound a meaning to the boy's indifference.

'I know Daniel,' Margaret said to Josef. 'I agree with his father. He's no murderer. He's an activist and they've framed him to get him out of the way.' Josef wanted, suddenly, to demand of her: 'How well do you know him? How close is he to you?' Her face was tight, her jaws clenched in a spasm of anger, but the sudden hatred in her eyes gave way to a softer expression, and she said to the man and the boy: 'Be here at nine on Monday. All right?'

The supplicant nodded and stood, still clasping his hat to his stomach, though one hand rested on the boy's shoulder. The two walked out together.

'Daniel in the lion's den,' Josef joked.

'Would you like some co . . . coffee?' she asked. 'I'm sorry I can't offer you tea.'

'Yes, thank you,' he said. Was she angry at his flippancy?

'Milk, no sugar?' she asked. 'Like your tea?'

'Absolutely.' He was complete in her company: all the fragments of his shattered ego were drawn together into a wonderful whole. If only she would accept him, life would be worthwhile, perhaps. He could start again, could build up a new life out of the mess of the old one. If only she would let him.

'Hang on,' she said and disappeared into the next room. She returned shortly with two polystyrene cups containing the coffee, and handed him one. Their fingers brushed as the transfer took place. His hand jerked as if he had touched a raw electric current. Guardedly, he looked at her face to assess her reaction, but she gave

146

nothing away. Perhaps there was nothing to give away. He had to sit. He chose the chair that had been empty when he came in. His skin, where they had touched, burned, and his heart beat erratically. He had to speak, to justify his staring at her.

'Tell me about Daniel,' he suggested. At least he was not as leaden-mouthed as the previous night.

She sat behind the desk and took a cigarette, which she lit, nervously. He did not remember her smoking in her flat: perhaps she only smoked at the office where the pressure was greater. Several cigarette butts had been stubbed out in the ashtray.

'Daniel is a sad case, but symptomatic of the problems we deal with,' she said. 'He was born on a farm and his parents did not get a birth certificate for him. When he was about four or five, his parents were killed in a car accident. There was no death certificate. He was brought up by his father's brother . . . the man in here now, on an adjoining farm. As far as Daniel was concerned, this man was his father, the wife was his mother, and the boy, Clifford, his brother. In fact they all speak of one another as if that's the family connection. Daniel lived with the family in a labourer's shack until he decided to come to Eisstad to look for work. He got a job on a construction site, casually employed, from week to week, and that was fine. But when the job ended, he couldn't get anything else. He had no identity papers at all, in fact no proof that he even existed. You can't get permanent employment if you don't exist.' She pushed the end of the cigarette into the ashes of its predecessors and lit another. 'So he came to us, and we've been trying to get through the tangle of red tape that trips us up all the time. He'd learned to read and write at the farm school and wants to get a job as a clerk. He's burning to succeed . . .' Josef S wondered wryly if his own burning would help him to succeed with her. '. . . which is why he didn't languish on the farm picking grapes, why he came to the city and got involved with the FDF. It's incredible: they can't get him a birth certificate, but he exists enough to be arrested on a trumped-up charge . . .'

'It's a very sorry story,' said the lawyer, 'but how can you be so convinced that he's been framed?'

'Daniel is the gentlest person,' she snapped at him, but smiled immediately, cushioning the impact of her anger. 'And that's the story of Daniel.'

The telephone rang. 'Hello,' she answered, gripping the receiver between her head and shoulder and reaching for a pen. 'Yes, I've got

147

the bail money right here. Tell her to come in and fetch it. Goodbye.'
Her brown eyes almost looked right through Josef. 'This woman's
husband was arrested for theft . . . we've got bail.'

'Where do you get the money? It's not your own, surely?'

'Oh no, we get donations from overseas.'

'You're a saint!' he burst out. 'Do you get paid for doing this? If
I may ask . . .'

'You may,' she laughed. 'Yes. I draw a small salary; I have no other
income. And I'm no saint. There're lots of people like me, like the
ones you met last night. University's in vacation now so I can be
here all day. During term I come in the afternoons, after lectures. I
love the work,' she added, pretending to be apologetic.

'What are you studying?'

She raised her cup, sipped, pulled a face. 'It's cold,' she grumbled,
then replied. 'I'm studying social work. What else would I do?'

'What else indeed,' he repeated. 'It's so easy for you. Your whole
background, everything you've done, everything you are, all rein-
force your position in this role. You *are* involved, you didn't have
the choice . . .' He caught her smiling at him curiously, realised how
high her cheekbones were, could not establish what it was about her
features that bewitched him — each taken individually was unre-
markable. What combinations found favour with that deep judge
which determines whom we shall love and whom not? He faltered
for a moment as he felt that she was playing with him, a cat with a
mouse (in these games of love and politics, the lawyer was new, raw).

' . . . For me, the choices have been difficult. I've had to reassess all
of my relationships. My wife is scared,' (he did not say: "and on the
point of leaving me"), 'my partner has read me the riot act. He believes that if the Government is overthrown by the people, there'll
be a harsh military rule, worse than anything that's happening now.
He foresees tanks in the streets . . .'

'But there *is* a harsh military rule,' she cut in. 'There *are* tanks in
the streets of the townships.'

'He means in the streets of Eisstad. If power is given over, he sees
a radical change, a very uncomfortable transition for us. He's not
interested in the people suffering now . . .'

'Josef,' she said softly as if she were placating a child, 'Josef. The
man is paranoid. Of course no one knows what will happen. But
this can't go on. You know this can't go on. That's why you've
decided to do something. That's why you've decided to defend
William Ngo.'

'It can go on,' he wanted to say to her. 'In a modern industrialised state, unless there's a mutiny by the armed forces, the Government can keep an insurrection down for ever. You're naïve and idealistic if you believe otherwise. Perhaps I am a more astute politician than you are!' Instead he asked: 'You know that I'm defending William?'

'It's in all the newspapers,' she answered. 'Why didn't you tell me last night?' He shrugged, and she, possibly interpreting his gesture as modesty, said: 'It's a very brave choice.'

'But I'm dragging others into it: my family, my firm. Others might get hurt because of my choice; that's what I'm worried about.' Did he want her to release him from his obligation, for her to say: 'No, Josef, you can't risk their lives. Don't do it.'? Is that why he had come to her? To have her take his responsibility away from him, his free choice?

'I used to be a good lawyer,' he said. 'I used to fight to the death. When I'd leave the arena, my opponents' blood would be dripping. But now I'm crippled with doubt. I've grown old and tired . . .' He rubbed his eyes. 'The omens are against me. On my way to you, it rained out of a sky that was clear only moments before. I saw a dead rat in a gutter . . . I'm not superstitious . . .' He pressed his hands together beneath his chin, a gesture simulating prayer. 'I'm sorry to burden you with these things,' he said bitterly. 'You're the only one who seems to understand.' Perhaps the freshness of her idealism appealed to him.

'Talk, I'll listen,' she said gently.

'Yes, I suppose you will,' he blurted out harshly. 'You have to at the Advice Bureau.'

She was too professional to be flustered by his sudden change of mood. 'I'll listen because I like you, not because I have to,' she said. 'Talk if you want to.' She did not stutter when she was dealing with clients.

The telephone rang. She answered it. 'Yes, tell her to come and see me when she gets off work,' she said.

He stood up. 'I must go. You're busy. You've listened to me long enough.'

She walked after him. 'I'm going away for the weekend,' she said. 'Camping up the coast with some friends. I'll be back by M nday. Here's my telephone number. Call me if you need to talk.'

'Yes, I will,' he said, accepting the note. He stuffed it into his pocket.

Outside, the clouds had begun to disperse, and he walked back to his office deep in thought, reflecting on the vulnerability that had made him turn on her, and the fact that he had still not told her that he loved her. He felt betrayed because she was going away, and wildly jealous of her friends, even though he recognised that she owed no allegiance to him. He bought the noon edition of the *Evening Times* and sat in his office, with instructions to Julia not to interrupt him, reading during the lunch hour.

CHAIN-PROTEST WOMEN ELECT TO GO TO JAIL. The women had appeared in court the previous day and had pleaded not guilty to contravening Section 48(1) of the Public Safeties Act. However, after evidence was heard, they were convicted and sentenced to twenty-five dollars or ten days. Declaring that they refused to pay money to an unjust system, they elected to spend the ten days in jail. Their attitude was welcomed by the FDF whose spokesman (unnamed as usual) said it was time that more of the people of Eisstad took such stands 'against oppression'. An editorial in the newspaper praised the women for their courage. Two more instant heroes, Josef thought.

Besides the obvious follow-up to the Buth story, another item was of interest: a magistrate and a prosecutor (unnamed also) had resigned from the Department of Justice rather than administer an unjust set of laws. Idly, Josef wondered if the beggar in the doorway had prayed for him. If he had, the prayers had brought nothing but far more heartache.

In the evening after work the carpenter was sitting in his van outside Josef's house, waiting. 'You've got a pretty good watchdog there,' Mark said. 'He was barking the minute I opened the gate.'

He didn't stop them hanging a dead cat from my doorpost, the lawyer thought. He asked: 'Why didn't you go in?'

'No one's home.'

For the second night in a row when he arrived home from work both Dorothy and Robert were out! Had Robert regressed to the viking-state, roaming the streets looking for trouble? And where was Dorothy? Her husband could not imagine.

Josef opened the front door and dropped his briefcase as Lex almost bowled him over, simultaneously trying to welcome his master and bark at the carpenter. Mark took refuge hurriedly outside, and Josef called the dog into the bathroom. As Lex had not decided that keeping the workman at bay was a priority, he followed, ecstatic at the attention he was receiving. Josef closed the door on the dog and let the carpenter in.

'Sorry about that. Do you want something to drink?'

'A glass of water will be fine.'

While Mark was installing the bolts, Josef studied his workman's hands, compared them to his own. Would the carpenter be able to repel a physical attack that much more efficiently than he? And had the lawyer been reduced to his brother's level: considering expression through physical violence, like children in a playground, the strongest dominating?

'There you are, Mr S.'

'Thank you, Mark. Will you send your account to my office?'

'Yes sir.' He put down the empty glass, wiped his mouth on his sleeve. 'Give my regards to Mrs S.'

'I will. Goodbye.'

'How long have you been married?' Josef wanted to ask as he let the workman out. 'Do you still love your wife enough to kiss her?' But the gate clicked shut, the car was started, the man was gone: the lawyer's questions were left unspoken. Unanswered.

On his release from the bathroom, Lex leaped on his master, lavishing Josef with spit. 'Come on,' the lawyer said, impulsively. 'I'm going to take you up the mountain.'

He hung his jacket over a chair and pulled on a jersey. Lex's excitement at the treat bubbled over into unmanageable joy. In the car he was on Josef's lap, slobbering against the windows, steaming the windscreen with his hot breath, barking at every dog he saw in the street. Josef did not try to control him.

A few cars were parked in the lot on the Leeukop, perhaps belonging to visitors of Albert Poynter. Josef stopped near the path that led up the face of the mountain. He opened the car door and Lex hurtled out like a missile expelled from the cannon. More sedately, the master followed. Clouds billowed round the head of the mountain as if the lion were breathing fire.

The path stretched upward before him, seeming to go on forever. He could not think what had prompted him to come to this desolate place. A cold wind sprang up suddenly and the dog howled somewhere ahead, swallowed by the bushes that the dusk had painted black. Perhaps Lex had scented something dangerous, perhaps the last lion, settling down in its cave for the night, not expecting to be disturbed. Josef heard a rustling in the bushes behind him and he turned sharply to be confronted by the clown-face of a guinea-fowl, which, when it realised that it was exposed,

151

fled back into the undergrowth. The cold was cutting into his cheeks, leaving red weals, and his fingers became clawed. He understood, too late, how ill-prepared he was for this pilgrimage, but he could not go back. Stones gave way beneath his feet: he had to concentrate as hard on the path ahead as on the walk itself. He maintained a fast pace; if he walked quickly enough, he could keep the cold from cramping his knees. Soon he came to a section of the path where mist began to curl down the mountain like a raging torrent, a ghostly fall of freezing air, going nowhere. The cold smell of the mist was the prehistoric smell of swamps and caves. He stopped for a minute and looked down to his right, at the sea. It lay flat and grey as if it had been beaten into submission: a sullen monster waiting for a change of wind to raise it into the fury of which it was capable: the comparison to the situation in the country was so striking that Josef S turned quickly away and continued his walk. The dog had vanished into the mist and only muffled sounds indicated that it was still on the earth, had not been spirited off into space. And then Josef S entered the eerie, silent world inside the cloud. The confusion in his mind drove his legs with a strength that he would not have believed possible. Margaret's face haunted him: it seemed to hang before his eyes, on the surface of every rock, reflected by the white glare. The face was beautiful to him: it possessed a deep caring, a limitless compassion, and he was infinitely sorry that he had left her office so abruptly. But he could not have reacted in any other way.

Another rustle brought his mind back to the present. He saw thick animal hindquarters bounding off into the bushes. Some creature, brown or red, had been disturbed by the man and his dog. It could not have been the legendary lion. Surely the King of Beasts would not have fled like that. In the disguising mist, he could have taken his revenge for the elimination of his fellows, and there would have been no witnesses. The dog . . . where was the dog?

'Lex!' he called into the mist. 'Lex!' But his words were sucked by the malevolent whiteness: there was not even an echo to reassure him. The dog had no conception of its own size; it was a fighting machine possessing no fear; it would attack anything. Desperately, he willed it to barrel out of the bushes at him, wet from the mist. Instead, he nearly fell over the rotting carcase of a small buck whose legs stuck out stiffly from the dark mass that had once been its body. He made out a backbone which seemed too big for the thin legs and tiny hooves before he plunged on, more fearful than ever.

The path was crossed at various points by rivulets, streams coming down from the mountain, making the black rocks glisten as though they had been oiled. Somewhere, he heard the splashing of a water-fall: the afternoon rain had created new stream beds, new falls, where water-slides burst over ledges. As he ascended, he saw, through a gap in the cloud, a place where the wind drove the water back up-hill, over the grey scrub that clung impossibly to the sheer rock face, as if gravity had been turned upside-down. Josef S stood, soberly, in awe of this great wilderness to which he had such ready access. Ten minutes' drive from his house, a few minutes' walk, and he was in a primeval place where, it appeared, no other human had gone before. All around him was a whiteness of a misleading quality: one moment it was so dense as to be impenetrable; the next, the shield became transparent and he could see for some distance. Sometimes, the mist took on a drab, dirty grey colour; others, when it caught a rare beam of sunlight, it shone and Josef S was blinded by its brightness. In his wonder at these diverse faces, he had almost forgotten the cold, which now clamped its tight grip afresh on his bare lawyer's hands and bent his fingers further into a position resembling birds' claws.

'Lex!' he called again. No answering yelp, no heavy movement from the mist. He had to go on, as cold as he had become. The cloud shimmered in front of him. Now the path was open like a corridor lined by walls of mist, now it was blocked as though a door had suddenly dropped into place and he could go no further. And yet, by wading through this door, he was stepping into another reality altogether, where the air was white, where the sea below did not exist. He entered a white chamber. It was absolutely silent: the wind was not permitted to enter; traffic noises, which he had been able to hear before, suddenly ceased; there was not even the sound of water. The path climbed ever upward, the angle was steeper than ever, the higher he went, the further he had to go and the more dif-ficult it became. The cold, wet air stuck in his lungs: he was breath-ing in pellets of water. The dog could have been anywhere. That bounding beast could have pounced on it, torn out its tame throat with wild jaws, left the mark of the wilderness on its civilised coat, accustomed to soft couches in living-rooms. If he did not bring it back . . . Why had he been foolish enough to take it in the first place? To left and right the air was solid as walls, and he could see only a short distance ahead: his chamber moved with him, an inch at a stumbling time, up the mountain. From his searing throat, burning with the cold, he heard the cry: 'Lex!' repeated again and again. The word was absorbed into the padding of the walls but could progress no further; it was lost in successive layers of cloud.

By chance (or was it decreed?), the mist cleared to Josef's right and he saw the dog: a thick white lump lying in the bushes. A shrieking caught in his ears like the wind snagging on the branches of a dead tree. Lex must have dropped from the ledge above, blinded by the mist, trying to find his master. Perhaps he had slipped on a loose stone or skidded on a wet rock face, and, clumsy to the last, broken his neck ten feet below. Josef began to edge across the steep mountain face towards the body. He had an obligation to bring it back: he could not go home to Dorothy empty-handed; he could not leave Lex to rot in the open like the buck he had seen earlier. He was not sad, but numb with shock and cold. The ground was slippery as he left the path, as his lawyer's shoes sought footholds on the sharp stones. And he had no idea how high up he was because the mist was not only his walls; it was also the floor and the ceiling. And there was the dog, head twisted at an angle that was wrong, the tongue that used to leave its wet imprint on him when he came home from work now drying, and Dorothy, reproaching him for killing that which was dearest to her. His numb fingers could not grip properly, the chill went right through his jersey and affected his co-ordination. He had never liked the dog much: was it worthwhile risking his life to retrieve the corpse? But he had to, for Dorothy's sake.

He reached the animal after what seemed like hours of skating over a treacherous surface, but could not have been more than a minute. The proximity of death made him feel unclean and the death of something linked so closely to him in so remote a place generated a conflict: at the same time he wanted to leave it where it was and wash his hands of the whole affair, yet he needed to bring it back as a matter of duty to the heart of his family where proper last rites could be administered. He felt that he ought to experience sadness, and was disappointed to recognise in himself no more than disgust at his obligation to be intimate with death. Weren't parents supposed to clutch their dead offspring to their breasts, hugging the corpse? Perhaps if it were a child . . . but there would be no children. Certainly not with Dorothy.

He stood over the dead dog, and recoiled. Something had killed Lex: a red slash ran like a furrow across his face. Could it have been delivered by the swipe of a massive claw which gouged open the skin to expose the bone? Josef looked round nervously, but there was nothing to be seen, only the floating walls of mist. There was no noise, no angry grunt of a lion launching itself to attack. He bent down and tried to pick the dog up. But his foot slipped, sending loose stones down the slope and he thrust himself back against the mountain, grabbing onto bushes while he regained his balance. His breath came in quick gasps as he contemplated what might have been. He did not even know how far he would have fallen because he could see nothing below him. Gingerly, he took hold of one of the dog's back legs, and pulled. Never co-operative in life, Lex was not too willing to oblige in death. He moved grudgingly, snagging on stones and on the branches of low bushes while his master edged backwards towards the path, expecting to be knocked off the mountain at any moment by some hungry beast determined to reclaim its meal. How he dragged the dog to the path, he did not know.

When, later, he tried to recall those few minutes, in which he must have been clinging to a steep slope, attached, it seemed, only by the weight of the dog, he could remember nothing. All he remembered was the urgency to get off the mountain before its destructive forces overwhelmed him.

The lion, symbol of human cruelty and war, of human aggression, lived in flesh or spirit on the mountain that bore its name. The War Gods, fed by army and popular resistance alike, had taken up residence on the Leeukop. They sat and exulted, growing fat, as the humans on the plain below carried out their directives. These cruel gods had killed the dog, which was called Lex, as a joke to show the lawyer in what contempt they held his fragile system of law: human civilisation was their enemy and they used the lion, their symbol, to destroy its niceties.

Josef S saw these things as he carried the corpse of his dog down the mountain, fleeing from the mocking laughter of the War Gods. He realised that by rejecting Foster's offer, he had elected not to join those twisted deities and consequently he had become their enemy. They had summoned him into their stronghold to give him a taste of their power, to warn that they would defeat him in the end, that reason would not prevail in the Republic, and that those working for reason would be swept aside by the mighty paw of their agents. As the lawyer stumbled out of the mist with the body of the dog in his arms, crooked like a shepherd's carrying a lamb, he heard a shrieking in the bushes, the shrieking of a bird or animal in distress

155

like the shrieking in his dreams. A dead weight, a slashed face, a trickle of blood at the mouth, hair smelling of wet washing: these were the impressions that Josef S had, lurching down the mountain to the parking lot, to the shelter of his car.

She was waiting for him when he walked in. She had the front door open and the lights on: she could have been the angel waiting at the gates of heaven, or the other one guarding the place below. The dog lay in his arms like a bag of cement. Am I destined to walk up and down this path carrying dead animals? he wondered.

The tiredness wore him down so that the journey into his house took on gargantuan proportions. He was entering a furnace, lit by fires over which his wife had control. She whipped them into creation, driving them to a frenzy until they would burst out of the house and engulf him. She stood in silhouette so that he could only see her black shape and not her features.

'The dog is dead,' he said to her. 'Lex is dead.'

She did not speak: there was a terrible silence. It stretched from her form to his; it was the darkest place in the world, even darker than the Leeukop on this night of storms. Tentatively, he approached her, step by step, trying to retrieve some of the lost ground; trying, by covering a distance in space, to recover what time and neglect had destroyed.

'Josef,' she said from the threshold, 'I want to tell you personally why I'm leaving . . .'

'Dorothy . . .' He stood quite still, the dog clutched in his embrace like a dead lover whom he was trying to bring home.

'I believe you're seeing another woman,' she said, holding a piece of paper in her sharp fingers. 'I found Margaret's telephone number in your jacket.'

'I can explain . . .' he began, mildly perplexed as to why he was bothering. Was it not all leading to this anyway? Had he not fallen in love with Margaret as a substitute, already preparing himself for this inevitable confrontation? Whatever reasons she produced now were only symptoms of the failure of the marriage. If it were not these, she would have found others: why even try to answer them? He lowered the dog onto the path before her like a sacrifice.

'Despite my opposition, you've taken that case, and I wish to receive no more death threats on your behalf.' A suitcase waited for her in the hall. She lifted it, and began to walk towards him. 'And now you've killed my dog.'

He backed away from her. 'I didn't kill the dog!' he wanted to scream at her. '*They* did, on the mountain!' But all he could say was: 'Where will you go?'

In the street, a car idled. 'I'm going with Robert,' she answered. 'He has been very kind to me, and supportive. All you've done is push me away. I care for him very much.' She did not look at Josef as she skirted the dog and walked down the pathway, a refugee, suitcase in hand. 'What must I do with Lex?' he wanted to shout after her. 'Don't you want him?' The gate closed with a finality that he thought he would never hear, let alone survive. A car door slammed. And she retreated into the night with his brother.

The dog was buried; his wife and brother were gone. Josef walked on the promenade beside the sea, opposite the still-sleeping blocks of flats. The mountain showed a docile face: the War Gods were invisible or had left as well, the clouds had been folded away by the dawn. Once again, it was a bland impersonal hump of rock that had witnessed three centuries of Eisstad's history from its immortal security. The sea was as flat as a mirror: a row of black rocks echoed dangerously just below its surface. A jogger ran past him, a woman, smelling of a similar perfume to the one that Dorothy used. Josef avoided looking at her, and stared out to sea. A boat on the water belched a trail of smoke, seaweed floated in tangles inside the rock pools, a long black shape swam by and then disappeared. Was it a shadow? Or a dream? A yacht was out there, its mast stripped as bare as a tree in winter.

He could not remain in his house; the desolation drove him away. He could not bear to be surrounded by the familiar objects: the white plates, kitchen utensils, the pictures on the walls, her toothbrush which she had left behind. Her demure, girlish smile teased his imagination, the green eyes and shock of red that had once attracted him. Even though love was gone, dependencies had been created: the old comfortable relationship, worn as a blanket, had been discarded and he stood naked and alone. He contemplated the abyss of the sea, the black rocks as dangerous as the dark side of the psyche. A vision of absolute aloneness came over him, a desolation mirrored by the cold sea, blue-grey in the chill fragile morning. The blanket was off and the cold came rushing in with a force that suddenly left him breathless and weak, despite the protection of his overcoat, so that he had to lean against the railing and recover. He stood, gaping into the abyss, as a man might stand on a

157

platform overlooking a railway track while a train rushes headlong towards the spot where he intends to throw his body, hoping that his act of abandon will free his troubled consciousness from its torment: he demands relief in oblivion. Josef S stood before the pit, as his father might have done when his wife was killed, before escaping into the silent tapping of his typewriter, until even that silence could provide no further peace and his train was a bullet in the head. But the son had been expecting this, even encouraging it, and, as he stared into the depths, as the panic clouded his reason, he summoned his ghosts to him.

'How did you manage for so long after your wife died,' he asked, 'when I, who drove mine away, am facing this despair?' The sound of wavelets beating softly on the beach had the same monotony as the ticking of the keys, which was the music that used to put him to sleep at nights. 'Are we genetically programmed, father, you and I, to lose our wives? And what about Robert?' But he knew nothing about Robert: the State had seen to that. 'Is he really sleeping with Dorothy? Then how can she be so indignant at me? How long were they at it behind my back, how long did Robert secretly watch my movements, unable to face me out of jealousy and guilt? Did I drive my wife into the arms of my brother?' A sea-bird screeched, indicating that life was returning to the world; the bird was as white as the hair of the man who had shuffled into the house, night after night, to his bottle and his typewriter. 'How can I know so little of those who are closest to me?'

An old man walked slowly across the promenade. From a plastic packet he scattered breadcrumbs on the ground. Within seconds, a flock of gulls and pigeons had surrounded him: wings rustled dryly as overcoats. He held out his hand, palm flat, offering a crust, and a gull settled its sharp beak within a millimetre of flesh, removing the gift. For a while, the man watched the activity he had set in motion, then he adjusted his hat and returned to his car. Josef turned back to the sea and heard him drive away.

'Perhaps I'll be able to grow in new ways, and she too can grow . . .' he thought despairingly.

Suddenly a wind came in from the sea; it carried the smell of fish as heavy as stone, so rich that it stopped up his nostrils and made him gag. He disentangled himself from the rails, walked, skirting the edge of the gulf that yawned before him: the sea was viscous as blood, the rocks as sharp as razors.

'I drove her to go,' he said incredulously. 'I could have told her that I loved her, I could have lied to keep her . . .'

A shape, attached like a fungus to the side of a toilet wall, managed to remove itself and lurched towards him. He recoiled at the ugliness of the face: a meths-drinker deformed by her habit. He tried to step out of the way, but in his daze, in his stupefaction at the events that were rolling into one another, gathering momentum until they knocked him off-balance, he stumbled and collided with the woman. For an instant, he gasped at an indiscribable stench, the stink of ravage and disease: from the abyss, sent by the War Gods, this thing which had lost its humanity clawed at him. He saw, dimly, the apparition insert its thumb into the vagina created by its first two fingers, and grin at him. 'Wanna fuck?' the lips said, and the voice carried the tone of the depths. He pushed her away as he had pushed the hanging cat that had sunk its claws into his coat, and she sprawled on the ground, grinning all the while. Appalled at the violence of his reaction, he stood above her as she lay on her back and, in a mockery of intimacy, lifted her skirt. He ran from her as though the devil were chasing him.

From home, he called his office to report that he was sick but would be in later. So my practice is going to hell, he thought. Who cares? The people will have to support me with all their overseas funding. When no one answered, he remembered that it was Saturday.

He lay on his unmade bed, staring at the ceiling. She would not share the bed again. And who could blame her? After a while, he forced himself to get up and walk to the kitchen where the new shiny bolt smiled at him, making fun of his attempt to protect her. If he looked through the window, he could see the upturned earth where the dog was buried beneath the fig tree. He had worked as if drunk after she left, in the daze that followed the realisation of her absence. Some part of him knew that the animal had to be disposed of, another part performed the ceremony, turning the hard earth as if the challenge to his muscles would help his state of mind. If he had been tired from his rigours on the mountain, he had not known it. He had worked mechanically, shovelling as a stoker in an engine room, until he had dug a hole deep enough to put the extinguished fire into.

He reached for the bottle of gin that had appeared somehow, tempting, half-empty (had it not been full the night before?); his hand moved as if it had a will of its own, towards the bottle. The cool, clear liquid promised relief. His fingers folded around the

159

smooth glass, and he drew it closer. It scraped on the table-top, he shut his eyes, and then pushed the bottle away. 'No.' He shook his head. 'No!'

There was a knock at the front door.

'Dad, is that you?' he asked quietly.

The knock was repeated: he went to answer. The shy young girl who stood outside turned away from the unkempt face that peered suspiciously at her. 'Have I become so vile?' he asked, but she did not understand.

'Collecting . . .' she ventured, now looking at him because he had spoken, but avoiding his eyes. Did she wish to run from this monster she had called forth unwittingly? Did she fear it would reach out a bony hand and drag her into its lair? But perhaps she saw worse monsters in the place she came from for she dared to thrust a small black book at him, stamped with the name of a church. He snatched the book with ragged impatient fingers, opened it, saw that Mrs Milner had given five dollars. Was she buying peace from God?

'Here.' He fed a crumpled note into the book's hungry jaws — the denomination did not matter — and pulled back his hand before he was bitten. She mumbled thanks and returned the book to her pocket. Distressed as he was, he wondered if the money would ever reach the Church coffers. He slammed the door behind her and shouted: 'This has become a nation of beggars!' He heard the gate click as she let herself out and he went back to the kitchen. There the gin bottle enticed him, like a pagan God, from the altar where he had left it. Again he was tempted, again he stretched for the lure of impermanent oblivion.

'Dad,' he whispered, 'dare I?' And he saw the old man, at his desk, sitting behind the typewriter with a bottle in his hand, trying to focus on the teenaged boy who had surprised him at his 'work'. 'How many bottles did you put away, Dad?' he sobbed, and the old man scratched his head because he had no idea. Tired fingers clutched the bottle's comfort: glass, whereas they only wanted to touch flesh. Red eyes wept at the boy, and the old man said: 'Don't destroy yourself, my son, as I did. I had no other comfort . . .'

'Dad, don't!' Josef S cried and swept the bottle to the floor. It crashed against the wall and died in a wash of glass and liquid. 'Christ, what am I doing?' he asked.

He walked through the house, leaving the mess in the kitchen. He inspected the contents of the lounge: wooden kist, thick cream sofa, the fireplace, the bookcase with its books and bowls, heavy white curtains. It was a comfortable room but it offered him no comfort at all. The objects which had been pleasing, or at least neutral, to the eye when things were going well, when Dorothy was there, when he was not distressed, had become beasts: perspectives changed. Husband and wife had chosen styles together, and colours, during the years of their marriage, and to what end?

'Dad, was I too scared to love her because I saw what grief did to you? Did I drive her away, creating the situation that I feared most?'

Another knock on the door. 'Christ,' he said, 'it's a wonder she ever wrote anything if she was disturbed like this.' He stalked to the door and flung it open, expecting another beggar, about to exclaim: 'Go away and leave me to my misery!' But the woman had not come to beg. She smiled at him: 'Is Dorothy at home?' she asked cheerfully. She was chubby and listed like a ship taking water.

'No,' he said desperately, but his voice must have been too faint because she adjusted the volume of her hearing-aid and looked at him quizzically. 'No,' he repeated.

She extended her hand and automatically he took it. 'Hello Mr S,' she said. 'I am Iris Milner, your next door neighbour. I came to visit your wife.'

'You won't find her here,' he wanted to say. 'Go and scour the cheap hotels. Ask for a young viking and his mistress, his brother's wife. Somewhere on the beachfront perhaps.' He said: 'She's out.' But Iris Milner showed no signs of going away, and when the impasse became embarrassing, he invited her in.

'Thank you.' The old woman hobbled rather than walked, unpredictable in body: he feared she might lose control completely and collapse. She did not appear to be put off by his wild look and staring eyes, his stubble and drab grey overcoat, shadow of his father. Blind to the air of chaos that he exuded, she entered his house. 'Isn't it funny,' she said too loudly, 'that we've lived next door for so many years, but never met?'

'I suppose so,' he agreed. 'I work a lot . . . Come into the lounge.' She sat on the sofa. 'Do you want tea?' he asked. What was he going to do with her?

'Thank you,' she said, and then: 'You must be very proud of Dorothy.'

'Why?' he stammered.

'Her book, of course,' the woman beamed. 'You men are so involved in your business that you neglect your wives.' How much had Dorothy told her? What was she doing here? Did she know all

161

about him?

'Yes, of course, her book,' Josef echoed.

'You know, until your brother came to stay, I was worried about Dorothy,' Iris Milner said. 'She was so alone, so lonely, so sad.' Was there condemnation in her voice?

'She's close to Robert,' Josef offered.

'Oh yes, she's much happier now. I come and talk to her quite often; we have a lot in common. Now I'm not blaming you, please understand, but I do think you should take better care of her. Being a writer, she's a very sensitive woman. I am used to living alone: my husband is dead.'

'Oh, I'm sorry . . .'

'He's been gone for many years, but even while he was alive I never saw much of him. And I coped very well. I'm much more self-sufficient than Dorothy.'

Needing to escape, he said: 'Let me get the tea.'

When he returned (having avoided the broken glass in the kitchen without attempting to move it), she was sitting in the same position, as if she had been switched off and only reactivated by his entry. He carried a tray on which were a teapot, two teacups, a milkjug and a bowl of sugar. How unusual, he thought, that I should be entertaining Dorothy's friends, that I am being this domestic. But he would have to get used to it: no one else would get his food for him now. What would she say, he wondered, if I told her that Dorothy had gone off with my brother? Would she sympathise with me? But he could not tell her. She poured the tea.

'My husband was a doctor,' she informed him. 'He worked in the Northern Territories for forty years until he retired. I was born in the city, but I soon got used to the solitude. I was alone a lot, especially when my husband went away for days at a time on calls.' She seemed to have forgotten the point she was making and had become immersed in her reminiscences. 'I pity people who have never lived in the country . . . It was all so beautiful,' she said wistfully. 'I used to go out into the desert to paint. I loved the colours. I've got all of my paintings still . . .' But Josef did not accept the implied offer. '. . . Sometimes lions would come to the dam to drink. You know,' she confessed, 'I do miss lions.'

After the events of the previous night, Josef could not admit to any similar longing: the mysterious death of the dog had left him with very little affection for lions. He remained silent. What possible answer could he give to such statement? He wished that the woman would go: he could not understand her.

'Which is why I support Dr Foster,' she continued after a pause. 'Although Dorothy disagreed with me . . .'

'You support Foster?' he echoed, dumbfounded.

'He's a darling man,' she said. 'I'm with him all the way.'

He was too tired and self-absorbed to argue with her: she was as unpredictable in mind as in her unco-ordinated body. Any argument would be a fruitless exercise. 'Good,' he mumbled, passing his hand over his eyes. At least Dorothy had some sense . . .

'I even wrote to the newspaper,' she said proudly, dropping her head back and addressing the ceiling, 'and they published my letter.'

'You wrote under the initials of I.M.?' he asked. 'That was your letter?'

She nodded, smiling mischievously, like a child allowing him to share a secret. 'I didn't give my full name of course because I'm a retiring person . . . I didn't want the publicity.'

'I have such a revolutionary neighbour,' Josef murmured.

'I wouldn't have told you if I didn't know that you're a bit of a radical yourself,' she chuckled.

'But I'm not,' he protested. 'I'm not at all. I simply want to have justice served. I want to give William Ngo the best, possibly the only, chance he'll get. Does that make me a "radical"?'

'In this place, at this time, it puts you close to it,' she answered, sipping her tea. 'By the way, what d'you think of our friend's disappearance?'

'She hasn't disappeared,' he said, still reeling from the shock of discovering that this chatty woman, whom he had rejected as one of Eisstad's blinkered majority, was politically more extreme than he. He bit back his words. 'Who?' he corrected himself. 'Who's disappeared?'

'Haven't you heard the news?' she asked from the perspective of one who lives alone, for whom the radio is the principal companion, and who expects that everyone is in the same position.

'What news? No I've not listened to a radio for days: they're always playing that ghastly music.'

'Mourning the departed President,' she said sweetly. 'So you don't know that Dr Foster has disappeared.'

Iris Milner's visit was becoming a succession of surprises. 'But I saw him yesterday! He came to ask my advice . . .'

'And what did you tell him?' She put down her cup with a determined tinkle.

'I told him not to be stupid, and he walked out, threatening . . .'

'Well he's done it,' she said. 'Or claims to, in any event.'

'Done what? What has that madman done?'

'He claims to have set a lion loose on the mountain, and now they've cordoned it off and sent in the army. They've got soldiers looking under every bush. Isn't it all ridiculous? Listen, you can hear the helicopters.' She fumbled again with her hearing-aid.

'Lex!' He said, seeing again the red slash on the dog's face, the broken neck, the hindquarters bounding away into the mist.

'Excuse me?'

'When did he release that lion?'

'Nobody knows if he actually has,' she cautioned. 'No one knows anything, except that he's vanished'.

'Well his bloody lion might have killed my dog,' Josef snarled, and almost added: 'And put the last straw on the camel's back which was my marriage,' although he knew that the marriage was over long before the dog slipped down the side of the mountain, for whatever reason. Now that his attention was drawn to them, he heard the helicopters. The warriors had gone to pay homage to their masters on the Leeukop. 'That'll give the bastards something to do other than harass funerals.' She was frowning — either she had not heard, or she had not understood — but the lawyer was in no mood to explain. 'Maybe the press will forget about me now they've got lions to chase,' he continued, and then turned to his visitor; he feared suddenly that she would ask about the dog. Or give him more advice about Dorothy. 'I'm sorry, but I'm feeling ill,' he said. 'I must rest.'

'Yes, of course,' she answered, peering into the cup to see if any tea was left. Then she stood. 'Please tell your wife that I came to say hello.' She waved a warning finger. 'And remember to treat her well. Dorothy deserves the best.'

Well she got Robert, he thought, the soldier. Was that the best she could do? 'Thank you for your concern,' he said, ushering the woman out as quickly as she could hobble. 'I'll tell Dorothy when next I see her.' If this answer was mystifying, Iris Milner gave no indication that she was unsatisfied.

Outside, the helicopters buzzed around the hive of the mountain, eager to serve. Josef caught a bus into town: it was impossible to endure the ghosts in his house. The headlines screamed: 'I RELEASED LION ON MOUNTAIN': FOSTER. They must be selling a lot of newspapers these days, Josef thought unkindly. There hasn't been so much news for years.

164

He had not changed his clothes since colliding with the woman on the beachfront and he was sure that they carried her stench; that it had rubbed off on him. He saw the Supreme Court through a mist, and, like a drunk, he stood, swayed, and studied the building which had given him his living.

'While you were drinking yourself to death, my dear father, while you were hiding behind the flimsy protection of that typewriter, I was putting myself through law school so I could get married and support a wife, so I could build a future for myself that would be different from the life you'd condemned yourself to. But I've given it up, I'm afraid. I've inherited your desire for self-destruction; I studied your morbid self-obsession too carefully. How can I love when I had no instruction in love? My yearning for Margaret Spears is no closer to love than the cold bridge that joined me to Dorothy.' His hands were shoved deeply into the pockets of his father's over-coat. 'Is there any reason for me to continue going up those stairs with my gown over my shoulder? Is William Ngo to be my redemption?'

He looked at the facade of the familiar building as a stranger might have: the grey stone which he saw almost every day and which he did not notice. There were four pillars, two on either side of the massive wooden doors, a flight of eleven steps (he counted them), and the words: SUPREME COURT in brass, as polished as gold, fixed onto the wall. The Republic's flag fluttered half-mast, because of Buth's death, against the bright blue sky. Like the letters, the flag was gold. In its centre the crowned lion of the Republic's coat of arms reminded the citizens of the conquest that had given them a fatherland. If the Revolution succeeded, if the gold flag was torn down, if the yellow, red and green of the FDF went up in its place, would he still have a job? Would the present system of justice be retained in the New Republic? At least William Ngo is getting a fair hearing under this system, he thought. We haven't put him up against a wall and shot him out of hand. If the FDF was in power and Mkhize was President, and someone stuck a knife into him, would the assassin even have the formality of a trial? But Parry's words nagged in the back of his mind: 'The Ngo case is hopeless . . . He's going to swing.' How fair is any system of law which must protect the interests of the group which promulgated it? In fact isn't William Ngo simply being put up against a more sophisticated wall? Above the oak doors, a window in the shape of a half-moon created an impression of symmetry, of justice. Justice took up three storeys, with ten windows per storey allowing light into courtrooms and Judges' Chambers. If Mkhize was in power would he have enough trained bureaucrats from the townships to fill all that space?

A policeman wearing the blue fatigues of the riot police stood at the bottom of the steps, a submachine-gun slung over his shoulder. He eyed Josef S curiously as the lawyer scrutinised the building that he knew so well yet would not have been able to describe if asked to do so. Does he think I'm drunk? A potential saboteur, weighing up the pros and cons of an immediate attack, or assessing my future chances? A tourist, running out of money, living in seedy hotels? A lawyer, thrown by a most curious combination of circumstances into confusion? On innumerable mornings he has nodded me into court, cloaked in the protection of my black robes, while his companion body-searches the others seeking entry. But now he does not recognise the tramp in the stained grey overcoat, rambling and distracted, trying to find meaning by counting steps and windows.

But there was no meaning to be found in a policeman guarding a deserted building, and Josef wandered away in the direction of the cobbled square over which Gomez presided. On the way he bought a newspaper and cast his eye over the story of Foster's alleged escapades. 'They'll never find that lion,' Josef said to Gomez. 'Or Foster. They've gone forever. They've merged with the spirits on the mountain, who ensure that the civil war continues. My dog was not killed by a real lion: it was killed by an idea. Perhaps one day the FDF will put up a statue for Foster in your place, and proclaim him their visionary, the founder of the New Republic.' Or perhaps the lawyer had a hangover from drinking half a bottle of gin the night before.

5

Buth was being buried. The State-run media carried full coverage: ETV televised the funeral live, the radio broadcast a commentary. Josef did not watch or listen, even for the arguable satisfaction of following a dictator to the grave. The farm where Buth spent his childhood, the small cemetery where members of his family were buried, the arrival of the hearse, the Presidential Guard at attention, the Generals carrying the coffin, the propaganda that the Government commentators would wring from every possible aspect of the proceedings, exploiting public sentimentality: Josef imagined these things and avoided them. He even refused to buy the Sunday newspapers, and it was only from inadvertantly glancing at headlines that he learned that Clarke, who had been Buth's Minister of Education, had been named as his successor.

Perhaps because it was a day commemorating death (it was Mrs Idini's funeral as well), Josef decided to pay homage to his parents. The old cemetery was beside the coast in the industrial area to the north of Eisstad, overlooked ironically by Eisstad's hospital. But the former institution was not an inevitable next step from the latter: the cemetery was full, a memorial as dead as its inhabitants; the hospital could not supply it with any more customers. An overalled functionary, employed by the municipality, tended the cemetery, armed with a broom against the spirits of the restless.

Josef gave the man some money as he opened the iron gates. 'Are you looking after them well?' the lawyer asked.

The workman nodded. 'I brushed them off this morning. Gave them a good dust.'

'Good. I've brought some flowers.'

'I took the old ones away when they died,' the man volunteered. He leaned on his broom and complained. 'It's quiet here now. Only a few come to pay their respects these days. It's a shame. You've got to remember who went before,' he added piously and dabbed at the ground behind where Josef stood. He sighed. 'It's a shame.'

The lawyer nodded at him and walked briskly through the avenues of stones and crosses and angels. Sea sand covered the ground between the graves: it was blown in continuously by the wind, involving the cemetery attendant in a lifelong struggle to keep

167

it at bay. Josef's feet dragged in this soft material, this shifting sediment. By the time he got to the two stones, he was sweating, even though the sun was not particularly strong. His grey overcoat hung heavily on his shoulders, but he did not remove it. He reflected that no municipal attendants kept the Valhalla Cemetery in order.

An empty jar stood on each gravestone, clean but disreputable as a beggar. There was no alternative, however: vases could not be trusted; too pretty to remain in such a drab setting, they danced off at night to the music of a ghostly orchestra. Only empty jars were dull enough to stay. Josef divided the flowers he carried and put a bunch in each jar. The little festivals of colour immediately broke the harsh monotony of grey stone and white sand, and the dreariness of a horizon that contained only factories and the hospital. He knelt on the grave of his father and touched the stone.

'Where am I going?' he asked. 'I need guidance. Things are falling apart.' The wind swirled the sand around his feet and grit stabbed into his eyes. He rubbed where it burned and the burning intensified before it went away and he could see again.

A woman's face appeared to him, shy and proud, a slight smile touching the corners of her lips, a misty look in her eyes. She spoke, her mouth moved, but her son could not hear the words. And when he reached for her, she was not there. Instead, Josef saw a man sitting on her gravestone. Two boys stood before him. The elder held the younger by the hand and they watched the tears drip down the man's face into the dirt next to the grave, next to the flowers he had brought, as if he would make the desert bloom with his grief. The elder boy had sad eyes and he seemed to understand the sorrow, but the younger one was smiling. And then the tableau faded away and was replaced by a new once, consisting only of the boys, the elder grown to a man, standing beside the open grave of their father while clods of earth rained onto his coffin. The burning returned to Josef's eyes, a hot burning of loneliness as he knelt beside those desolate stones in the sand.

He walked slowly back to the entrance, past stone slabs and marble scrolls, past vaults like small cottages housing the more affluent dead, past an angel with ragged wings bestowing blessings no more effective than those conferred by the beggars of Eisstad. 'In loving memory of . . .' was repeated a thousand times. But who remembered? He took some comfort from the sight of the Leeukop: for a moment he considered that the mountain was the only stabilising factor in his life; it was omnipresent, it was the dark corner of the psyche populated by wild forces, it was a monument to constancy. You could reach out, touch it, and it would always be there, solid and mysterious, a paradox that helped to soothe the troubled mind. The sun was striking the mountain at such an angle that it glowed, and was difficult to look at, and no detail was visible; its glassy surface could afford no foothold for the War Gods which had despatched the dog and given notice that reason was not to be tolerated.

At the entrance, the attendant still leaned on his broom. 'See you next time,' he said. This place of death was his home; he was the custodian of an area which the living would rather forget. Perhaps he was a creation of the grief of the bereaved, a sponge collecting human misery. But he was not morbid or suffering; Josef knew that he projected his own pain onto the man.

'Please water the flowers,' the lawyer said, unconcerned that his eyes must have been red. He gave the attendant more money and the offering was secreted into an overall pocket somewhat cynically as if to say: 'You give me a tip to look after your dead. I am the keeper of your memories. I am Pluto, the guardian of your dead. While you come and go between the living world and this one, I have to remain here because it is my job. I am the one who dusts off the old bones of your ancestors, keeps them clean for your visits.' And then he might have added: 'But none of my people are buried here in your cemetery. Come the Revolution, my people will despoil these graves that I have spent a lifetime keeping clean. They will enter the tombs and rip open the caskets and fling the bones into a pile, mixing up ancestors so thoroughly that history will be irrevocably confused and chaos will rule. That is my prediction for this neat cemetery.' Instead, he commented with the knowing air of one who is in the business: 'They're planting Buth today.' His grin revealed an absence of front teeth which emphasised a wicked set of canines.

'Do you think he'll go to heaven?' Josef asked, thinking about William Ngo.

'Where's that?' Pluto winked, and then said: 'Heaven is a place where cooking pots full of fat are on the boil all the time.'

'Maybe the President will fall into one of them,' Josef suggested.

'Then it will no longer be heaven,' Pluto retorted, and opened the gate for the lawyer to leave.

The Abyss split the plain, snaking through it forever. A tall, frail figure stood at its lip and contemplated the pit as if he were seeking salvation in its depths. He jerked: the shrieking seemed to pass through him like an electric current, forcing him to dance to a painful tune. Josef was impelled towards the Abyss but he dragged his feet in the dust, his dread competing with the desire to hurl himself in, to be swallowed by those inviting jaws.

The mourners had dug their own pits in the sand, directed by a wild man, wearing the skins of a lion, who danced in the dust, thrusting a short spear repeatedly into the air. The wind pulled at the tufts of lion-hair that dangled from his shoulders like a mane. As the earth accepted the coffins, a bell tolled: 'Dolente, dolente.' The shrieking continued like a steady cloud cover. Above it, the peals of the bell rose up like two mountain peaks.

The tall figure at the ravine's edge who watched over the funeral wore a uniform the colour of the dust. He straightened as Josef drew nearer, but the lawyer could not yet see his face.

'Let's go, Mr S,' Ben said, peering round the door.

The lawyer spoke into his dictaphone: 'That will be all for now, Linda. Type the opinion in the Kerr matter so long and I'll do the pleadings when I get back.' He clicked the machine off and removed the cassette. 'I'll meet you at the front,' he told Ben. He took his jacket, a pen and a note-pad, looked around the office to see that everything was in order, smiled at the photograph of his wife that now stood on his desk, and gave the cassette to his secretary. At the reception desk he told Julia that he would be back before lunch.

'I'm so pleased the press aren't phoning you any more,' she confided. 'I was overcome with calls last week.'

'They've found other news.' He smiled. 'Lions on the mountain, Buth's funeral, the appointment of Clarke; they have no more time for a lawyer who won't talk to them.'

'Well I'm glad they've decided to leave you alone,' she said staunchly.

So am I, he thought. Imagine if they were to ferret out my domestic secrets: LAWYER'S DECISION TO TAKE NGO'S CASE CAUSES WIFE TO ELOPE WITH BROTHER! I would never live it down.

Outside, helicopters continued to search for Foster's lion, but with less hope every day of finding it. 'It's a hoax,' Ben said. He walked briskly, struggling to match the long strides of his employer. He carried a brown folder, marked: STATE v NGO.

'What is?' Josef asked, deep in thought. Despite his legal experience, he was uneasy. He had not been to the Tower since the early part of his career when he had cut his teeth on criminal work. Then he had routinely consulted with awaiting-trial prisoners, then the Tower had been an extension of his workplace. Now . . .

'That lion story,' said Ben. 'It's a hoax. Foster didn't let any lions loose.'

'You think or you know?'

'I'm sure. That's the talk in Valhalla. Some of the people say the man is mad, but the firebrands like him.' They continued to walk in silence, Ben breathing heavily from the strain of keeping up.

A young man with a shaven head stood outside a bookshop, looking in. He was too small for the age that his face betrayed: one of the township's malnourished children. Glassy eyes stared at the display of books in the window, fascinated by the pictures on the covers, hinting at worlds to which, Josef guessed, he had no access because he could not read. The boy flexed a leg (feet, disproportionately big for his small body, grew out of his blue tracksuit trousers, solid as hammers), and then loitered away, peering into dustbins as he went, with much the same intensity as he had gaped into the shop window.

'Almost there,' wheezed Ben in relief. A yellow mongrel fixed them with a baleful look as they entered its territory, the run-down eastern side of the city. It urinated against a fence, then slunk away.

'Out of breath?' Josef teased. 'You're half my age!' Would Margaret not be proud of him, going into battle on behalf of the oppressed, note-pad and pen tilted at the walls of the Tower that had become visible ahead?

'Yes,' said Ben, 'the teargas has made my asthma worse.'

Immediately, Josef slowed his pace. 'I didn't know you suffered from asthma.'

'It's not important.'

'Why d'you go out in the streets when there's teargas around?'

'It comes into my house. Some nights the soldiers drive up and down in their Leeus and put us to sleep with teargas, as they say. They pump it into the streets so that it lies there like smog and people can't go out. It makes my chest close up. But it's nothing.' Perhaps he saw the anger in Josef's eyes. 'Come,' he said. 'It's almost ten o'clock. We must be there on time.'

The Prison's facade consisted of a gaunt red clock tower, which marked off the time of those sentenced to waste their lives behind

171

the yellow steel doors. It hung over the street like a great, one-eyed bat. In deference to the Republic's sensitivities perhaps, the Prisons Department was attempting to ameliorate the harsh effect of the building. Gardeners, who were prisoners, hunched on their knees, unguarded, in servitude to the State. Why did they not fly away from the cage to which they would have to return at the end of their day's work? Their wings were clipped, they had been robbed of the courage to escape; defeated, they spent their days outside the bars until it was time for them to turn themselves in once more. They were imprisoning themselves, doing the State's work voluntarily. As if to mock this servility, two starlings gambolled past, rolling in pleasure at their freedom.

To either side of the facade, high grey walls extended, prettied by the work of the gardeners who had constructed rows of trees and beds of red and purple flowers; but the beauty only went as far as the walls and stopped there. Inside those walls there was the suspicion of drab horror. Josef's legs grew reluctant to ascend the eight steps that led from the street to the level on which was the door. No one stood on guard in the sentry-box, for who could have escaped the thick steel bonds, who could have slipped out of the half-moon windows (echoes of the window above the Supreme Court's door) blocked off by black bars, who could have scaled the fortress walls, to give a guard something to do. Certainly the tame gardeners needed no safe-keeping.

On the landing, Josef S turned and looked at the last sight that many had for a long time, of freedom: it was not inspiring. Two service stations, a block of council flats, a desperate office building with TO LET signs in the empty windows, and a desolate tennis court across the chipped surface of which the wind blew ice-cream wrappers and old newspapers. He shuddered, but Ben appeared to be unaffected: his breathing was even back to normal. They stood under the red clock tower with its tiny ineffectual lamp which could not have even begun to light the darkness. The Republic's gold flag fluttered from a flagpole next to the sentry-box.

'To think I used to visit this place without any qualms when I was young and innocent,' Josef said, trying to joke. 'I suppose those two women are locked up in here.'

Ben touched the lawyer's arm encouragingly, then rang the bell set in the wall beside the steel doors: an incongruous thing to do, as if they were visiting the house of friends on a Sunday afternoon for tea. A porthole opened and a fat cheerful face asked them what they wanted.

'We have a consultation with William Ngo,' Ben said, 'This is Counsellor S.'

'Come in,' as though the tea were poured, the cakes waiting on dainty plates. One of the doors slid open, admitting them, and sealed with the solid 'thunk' of a closing bank vault. The air seemed to be expelled before it and they were left inside the dark vacuum. A series of offices and rooms flanked a passage that led to a barred door. 'In here.' The warder, wearing the brown uniform of the prison services, showed them into a bare room containing a table, two chairs and a high barred window. The morning sun struggled to enter.

'I'll get him for you,' the big man said and melted away as the weak light fell on him.

'The Tower,' mused Ben as they waited. 'I've never been in the Tower before. I hope I never have to live here.' He laughed; the sound came out as sharply as a cough, puncturing Josef's tension. After fifteen minutes, no one had come and Ben looked at his watch. 'I arranged for ten,' he said apologetically.

'They keep you waiting,' Josef answered. 'It's a favourite trick of theirs. They haven't updated their tactics.'

'Part of the intimidation.' Ben stood and wandered out into the passage. He glanced up and down, then said to someone out of sight of the doorway: 'Please can we have another chair in here? We'll be one short when our client arrives.'

Josef S inspected the room, this ante-room to deprivation. It possessed the claustrophobia of all such Government-controlled institutions where the individual has no control; the faded green walls could have belonged to classrooms or hospitals, to courtrooms or lunatic asylums. The wooden chairs and table were there to give the players in this charade the barest minimum to perform their functions: there was no pretense at comfort, no attempt at disguise as there was outside, no team of interior decorators, gardeners for the inside.

Ben returned with another chair and, in his eyes, the glint of victory that indicated he had fought for a right and won. He put the chair before the table with a satisfied turn to his lips, and then sat in it proprietorially. They continued to wait. From time to time, doors clanged and prison officials and policemen walked past.

'I could go and hurry them up,' Ben suggested, flushed from his small success.

'Don't bother,' said Josef. 'They'll take their time. If they know

173

you're annoyed, they'll keep us waiting even longer. It's all a war of nerves. It always is.'

'Don't you have appointments?'

'I'm clear until after lunch,' the lawyer said. 'I kept the morning open.' He did not say that he would have gone on into the afternoon if it were necessary: William Ngo had become so important to him. 'I know their ways.'

At a quarter to eleven, a commotion outside heralded the arrival of the fat warder, the Charon who led the dead across the river, a cherubic ferryman, quite unlike his gloomy mythological counterpart. He smiled grandly, and produced the prize, magically back from the netherworld: this Charon had the ability to bring the dead back to life, and he flaunted his power with the showmanship of a professional magician. His keys were his oar; they rattled like the chains of the ghosts that he escorted across the boundary to the real world.

William Ngo was not bowed. He stood, tall and terribly thin, handcuffed and in leg-irons, beside the warder.

'Does he have to be chained like this?' Ben protested.

Charon's smile broadened. 'We can't take any chances, can we?'

Josef put his hand on the clerk's shoulder, to quieten him. 'Thank you,' he said. 'And now, would you mind leaving us alone?'

'I'll be waiting outside,' Charon answered, and left the room. A chair scraped against the stone in the corridor.

Josef motioned for Ngo to sit and then followed the guard. Charon had positioned himself just outside the open door. 'I'm sorry,' the lawyer said, 'but I'll need to conduct my consultation in private.'

The man began to argue, but Josef frowned him to silence. He shrugged his heavy shoulders, hauled his chair across the passage and gave the lawyer a meaningful look as if to say: 'Don't try anything.'

'Stupid officiousness,' Josef muttered as he returned to face the accused. 'I am Josef S,' he introduced himself. 'And this is my clerk, Ben, from the FDF. He has approached me on behalf of the FDF to represent you.' The handcuffs would have made it awkward to shake hands and Josef did not attempt to do so. William Ngo sat upright, staring directly into the lawyer's eyes.

'I don't want to be represented,' he said.

'I see.' Josef looked at his assistant, who squirmed. 'Did you know that, Ben?'

'The FDF has collected the money for the defence,' the clerk

174

said to Ngo. 'We assumed you'd want to be defended.' And to Josef: 'We hadn't spoken to him; he's been held incommunicado. We naturally assumed . . .'

'Why don't you want a lawyer?' Josef asked patiently. 'Surely you must be aware that it will be better for you.'

'I don't want it to be "better for me",' William retorted.

'You've been charged with murder,' Josef referred to the charge-sheet in the brown folder, 'for which death is a competent sentence. You don't want to hang, do you?'

'I appreciate your offer, Mr S,' said William; then turned to Ben, 'and that of the FDF, but you know as well as I that I'm going to hang in any case . . .'

'That's by no means a foregone conclusion,' said Josef, aghast. 'I can get experts to plead in mitigation of sentence, psychologists . . .'

'I am not mad. I'm as sane as you. I won't get off on the grounds of insanity.'

'Political scientists, sociologists,' Josef persisted.

'To what end?' asked Ngo. 'So that I'll be imprisoned for the next twenty-five years? Do you think I want that? When I stabbed him I knew what I was doing. I'd planned it. I wanted to do it, and I'm not sorry I've done it. I don't want mitigation of sentence. I don't want to rot in jail. Now can I go back to my cell?'

'But my wife has left me and Mrs Idini was murdered because she was going to defend you, and . . .' Josef was going to say, but he realised that these things had nothing to do with William Ngo. What a waste of life. My marriage was over in any event. But Mrs Idini could have contributed so much. Ben simply looked flabbergasted.

'Wait,' Josef waved Ngo back down as he made to stand. 'Tell me, please, tell me, if you would, just for my interest, why you don't want to get off. Why d'you want to be a martyr?' Belatedly it occurred to the lawyer that the room might be bugged, but there was no place for a hidden microphone in those bare walls.

'You can call me a martyr if you want,' William Ngo responded. He narrowed his eyes and pulled in his chin so that it was tucked into his chest like a boxer's. Nevertheless, he allowed himself to sit.

'I recognise you,' Josef said. 'You have a beard now. You were at the demonstration outside Parliament, when those women chained themselves to the fence . . .'

'Would you call them martyrs too?' Ngo asked, mocking, aloof. 'They're also inside. Their choice. They didn't have to be.'

'Yes, but only for a few days,' Josef reasoned. 'You're throwing away your life.'

'No, not throwing away. I'm sacrificing myself for my people.' He spoke jerkily. His anger bubbled under the suface and he strove to contain it, tried to be dignified. 'Do you understand?'

'No,' said Josef. Ben was silent. 'All I see is a young man with so much potential preparing to waste himself. After the struggle is over, people like you will be needed to rebuild the country.'

'My potential is needed to perpetuate the struggle, not to wait until it is over,' Ngo answered. 'How can you judge me? Your people have oppressed ours for three hundred years. What do you know of our struggle? The Revolution needs sparks to ignite it. A thousand, a million sparks. We must keep lighting the fires again and again, every time the Leeus put them out. That's all I am: another flame. If I can fire the struggle even for a little while, I'll have done my job. I intend to plead guilty and make a speech in court explaining my position. The speech will go out worldwide and galvanise world opinion against the Government. I welcome the death sentence.'

'Does the State know this?'

'Not unless they're listening now. I tell them nothing. I won't co-operate with those pigs. They tried to force me to confess to the murder, and to admit that I'm part of a conspiracy involving the FDF. They even asked me about an astrologer who predicted that I would kill Buth. They said he was part of the conspiracy. But they couldn't get me to say anything.' He laughed bitterly. 'I was prepared to die in there, just like Gavin Davids, but they were too careful to kill me. They know the whole world is watching. They couldn't have me die in detention. They need to get me to court to show how civilised they are.'

'How did they try to force you?'

'Torture,' William said, but did not elaborate. Of course Robert had been correct that the police would 'beat the shit' out of Ngo. What sort of country wasted the youth like William and Robert, pitting them on opposite sides, both prepared to die for their beliefs?

'Was it bad? Are you all right?'

'No worse than the torture Christ endured.'

'Are you a Christian?'

William permitted himself a rueful smile: the angry pucker left his face and a gentleness shone through. 'A sort of fallen one, you could say.' He tried to scratch his head, had to use both hands, and swore at the restriction to his movements. 'I was a lay preacher once, counselling people in need. They came to me in the street in Valhalla, to my house, to my office, with their problems. I used to believe I could help by counselling. I used to believe I could impart a wonderful vision of life to them when they were suffering under the system. I wanted to believe!' He slammed both fsts on the table. Ben winced. Josef could almost hear the skin on his wrists tear. 'I wanted to believe that I could make people happy by reading the Scriptures to them. But how could I spread love and peace when there was such turmoil? People would ask me what was going on, why a Government claiming to be Christian was uprooting communities. I could not answer. In the end, I decided that, like Christ, I'd have to suffer to serve my people. So I had to sacrifice myself in the interests of my people. Do you understand why I am going to plead guilty?'

Josef rubbed his eyes. 'I know little of theology. I'm a lawyer, not a religious man . . . Does one have to murder to solve a dilemma such as yours?'

'I told you I was fallen,' William joked, then said: 'Violence is inherent in the system and must be met with violence. Only a madman would wish for violence, and you may still think I am mad . . . only someone insane would turn his back on the prospect of peace . . . but I had no alternative. I had to do what I did.' He looked deeply into Josef's eyes. 'Perhaps you and I have this in common: we're both ready to die for the redemption of those who remain behind.' He started to get up again. 'Now can I go?'

'Why are you so anxious to be back there?'

'Because that's where I've decided I must be. That's where I must return.'

'In case you change your mind,' Josef suggested.

'My mind is made up,' said William Ngo.

'There's something I want to tell you, if you don't know already. Just so that you don't get taken by surprise.' William sat. His dark eyes were now untroubled and Josef remembered his own haunted reflection in a bus window. Perhaps peace only came to those who fulfilled their promise to themselves. 'A lawyer by the name of Mrs Idini took your case before me. She was murdered, presumably by a Republican death squad. Obviously they were unaware of how you were going to plead . . .'

'I know,' said William. 'My interrogators told me. They were baiting me, trying to force me to co-operate with them' He smiled;

there was no evidence of his previous anger. 'You're a brave man, Counsellor S,' he said, 'risking your life for me. I must thank you. But now you're off the hook. You can tell the newspapers that I intend to represent myself, but don't say how I'm going to plead. I don't want to make the State's job any easier.' The smile widened. 'I know it's a silly game, but it's the only one I can play. I have very few cards left, and my hand is restricted.' He leaned back, apparently unconcerned as to whether they had caught the pun. 'I'm sorry that she died, but I didn't ask her to defend me, and I can't take the blame.'

The warder's head appeared in the doorway. 'How's it going?' he asked. 'Planning escapes, eh?'

'We're nearly finished,' Josef answered impatiently; his tone was strong enough to drive the head back into the passage.

'Okay, okay.' Charon submitted. He knew his time would come; he had merely to wait. No one needed to hurry in this machine that was the Eisstad Prison. It had a quiet dignity, the grandeur of finality. Everyone had a place, everything ran according to a hidden time-table. Hospitals also have such an inner clock directing the pace of their workings. And courtrooms. And lunatic asylums.

'Why did you take my case?' William asked. 'Why did you put yourself at risk for me?'

'Does it matter?' Josef asked wearily.

'Was it because of the publicity?' William taunted. 'So that you could become famous on my back?'

'Is fame worth death threats and your wife leaving?'

'Your wife, Mr S,' Ben interjected. 'I didn't know . . .'

'I'm sorry. I didn't intend to mention it. She didn't want me to take the case. But she left for other reasons as well. This was simply the last straw.'

For a second, the mask fell from William's face and a worried look betrayed the compassion that Josef knew he was hiding beneath the bravado. But his features composed immediately: his vulnerability demanded the protection of arrogance.

'There must be casualties in the struggle,' he declaimed, acknowledging then that Josef was part of the struggle, even if the lawyer was not going to take his case. Did Josef need Buth's murderer to give him an identity, to give him substance, to make him whole again? Could he deny that he felt cheated because the young man was depriving him of the chance of making a public statement? But what right did Josef S have to demand that he be given the opportunity to act for Ngo? Perhaps the struggle *would* benefit more from a martyrdom than a successful defence. The FDF, it seemed, also wanted to bask in the reflected infamy of this maverick, even if it could not endorse his conduct. But it too was destined for frustration, as evidenced by Ben's chastened expression. As though he were following the lawyer's train of thought, William said to the clerk: 'Even if I wanted a lawyer, I think it would be very foolish for the FDF to give me open support. Don't you? The FDF must walk very softly now. The Republicans are sore at what I did. They're looking for ways to lash out. Be very careful.'

'As I've explained to Mr S,' Ben said, 'we never intended to be linked openly to you. We just wanted to give you the best possible defence. We don't want you to die in the struggle, but if that's your choice . . .'

'I was born in Waterfront,' William Ngo said. 'My family had a house, we had neighbours, we were a close community. And then Buth's Government decided to remove us to the townships. Do you know what that did to my family? My father was a hawker: he'd lived in Waterfront all his life. It was all he knew. He sold fruit and vegetables on a street corner. He was a proud man, my father, as territorial as a dog. It was *his* corner, and if anyone else intruded, my father chased them away with a stick. The community supported my father; we were loyal to each other. I went to school in Waterfront; one of those buildings that's now deserted was a classroom. And then Buth wanted it all and kicked us out. Just like that. He promised us new houses in Valhalla. We didn't want his houses, but we had no choice . . . My father died as a dog would die, proud and starving in an unfamiliar place. My mother struggled to put us through school; she had to commute into Eisstad every day to clean people's houses because there is no work in Valhalla. We have been turned into beggars, Mr S, and I swore to avenge the death of my father. He was a good man, an honest man, and they killed him as surely as if they'd shot him. I tried to be a Christian, but the people came to me day and night with their stories, which were so like my own story that I knew I would have to accept violence out of love for my people.

'Buth grew up on a farm on the land that was stolen from our people three hundred years ago when we were enslaved. Now I have sent him back to that land.' He stood up firmly; the discussion was over. Josef stood too.

'This place is going to burn,' William Ngo warned. 'For too long,

179

the Republicans have feathered their nests by impoverishing my people. One party rule is over, my friends. Democracy will come soon. The workers will rule.'

'I'll see you in court,' Josef said. 'I'll be there.' But the gangly young man who had stalked away from the taunts of the crowd outside Parliament did not answer as he walked out, stiff in his shackles.

'How many files have they given you, my boy?' the warder exclaimed. 'A machine-gun hidden in your arse, eh? Come on.'

The corridor smelled clammy, unhealthy, suffering from an absence of sunlight. A rattle of keys, a clap of steel, and Charon had led his charge back across the Styx into the murky world beyond. A young warder, groomed in crisp brown, doomed to grow old in these caves, even less free then the gardeners, showed them out.

'If more people were as committed to the struggle as William Ngo, we would surely have won already,' said Ben. Anger glowed in his eyes.

The sunshine blinded, the birds rejoiced, and Josef put his unopened note-pad back into his pocket.

So William Ngo is not going to save me, Josef thought. He's going to die for the people of Valhalla, but he will engineer his death alone. He assumed we're both prepared to sacrifice ourselves to redeem those left behind. But he was wrong: he is ready to die out of conviction to his cause; I, simply out of despair.

A small boy — perhaps one of those from the fish factory — cringed up to him, hands cupped, face pained. 'Please boss,' he whined. 'I'm hungry.' Josef gave him a coin and the boy leaped away as though he had been scalded.

'You mustn't give to them,' Ben admonished.

'He was hungry,' said Josef absent-mindedly.

'He'll go back to Valhalla and show the other children how much money he's made by begging from people like you and tomorrow ten more children will come into town to try their luck. We don't want the children to be beggars, Mr S. You must not give. Harden your heart: it's better for them in the long run. They have places to go for food. There are welfare offices, and the FDF runs a soup kitchen on the Flats. They must learn not to beg.'

'Yes of course,' said Josef, buying a newspaper from a vendor in a doorway.

Back in his office, he called Margaret. She had returned from her camping trip and sounded pleased to hear his voice. She reminded

180

him that the Peace Rally marking the end of Albert Poynter's fast was the following night. They arranged to go together and he was encouraged that she appeared to prefer his company to that of the many friends she must have had in the political movement. He agreed to fetch her. His heart beat faster; again he experienced the thrill that he had first felt for her in the Hunting Lodge.

The front page of the newspaper was split in half under the heading: A TALE OF TWO FUNERALS. One section was devoted to Buth, the other to Mrs Idini. Buth's funeral had been a stiff, formal ceremony befitting State mourning; Mrs Idini's had been chaotic. The restrictions imposed on the latter had been flouted, political speeches had been made to the crowd of over thirty thousand, and the police had entered the stadium shooting teargas. Scores of people had been arrested or injured in the stampeding panic. It was not far-fetched to assume that Ben's asthma was partly related to these events.

Josef also read that Gille Sutton and Sally Patterson, the 'chain-protest women', had been released from the Tower earlier that morning (there was an automatic remission of sentence for good behaviour). Interviewed at home by a reporter from the *Evening Times*, Mrs Sutton expressed surprise and joy at the support she and her companion had received from the public in the form of telephone calls, flowers and letters. She said that she and Mrs Patterson had been kept together in the women's section of the prison for the duration of their sentence. The experience had been 'unpleasant but valuable' in that it had given them a taste of what thousands of people suffered because of their opposition to the Republican Government. She believed that ordinary citizens of Eisstad could do more to show their concern, for example by writing to the families of detainees. Such support helped to spread goodwill and was more fully appreciated than one imagined. In answer to a question, she said that she would rather not go to prison again, but could not predict what circumstances might cause her to be arrested in the future. She concluded: 'I have a boy of ten. In the townships boys of ten are being shot by the police in the name of State security. This is an appalling indictment of the country we live in. I know mothers who are mourning for their children. I share their grief.'

The people massed up the steps into the City Hall, a hot, noisy, excited group who had come to celebrate the Peace Rally. Josef kept Margaret in view although he did not touch her. Her fingers curled beneath the sleeve of her white shirt; he longed to take them in his own. Perhaps Robert, the impulsive one, would have done so without even thinking; his cautious brother could not.

The marshalls at the door wore red armbands and FDF T-shirts and carried walkie-talkies. Margaret exchanged a few words with them and with the workers in the foyer who sold FDF paraphernalia from trestle tables bedecked in the organisation's colours. Then she and Josef entered the auditorium. The City Hall was dressed for the FDF that night. Huge yellow, red and green banners hung from the walls, from the boxes, from the gallery. They proclaimed that the FDF presented the true aspirations of the people; they demanded the release of Raymond Mkhize and the removal of the army and the police from the townships; they condemned the assassination of Mrs Idini; they saluted the courage of Albert Poynter.

'Just as well we came early,' Margaret said as they chose seats near the front. It was only half-past seven but already the hall was almost full. A group of men sat behind them eating fish and chips wrapped in newspaper, a woman breast-fed her baby. For those who had come straight from work, supper had to be taken in public; there was no question of going home to Valhalla first.

On the stage were a table draped in an FDF flag, a number of chairs, and a podium to which a microphone had been attached. The table was dominated by a red vase containing yellow flowers and a large white candle circled by a strand of barbed wire: a water jug and tumblers for the speakers blended humbly into the background. The camera crews, who formed a clique of their own that went from story to story (and the Republic was full of stories), were setting up their equipment, taping their microphones to the stage, aiming their video cameras at the podium, joking with one another, relaxed now after a day probably fraught with confrontation. Josef recognised Mike, who had photographed Albert Poynter in the Hunting Lodge, staked out like a sniper on a corner of the stage, waiting for his target to appear in his sights. John, the doctor, was also there, sitting beside a woman whom Josef took to be his wife. Eyes met, and John returned the lawyer's smile.

Josef and Margaret did not speak. They sat in silence as awkwardly as strangers. She wore her hair in a pony tail as she had the first time he had seen her, and the soft skin on the back of her neck was exposed, as open as an invitation. But, even though she smiled when he stared at her, there was in fact no invitation. She could have been a picture, a beautiful photograph placed on the chair beside him: so little warmth did he receive from her.

The activity was intensifying: the hall began to hum. The speakers were taking their seats although, as yet, there was no sign of Albert Poynter. Two members of a press crew crossed the stage like two clowns pretending to be a horse, but without the costume. The man in front carried a video camera; the one at the back, bent over, wore earphones. They were connected by a wire leading from the camera, and, as though their imitation were not yet perfect, they bumped into each other as they trotted across the front of the stage. The cameraman sideswiped the table and the vase trembled but did not fall.

The hall was getting hotter; the atmosphere was charged as the crowd waited for the proceedings to start. Suddenly someone shouted: 'Power!' Immediately people sprang from their seats, fists clenched, echoing the salute: 'Power! Power! Power!' And out of this chanting rose the first notes of a choir singing, like a bird out of flames, and Josef felt electricity rush through his body as the words: 'Oh Lord send us peace' soared through the auditorium, shivered, to be followed by: 'Deliver this troubled land'. Each new line was as strong, yet beautiful, as one of the gulls at the seafront: haughty, yet delicate. They stretched their wings, and, watched by the mass of people, swirled in play above their heads. A woman began to ululate, her voice weaved round the words of the singers, raising their prayers even higher. Josef closed his eyes, and longed for peace, and remembered that Margaret Spears had caused him to experience such immense peace, but was now troubling him as greatly as the events in the country: for the external tumult seemed to be mirrored in the desolation he experienced, that was now enhanced, rather than diminished, by her proximity.

'Thank you to the Valhalla Community Choir for starting the meeting,' the chairman said. In answer, the 'Power!' chant began again, staccato as boots marching on gravel. The chairman put his hands up, palms out, and using his enormous presence, waved the crowd to silence. The voices died and the people sat. 'I have some announcements,' he said, smiling and obviously enjoying himself. 'The organisers have requested that I ask you not to stand on your seats.' A ripple of laughter greeted this remark and chairs squealed from bodies rocking in mirth. 'Also, please use the ashtrays if you smoke.' Josef could see no ashtrays. 'And now, I am sure you will give Albert Poynter a big welcome. He has just come down from the Hunting Lodge on the Leeukop, and he promises that he saw no lions on the way.'

The applause deafened: the audience stood and welcomed the man who had brought them together. He walked uncertainly onto the stage, blinking as if dazzled by the bright lights, a chunky figure despite his three-week fast. He wore a shaggy fisherman's jersey knitted in FDF colours, faded blue denim jeans and running shoes: a modern hero, crying at the response he had evoked. He took the microphone from the chairman, and in a cracking voice said: 'Thank you for coming.' He wiped his eyes with a handkerchief and tried to continue, but could not. He smiled through his tears and sat down in the seat that had been reserved for him. The crowd shrieked. A group near the stage began to dance and chant: 'Free Mkhize!' and 'Power!' After a few moments of pandemonium, Poynter recovered. Immediate silence greeted his return to the podium; whoever had a seat, sat.

'Again, thank you for coming,' Poynter continued. 'We hoped the meeting would be big, but we didn't think it would be this big.' Suddenly there was a sound of chanting in the passage outside: a few people turned in their seats, but Albert Poynter kept on speaking. Josef felt trapped, as if he were in the tube of an underground railway system with the train bearing down, pushing the air before it, with no way to escape. Margaret was listening closely to the speaker and did not seem to have noticed the commotion. Josef trembled: how could the hall accomodate any more people? It was already packed to the rafters: people stood in the doorways and in the aisles; some stood flat against walls, balanced, it seemed, on air. But the rush stopped; the train did not arrive. 'Troops must get out of the townships,' Albert Poynter was saying, 'and Mkhize must be released: these are our demands.

'My fast was a way to focus attention on the suffering of the people in the townships, in some way to identify with that suffering . . .' Josef had heard it all before: it was the same message, repeated over and over, the *leitmotif* of the struggle. He felt a terrible ennui, verging on cynicism, despite the hugeness of the occasion. Everyone said the same thing; and the Republican Government chose not to listen. It had lost a leader for its deafness, but would take its revenge, and already the new President was installed, carrying on where Buth had left off. And the trains of the oppressed, hurtling in from the Flatlands, would continue to chant and dance and demand and die.

'Thank you,' Poynter said. Thunderous applause escorted him to

184

his seat.

The chairman's loosely fitting shirt made no attempt to disguise a massive stomach. 'Our next speaker,' he boomed, 'is Rodney Baker, the acting secretary of the FDF.'

The elderly man in the drab brown suit looked the antithesis of a hero: in fact he could have been one of the messengers in Josef's office. But he had a quiet authority which stilled the noisy crowd as he walked over to the candle. He stood above it for a moment, facing the auditorium, and then took a box of matches from his pocket. In a very deep voice, he said: 'This is a candle of freedom, for those who have suffered in the cause of freedom, for those who have died, for those who have lost their loved ones . . .' He lit the candle, and the light flared through the barbed wire. He began to sing, and the song was a perfect continuation of his words: nothing was out of place. He closed his eyes: the beautiful voice harmonised with the flickering candle, entrancing, and so great was this man's power that the audience sat, hypnotised to silence. When he said: 'Power!' the word lashed like a whip.

Margaret whispered to Josef — the first time she had spoken to him; it required Rodney Baker to break her mood tonight. 'He's a very powerful man,' she said. 'One of the future leaders.' Josef nodded: he did not know what to reply. Would Baker not be dead of old age by the time the people triumphed? The candle made him think of the possibility of fire, and the danger of blocked entrances. Every now and then, a sharp sound, as of barking, entered the hall. Baker had gone over to the podium, and was speaking.

'We have been accustomed over the years to having our leaders banned, muzzled . . .' Someone shouted: 'Murdered!' and Baker smiled before he continued. 'We have the army quartered on an unarmed civilian population, and we ask who the enemy is. I will tell you, friends. The Republican Government has declared war on its people.'

'What's the alternative?' came a cry from the audience. A thickset man with short hair and a puffy face had leaped up, unable to contain himself. 'Chaos?' he demanded and sat. The people next to him giggled, embarrassed, and shifted away as if they would be infected, or adjudged to share his opinions. A clutch of marshalls descended on the heckler and he was escorted out, unprotesting, accompanied by a group of journalists looking for incidents.

'Friends,' Rodney Baker said, unperturbed by the interruption, 'let me tell you that we of the Flatlands do not hate the people of

185

Eisstad. We recognise that they are not demons. They are ordinary, scared human beings. And those who are prepared to sacrifice for us — their sacrifices touch us very deeply. Albert Poynter has gone without food for three weeks, two housewives went to prison on our behalf: these actions mean so much to the people of the Flatlands. They help to build bridges, my friends, when the Government and the police are doing their best to break them down.

'I feel sorry for the police,' he said, drawing raucous laughter from hundreds of throats. 'They have an unenviable task. They have to carry out the immoral laws of an evil system. I would like to regard the police as my friends, but they are seen to be defending something which is utterly indefensible. Indeed, they seem to relish their job. They are going to have their work cut out redeeming themselves. Peace and justice won't arrive at the barrel of a gun. Peace and justice will only come when the cause of the trouble is eradicated. And the cause of the trouble is this Government.

'This Government has turned us into aliens. They have uprooted stable communities and dumped people into resettlement camps. You don't dump people like you dump garbage! The Republican Government has stripped the majority of the people of their rights in the country of their birth. They have separated us, Eisstad from Valhalla, so that the one does not know what the other is doing or thinking, and mutual suspicion builds up, and we are drifting towards civil war.'

'We are already in civil war!' a man with fiery eyes shouted.

'I have a story to tell you,' Baker continued, 'about a labourer who lived in a shack in Waterfront. When the removals took place, he asked the officials from the Resettlement Board if he could destroy his own shack: he wanted to do it himself. Well, they thought about it for a little while, and then, because they have big hearts, they gave him permission. So he took down his own shack of corrugated iron, sheet by sheet, and stacked the sheets neatly on the ground where it had stood. The next day he was found hanging from a tree nearby. A shop was built on the site and a citizen of Eisstad is trading there now. What sort of person, my friends, can benefit from the misfortune of another in this way?'

'Devils!' yelled a companion of the man with fiery eyes, to murmurs of approval.

A marshall scuttled onto the stage and handed a note to the chairman. The two conferred briefly behind the speaker's back.

'Freedom is indivisible,' Baker was saying. 'Whether you live in

186

Eisstad or Valhalla, you are not free. I call on you to commit yourselves completely to this great struggle for freedom. We cannot afford to waste time and energy and resources. We must make it clear that we want a just, democratic society. Now!'

The audience erupted as the acting secretary walked slowly back to his chair with the shuffling gait of an old man. Margaret was applauding ecstatically. Even Josef was sufficiently moved from his cynicism and self-absorption to clap.

The chairman had reclaimed the microphone: his former jocularity had gone, but a woman in front of Josef giggled in pleasure at the reassuring sight of his bulk.

'Ladies and gentlemen,' he said sombrely. 'Ladies and gentlemen. Please be quiet. Please . . . We still have two speakers from the FDF, but I am afraid that, due to circumstances beyond our control, we are going to have to end the meeting now.' The silence was sudden and electric. 'I know that we are jammed like sardines into this hall, but I must ask you please to leave as quickly and quietly as you can. There are police outside.' An angry muttering grew out of the bowels of the crowd and the chairman raised his hands for silence. 'I ask you not to provoke them or to allow yourselves to be provoked. We must show them that we will not sink to their level. People from the townships: please wait inside until the buses have moved into position. Will the bus drivers please go to the entrances. Thank you all for coming. Peace be with all of you.'

The speakers collected their papers and exited through the wings: the show was over. The crowd began to file out, watched over by the chairman, a great paternal figure concerned for the welfare of his children. Many men had their hands on the shoulders of their wives or girlfriends, but even in this time of stress Josef dared not touch Margaret. The cameras were panning the people leaving, concentrating perhaps on expressions of fear, of anxiety, of excitement even, to which words of explanation would be added when this audience fled across foreign television screens. The fear of walking out into chaos, the trembling in the knees, stomach turning to water: the lawyer recognised that these things were part of the daily reality of the township residents.

But outside, the feared confrontation had not materialised. Instead, a singing mass of people had virtually closed off the street in front of the City Hall. Buses were edging through the crowd which danced and chanted to meet them. The only sign of the police was a solitary yellow van, parked a block away: black dogs barked hysteri-

187

cally from a dark cage at the back; two policemen sat in the cabin, impassive, watching. A section of the crowd broke away and moved off towards Gomez Square, stamping and singing, a carnival, a festival in the middle of the City of Ice. Margaret recognised some-one she knew and excused herself while Josef waited for her. A gust of wind blew her skirt against her legs, beautifully outlining the backs of her thighs.

Josef tore his gaze away and he saw them, then, on the southern edge of the square: the armoured personnel carriers designed to sur-vive landmine explosions, called Leeus because of their alleged ferocity in battle, lying incongruously in wait in the dark streets of the city. Once his eye got used to their shapes, he could distinguish three of them against the backdrop of the night, naked expressions of State power; it was like finding the hidden objects in a child's puzzle-drawing. And before them stood a row of men wearing visors and holding long guns.

Margaret returned. 'It was a bomb scare,' she reported.

'Come on, let's go,' Josef said, and she nodded, and only then did he lay the lightest of guiding hands on her shoulder.

She made the tea: she remembered how he liked it. He noticed that her hands were trembling; so was he. The shiver sprang from deep inside his chest; only his overcoat prevented it from chilling the room.

'Joe didn't announce the bomb-threat in case there was pa . . . panic,' Margaret said. Her face was pinched with anger.

'Do you think there was a bomb?'

'No. But Joe didn't want to take any chances. Not with so-so many people.'

'At least Albert and Baker spoke.'

'The main speakers always go on first,' she said. 'We've learned from experience. This is an excellent way to break up a meeting,' she added bitterly, 'and to intimidate. Some of those old dears in the audience must have been terrified out of their wits. They'll never put a foot out of their houses again.'

Not if those old dears are anything like Iris Milner, Josef thought. 'Do you always stop your meetings when there's a bomb-threat?' he asked.

'It depends on the chairman; it's his decision,' she answered slight-ly too sharply.

'Perhaps Joe gave in too easily,' the lawyer suggested.

'They'll certainly see tonight as a victory,' she said. 'Now they'll believe they can get away with it whenever they want. After Rodney's speech about committing ourselves to the struggle . . .' She shook her head. 'We *have* to bargain from a position of strength. If the marshalls hadn't negotiated with the police to back off, there would have been chaos tonight. We can't be seen to be weak.'

'I feel bad that we can choose to leave and come home, but the people from the townships are stuck with the situation.'

'What does guilt help?' she retorted. '*Do* something.'

'I wanted to help William Ngo,' Josef said. 'That was my contribution. But it came to nothing.'

'You could take other cases. Less newsworthy perhaps, but needy all the same: children arrested on public violence charges, victims of police brutality suing for damages . . . You could act for any number of people.' She was accusing him, indirectly, of snobbery. He stared at her over his cup of tea like a dumb animal at its tormentor. Echoes of the speech he had given to Foster reverberated in his head. 'The State is trying to depoliticise political activities, to pretend they're criminal,' she said, visibly upset, talking at him. 'That's why there are so many public violence cases now. I have a friend who works in legal aid. Last week she was called up-country to defend a group of twenty-seven children who'd been involved in a skrimish with the police. She wan't given time to consult with them and her application for a postponement was refused. If she'd appealed, the children would have had to sit in jail until the appeal was heard because the magistrate wasn't going to give them bail. Either way she was lost. That's how the State is using the courts to do its dirty work. William Ngo is the tip of the iceberg. If you want to do something, you could start by spreading the information among your lawyer friends that there is no such thing as an independent judiciary in the Republic . . .'

He did not say that Ben was probably the only friend he had left in the legal fraternity. Outside, the noises of the traffic in the city indicated that life was continuing normally for some. 'You know a lot about legal procedure,' he said eventually.

She managed a strained smile at the compliment. 'It's part of my work at the Advice Bureau,' she answered. Her white shirt held the shape of her breasts like a hand; he hoped she was not aware that he was looking at them. Although it was a warm night, his shivering continued: he felt as nervous as when he had first stood up in court. His heart beat so loudly he was certain she could hear it. He did not

189

know how to approach the subject, but knew that he had to take the initiative, get it over with.

'My wife left me,' he began tentatively.

He had won her attention; he could see it. She shook her head slowly. 'I'm sorry.'

'I was upset at first,' he said. 'But I've come to terms with the loss. I didn't love her . . . I hadn't loved her for years. We stuck it out, from habit . . .'

She looked at him mutely, not offering the usual aids to conversation — the noises of encouragement, the smiles or frowns — as if she were waiting for the punch line that now had to come. The wife was gone and could no longer provide the padding between them. Josef did not want to continue: it was all wrong. She had not smiled, happy that he was now free to be with her, but he could not stop himself. He was the train rushing through the subway and she the innocent, trapped on the tracks, unable to get out of the way.

'I am in love with you,' he said.

She did not answer him, but continued to stare as if he were speaking in a foreign language, or as if he had hypnotised her into immobility. Her lips were drawn into a tight line, her jaw was rigid. After a while, he grew uncomfortable and dropped his eyes, transferring his gaze to his long fingers locked around the cup of tea; for a moment he feared that he would need pliers to release them. He saw them, his father's fingers, squeezing life from whatever they touched: life-denying fingers. And she sat there, horrifically silent, while he had to find words to patch up the rift, to replace Dorothy as a buffer for the onrushing train. But he was being crushed, not her.

'I don't know if you knew that . . . I had to tell you . . .' He discovered that his fingers could move, and he flexed them, and the genius of their construction almost distracted his monologue: the folds, the blends in the flesh, the small hairs that had decided of their own accord to sprout in certain areas, but not in others, the knobs of knuckles; long lawyer's fingers. '. . . I've loved you since that day in the Hunting Lodge. I am aware of you as if you are inside me . . .' He faltered, and looked into his hands. Silence existed except for a clock ticking somewhere inside her bedroom, and the traffic noises. 'Is there any chance that you might love me?' he asked, suddenly angry, although he kept his anger hidden. Had he to force an answer out of her?

'I have recently broken up with someone,' she said then, slowly, choosing her words by weight, like a butcher weighing meat. 'And I need to be independent for the time being. Can we be friends until I sort myself out? I do enjoy spending time with you.'

'Is there any hope?' he asked. The anger, and the passion, had subsided, and he was numb. Now that he had exposed himself, why not go the whole way; why not lie with his face in the dirt? 'Please tell me if there's any hope at all. I can wait. I have no one else . . . Please, I have been honest with you. Be brutally honest with me.' What had he to lose? His pride? He had lost that already. She could think no worse of him: she could not despise him any more. He had robbed her of her power, had drawn her sting.

'I will let you know,' she said. 'I don't know now.'

'I want to make it clear that you don't owe me anything. All these feelings are mine. I feel the love; I must deal with it.' In all the time they had spoken, she had not moved. 'It's too easy an explanation to say that you are a replacement for Dorothy. I don't believe that. If I'd met you at another time in another place, I'd like to believe that my feelings would have been the same . . .' Reason was all he had left; he was empty of emotion.

'I'm glad I "found" you in the square,' she mused. 'I saw a tall thoughtful man, and I wondered what he thought of us. I wondered if he was politically aware.'

Josef put down his cup: he had to get away. 'Thank you for taking me to the meeting,' he said, ' and for the tea. I'll speak to you soon.' He knew that the last statement was a face-saving lie. He knew that he would have to be apart from her while he gave himself a chance to recover from this sickness. All of the heart-thumping madness was to come to nothing. And another reason that Dorothy had used to leave him no longer applied. He walked to the door and she followed, now as unapproachable as a fortress. He turned to smile at her, to show he was neither hurt nor angry, that everything was fine; but his facial muscles would not perform the function properly and all he could produce was a lopsided grin. She leaned over the abyss that had opened between them, and kissed him on the lips. The contact burned. The door that closed was the slamming of a chapter of his life. He walked down the steps to his motor-car, past a cat that slunk off into an alley. Could it have been Walter?

He drove past Gomez Square on his way home, but everything was quiet. The lights of the City Hall were off; the building was a ship anchored in a port, its crew asleep for the night. Outside, an empty police van was parked. The sleepers in the square had wrapped themselves in cardboard and plastic; a man, dressed in white, lurked in a doorway, shifting his gaze up and down the street. Everything was normal, except that Josef was stripped bare.

He woke suddenly. The heavy white curtains hung like ghosts in the darkness. The room had grown suffocating even though it had only one occupant now. He stood, and parted the curtains. The shutters were open. Through the window he saw the car, a white one with an aerial, parked directly opposite his house; he could not see if anyone was inside. Shivering, he let the curtains drop into place. He did not open the window.

In the morning, he read in the *Daily News* that Albert Poynter had died in a motor-car accident on his way home from the Peace Rally. Poynter's car had collided with a stationary vehicle on a freeway and he had died instantly. The police were investigating, but no crime was suspected.

6

The tall man in the grey overcoat glanced at the houses as he passed in the dusk: perhaps they were not isolated, perhaps families lived in them, husbands and wives, and children and dogs, but they were unlit. Windows as dark as sunglasses reflected the encroaching night. No one was in the street, not even a tramp, to suggest that life continued. Everything he looked at was lonely. The walls were grey, the cars empty, the trees in the gardens had lost their colour: shabby oaks and tatty palms; figs as bare as dying veins branched into the grey evening.

His house was dark too. Once, when he had come home, the lights were on, a dog had barked, a voice had called in greeting when his key turned in the door. Once, there had been a reason to come home at night.

His footsteps rang on the hollow floors and the dark rooms swallowed the sound. He walked past his bedroom where the bed was unmade. He put down his briefcase; the noise was too loud in the empty house. In the kitchen, he opened a can and poured its contents onto a plate. And then he reached for the bottle of gin that stood waiting on the counter. He took plate and bottle with him to the lounge and sat down in the brown armchair. He did not switch on the light. Newspapers and magazines were strewn on the floor where he had left them, but he could not recall when. He put the plate on a table and drank, straight out of the bottle. Why worry about the nicety of a glass? The purpose was to transfer liquid to stomach as quickly as possible for distribution to the brain, to dull the longing, to ease the tension, to kill the families of faces that insisted on parading before him. Margaret Spears was the worst: she appeared as an innocent, as a child, pleading with him to stop drinking: she would come right over, switch on the lights, cook him a decent meal, make the bed, if only he would put down the bottle. Her smile under the shadows of her eyes was warm, full of love. Had he given her up too easily? Should he not have persisted? Or was he heir to his father's faint heart? Had he inherited a ready acceptance of defeat without the will to fight back? But he knew he was not able to inspire love in others. Not in Margaret, nor in Dorothy. Nor even in his brother. And the faces winked their eyes or bowed at the neck, bidding him goodnight once more, as they left the stage he had created for them. Margaret's was the last to go, pale and distracted, lovelier than anything else in the world.

He finished the bottle, and stumbled in the dark to the kitchen to fetch another. The beauty of living alone, he mocked himself: I don't have to demean myself by hiding bottles of liquor and having my wife find them in the toilet cistern, buried in the garden like the dog, tucked away in a drawer with my socks. He retreated to the bedroom, leaving supper uneaten in the lounge. The ache was gone, drowned. Margaret Spears was by now a numb spot in a raw wound. She had not come to stop him drinking, nor to make his bed, and he climbed fully clothed into the tangle of sheets and blankets. How many nights had he buried himself, and her, like this? He had no idea. Somewhere into the second half of the bottle, he fell asleep.

'The situation is,' Josef spoke into the telephone, 'that a contractor can't take it upon himself to effect unauthorised repairs. That cannot be implied in a contract . . . Do you follow me? You're welcome to come in and discuss it. My secretary's away this week, but you can make an appointment with Julia.' He put down the receiver, touched his half-empty cup to his lips, preoccupied, and paged through a law report looking for a reference. The phone rang again. 'I'm sorry,' he said. 'I'm in court today. I won't be able to see you . . . Goodbye.' But when he left his office, he did not take his court-gown.

Ed Parry greeted him in the corridor with no more than a nod. Josef nodded back politely, without warmth. He kept his eyes averted. He did not want his partner to see how red they were. Parry turned as Josef passed, his mouth open as if he were going to say something, but Josef pretended not to notice and walked by, looking down, apparently deep in thought. Was he about to ask if I'm off to court? Josef wondered. Was he going to say how pleased he is that I'm not involved?

'I'll be out this morning,' Josef told the receptionist. 'Take messages.'

'Will you be back at lunch-time?'

'Probably. If anything urgent comes up, pass it on to Mr Parry.'

'Dare I?' The corners of her mouth lifted in amusement and Josef grimaced in reply.

'Ben's coming with me,' he said, implying that he still had allies within the firm.

'I'll pass Ben's messages on to Mr Parry as well,' she joked.

Outside, the sun shone weakly, as if it did not know what season it was in. A spattering of rain on the pavement released a rich, fertile smell which filtered through the stale city air. Steam rose from the surface of the road as if the spirits of those who had settled this country were fleeing from the confrontation to come.

The Supreme Court was under siege: the police had erected barriers, closing it off to traffic. Five yellow vans, wire-meshing on their windows like braces on adolescent teeth, straddled the section of road in front of its entrance. Pockets of riot policemen lurked in doorways and alleys, thugs in uniform, smiling in anticipation of violence, gun butts protruding ostentatiously from holsters as their jackets fell back. In the street beyond the barriers, a crowd seethed. A squad of policemen, rifles pointing at the ground, held it at bay. Josef recognised the colours of the FDF woven into jerseys, scarves and hats; T-shirts and placards demanded the release of Ngo and Mkhize, or called for urgent political reforms, or made uncomplimentary suggestions as to the future of certain Republican leaders. The crowd did not try to move forward; it seemed to be waiting, prepared to maintain its side of the impasse without breaking the equilibrium. The opposing policemen, helmeted, were equally impassive. The two sides were like boxers sizing each other up before the bell sounded to begin the fight. The press was there, as always, recording the latest in the soap opera from the Republic to entertain families around the world when they sat down to dinner that night.

On the landing at the top of the stairs, a mountain of a man blocked the doorway to the court. 'People,' he was saying through a megaphone, 'the court is full. There is no more place inside. Please disperse. Believe me, if there was room you could go in, but it's jam-packed in there.'

The crowd made an angry rumbling noise as though the people were expressing their fury through means other than mouths, by rubbing carapaces or rasping wings. This steadily growing mob was nothing like that other, joyful, crowd that had chanted and danced its way out of the City Hall after the Peace Rally: this one carried with it the intervening months of frustration. FREE WILLIAM NGO on a huge banner, raised as Josef watched, focussed the discontent.

'Be reasonable, people,' the giant said, but he was dealing with an unreasonableness that was not based in the present.

195

Suddenly Ben was there, ubiquitous Ben, taking Josef's arm. 'Come on Mr S,' he urged, 'let's get into court before it's all over.'

'We'll have to go in the back,' Josef said. 'But don't you want to watch this?'

'Nothing is going to happen yet,' answered Ben, the prophet. 'They're angry, but this is the centre of Eisstad. They need the spark, and they'll get it. William was right. He *is* the spark. You'll see fireworks when the case is over.' The prospect of upheaval, the township violence imported into the central city, the meeting of his two worlds, filled Ben with a heady energy. 'They won't dare shoot in Eisstad like they do in the townships. Come!' he wheezed, and grabbed Josef's hand. The lawyer allowed himself to be led to the administrative entrance on the other side of the block.

Two policemen, dressed in the roguish blue uniforms of the riot squad, stood guard at the back door: one carried a submachine-gun, the other a walkie-talkie. With them was the door's usual keeper, a man who had occupied this position for longer than anyone could remember. He always wore a single brown glove (no one knew why) and a slate grey uniform which had taken on the colour of the stone walls. His dour face was too forbidding to invite conversation; his eyes were red as if he had been drinking. Eisstad is populated by gatekeepers, Josef suddenly thought. And alcoholics.

'Excuse me, sir,' said one of the policemen. 'We'll have to search you before you go in.'

'I'm a lawyer,' Josef snapped, 'and this is my clerk.'

'Are you invoved in the case, sir?'

I was briefed but the accused did not want me to represent him, Josef thought, but he only said: 'No', before submitting to the search; there was no point in arguing with these people. The gate-keeper looked through the lawyer without recognition; he had joined forces with a mightier power.

'Fine, sir, you can go through.'

The benefits of the system, Josef reflected wryly. Access to the gates.

The entrance was paved with mosaics that might once have been bright but now were dulled with use. They gave way in turn to a dark wood inside the dim corridors. Most of the doors were closed. Every now and again, the staccato blast of the megaphone tried to impose order on the storm that rumbled outside. A few officials walked quickly up and down the corridors, as if they needed to complete their business before the storm burst.

'It's in court four,' said Ben, breathing heavily. 'It's the only case on the roll today. All the others have been postponed.' But he was talking to himself, intoxicated with Revolution. Gin bottles floated past Josef on a sea of dust particles ;he reached to pluck one out of the air, but his fingers curved around emptiness. The bottles were moving targets at a funfair shooting range, but, carefully as he aimed, he could not bring one down. His head throbbed with the effort. Gin bottles took off from the surface of a lake like a flight of migrating ducks; they would not return before the spring . . .

A number of policemen carrying submachine-guns patrolled the corridor outside the court. They watched incuriously as Josef and Ben arrived out of breath at the lawyers' entrance and edged in between the spectators cramming the doorway. The courtroom had the atmosphere of a football stadium rather than a place where justice was to be administered; it hissed with expelled breath, pulsated — the heart of the still building. Its gallery was too small to seat comfortably all those who had crowded in to support William Ngo.

The accused stood in the dock, upright, manacled, the archetypal martyr. His beard had grown thicker in the months since Josef had seen him, and this accentuated the hollows in his cheeks. A cordon of policemen circled him, a belt of well-fed flesh fitting loosely on a slender waist.

Josef glanced at the gallery and the blood began to beat wildly in his head. He had to rest his hand on Ben's shoulder for balance. A lawyer whom Josef knew whispered something, but the words were drowned in a flood of competing stimuli. Up there, in the middle of the crush, was a face that all but rendered the proceedings irrelevant.

'Rise in court!' The orderly's voice rapped like a cane on a desk top, and Judge Salmon entered. His red gown was far too strident, melodramatic, on his stooped frame: the system institutionalised the drama by directing that he wear red. His white hair and gentle face were out of keeping with the severity of his dress and his task. The assessors, two elderly men in dark suits and civil service ties, followed him in.

The spectators in the gallery were settling themselves again, squeezing back into their seats, and Josef lost sight of her for a moment. Anxiously, he willed her back into view.

'Mr Ngo,' the judge was saying, 'are you not represented? You're entitled to a lawyer, you know.'

'I have refused,' William Ngo answered. 'I can say what I want to say alone.'

Josef's eyes sought her out, pleaded for her to look at him, but her attention was fixed on the principal players.

'You are charged with murder,' Gough, the Senior Public Prosecutor was saying, 'an offence which can carry the death penalty. How do you plead?' He looked across at William with pale blue eyes.

Ngo spoke softly, but clearly, with no hint of the arrogance that he had displayed to Josef: he was humble, he was the servant of his people, he was the spark that was to ignite Eisstad. 'I plead guilty,' he said.

The heart that was the courtroom missed a beat: there was a deathly hush. The prosecutor's mouth hung open slackly. The assessors looked glumly at each other across the judge's back: William Ngo was not to be their meal ticket. Even the press pencils stopped in mid-air. Then a roar escaped from hundreds of throats, a continuation of the noise begun outside, as the lion expressed its satisfaction at Ngo's defiance. Salmon slammed his gavel and demanded order. Josef felt a malicious joy at the expression on Gough's face: the wind had been taken out of the State's sails. Months of preparation, months of collecting evidence and grooming witnesses, had been for nothing. It was obvious that the State had had no inkling of the way that Ngo would plead. The torture to force a confession, the attempts to prove a conspiracy, to implicate the FDF in the murder, had been futile exercises. The State had won, but what a hollow victory! And in the end, had the State won? In the gallery, a woman started to sing a freedom song.

'If there's no quiet right now, I'll have to clear the court,' the judge threatened, 'and continue the proceedings in camera.'

The song trailed off, and the gallery, having expressed itself, grew quiet, waiting for the next twist in the drama.

'Would you like to tell the court the circumstances surrounding the offence to which you've pleaded guilty?' Salmon spoke to Ngo as if the two were alone in the room, as if the world were not watching. It was an intensely personal interaction, the concern of a father for a child who has admitted he has done wrong, but whose guilt must be absolutely determined before punishment can be administered. The press pencils had resumed their manic scribblings, the assessors had arranged their features so as to conceal their disappointment, Gough had closed his mouth.

'Yes,' William Ngo said, 'I would.' He did not refer to the Judge as 'my Lord', as though he were showing, subtly, that he did not accept the court's authority.

At that moment, something made Josef look up at the gallery. Margaret was staring at him. Their eyes met and she smiled, an impersonal twist to her face that she could have directed at any acquaintance. He was too dumb-struck to respond. Suddenly he was jealous of all the other recipients of that smile, whoever they were: all the Daniels who came to the Advice Bureau seeking her help; all the previous, and future, lovers, of whom he was not destined to be one.

'Proceed then, Mr Ngo.'

The gallery was a carnival, festooned with FDF colours, yellow and red and green, and packed with revellers who were waiting for the right moment to explode once more. Garlands of flowers crowned a hundred heads and the sweet smells of jasmine and orange blossom filled the court. This was a celebration, not a time of mourning. William Ngo was a high priest whose pagan congregation worshipped him, were prepared to die if he gave the command. Margaret Spears had flowers woven into her thick dark hair, and her dreamlike eyes cast a spell over the entire proceedings: she alone could unfreeze the tableau . . .

'. . . this is an iniquitous, evil system,' William Ngo was saying, 'and my function is to draw attention to the repression . . . I'll tell you how I killed Buth. I'll tell you because I want his successor to live in fear. He'll not know when another killer like me will emerge from the shadows. This society breeds assassins: those you trust most implicitly have a dagger hidden in their sleeves. This society divides people, and out of these divisions fear creeps, and stalks the land.' William Ngo spoke strongly and clearly; he seemed to be enjoying himself. 'Yes, I'll tell you how I killed the President,' he said. 'I got a job as a waiter at a restaurant called The White Horse where I knew he used to eat regularly. And because he went there so often, the Security Police checked me out thoroughly. But my credentials were impeccable.' He smiled slightly. 'I had been a fairly good lay preacher, but I turned into an excellent waiter.' The court chuckled. Even Salmon could not prevent his cheeks from creasing in the briefest of grins. Aware of his charisma, Ngo continued. 'I watched the President when he ate, I watched how he sat, where his guards stood. He always sat at the same table, in the same chair.' His smile grew wicked. 'I hope that President Clarke's security men look after him better. But there's always a way through. He must live in fear.

199

Someone will get to him.

'President Buth began to recognise me, and after a while I was so familiar that he did not see me any more: I was a ghost. And when the time was right, I had the knife, the murder weapon you see over there, on my tray as I was serving him his grilled sole. I put the fish in front of him, and when he leaned forward to eat, I stabbed him in the chest.' The court breathed out slowly. 'He did not tip very well, but that wasn't why I killed him. I killed him because he was an evil man who caused untold harm to my people. I have known oppression and brutality in this, the country of my birth. I have seen old women teargassed and beaten in the streets by young policemen with smiles on their faces. I have had friends shot dead while protesting peacefully at legitimate grievances like poor schooling and forced removals.' William Ngo's voice had lost its humour. Now it lashed at Salmon who represented the system he hated so much.

'When I was arrested, I was viciously beaten up to make a confession, but I refused to co-operate with them. They gave me electric shocks on my genitals; they made me stand naked in one spot for over twenty-four hours; they even dangled me out of a window and threatened to drop me. But I would not talk to them.' The courtroom buzzed and a group of women began to sing.

'Quiet!' the judge warned.

'I want the world to know what goes on in their police cells,' Ngo said, softly so that the journalists strained to hear. 'I have no reason to lie. I have nothing to gain. I've pleaded guilty to murder. As the court has heard, my act was carefully planned, so there can be no extenuating circumstances. I wish to stress that I have no affiliations with any anti-Government groups. I acted entirely alone.' He looked up at the ceiling and his eyes were cold. 'I cherish the ideal of a Republic in which all the people can live together in peace and harmony, where no one is oppressed.' Then he addressed the judge directly. 'I have elected to die for my ideal.'

'Extraordinary,' someone said.

Ben nudged Josef, who bent over. 'Why didn't he tell them about his father?'

'Because he doesn't want the court to find any extenuating circumstances,' the lawyer guessed. 'He knows the law. He wants to leave no doubt at all about the death sentence.'

'Have you anything to add, Mr Gough?' the judge asked the prosecutor.

Gough stood briefly. 'No, my Lord,' he answered.

The women began their song again; the gallery was electrified.

'The court will adjourn until two o'clock,' Salmon said, aware that there was no way he was going to impose order.

'Silence in court!' the orderly yelled and the judge together with his assessors escaped from the courtroom under the cover of his voice. Then three policemen escorted Ngo back into the cells: the 'ghost' who had murdered Buth clanked down the stairs, in his manacles, to the underworld. Gough was speaking to a group of men with hard expressions. Despite their victory, they did not smile; perhaps they realised they had been outmanoeuvred. And, as the courtroom emptied, the song continued, the melody ringing from the buxom breasts of the matrons in the gallery.

'Shut up will you!' a policeman, overwrought, screamed, but his hysteria only spurred the singers to greater heights. This austere place where 'Justice' was dispensed, with its panelled walls and high judge's chair, with its long lawyers' tables and daunting dock, had become intoxicated with celebration.

Josef and Ben were propelled by the sweaty crush of spectators towards the main exit, and thrust out into the street, where, as Ben had predicted, the people and the police still faced each other across the barrier, each side waiting for the other to make its move, each side for its own reasons holding back. But, as those who had witnessed Ngo's admission emerged, they transferred their excitement to those waiting below. People split into small groups and earnest discussions took place, watched by press and police. The police had dogs now, sleek and mercenary, eyeing the crowd with a frightening hunger.

'Hello Josef,' she said calmly, as if months had not separated them.

'Hello Margaret.' If he smoked, he would have lit a cigarette and put it nervously to his lips. He looked at her for a moment, searching for words, and then turned away as if she were shining so brightly that the sight of her hurt his eyes. He was again the infatuated adolescent who had sat in her living room, tongue-tied, on that first night after they had come down from the mountain. And again she took the initiative: it was a trait she might have acquired from dealing with the speechless. Although he could not forget that other side of hers: when she had been struck dumb in the face of his declaration of love.

'Would you like to go for coffee?' she asked brightly.

Why not? He turned to Ben. 'Tell Julia I'll be back later,' he said,

201

and the clerk slipped away, grinning.

They walked together, silently, until they came to a coffee bar at the top of town, across the road from the offices of the *Daily News*.

'Here?' Margaret suggested, and Josef followed her inside. They forced a passage through groups of journalists, involved in animated discussion, to an unoccupied table. The warmth and the smell, the sizzling sounds and hubbub of voices, cast a veil of normality on an abnormal day, but could not thaw the coldness in Josef. William Ngo's name sparked every conversation around them.

'How have you been?' she asked after they had ordered.

'The truth, or the glib version?' he said, unable to mask the bitterness that he heard in his voice.

'Whichever you wish,' she answered, the counsellor dealing with just another problem. Did she regret her invitation, opening up this can of worms?

'The glib version is that I'm fine,' he said. Why should he present a strong front to her? What difference did it make now? 'I'm divorced. My wife, ex-wife, served the papers on me: "Irretrievable breakdown of the marriage". I didn't oppose it. There were no children to fight over and we sorted out the property side as equitably as we could. I got the house,' he smiled bleakly, 'and the char, but I have to work pretty hard to keep Dorothy living according to the standard that she's been accustomed to. I'll have to continue paying until her books become bestsellers. So, there you are, I'm fine.' He did not mention the drinking; no one knew about that.

'What about your brother? Have you settled your differences?'

'I don't see him . . .' Josef sipped the coffee, willing it to be a different drink, but it disappointed him. 'In fact Robert's gone back to the army. He's joined the permanent force . . . No, I don't see him at all.'

'The permanent force?' Margaret asked.

'I suppose he wanted to go back to the home he knew best. He needed that kind of structure in his life. Maybe he just missed the excitement.' The lawyer studied his hands. 'Maybe he wants to earn a steady income to show Dorothy that he can support her. Which, of course, will be a relief for me.'

Margaret looked up curiously. 'What do you mean?'

'Dorothy's living with him,' Josef said.

'How strange. From her books, you'd hardly think she would go off with a soldier.'

'The system corrupts and co-opts.' There was an edge to his voice.

'In the end, most people just want security. Maybe this is how she's found it. At least she won't get death threats now. Who knows? She claims to love him. People do unnatural things when they are in love,' he said with a wintry smile. 'There might be a family resemblance between Robert and me that she finds irresistible. Or maybe she's gone with him because she wants a child,' he added meanly. 'And what better child to mother than Robert?'

But Margaret had drifted away. She was staring over Josef's shoulder into the rain with a faraway look in her eyes. The lawyer twisted in his seat, expecting that someone was watching him through the window. As if the steam hissing from a percolator were the shrieking in his dreams. As if the figure standing before the pit had revealed his face and was moving towards Josef with arms outstretched. But of course no one was there and Josef returned his attention to Margaret. He was shocked to see pain reflected in her eyes, such pain that his own discomfort seemed trivial in comparison, and he was moved to chatter to distract her.

'A few months ago I was hiding from journalists,' he said crookedly, 'and now I'm sitting in the middle of them and they don't even know who I am. They're talking about William with such authority — political analysts at every table — as if they know what he's thinking. But *I* spoke to him, *I* know what he's thinking. No one remembers to ask me. Anyway, this anonymity is bliss. Even the security people have stopped watching me.' He looked into her eyes, trapped them as tightly as he wanted to hold her physically, trying to squeeze away her pain. 'They watched me for months, day after day, sitting outside my house. God knows what they thought I was up to. What a waste of money! My money! I was paying for them to watch me!' It had been a small quest: to make her smile. But he had succeeded. He ached to touch her.

Her voice was small, but she managed to joke. 'That's the price you pay for mixing with subversives,' she said. 'As long as they only watch . . .'

'What's the matter?' he asked suddenly. 'Are you all right?'

'Yes, I'm fine,' she answered curtly, her voice sounding as it did when he had first heard her, giving orders in the square. But then she added, 'Actually I'm not. My father died last week.'

'I'm so sorry,' he said. He put his hand on hers, but she pulled away sharply. 'Can I do anything for you?' he asked. 'Anything at all?'

'No.' She stared again into the distance, and her bottom lip began

203

to tremble. 'I must go,' she said abruptly. She picked up her bag and opened it, fumbling for her purse.

'Don't worry,' he said, wanting desperately to cling to the tenuous contact he had with her, as she slipped out of his grasp again, perhaps for ever. The exhilaration he had felt in court had been replaced by a dull bitterness, a bad taste in the mouth that was anger at losing something fragile and beautiful.

'Are you going back to court?' he asked.

'I don't know,' she answered. 'Are you?'

'No,' he said. 'I have no desire to see the morbid conclusion.' He paid and tipped the waiter, and they walked out into the cold. She adjusted her scarf, tightening it around her throat.

Formally, he extended his hand to her. 'Goodbye.' She kissed him on the lips as she had done once before, impulsively, or with a pretense of impulsiveness, and then walked away hastily. He watched her go, head slightly bowed, mingling with the crowds in the street. He felt that he had aged, that he had passed through another stage of his life, a snake shedding skin into middle age. She disappeared from his sight into the labyrinth of Eisstad while the light rain created a mist that obscured the labyrinth's entrance like a silken curtain.

A clown, painted white face and red nose, walked by carrying two empty gin bottles. His big shoes slapped on the pavement; his hobo's dress might have been funny in a circus ring, but in the street only succeeded in making him look sad. He shouted over his shoulder: 'You mustn't think I was drinking this, eh?' But when Josef tuned to see at whom the words were aimed, the clown vanished, seemingly into thin air.

The rain was plastering down the lawyer's hair and running into his eyes and mouth, but he neither took cover nor walked any faster. He stopped to examine the window of a fish shop. There were red speckled corpses with blind discs for eyes and fins like wings ; and others as floppy and broad as the shoes of the clown. The smell was overpowering. Inside, the proprietor chopped viciously on a board. Outside, one of his workers, clad in wellington boots, a woollen cap and green overalls dragged a crate towards a truck.

'It is a time of death, my son,' the voice warned inside Josef's head. 'These are grey days, my boy, days for dying.'

'No father,' Josef pleaded. 'Put away that bottle. You're drunk!'

'So what?' the old man slurred. His grey hair, which should have bestowed dignity, was awry and greasy; its lank strands fell across his eyes so that he could not see and he had to wipe away the blindness, but it returned. 'I've been drunk for years,' he boasted, but added sadly: 'It doesn't help though, Josef.' Then he ranted: 'You think I'm mad, sitting in my room, year after year, brooding over your mother. Well I don't care what you think. I'm dead, Josef. I died with her.' He hit the bottle savagely on his desk and the noise made his son start but the bottle did not break. He returned to his typewriter, seeming to forget that Josef was there.

'What about us? Robert and me? What about us?' the young man demanded with tears in his eyes. 'We're alive. Don't you live for us?' But his father looked at him with eyes that betrayed such incomprehension, such total absence of recognition, that Josef turned in sudden terror and fled from the presence of this stranger, slamming the study door shut behind him. Robert waited in the passage, his eyes mirroring their father's bewilderment.

A few moments later the boys heard a sharp crack in the study. They rushed into the room together.

'Oh God, no!' Josef screamed. The old man slumped over the typewriter in a final obscene gesture of union with it. His hair, what was left of it, was red and matted. The hand which had fired the gun hung behind the desk. Robert turned and glared at his brother. 'You were his favourite,' he charged. 'Why didn't you stop him?'

Another member of the uniformed army of fish workers emerged from the fish shop, dragging another crate. And then the walls of buildings were rushing by, alleys, doorways, signs, invitations to eat and buy clothes. 'Hello boss,' Josef heard. The clown sat in an alcove surrounded by bottles like stalagmites; water ran down his startling white face as if he were crying. The lawyer averted his eyes.

'Are you going to blame me for ever?' Josef demanded, but Robert's face eluded him when he sought a reply. The clown began to rise, kicking over bottles; he had no control over his big feet. Laughing raucously through thick red lips, he thrust an open bottle at Josef. 'Drink with me?' he mocked. 'Brother?'

'Yes!' the lawyer yelled, grabbing temptation from the clown's hand. 'Yes!' he raged and jammed the glass to his lips. But when the poor liquid dribbled into his mouth, he spat out furiously: it was water! He dashed the bottle on the ground while the clown sat amid the broken glass doubled over in laughter. Then he staggered away, leaning against walls in case he fell into the gutter.

Outside the Supreme Court, the crowd had grown: the townships seemed to have emptied into the central city. Press, police, people: the eternal participants in the game of Revolution. The crowd was

205

swelling constantly and the police had called in reinforcements: each was a pool being replenished from a swiftly flowing stream. The police were no longer talking: they were ready for battle, their armour and firepower against rocks, their helmets confronting naked faces. 'Free William Ngo!' someone called, and someone else ululated: a spine-chilling challenge to the State.

'It's getting nasty out there,' Josef said to Julia as she handed him his messages. She shrugged at his comment as if to say: I have no experience of these things. They do not exist for me.

Josef was aware of Ed Parry, hovering just out of sight in the boardroom. He had the impulse to shout: 'Don't come out now Ed! Your fears are about to be realised. You should have followed Gavin Davids' advice and emigrated when you were young. But it's too late now. Stay hidden, Ed Parry! Our ideas of law are going to be tested on the streets of Eisstad today. Don't come out now, Ed!' But the moment passed, and Josef was silent.

Ben was waiting in Josef's office. 'The townships have been sealed off,' he announced. 'What will Salmon decide?'

'He's got no option,' Josef answered wearily. 'Ngo has tied his hands. He's imprisoned them all. He's prepared to bring the pillars down with him. Don't fool yourself: the police won't hesitate to shoot. Even in Eisstad.'

'It's a pity *The Voice* won't be publishing the story,' Ben mused, and when Josef raised his eyebrows, the clerk explained: 'Most of the staff have been detained. There aren't any reporters at the moment. But don't worry. *The Voice* has its roots in the community. There'll always be someone to carry on the work.'

Was I worried? Josef thought. Do I have any emotion vested in the struggle? Do I have any part in it after all? Do I support it? Have I become involved in someone else's fight because I've been unstable, because I've been going through changes of my own that needed expression?

'I was not worried,' Josef said. 'There's an army of journalists on duty today. I'm sure the story will be covered adequately.' He reached for his dictaphone, implying that he wanted to work.

But Ben did not take the hint to leave. 'Are you going back to court?' he asked.

'No. I couldn't bear it. I won't witness the loss of a life that I could have saved.'

'He didn't want to be saved . . .'

'You go,' said Josef, 'but be careful.' The clown rolled in hysterical laughter on the broken glass; a peacock shrieked . . . 'But I expect you know how to handle yourself. From what you've told me.' He regretted the irritability in his voice, and hoped that Ben would not take it personally.

But the clerk continued to sit. 'Mr S,' he said, 'can I talk to you for a minute?'

Josef put down the dictaphone.

'Mr S . . . I want to be a lawyer.'

'Is there a problem with that, Ben?'

'Mr S . . . I've got friends in the townships who are devoted to the struggle . . . Their lives are an endless circle of meetings, distributing pamphlets, fear, hiding, detention for six months, release, and then it starts again . . .'

'Yes?'

'Mr S . . . My friends want me to be committed like they are. They think I'm selfish, following my own career while they're on the front line.'

'And what do you think, Ben?'

'I don't know, Mr S. Part of me says I should be completely involved . . . But another part sees how futile it is. I can contribute more as a lawyer, even if it takes me years to get there . . . I don't know, Mr S.'

'But surely your contribution doesn't have to be all or nothing . . .'

'You mean I should be a week-end activist? No, that is not an option . . .' He stood up then to leave. 'I'm sorry I troubled you with my problem. You cannot advise me.' His face had grown taut as if the skin had been stretched across his cheekbones.

Josef walked across the room and put his arm around the bony shoulders of the young man: a rare gesture of affection. 'Come back immediately, and tell me what the sentence is. Come, I'll walk out with you.'

In the reception area, staff members were as overwrought as tightly wound clockwork dolls. Suddenly everyone had hopes and fears and anecdotes. 'My husband's shop had a rush on foam this morning,' one of the women was saying. 'People are buying mattresses for their workers to sleep on tonight . . . in case they can't get back . . .'

'Be careful,' Josef repeated to Ben, and returned to his office, pulling the door shut behind him. But instead of working, he approached the typewriter. Sometimes if he looked very closely, he thought he could still see the blood stains. Sometimes, even after all these years, the smell of blood came back, sweet in his nostrils.

207

'I'm glad I'm not a parent, Dad,' he confided. 'I don't want to bring up children in this unhappy country. I'm worried about Ben. How much more would I worry about a child of my own? Do you understand my fears about children? Do you understand why I don't want to be responsible for the suffering of something I've created?'

In the silence that followed, the echo seemed to say: 'One day you will be old and lonely with no one to take care of you. Beware, Josef. Beware the enticing eye of the revolver.'

'But you had children,' Josef retorted. 'And that didn't stop you . . .'

He stared at a law report that lay open at a reference he needed, but the words made no sense: they refused to enter his brain; they seemed intent on floating across the page, elusive as smoke. He flicked open his appointment book: he was free until late afternoon. He called Julia on the intercom. 'Please phone Malcolm and cancel, will you? Then you can go . . . I think the staff should go home early today . . . there's going to be trouble. But check with Mr Parry first.'

'Yes Mr S.' Her voice, roughened by years of smoking, betrayed no fear.

Josef sat back in his chair and closed his eyes. Foster had disappeared, Albert Poynter had died, Dorothy had abandoned her liberal principles to live with a soldier, Ed Parry was not speaking to him, Margaret had retreated, traumatised, into the mists, William Ngo was about to be sentenced to death. What a toll! The Republic chewed up its citizens in its machinery of conflict, so aptly depicted by that gruesome statue in the Revenue Building.

He did not know how long he had been sitting there, dreaming, when Ben burst in dishevelled and wheezing with asthma. The clerk had lost his tie and the top button of his shirt was undone. 'Mr S . . . Come quickly!'

Josef was too tired for words. He wiped his hand over his face, feeling the ridges and crevices as if he were exploring a foreign landscape. He rubbed his eyes slowly: there was pleasure in the caress. 'What is it, Ben?' he asked.

'They're rioting, Mr S . . . in Eisstad.' Ben was wringing his hands in agitation.

'What happened to William?' Josef refused to be hurried or flustered: he was too tired for that.

'Death sentence. The judge said he had no option, no extenuating circumstances . . . William lifted his fist and shouted "Power!" and everyone in court shouted back. When they took him away, he was smiling, Mr S. The police cleared the court quickly, but as the people hit the streets, they carried the spark with them. It was what everyone's been waiting for, Mr S.' He shook his fist excitedly. 'It's just like in Valhalla, but it's happening here! Come on, Mr S.'

'Do I really need to be part of a riot?'

'It's history, Mr S.'

The floor was eerily deserted: there was no sign of the staff or of Parry. The front door was closed, but not locked. Josef clicked the latch as he left.

The world in the street was the familiar coloured by the extraordinary. Perhaps the better known a sight, the more outrageous is any departure from the normal. There was no traffic, nor was there any noise of traffic except for an occasional rumble, as of a truck. The streets were empty, as empty as on the day of the work boycott when Josef had visited the fish factory. It was the emptiness of a disaster area. A faint, acrid smell clung to the air.

Josef and Ben walked, side by side, warily. The lawyer felt ridiculous: a character in a cheap film expecting the villains to jump out of the alleys and side streets, a survivor in a fictional country ravaged by a killer virus.

'Where's the riot Ben?' he asked. 'What's happening?'

'Come, Mr S,' the young man replied, and led him deeper into the city, a guide into a low place: a forest of buildings suffused with a mist of teargas. In the street outside the new Civic Centre, an army Leeu had crunched into a parked car and the two machines, military and civilian, were locked in an embrace from which it seemed that neither could be extracted. A soldier stood on the nose of the armoured creature, his uniform the same colour as the vehicle, so that they were one beast, a mechanical centaur bearing the flag of the Republic and the identifying number: '66'. The soldier held a rifle in his crooked arms and observed the man in the suit critically from his vantage point.

'Is this history, Ben?' Josef's repulsion at the sordid, sombre atmosphere was balanced by a low fire of excitement and fear, sparked by the sight of the soldier and fanned by the smell of teargas and smoke from the central city. He noticed that the Leeu's khaki was rusted in places, and that one of the sixes was peeling off. Behind the smoked glass of the driver's window hung a pale mask, the face of a ghost.

'Eisstad is burning,' Ben replied, and this answer was sufficient.

Around a corner they came upon an articulated orange truck belonging to the Transport Services, slewed across the road and belching black smoke. People stood at a respectful distance watching the demise of this monster, abandoned by its owners to the mobs. Flames licked at its body; its tyres had collapsed and were on fire. An explosion burst from its bowels sending the onlookers scrambling for cover.

'Petrol tank!' somebody yelled in triumph, but it was only another tyre succumbing to the heat. And then the people laughed and nudged one another with relief, like schoolchildren waiting for the fright of the next explosion. A woman standing next to Josef was examining her handbag: the strap had snapped as she had jumped.

'Where's the fire department now?' someone asked, but no one bothered to answer: the burning hulk commanded full attention. Presumably to those who had set it alight, it represented the wealth, the infrastructure of Eisstad, from which they had been excluded: the workers' revenge. The symbol rested, defeated and dying, presenting a spectacle of majestic innocence to a fascinated audience of secretaries and messengers. And lawyers.

There was no warning beyond a screech of brakes, but Ben took Josef's hand and was pulling and dragging him away. Josef, hypnotised by the flames, could not tear his eyes from the burning wreck.

'Is this history?' he repeated. 'Am I prepared for this change?'

'Come on Josef!' Ben shouted. 'We've got to go!' He had never before called Josef by his first name: now they were equal. Dimly the lawyer realised that township instinct guided Ben's judgement, that Ben had heard the sound of those brakes before and knew what they signified.

The police van rolled to a halt and disgorged a thickset man in blue fatigues. As Ben and Josef hid in a doorway, he ran into the middle of the road, crouched, and fired his heavy gun. Puffs of white smoke burst on the tarmac and on the pavement as the crowd scattered in all directions like dandelion seeds in a strong wind. The smoke spread rapidly, enveloping a girl who had taken refuge behind a pillar in the foyer of a building. She collapsed, coughing and desperately clawing at her face. People close by ran to her and dragged her away; she appeared to be unconscious. The lawyer's eyes streamed and burned. 'Don't rub it in!' Ben shouted holding his chest, as he and Josef ran.

'I'm going back to the office!' Josef replied. 'I've had enough.' But a Leeu trundled into place before them and they were cut off.

Someone hurled a rock at it (where did they find rocks in the middle of the city?) and the metal rang with the force of the impact. A head, protruding from the top of the vehicle, was retracted hastily. The behemoth stopped and riot policemen tumbled out, carrying shotguns or quirts. Josef looked around anxiously for Ben, but the clerk had vanished. There was no way out: one side of the street was blocked by the truck and the teargas; the other by a wall of flesh machines, flexing their quirts, beating their batons on the palms of their hands in anticipation of striking flesh. Josef pulled himself upright and straightened his tie. He had his handkerchief out, dabbing at his mouth. The burning in his eyes was almost more than he could bear, but he held his head up and marched straight at the Leeu. Ben would have to take care of himself: he knew these situations.

'Please let me pass!' Josef demanded, hearing that his voice was out of control.

'What are you doing here?' a policeman screamed at him, coiling a quirt like a scorpion's sting.

'I'm a lawyer,' Josef coughed. 'I'm on my way to the office. I got caught in the teargas.'

The man eyed him suspiciously, a dangerous look, hinting at an unpredictable temperament, capable of sudden violence. 'All right, hurry up,' he ordered. 'Get off the street.'

Josef stepped gingerly between the policemen and their Leeu. I am part of the system, he thought again. I'm saved because I'm on the right side today. These people are protecting me from the mob; I am privileged. Nevertheless his 'saviours' seemed on the point of turning on him, as if he were a threat to the peace simply because he was there. Another rock clattered on the side of the Leeu and a blue stampede set off towards a section of the street where pockets of teargas billowed up like mists from a field in the early morning. A shoulder slammed (purposefully?) into Josef, sending the lawyer reeling away.

The low cloud, combined with the smoke and teargas, had turned the city dark. An artificial night had descended. In the gloom, Josef saw a young man behind a wire-mesh fence, tense as a dancer, balanced on the balls of his feet. This haunted figure carried a baseball bat and poised for a moment as in a photograph, fear etched in eyes that darted from side to side. Josef hurried by, but shouting made him glance back. Policemen were converging on the youth, quirts, batons and moustaches twitching. Josef ran, a man possessed by devils: he had seen too much.

But he was not spared yet. The rioting had spread through the city, a disease imported from the townships, infecting whatever it touched, its rampaging cells devouring order. The clown appeared, weaving in and out of the chaos, seemingly unaware of the danger he was in, yelling: 'Police! Police!', hailing the coming of a Messiah in whom he did not believe. He disappeared into the acrid murk, still chanting, protected by the alcohol in his blood. Josef ran on, past an intersection across which a Leeu crouched, brown against a purple background composed of smoke and cloud.

Breathing was difficult because of the teargas and the lawyer leaned against the window of a bottle-store whose doors were locked. As he rested, a group of youths advanced up the street. Scarves and bandannas disguised their faces. Acting as a single entity with a central brain, the group bore down on a parked van and heaved it on its side. It went over remarkably easily, a willing participant in this assault on the status quo, crunching to the ground as the rocks of its tormentors thudded through the windscreen, leaving it blind. No one spoke: each member of the attacking party acted with a silent methodical fury. The van surrendered, sighing black smoke. 'Let's go!' someone cried, and, as the group retreated, Josef caught sight of a face hidden behind a pink scarf: the eyes dazzled with delight.

'Ben!' Josef exclaimed. 'Ben!' The young clerk who shuffled nervously in the presence of authority, who had been Josef's guide in a complicated political landscape, who was torn between allegiance to his comrades in the struggle and his desire to advance himself, was turning over cars in the streets of Eisstad! But before Josef could verify his identification, a policeman ran towards them and everyone, including the lawyer, fled. Behind him, Josef heard a sound as of wood being beaten.

A terrible stillness hung over the city, as if everyone had died leaving Josef S the only survivor of the war, picking his way delicately as a grasshopper through the ruins. A cat sat on a wall at the bottom of his road, still as a gargoyle, watching the passing show. The wind had blown loose bougainvillaea flowers from a neighbour's garden into a purple mat like a pool of dried blood against his front gate. Exhausted, Josef let himself in.

Everything was safe, everything was as he had left it. The riots had taken place somewhere else, involving other people, issues which did not affect him. Nothing mattered. He slumped into a chair, too tired to take off his coat, aware that his clothes stank of teargas. He sat and stared at the photograph on the wall: the hopeless couple stared back. He sat quite still for a long time. He could not make food for himself: he was not hungry. But a bottle had appeared mysteriously at his elbow. Thankfully he tilted it to his mouth. They stared back: the pretty young woman and the faded man, projecting on him the hopes they could not fulfil for themselves. As nausea built up, Josef forced himself away from them. By the time his face was numb, darkness had fallen on the house, and he reached across to switch on the radio. His bloated fingers got lost on the dial, but suddenly there was sound.

'In the aftermath of today's unrest in the centre of Eisstad, the Government has placed curbs on the press,' a honeyed voice said. 'In terms of an extraordinary Government Gazette, the press, from midnight last night, may not report on the actions of the security forces in curbing unrest, on boycotts, stayaways, illegal strikes, restricted gatherings or detentions without trial; nor may the press repeat calls for the release of detainees. Journalists found guilty of contravening the new regulations face a fine of twenty thousand dollars or ten years in jail, and foreign journalists could be deported...'

Despite the darkness, Josef was not sorry that Dorothy had gone. He was sorrier at the loss of his brother. Even Margaret Spears, whom he believed he had loved, now seemed millions of miles away. Nothing mattered at all: not even what happened to Ben.

'Also in terms of the Government Gazette, the organisation known as the Flatlands Democratic Front, or FDF, has been banned,' the disembodied voice continued in the night. Josef managed to turn a knob and the voice went away.

The shrieking reached a crescendo: Josef had to cover his ears. He was standing at the lip of the Abyss, which had gouged a sinuous wedge of earth out of the plain. He had expected a sulphurous, smoking pit; horned devils lashing the backs of tormented souls with enormous whips. Instead, the ravine was packed with dense vegetation, a lush paradise devoid of human life. Sheer white cliff faces dropped through layers of trees and bushes to a dark languid river that wound through reed beds. Shocks of red flowers burst out of ash green backgrounds like wounds; wild grasses hissed at the stirrings of subterranean breezes. A red path, its roots lost somewhere in the depths, provided access to the outside world: the footprints of the mourners were embedded like fossils in the hard earth. Amazed, he compared the luxuriant pit with the dust-bowl he had crossed. Was this where life had begun?

The figure stood beside him, had arrived unseen, striving to stand upright but crippled with pain. It was Robert! The brothers looked into each other's eyes. Josef took his hands from his ears to embrace th' soldier, but he was confused by the shrieking, and when Robert pushed him, Josef was off-balance and powerless to prevent himself from falling into the Abyss. 'You were his favourite,' Robert said.

A bell tolled, the sound punctuating the shrieking. Josef's body cracked against the rocks and came to rest in a thicket: his grey coat was covered in blood.

The streets were quiet. Josef took the bus into town, not knowing what to expect. But everything was normal: there was no broken glass, no Leeus, no soldiers. People were going to work as if nothing had happened. The chaos of the previous day had been swept away as if by an army of municipal cleaners. A woman in blue overalls in charge of an orange bucket and an assortment of rags was vigorously wiping the brass letters: SUPREME COURT set into the stone wall at the entrance of the court building. A section of the staircase, shining as if oiled, was cordoned off with rope and a hoarding warned that the steps were slippery when wet.

The boil of tension had burst and the State was still in control. Had William Ngo surrendered himself for a brief day of violence? Was his spark able to ignite the people to no greater fury? The rebellion had been crushed and William Ngo had been sentenced to die. The sun shone: even God was smiling at the restoration of order. Had He turned his back on a young man who had been too arrogant? The previous day, He had set the stage with storms to reflect anarchy; now He directed the sun to shine.

'Did you hear?' Julia greeted Josef and the lawyer, suddenly fearing for Ben, went cold.

'What?' he barked.

'The clerk of the court told me that Judge Salmon's son hanged himself last night.'

Josef sat down; his legs had turned to water and could not hold him. 'Why? Why did he do it?'

'He was protesting against his father's decision. He left a note in his bedroom . . .'

'Oh God, no.' Robert stood beside him next to the Abyss . . .

214

Where was Ben?

'The clerk of the court said they found him this morning, hanging from a tree in the garden.' Julia seemed to enjoy repeating this bad news: knowledge gave her importance. 'He belonged to the FDF,' she added.

'Send a telegram of condolence from the firm,' Josef instructed wearily, 'and one specifically from me. Ask Mr Parry if he wants one sent in his name too. Have you seen Ben?'

'He hasn't come in today, Mr S.'

'Get someone to call the hospitals and the police stations,' Josef said.

'Yes Mr S.'

Ben arrived in the afternoon, without offering any explanations as to his absence or the bandage that was wrapped around his head. He set about his work, not speaking to anyone, and Josef called him into his office. The young man was sullen and defiant: gone was the comradeship of the previous day.

'Sit,' Josef offered him a chiar. 'Are you all right? We've been worried . . .'

Ben glared at his employer: for the first time, hatred was evident in his eyes. Josef's relief turned briefly into anger but was replaced by a flickering fear. Did Ben perceive him to be one of the enemy? Josef turned his back on the clerk and stared at the mountain, bathed in bright light, the mountain that swallowed dreamers, that had unleashed the might of its War Gods and was now smiling, satisfied at a job well done.

'We called the hospitals, the police stations . . .' Josef said after a long silence, ' . . . but not the mortuaries. I didn't want them to call the mortuaries . . .'

'When the Revolution comes, you won't be needed any more,' Ben said cruelly. 'In the townships we have our own courts. We settle our own disputes. We have our own magistrates and prosecutors and punishments. After the Revolution, there will only be People's Courts.'

'Then why are you here?' Josef asked sharply. 'Why did you come into work today? Why do you continue to train to be a lawyer?'

But Ben did not answer. Tears flowed down his cheeks. 'The FDF has been banned,' he said softly. 'We were peaceful and they banned us. Now we will have to go underground. We will have to continue the struggle with more and more violence. Do you know what this

215

means? You will have bombs in your railway stations and your supermarkets. You will have to look out for yourself, Mr S. You are not one of us, nor are you one of them. That means you are at the mercy of both.'

Suddenly he smiled. 'Do you want to come to Valhalla tonight with me? We are having a candle-light vigil for William Ngo and for those who have died in the struggle. I thought you might like to see it.'

'Of course,' Josef replied. 'But aren't there roadblocks?'

'You'll get in,' Ben said. 'And I need a lift home. The buses aren't running today.' He stood up.

'What about the danger to me?' Josef asked.

'It's your choice.' Ben walked out.

The press restrictions were the major news item in the noon paper. A Bureau of Information had been set up to supply the reports that the journalists were forbidden to investigate and write themselves. The Bureau had announced — and the *Evening Times* was therefore at liberty to publish — that the FDF had been banned, and that there had been disorder in the centre of the city: the Battle of Eisstad, as it had been dubbed. In a gesture that might have been construed as confrontational, as testing the limits of the press ban, the newspaper's political columnist had written a piece conjecturing that there had been a military coup, that the Generals (of the Police and the Armed Forces) had taken power and that Clarke was being retained as a figurehead only.

It was a normal lunch-hour, one of countless lunch-hours that were all alike: the previous day's had been an aberration. Eisstad was pure again; the trouble had been relegated to the townships. Until, as Ben warned, the bombs began to burst in the supermarkets.

A display in the window of a bookshop caught Josef's eye. He entered and was drawn to the new fiction stand, to a slim hardcover with the picture of an ox-skull on the cover: *Stories of Exile* by Dorothy Knox. His fingers trembled as he took a copy from the shelf, as he found her photograph on the inside back flap. His breath came quickly at the sight of his wife, his ex-wife, her hair framing her face like a mane: she was strikingly beautiful to him. He thought of the empty, dark house to which he would have to return that night — and every night for the rest of his life — to sit alone in a chair with only the numbing comfort of the gin bottle for company. No children. Only an old wedding photograph of a faded man and his pretty wife on the wall, wondering what had gone wrong with the life they had planned.

The blurb read: 'A collection of striking stories . . . highlighting the contrasts in our divided society . . . a tour de force by a talented writer . . .' What did Dorothy know about the contrasts of the Republic? Day after day suffering a self-imposed house-arrest: not venturing out except to the supermarket or perhaps to talk to the lunatic Mrs Milner. Where did she get the ideas for her stories? From their neighbour? From the nightwatchman who had lived in the parking lot across the road? From the char who came from the Flats to work in the mornings? Could those scraps have provided sufficient material from which to construct a book?

Josef realised then how little he really knew about her, how difficult it would be to reconcile the discrepancies, how self-absorbed he had been. Perhaps he would learn something of her feelings towards him if he read the book, perhaps she had written him into some of the stories. Would he have been portrayed as a weak husband who could not love, a man too scared to give her children? Or was her judgement harsher, making him hard, uncaring, the villain? The book was dedicated: 'To Robert, who set me free.'

Josef looked up. And his bones turned to ice. The grey head of a woman, rigid as a corpse, had materialised eight foot above the ground. Then it descended from sight behind a gondola of books. The lawyer continued to tremble even when a hand returned the grey woman to the topmost shelf from which it had removed her.

He bought Dorothy's book and received an approving glance from the assistant, a short dark man with a beard and intense brown eyes, as if *Stories of Exile* were the recommended reading of the liberal intellectuals, their book of the week. Do you know that she's dedicated it to her viking lover? Josef wanted to shout at the smug salesman. The joke's on you!

On an impulse, he went into a toyshop and bought the blue plastic toy called ZAPMAN, which possessed movable limbs and an arsenal of detachable weapons. Once, months ago, a boy on a bus had confronted him with a ZAPMAN and had evoked childhood memories of war games with Robert. Josef gave the toy to the first newspaper vendor he came upon. The child's wizened features bloomed with delight; he forgot about the newspapers he was supposed to be selling and sat down on the pavement, tearing open the plastic wrapper and thanking his benefactor at the same time. Josef left him shooting imaginary enemies (policemen?), his stack of newspapers abandoned on the pavement.

217

Back in the office, Josef paged through the newspaper. A small article tucked away on an inside page caught his attention. It was headed: ACTIVIST ARRESTED. As he read, a shadow fell over the city. 'Ms Margaret Spears, a member of Students for Justice and a voluntary worker at an advice office in Waterfront, was arrested last night for the possession of illegal drugs,' the newspaper announced. 'Ms Spears has in the past been detained, interrogated and searched by the security police and harassed by right-wing elements. Investigations into the case are continuing.'

Below the article, the daily horoscope appeared. The lawyer's eyes wandered, unseeingly at first, to his star sign. But then he focussed on the words and a small grin twisted his lips. 'Don't venture too far from home,' he read. Could the warning have been written by the same astrologer who had foretold Buth's death?

A dead fly curled on the dashboard of the car, wings splayed at awkward angles like a signalman's arms. Josef lifted the insect in the palm of his hand. It was as beautiful as a bead, so shiny that he could see his reflection in the green surface of its polished abdomen. Josef blew and it fluttered to the ground in a parody of flight. The idea of the Revolution, too, was a beautiful shell which could not fly.

Josef took a swig from the gin bottle, then hid it under the seat as Ben approached the passenger door. Ben climbed in and Josef started the engine. They drove in silence, into the gathering darkness: there was nothing to say any more. The lights of the township showed up ahead, denser at the entrance but thinning farther inside where the electricity did not extend. Three or four enormous spotlights threw bleak orange light over areas as large as football fields. And in the black heartland of the vast township angry red glows warned of private vendettas, secluded hatreds, sporadic acts of defiance. Ed Parry had once said that it was still pioneering country in there; the frontiers were still being consolidated.

The presence of the so-called 'security forces' grew stronger the closer they came to the entrance: riot policemen packed into landrovers, Leeus bearing soldiers, yellow police vans brimful with uniformed men. 'They won't stop us with Leeus,' the Reverend Lode had challenged at Freddy Pietersen's funeral. 'I call on you to commit yourselves completely to the struggle for freedom,' Rodney Baker had exhorted at the Peacy Rally. And William Ngo had prophesied that the workers would rule. But all those words were meaningless now. Steel ruled: the brute force of the State.

The traffic was being channelled into a single lane of the freeway. Josef's pulse beat faster as a queue of cars and minibuses developed, approaching the road-block which was hidden behind a shoulder of road ahead. He re-experienced the excitement he had felt the previous day, the adrenalin rush, and wondered fleetingly if he could become addicted to it the way that soldiers did. He reached for the gin bottle, then remembered where he was and stopped himself. They slowed down to a crawl, having entered a steel corridor, and Josef realised that he was sweating under his grey overcoat — his father's coat. His shirt was wet at the small of his back and the material clung to his skin. But it was too late to go back. If he swung his car out of the queue and drove away now, would they not pursue him and force him at gunpoint to stop, and demand explanations? Would they not decide that he was dangerous, and, edgy from tension, arrest him?

Ben, his mute guide, sat beside him, draining even more energy, silently demanding in his corner, demanding that Josef talk, that he reveal himself. The young man's eyes bored into him and Josef put his hand over his face, protecting it from the scrutiny of the clerk.

In the darkness now, even the Leeukop was obliterated. Once, Josef twisted around to look for it so that he might take some comfort from its steady bulk. But the sky above Eisstad was uniformly black, had swallowed the mountain or merged with it. The War Gods were released tonight, not confined to their lump of rock. They had clear passage across the heavens, rolling their tanks of clouds towards the townships.

The car inched forward. As they rounded the final bend before Valhalla, arc-lights flooded the road with a harsh white glare. It was too late to pull out the bottle, too late to escape: they were in the eddy of the whirlpool. Ahead was a barricade of men and machinery, flashing red lights, vehicles anxious to be cleared so they could enter the township: to seek the dubious safety of home. A separate queue of cars and minibuses in the cordoned-off lane waited to be searched, their occupants milling about like stray cows at the site of an accident involving a cattle-truck on its way to the abattoir.

Josef's hand was shaking almost uncontrollably on the steering-wheel. When he heard the first shriek, his body jerked as if he had been shot. He ventured a fearful glance out of the window. To what agonies was this unfortunate creature being subjected? What soul

219

could be so overcome by grief? Ben, hardened to the realities of police torture and township retribution, was unmoved. Disbelieving, seeking an answer to the mystery of his dreams, Josef at first did not understand.

'What's that noise?' he asked.

'Peacock,' Ben answered sullenly.

And so it was. On the white gravel before the amused eyes of the policemen and soldiers, a metallic green bird strutted, in the full glare of the arcs, showing off its jewels like a celebrity. Its fat blue neck jerked as it uttered its bloodcurdling shrieks; it made a mock charge at something that the lawyer could not see, and then suddenly fanned its tail-feathers. Hundreds of eyes stared alarmingly at Josef, warning that he was in danger. One of the soldiers raised his rifle, but a companion whispered in his ear and the gun was lowered. The bird, believing in its invulnerability, turned, its tail-feathers sweeping round like the train of a fantastic outfit. Still shrieking, it made a showy exit from centre stage, flouncing between steel curtains to a dark dressing room beyond.

The shaking and sweating were unbearable. Even though Ben was with him, even though the roadblock was just ahead, Josef had to have a drink. He fumbled under the seat . . .

A torch at each window broke the familiar darkness in which he was swimming like a goldfish in a bowl. Guiltily, Josef returned both hands to the steering-wheel.

'Can we see your identity books please?' The face behind the torch that shone into Josef's lap wore a moustache. Its request was backed up by force: a burly policeman stood by, his rifle butt resting in the dirt, the barrel against his paunch. Josef imagined rifles aimed at his head in the darkness behind the arc-lights.

Ben and Josef handed over their books.

'What are you doing here?' the rough voice asked. 'Why are you going into Valhalla?'

Because I'm seeking oblivion; because I've inherited my father's self-destructiveness together with his overcoat; because I'm tempting God to destroy me for my impudence; because I'm stripped of my beliefs and my loved ones and I am naked as a child in a cold world; because I am prepared to die at the hands of this Revolution, sacrifice myself like William Ngo, and my death will be as meaningless as his; because I wished to be a voice of reasonableness but there is no place for moderation in a polarised society; because I cannot bear to eke out my days drunk in a tomb in Eisstad. Are those reasons sufficient? Sweat beaded from his hairline.

'I'm a lawyer,' he said, 'and Ben is my clerk, and I'm giving him a ride home because the buses aren't running.'

'I advise you strongly not to go in there tonight, sir,' the policeman said. 'They're mad in there tonight. Even our patrols are heavily guarded and we're keeping them to a minimum.' He gave the identity book back. 'If you go in, we can offer you no protection at all, sir.' Josef nodded patiently. In the distance, he could hear the peacock shrieking. 'They're burning people in there, sir. Their own people. I would advise you to drop your chap off here and let him get a lift with one of these others.'

'Thank you for your advice,' Josef said, politely, firmly, 'but I'm going in unless you order me not to, and I'll take my chances.' The blood was hammering in his head, and he could feel sweat rolling down his face. His hands burned with excitement.

'It's up to you, sir,' the policeman replied, and waved him on.

The road slanted down into the township, tarred and graced with street lights at first. Josef edged the car into the Abyss. His fear had gone; he felt a wild exultation as he entered this alien territory, the ghetto of Valhalla.

'Why are they burning people?' he asked.

The road was still part of Civilisation. Tarred, it ran past the Valhalla Police Station, blue light a last beacon before the frontier began.

'They're burning people from Valhalla who support the Government, and informers, and policemen with their families. They're burning the schools where the children get inferior education and the beer halls which provide the alcohol that turns the people into slaves. Tonight is the Night of the Candles,' Ben said.

The car began to jolt as they drove over the first corrugations. The Night of the Candles. People, dressed in white for the vigil, shimmered like ghosts in the massive darkness, punctuated by deep flickering eyes that seemed to be judging the iniquity of the Republic. Everywhere, the candles burned: in windows, on verandahs, on the boundary walls of houses, on post-boxes, in rows or standing singly, as beautiful as the fiery eyes on the tail-feathers of a huge black peacock.

'You must tell me where to go,' said the lawyer. He pulled out the gin bottle, greedily unscrewed the top and drank. The peacock shivered its tail, the eyes sparkled and danced, and threw their flames into the road: Josef swerved furiously to avoid a burning

221

tyre. Faces slipped past the windows of the car; Ben was clutching his seat, frozen at the near miss.

'You're drunk,' he spat, and Josef could not contradict him. 'Left here. Drive slowly.'

As they progressed deeper and deeper into the heart of the township, the number of burning barricades increased: burning boxes and mattresses and tyres. A car skidded past them, headlights switched off, but with a candle alight on the dashboard revealing eyes crazed with elation. Josef held the bottle in his lap; now his hand was steady on the wheel. Houses had given way to shacks: the car lights flashed off corrugated iron. Even here, candles burned, in single windows like blind eyes; hubcaps and tin basins were candle-holders.

'In here' Ben instructed. The white bandage had slipped and lay at a rakish angle across his forehead. Somewhere a dog howled. 'Stop.' Josef obeyed.

Ben opened the door and got out. 'Goodbye Mr S,' he said. 'I won't see you again. I'm resigning. My struggle is here. You go back to Eisstad where it's safe.' Josef shook his head numbly, but in the darkness, Ben might not have noticed. 'We don't need you. Go home.' Perhaps a smile twisted Ben's face. He did not say: 'I can't work with alcoholics', but that was what Josef understood.

'How do I find my way back?' The night was cold; the candles continued right up into the sky as if the heavens were saluting William Ngo with fires of their own.

'It's easy,' said the guide. 'You go left and right and right again and then after two blocks left and you'll be on a main road, and then you take the fourth street to the right past the stadium — you remember the stadium? — and then you know your way. Just watch out for the roadblocks. Drive slowly when you approach a roadblock. If you get lost, ask someone . . .'

'I've got a map.' There were chickens in the road.

'So you'll be all right. Thanks for the ride . . .' Ben flung the door closed violently, and was wrenched away by forces which the lawyer did not understand. Josef started the engine, took another drink, and set off. He had no idea where he was or how to get back to the entrance. There was no mountain by which to navigate and one street looked very much like another. Candles and white-clad figures slid by monotonously; Josef could have been driving in circles. The street numbers whirled and danced in front of him: VA 113, Avenue 39, VA 246, Avenue 75, in no order, as chaotic as the night.

'I'll drive until I'm stopped, or until my petrol runs out, or until it's light again, or until I fall asleep at the wheel,' he said aloud. But then his breath snagged in his throat. A mob was running towards his car, either in pursuit or being pursued, he did not know which. In the headlights, he saw knives and sticks and axes, and youthful faces, teeth clenched in grins or in anger. He slowed almost to a stall and closed his eyes, all at once warm and resigned. Rocks would hammer against the bodywork and smash the glass; sharp blades would stab inside, flailing in the darkness until they punctured flesh; and, at last, furious fingers would slosh petrol out of a battery of wine bottles, throw in a match or two, and ignite wreckage and corpse in a glorious bonfire that would serve as a warning to outsiders: 'The townships are ungovernable!' For a moment he was overwhelmed, stifled by the density of the rampaging bodies with their musty stale smells and battering limbs, by the rocking seasickness of his car as the mob lurched and tottered and tumbled against it, by the panting breaths and ululations and war cries expelled from lips that were perilously close to his window. But as suddenly as they had descended, the youths had stormed past, leaving him shaking his head in disbelief that he was unharmed. Josef drank again, for courage, and then drove on, his car bouncing and bobbing over corrugations.

Ahead, a form lay in the road, long and black, probably a dog; his headlights picked it up. One bent leg feigned movement, as if it were still attempting to run, as if it did not know it was facing the sky. Slowly — he was going nowhere so it made no difference how fast he travelled — Josef drew level. And in horror accelerated immediately. The thing in the road was a man, dressed in overalls, lying on his back, eyes and mouth partly open, clasping a stick in his tight fingers. The weapon had not managed to save his life.

He did not know for how long he had been driving — the pointer was sliding alarmingly low down the face of the petrol gauge — when he found himself under one of the enormous orange spotlights. Its foot was a thick wad of concrete, sunk into the sand; its ambit was a town of tents which could have been any colour during the day but which showed up as black at night. They stretched in neat rows, gently undulating along the white sand, until they extended beyond the range of lights and either stopped or continued, perhaps as plentifully: it was impossible to estimate. A black cylinder with a triangular lid serviced each row: from photographs, Josef recognised the infamous 'bullet toilets'.

The gin bottle was almost empty and the lawyer's hand shook only slightly as he poured the last of the liquid down his throat. And then the cold glass would yield no more. Josef swore. Outside, a woman walked past the spotlight with a bundle of wood on her head: the orange cyclops glowered over a town that had no electricity. Here and there braziers flared like the eyes of wild beasts in the night, and tufts of white smoke indicated where cooking fires were being doused. Everything was peaceful here: perhaps the rioting had not reached this section, perhaps the people, so isolated in the very heart of the township, lived as if on an island, cut off from the rest of Valhalla. The woman took no notice of the car cruising by and disappeared in between two rows of tents without looking back. Josef opened the window and flung out the bottle. A cold damp mist entered the car and settled on his forehead.

He was at a banquet; plates of foodstuffs were spread out on the table before him, an enticing array of colours and smells and shapes.

'Try this,' suggested the fat man next to him.

'I don't eat meat,' Josef replied.

'Just try some. Here,' the man, who was Ed Parry, insisted. 'It's excellent.'

The dish in question consisted of chunks of meat floating in a thin soup. Josef transferred three or four of these to his plate and then put one in his mouth. Very slowly, he chewed. The juice was sickly rich: he gagged and could not swallow. But neither could he spit out the distasteful thing. He was trapped by this chewed meat; it had made him its prisoner. In desperation, he turned to Parry for help, but the fat man was convulsed with laughter at Josef's misfortune.

He did not see the cow until it was too late. The animal galloped into the road, eyes dilated and nostrils flaring. A slice of meat had been cut out of its flank. Josef saw this in the few seconds in which he had to slam his foot on the brakes. The car skidded in the sand, there was a jolt as the front bumper collided with the terrified creature, and then the cow was gone, helter skelter into the darkness. Only the tinkling of its bell lingered in the cold air.

No one came to investigate the noise of the collision: besides the lights from the braziers and the distant puffs of smoke, the tent town seemed deserted. Surely the thundering of the maddened cow and the squeal of brakes should have drawn some interest? But perhaps people were too scared to leave the fragile security of their tents on a night like this. It did not matter. Josef wiped the sweat and mist from his eyes and pushed his foot on the accelerator. The car would not move; the wheels slipped uselessly in the sand. A rush of fear momentarily displaced the numbness which was the gift of the gin. He sat forward in his cold seat, pumping the pedal, but the wheels moaned apologetically and dug themselves in deeper. Tiredly, he slumped against the headrest and switched off the engine. For a long while he sat and stared into the desert. This was truly the end of the line.

After an indeterminate time, when his heart-beat was down to almost normal, and satisfied that he was in no immediate danger, Josef got out to survey the problem. The cold wind turned his breath to steam and stiffened his fingers. The skid marks were clearly visible, curves gouged out of the surface of the road, and the hoofmarks of the cow. The car was buried, axle-deep, in a ditch. What to do? Beat on the fabric of the nearest tent, demanding help? He took out his map and studied it under the baleful orange light. But the map was no help at all: the area where he must have been was indicated only by a blank space.

The newspapers used to give such good coverage, he thought. Now, with press censorship, my death won't even be reported. Or perhaps the Bureau of Information will issue a terse comment: 'An adult male from Eisstad was burned last night in Valhalla. His identity is being withheld until his next of kin have been informed.'

Who lived in these tents? Josef wondered absently. Refugees? Were these the poor souls whom the Government continually ejected from areas such as Waterfront and sent to Valhalla? Was the blank area on the map one vast resettlement camp: a ghetto within a ghetto? Under the unremitting light, the tents rolled away, a swelling sea of crests and troughs. Josef kicked the car, the door buckled and he hopped in pain, embraced by a cold mist without and invaded by a chill within. He pulled the coat tightly around his body. A dog barked.

Thirst was fire in his throat; he reached for a bottle that would bring relief to his tortured gullet; he longed for the sweet liquid to quench the burning thirst, to dull the senses and send the sodden spirits soaring, to kill Josef S, the clown who sat in alleys amid forests of glass tempting strangers to join him in his damnation. But the bottle was gone, and there was nothing, not even water, to put out the raging flames. Even if the mobs of Valhalla did not get him, how would he last the night?

The deep cough of an engine made him spin around. He overbalanced, and fell against the car, and lay spread-eagled while a solitary Leeu prowled into view, rangy and long-limbed, over the white sand tinted orange by the spotlight. Is this my enemy? Josef thought. Or has it come to save me? Must I run out into the road waving my hands to attract its attention? Or must I hide? Must I call the War Gods, with whom I have forged an intimate connection, to come to my assistance? Or has the army, aware of my need, brought just one bottle . . .?

The tawny machine stopped, and stood, huge, across the road, surveying him, a beast come in from the desert to find an easy prey: a wounded animal, limp and ready for the taking. It coughed again and yawned, showing off its long canine teeth. Josef's blood began to boil.

'Come on, damn you!' he yelled. 'Get it over with!' But the windows remained dark; the predator allowed no insight into its intentions. For hours, it seemed, man and Leeu examined each other across a strip of road so isolated it was not even marked on the map, while the sweat formed and froze on the lawyer's face and the Leeu's engine rumbled like a hungry stomach. But then a door opened. And a soldier stepped out, onto the mudguard, and landed nimbly in the sand. He wore boots which must have been brown but which looked black in the orange light, tired army fatigues, a belt with two stripes (one light, one dark), a buckle bearing the insignia of a wolf, and a helmet which came down to his eyes. He carried a combat rifle, a type used extensively in the northern war; like the toilets, Josef recognised it from photographs. While the War Gods swirled overhead, the two men squared up to each other in the desolate heart of the township, one backed by the might of the army, the other crippled and trembling, from anger and cold, and the need for another drink. If there were other soldiers in the Leeu, they had not dared alight. Only this one was brave, or mad, enough to descend into the wild streets of Valhalla dressed in the uniform of the enemy.

'Hello Robert,' Josef said, accenting the name mockingly. 'Looking for someone to shoot?'

'Josef . . . I'm on patrol. I recognised your car.'

'Didn't you recognise the overcoat? Dad's overcoat? It keeps the wind out, but not the chill.'

The soldier was young and tall. He had lost weight since his brother had last seen him, but perhaps that was imagination aided by the afterglow of the gin and the trickery of the thin light which diminished everything. The smell of burning seeped across the white wasteland and tickled the lawyer's nose. He wanted to sneeze it out, to sneeze out all the rot that had accumulated in a body which had once striven to be pure. He stood upright, pulled himself to his full height. 'How's Dorothy?' he challenged.

'She's happy.' The voice across the street was thick with tiredness and strain.

'*You've* made her happy?' Josef's words stung and Robert winced. The rifle went up an inch; Josef saw the reflex but he did not care.

'She's got rid of her radical ideas . . .' Robert spoke hesitantly, perhaps unnerved by his brother's aggression.

'Ah, you've tamed her! Now she won't be able to market her book! Have the two of you thought of that? All her hard work . . .' Josef sneezed and the stars collided in the sky. He had not known her at all! Who was this woman he had married? A woman who changed her political convictions with her lovers, who had made a love-pact with someone whose values she used to abhor? Or was Robert lying to him? Was the Devil tempting him to disbelieve in the goodness of his ex-wife? He tried to visualise her, but she eluded him, and the only memory he had was the brush of her fiery hair which burned where it touched his cheek.

'What are you doing here Josef?' Robert counter-attacked. 'Are you inciting these poor people to riot? Leave them alone. Their lives are miserable enough. The FDF is banned now. You'd better be careful. Your radical ideas are dangerous.'

Was this indeed Robert, or an image thrown out by the feverish workings of the lawyer's mind? What divine irony had set the two brothers together in this most inaccessible, almost dreamlike, of places? Could Robert have followed him here, waited until he was helpless before accosting him . . .? Impossible! Or was their meeting the accidental end to a lifetime of guilt and conflict? On the other hand, was it so unlikely that Robert, being on one of the few patrols that the policeman at the roadblock had spoken of, would pass him sooner or later during the night, trapped in the ditch?

'I'm waiting for my contact,' Josef lied and looked around vaguely, pointing into the refugee camp behind him. 'Run along now, little brother.' He waved dismissively towards the Leeu which stood by, armoured backdrop, engine idling. 'Go and play soldiers with your friends in there.'

The rifle was up now, ready for trouble. Long terrible fingers held the trigger. The eye at the end of the barrel stared unforgivingly at the lawyer. The stock rested against Robert's shoulder. Was his slender frame strong enough to absorb the shock of firing such a weapon? Would the recoil not knock him back into the jaws of his Leeu?

'You've become a revolutionary!' Robert exclaimed. 'You *have* joined them.' A fringe of hair fell over a small boy's face as he laughed, as he aimed his toy pistol at his brother.

'You ran away with my wife.'

'She isn't your wife any more,' Robert sneered. 'She needed someone to love her and give her a child. Not a cold fish like you. You're more interested in defending revolutionaries . . .' His eyes were invisible, hidden in shadow, his helmet grew like a mushroom over the top of his head.

'To give her a child,' Josef repeated woodenly. 'Is that what you've done?' This arrogant youth had shot his seed into Dorothy, had contaminated her with flawed sperm that would produce who knew what monsters to patrol future townships, to wade through valleys of blood. Josef's brother . . . a supposedly tormented soldier who had wrought havoc in a northern village, yet claimed to be haunted by the experience. Was this sort of conflict in a young man irresistable to a married woman in the present Republic, fed on a diet of violence and guilt?

Robert grinned, a reflex twitch to the lips. 'She's pregnant,' he boasted. 'She's going to have *my* baby.'

This *is* my enemy, Josef decided, and turned to look for the bottle he had thrown away. He needed a weapon of his own. He could not face the boy empty-handed. He dropped onto his knees beside the stranded car and searched in the sand, throwing up handfuls like a child on a beach.

'What are you doing?' Robert asked, tension wracking his voice. 'What have you got hidden there?'

'*I* don't kill, I don't even eat flesh. Aren't I a good person?' Josef muttered, almost toppling over before he managed to regain his balance. And then he accused: 'How can you, steeped in blood, love my wife?'

'I've risked my life for you!' Robert cried out. His feet were balanced shoulder-width apart, his back and legs were ramrod straight, his cheeks were tight with tension. 'I've fought on the borders! I've had friends killed in front of my eyes! I did it for Dorothy and for you! And you don't even care . . .'

'Your child will be born in blood,' Josef taunted. Somewhere a bell seemed to toll: 'Dolente! Dolente!' And a train rushed in towards a station. He could not find the bottle: but it did not matter; he would have to confront the enemy unarmed. The enemy that God or Fate had placed before him in the centre of the township under the pillar that spat out an orange light, a light of prisons and concentration camps. The enemy with whom he now had the opportunity to conduct unfinished business, his perverse alter ego, his Hellish nemesis.

'What have you got there?' Robert demanded. 'Don't do anything stupid . . .' The rifle's eye stared unflinchingly into the lawyer's.

Josef leaped to his feet. 'You've fucked my wife!' he screamed, hurling a handful of sand at his adversary.

'Josef! Don't!'

He saw the bright burst of fire and heard the rifle's crack, but mercifully there was no pain. An invisible hand lifted him off his feet and tossed him effortlessly and contemptuously into the ditch. He lay on his back, and his open eyes could not keep out the stars while a cold mist, vehicle of the War Gods, washed over him. A lion snarled triumphantly nearby, and then receded, growling, into the distance until it was swallowed by the silence that was overwhelming the land. He felt a strange relief that it had gone and that the game was finally over.

Dad please help me, he begged, I need a drink; my body is burning for a drink. And then charged: I could never be a father to Robert; that was your job. He wanted a father so badly . . .

The train gathered momentum. He was aware of it by feeling, not by sound, by the smell of stale air it pushed towards him, the pressure as it got closer. Oh dear, he sighed. I've got blood on your overcoat, Dad. And now Robert's gone and no one will know the truth . . .

A face peered into his: two huge eyes and a tower of a nose. 'Comrade,' he heard, and this made him happy because it included him in the fellowship of the Oppressed; and then a babble of voices as if a hundred people were all talking at the same time.

No good . . . bleeding . . . Leeu . . .

. . . soldiers . . . bandage . . . tent . . .

Bleeding . . . soldiers . . . no good,

No good at all, he thought. Have they read that article in *The Voice* which gave first-aid hints? Can they read?

He was in a procession in which everyone held a candle up to the night sky; the flickering lights were the eyes in the tail of an

229

enormous jewelled peacock. This was his funeral and the vanguard carried him aloft with intertwined hands while the mob shouted: 'Power! Power! Power!' He was gently jostled as his comrades bore him on a wooden bier across a dusty plain towards a grave at which the world's television cameras waited. The procession was twenty thousand strong; it wound back over the plain, snaking in and out of the light provided by a row of huge orange spotlights. An army helicopter threatened overhead, but defiant fists waved it away and it rolled from its course to disappear behind the distant hills. A wild priest, dressed in the skin of a lion, stamped the dust, making it rise to ankle height, then up to the knees, waists, and eventually shoulders, until the procession was a long train of dust, converging on a grave lit by the bright spots of the television journalists. The rocking was making him sleepy, and the chanting: he did not have long to travel. The pit waited, six feet of sheer drop. Earth would clod, stifling, onto his face, a few flowers would be thrown in for the sake of sentiment, and that would be the end of it.

The peacock rested its beak against his ear and shrieked. Or perhaps that was the whistle of the train which was upon him. While the lion priest chanted incomprehensible prayers at the lip of the grave, Josef's comrades lowered him, gently, still wrapped in his father's overcoat, into the ground.

THE AFRICAN WRITERS SERIES

The book you have been reading is part of Heinemann's long-established series of African fiction. Details of some of the other titles available in this series are given below, but for a catalogue giving information on all the titles available in this series and in the Caribbean Writers Series write to:
Heinemann International Literature and Textbooks,
Halley Court, Jordan Hill, Oxford OX2 8EJ;
United States customers should write to:
Heinemann, 361 Hanover Street,
Portsmouth, NH 3801-3959, USA.

BIYI BANDELE-THOMAS
The Man Who Came in from the Back of Beyond

Maude, a strange schoolteacher, tells the tale of a man from his girlfriend's past. As the naive student Lakemf listens, a tale of incest and revenge slowly begins to unfold.

CHENJERAI HOVE
Shadows

As the war for liberation rages around them, two young Zimbabweans must decide whether they will continue to live and love in such a barren land. A telling portrait of rural life and the strictures of colonial law.

NIYI OSUNDARE
Selected Poems

This collection contains the very best of Osundare's poetry. The verse testifies to his commitment to a popular 'total poetry' – words to be listened to in conjunction with song, dance and drumming.

TIYAMBE ZELEZA
Smouldering Charcoal

Two couples live under the rule of a repressive regime, and yet their lives seem poles apart. In this compelling study of growing political awareness, we witness the beginnings of dialogue between a country's urban classes.

NGŨGĨ WA THIONG'O
Secret Lives

A new edition of Ngũgĩ's collection of early stories revealing his increased political disillusionment and foreshadowing the novels which have made him one of Africa's foremost commentators.

ALEX LA GUMA
In the Fog of the Seasons' End

This is the story of Beukes – lonely, hunted, determined – working for an illegal organisation, and of Elias Tekwane, captured by the South African police and tortured to death in the cells.

CHARLOTTE BRUNER (ED)
The Heinemann Book of African Women's Writing

A companion piece to the earlier *Unwinding Threads*, also edited by Charlotte Bruner, this anthology of writing of the post colonial era provides new insights into a complex world.

CHINUA ACHEBE & C. L. INNES (EDS)
The Heinemann Book of Contemporary African Short Stories

This anthology displays the variety, talent and scope to be found in contemporary African writing. The collection includes work written in English and translations of francophone stories. The magical realism of Kojo Laing and Mia Couto contrasts with the styles of Nadine Gordimer, Ben Okri and Moyez Vassanji.

AMECHI AKWANYA
Orimili

Orimili takes his name from the great river that flows through his home town of Okocha. But while the river flows on to the wider world beyond, Orimili is anchored to his home town, and yearns to push his roots yet further in. His ambition is to be accepted in the company of elders, to wear the thick white thread of office round his ankle.